HIDDEN COVENANT

ORDER OF THADDEUS • BOOK 3

J. A. BOUMA

EmmausWay
PRESS

PROLOGUE

D ark and troubled thoughts haunted Rabbi Hilkiah as he hobbled down the cobblestone road toward his simple, single-room home, taking care where he placed each step. His old bones demanded it.

The sun was setting hard and fast, deep oranges enflaming the horizon. He hoped to reach the safety of his house before the night emerged in force. Ever since the Roman visitors had arrived, the city he had given his life to for nearly a century felt foreign and frightening, like a miasma of evil had descended upon the land—violating it, desecrating it. Such was life for *Haaretz*, for the Land of his people stretching back to the patriarchs and kings of old. But this latest episode was a different sort of blasphemy.

And he blamed one person above all.

Months ago, Helena Augusta of Constantinople, the consort of Emperor Constantius Chlorus and mother of Emperor Constantine the Great had arrived, towing along with her a large entourage and an even larger army of Roman soldiers. Even before she arrived, news had reached the old rabbi that Emperor Constantine had appointed her as Augusta Imperatrix, giving her unlimited access to the imperial treasury in order to locate the relics of Judeo-Christian tradition. So she had set out on a pilgrimage to Palestine, where she had been quite busy of late.

Ever since Constantine had signed the Edict of Milan proclaiming religious tolerance throughout the Empire and enacting a period of favoritism to the Christian Church, thousands of Christians had flocked to *Haaretz Yisrael*, the precious, holy land of the Jewish people. It was only a matter of time before the converted Emperor himself took an interest in the artifacts of the Christian faith. And his mother had been making quick work to preserve and extract those precious relics.

She immediately ordered the pagan temple dedicated to Venus that Emperor Hadrian had built over the site of Jesus' tomb near Calvary destroyed, and the site excavated. Apparently, she had made interesting discoveries, with rumors swirling she had recovered such artifacts as Jesus of Nazareth's scourging post, the crown of thorns, and even the cross from his crucifixion. While fascinating if proven to be true, those discoveries weren't what interested the rabbi or sent his teeth on edge.

He continued inching forward through the street, deep in concentration, deeply troubled. Earlier that morning, the Queen had paid the man an unannounced visit, believing that her honorific title and imperial mandate gave her blanket rule over the affairs and people of the ancient, holy city. Including the ruling Rabbi.

The conversation started pleasant enough, but quickly turned to the matter of her inquiry, an ancient relic from old that hadn't been spoken of for twenty generations stretching back to the Babylonian exile.

She had made mention of an ancient, Jewish relic made of acacia wood and overlaid with pure gold, protected by a lid of golden-winged creatures guarding stone tablets of a divine covenant.

He couldn't believe his ears when she voiced her request. "You are speaking about the Ark of the Covenant? Is that right?"

"Correct," she had said curtly. "And as the ruling Jewish Amora sage, Rabbah bar Hilkiah, I assume you have insight into its whereabouts."

What brazenness, what arrogance that Roman woman had to demand such information! Information which he had pledged to preserve and protect—even unto death if need be.

"This object you seek," he had replied, "has been lost for generations, ever since the great Babylonian exile. No one has seen of it or has spoken of it since its disappearance."

She leaned in closer, the scent of lavender setting his skin on edge. "I cannot imagine a holy object of such great import would have simply vanished from the face of the earth. Surely its whereabouts are known. Surely you know its whereabouts, Rabbi."

Yes. He did. But the curses of a thousand suns would fall upon him if he broke his vows to this heathen.

Rabbi Hilkiah shifted and rubbed his nose, then leaned back and smiled. "Empress Helena, as the prophet Jeremiah stated in his book, 'And it shall come to pass, when ye be multiplied and increased in Haaretz, in those days, saith Hashem, they shall say no more, The Aron Brit Hashem: neither shall it come to mind: neither shall they remember it; neither shall they ask for it; neither shall another be fashioned.'"

Helena sat stone-faced as he quoted the ancient, prophetic passage related to the Ark, clearly not used to being denied her wishes.

The rabbi continued, "The prophet Jeremiah from the ancient days declared that the Ark you seek would neither enter the Jewish peoples' minds nor be remembered; it would not be missed, nor would another one be made. And, as I said previously, it hasn't since the time of the Exile. So, you see, there isn't any reason for someone such as myself to possess information relating to the Ark's location, secret or otherwise."

One end of the old woman's mouth curled upward. She said, "I see, Rabbi Hilkiah." She paused, then continued, "As you know, my people have made quick work and great progress at unearthing the ancient relics of my faith, particularly relating to the events surrounding the new covenant, the crucifixion of Jesus of Nazareth. Would you allow us to apply the same techniques to the site of the original Temple? Excavate it to determine whether any other Temple treasures had been secreted away?"

The rabbi felt his mouth go dry and quiver in disgust. His eyes widened involuntarily, and he quickly blinked them and swallowed hard, trying to suppress the urge to shout down this woman for such a suggestion.

"I cannot allow such a..." he had meant to say *desecration*, but thought against it. "Such an intrusion into our sacred space. Surely you can understand."

"But the Emperor desires that all relics connected to the Christian faith be recovered so that their memory will be preserved for future generations. Surely the Empire would benefit from the memory of the former covenant contained within the Ark. And surely an official designee of the Jewish faith would want to help the Empire."

Hilkiah had felt himself grow warm with anger at the suggestion.

He simply replied, "Helena Augusta, I am sorry I could not be of more service to the Emperor."

She smiled weakly. "We shall see."

What was that?

A clay pot toppled behind him, crashing to the narrow cobblestone pathway and breaking his troubled recollection.

He turned around sharply, his breath catching in his throat, his heart beating faster with anticipation in his shallow chest.

The dusk seemed to envelop the world behind him, but the remaining sunlight cast a long, dark shadow of a cat scampering along toward him. It slowed to a trot as it approached him, then stopped to rub against his leg, purring contentedly.

The rabbi chuckled. "There, there," he said softly, bending

slightly to scratch his new friend as his heart rate and breathing eased back into a normal rhythm. "You gave me quite the fright. Yes, you did."

A loud cheer arising from a group of Roman revelers tumbling out of a house startled the cat, causing him to run off to a place of refuge.

"Until next time, my friend."

The rabbi continued along the road, avoiding a drunken man who had stumbled down the curbstone and his fellow revelers who were trying to help him back up.

He continued on his path toward home, troubling over the meaning of Helena's advances and insistence on violating the former Temple's ruins. What if she went forward with the excavation, searching the tunnels underneath and probing its secret chambers?

Another thought stopped him from walking: *What if she found what she sought? What impact would that have on her son's faith?*

On his own?

He started back up toward his home, hurrying his pace as the setting sun made the journey more difficult.

"Won't you spare a double denarius or two, kind sir?"

A near-naked man hunched over against a low-rise wall off the road caught the rabbi's attention. He squinted at him in the dark, his eyes not what they used to be.

The man seemed encouraged by the attention, for he sat up straighter, motioning to a small, open-mouthed clay pot at his feet.

"A double denarius, please? I haven't eaten in a week."

The old man gently smiled at the poor soul. He carefully walked over to him, reaching into a purse hidden within the folds of his cloak. He pulled out two of the silver coins embossed with the likeness of that dreadful woman's son, the emperor, and reached down to deposit them into the pot.

His wrist was suddenly seized. Instinctively, he tried pulling away, but it was no use. The man grinned, darkened, crooked teeth showing through a broad dark smile. "Hello, Rabbi Hilkiah."

The recognition of danger immediately pinged the rabbi's gut. He tried pulling away again, yanking his arm with everything his spent body had left inside. The man's grip was firm, betraying his feeble appearance.

Then the world went black in a blossom of stars and pain.

A PITCHER of cold water brought Rabbi Hilkiah back to consciousness.

"Ahh, back to the land of the living, Rabbi. How good of you to join us."

What? Where am I?

The rabbi tried recovering his breath from the drowning sensation and opening his eyes, but they stung from the cold liquid running down his face. After wiping it and recovering, he tried lifting his head, but a lancing pain sent him sinking backward. He was lying in a bed, the burnt-orange hue of the just-setting sun replaced with the yellow flicker of a single candle doing its best to light the darkened room. Recognition hit him: he was home. But how had he arrived?

Then the fog of confusion was replaced with remembrance. The cat, then the beggar; the footfalls of two or three men behind him, then the pain; the darkness, then the dimly-lit room in his home.

Hilkiah moaned. He tried focusing, but the dim light and the even dimmer eyes wouldn't allow for it. He caught sight of a figure. Not-all-that visible, barely recognizable, and yet...

No. It can't be.

The face of an ancient threat long thought gone. One his people had dealings with stretching all the way back to Egypt, before the great Exodus to the time when Yahweh's people suffered under oppressive slavery.

The dreaded Ibis Bird-Man. Thoth, the Egyptian god of knowledge.

The rabbi could barely make out the man, but it was unmistakable: the man who wore the ancient face was bare-chested and tanned to a burnished bronze, his upper shoulders ringed by an intricate weave of gold and turquoise beads at the base of his neck. A long beak of onyx black peered down at him. Silent and probing.

Hilkiah shuddered. *Yahweh, save me...*

"Hello, Rabbi Hilkiah," the Bird-Man intoned, deep and commanding.

The rabbi was trembling, his mouth had gone dry. He tried to speak, but his tongue stumbled over itself.

"What was that? Here, let me help." Bird-Man brought over a ceramic tumbler of water and offered it to the old man. He took it and drank greedily. "There you go. Now, you were saying?"

"What...What...?" He caught his breath, then finished the water down to the last drop. "What is the meaning of this?"

"It's simple. You have something I want."

Hilkiah pushed himself off of his bed, propping himself against the hard, stone wall of his simple home. "And what is that?"

"First things first," Bird-Man said, turning around to pull a wooden chair over to the bedside. He sat down, his large frame looming over the short, rotund Rabbi cowering under the covers. "You were visited upon by Helena, consort of Emperor Constantius Chlorus and mother of Emperor Constantine the Great, is that correct?"

"Yes," he said quickly. No use denying it. "Are you with her entourage?"

Bird-Man launched into a loud, long cackle-of-a-laugh. "With Augusta?" He laughed again, nearly falling out of the chair.

"In a word, no. I'm something of a foil to the Empress. But

then again," he said deeply, standing up and leaning over the bed, "you already knew that, Rabbi."

His eyes grew wide, and he felt himself sinking under the thin blanket covering him.

Bird-Man sat down, then continued. "She spoke to you this morning, asking you about the location of an ancient weapon of power, a vessel of secret, divine knowledge, of a divine covenant that's been hidden away for generations—unseen and unsought. Yes?"

Hilkiah nodded vigorously.

"There we go. That wasn't so hard. Now, what did you tell her?"

"I...I told her the truth. Not since the Babylonian exile have we caught sight or caught word of such a relic. Yahweh's holy Ark has been lost to history."

"Good," Bird-Man said silkily. "Of course, you and I both know that the ancient relic has been kept safe as much as kept secret for the past twenty generations. With only a handful of Guardians knowing its true location." He leaned forward, heaving heavy, sour breathes of air inches from Hilkiah's face "Including you."

The rabbi's mouth went dry again, his heart galloped forward uncontrollably.

"And you will tell me where those Levites carried it off to."

He couldn't speak. He couldn't move. He couldn't think.

Bird-Man stood up. From behind him, he pulled out a gold-sleeved object the length of his forearm. Sticking out was a handle, a golden cloisonné with precious stones and pieces of glass in blues, reds, and greens.

An ancient Egyptian ceremonial dagger.

The masked figure unsheathed the object, its golden strength glimmering in the dimming candlelight. He held it out in front of his chest and over Rabbi Hilkiah, the blade perpendicular to his body.

"Yahweh," the old man whispered, delirious from the moment, "the secret of your hidden covenant is safe with me."

"Really? We shall see about that. Because mark my words: one way or another, you will tell me, Rabbi Hilkiah."

At once Bird-Man was on top the old man, wrenching his lower jaw open and positioning the dagger's tip just inside his mouth.

"O Osiris, King Unas," he intoned, head tilted back, "I offer this sacrifice to you." Then he began speaking in an unknown dialect, his body rocking back and forth as if possessed by the forces of Sheol itself.

Eli, Eli lama sabachthani? the old Rabbi thought.

My God, my God, why have you forsaken me?

DAY I

CHAPTER 1

S ilas Grey was running late. Again. To make matters worse, he was running late for a hearing with the administration over their impending verdict.

Not good.

To make matters doubly worse, the idyllic campus of Princeton University he was hustling across was deluged by relentless morning rain. And he forgot his umbrella. He tried adjusting the collar of his raincoat to shield his head, but it was no use. It was going to be one of those days.

As Silas came up on the administrative building, he outstretched his arm to check his watch, a fake, gold-plated Seiko his father gave him as a high school graduation gift. It was pock-marked with ten years of age and three tours of duty across the Middle East. Cheap thing, but it still worked, and it still meant the world to him. The last remaining tie he had to keep Dad's memory alive after his death on 9/11. He channeled the man's strength to get him through the hearing. He was going to need it. It was now 7:04 a.m.

He opened the door to the ivy-covered, red-bricked building still standing after two centuries of educating America's rising youth. The administration may be different, but the roots of its deep tradition sank deep into Princeton's past. Every day he was thankful to have found a place at the institution, despite not quite fitting in. Though its history is steeped in Protestantism, having churned out Presbyterian pastors for generations before turning toward a more liberal-arts persuasion, his career as an assistant professor of religious studies and Christian history made him an outsider. And given his specialty in religious relics, particularly the Christian kind, even black sheep denied he was one of theirs.

Silas tried to labor his breathing as he quickly ascended the stairs to the third floor. Waiting for him was a conference room with a panel of his peers ready to bestow upon him one of the most sought-after milestones in academia: tenure. He hadn't anticipated it would happen this quickly. But he had relentlessly pursued the goal of clinching it within five years of receiving his professorship. He was now seven months shy of the finish line. He told himself to feign surprise and enthusiastic delight, even though he thought he deserved it a year ago. Anything less would offend the stodgy group, which wasn't what he needed now that he was ten minutes late to the most significant break of his professional career.

Before entering the well-appointed, mahogany-lined executive suite, Silas adjusted his tie and took a few breaths. He stepped forward, took another few breaths—in and out—and then opened the door.

"Gentlemen," he started as he walked inside, "please forgive me for my severe tardiness. I misjudged my commute and forgot an umbrella. Of all days!" He sat down at a short, cherry table in front of a longer one full of the tenure committee and smiled.

No one else returned the gesture, though he thought he caught a grin from the academic dean, Dr. Michael Brown. He scanned the panel assembled for his coronation, thinking that it seemed lighter on bodies than he remembered.

And then his eyes met two others attached to someone at the end he hadn't expected.

Dean Mathias McIntyre.

Perhaps it made sense that the dean of his department would take part in these procedures. But he had assumed the process was a formality at this point after months of documentation and several submissions. So why was his presence necessary, someone whom Silas was sure had it out for him?

McIntyre's mouth sat closed and flat, eyes slightly narrowed as he peered down at Silas from across a small pair of spectacles perched low on his nose.

This can't be good.

"Dr. Grey, thanks for joining us," Brown said. "Let us get on with this, shall we? I'm sure you've got a class to get off to at eight. And we certainly don't want to shortchange our students as much as you've shortchanged us this morning."

Nope. Not good.

"As our letter informed you, we've requested your presence here this morning to commence a hearing for your tenure as full professor of religious studies at Princeton. And while, at this point, such a gathering would merely serve as a formality in our procedure, there are a few...*issues* that have arisen in our process that we would like to address with you this morning."

Silas's mouth went dry. A full pitcher of water and a single, crystal goblet stood at one end of his table mocking him, begging him to show weakness. He wouldn't dare. Instead, he swallowed hard and stared forward.

Dean Brown opened a leather portfolio with a seal of the university emblazoned on it and brought out a piece of paper, which he used to begin cycling through Silas's "issues."

"First of all, there is the matter of neglecting your professional academic duties and absence earlier this year."

"Excuse me?" It came out before Silas had realized it. Which he instantly regretted.

Brown appeared to have been thrown off, not expecting Silas to utter a word as he read his victim the Riot Act. He cleared his throat, then said, "Yes, Dr. Grey. Earlier this year when you were absent two weeks without any notification."

Oh, you mean when I was nearly blown to smithereens making a name for the university while presenting a paper at one of the most prestigious religious artifact conferences in the world? The one where I was subsequently apprehended by special-ops agents working for a little-known religious order in order to save one of the most important relics of the Christian faith?

Which I did, by the way, Dean Brown.

Is that the two-week absence you're referencing?

It took everything within him to keep these thoughts to himself. Instead, he sat still, merely nodding his understanding.

"Then there are the multiple reports of tardiness to class, which I submit this morning certainly testifies to. There's also the paltry amount of articles and monographs you've brought to publication for someone in your position who is normally considered for this honor. And then the matter of conflicted relations you seem to have with colleagues, most notably the good Dean McIntyre, whom you report to as the head of your department."

Humiliation was sinking deep into Silas's bones. Satisfaction was spreading across McIntyre's face.

Brown continued, "It is because of these issues that we have decided to hold off on granting tenure at this time."

Silas felt himself sink back into his chair, not realizing he had literally been sitting on its edge. He sighed, but straightened quickly. He wouldn't show weakness before these executioners. No way.

"Now, this doesn't mean you are off the rails of tenure track. We're merely postponing granting it until you have worked through some of the issues of your development plan. And we are fully confident you will come out on the other side a better professor."

They're putting me on STEPs?

Steps to Track Employee Progress was virtual purgatory for the university ecosystem, a cycle of penance for the academic to earn their way back into the graces of the administration. It was also a death knell for a professor, a clear signal that Silas's academic career was in jeopardy, despite Brown's reassurances.

"Do you have any questions, Dr. Grey?"

He didn't. No questions, no thoughts, no feelings. No nothing. He knew there might be consequences from helping the Order with rescuing the Shroud and from his own pursuits of scientifically validating its authenticity—all the while temporarily neglecting his academic duties. Definitely not a bright spot in his career. But did none of his accomplishments mean anything to these empty suits?

"No, sir," Silas said simply. "I understand."

"Alright, then. Dean McIntyre will coordinate where we go from here and get with you to outline the path toward moving you beyond this little blip in your career. And we will look forward to getting you back on track to become your fullest professorial self in order to serve the Princeton family to its fullest potential."

What a load of crap.

CHAPTER 2

Why do they schedule me for these blasted 8:00 a.m. classes!

Mornings were a sore subject for Silas. He much more preferred nocturnal exploits to sunrise ones. This one was made more painful by the browbeating from administrative bureaucrats and the decimation of his professional goal of tenure.

He was still seething with the outcome of the hearing. On top of it, he had a lecture to get to. That he was now late for. Already he was falling down, barely an hour into his new "development" plan.

After leaving the hearing, Silas had gone to his car to stew before class. He didn't know what else to do. He sat in his aging, sagging Jeep as the rain assaulted its windshield. He pounded his steering wheel with the palm of both hands in anger. Then he closed his eyes, sighed, and leaned his driver's seat back. He started counting backward to quell his anxiety, a trick he had learned back in Iraq during the post-9/11 conflicts. When he had returned home to the states, he used it to deal with his post-traumatic stress—along with the little pills sitting in his glove compartment.

Silas popped the latch and found the plastic container that would help him negotiate the rest of the day. He opened a thermos he brought along to celebrate and poured himself a cup of steaming black brew. He popped a pill and took a swig. He hesitated as he twisted the cap back on the bottle, before taking it off and popping one more.

Extra insurance.

He leaned back in his seat and sat still, the patter of rain a balm for his heart rate and anger and disappointment. A few minutes later, he had jolted upright and checked the gift from his father. It read 8:01 a.m. Class had already begun.

Silas swung open the door, stepped back into the rain, and headed for his lecture hall.

"Just great," Silas mumbled as he hunched forward struggling with the collar of his raincoat. From across the sidewalk, he spotted Dean McIntyre, all dry and comfortable and not wet underneath a massive, black golf umbrella. He glanced at his watch, almost dropping the thermos of his precious brew. 8:04 a.m.

"The last thing I need is another snarky comment about running late again. Especially after that blasted witch trial."

Lucky for Silas, another sidewalk opened up to his left. It would take him the opposite direction he needed to go. But the escape was welcomed. So he made it, avoiding He Who Shall Not Be Run Into.

The trees above his alternative route were thick, heavy blankets of reds and oranges and yellows, a welcomed relief as the rain began to pick up the pace. His mind flashed to a memory of camping one summer with his father and twin brother, Sebastian, along the Appalachian Trail in Northern Maine.

Dad had the fantastic idea to go camping with nothing more than pup tents mid-April. They don't say "April showers bring May flowers" for nothing. After a night of saggy, soppy, wet canopies, they called it and drove to a Holiday Inn. The indoor water park more than made up for Dad's folly. Now, he was dead, thanks to the plane that slammed into the Pentagon. And Silas and his brother were on less-than-speaking terms. Especially after what Sebastian pulled over the summer with the Gospel of Judas nonsense.

Silas pushed the memory and the painful fallout from his mind as he double-backed toward his lecture hall. 8:09 a.m. *Move it, Grey.*

He hustled faster and made it to the door as thunder rumbled in the distance. Heavy drops joined the morning chorus. Two coeds twenty-feet back squealed as the rain fell with fury. Apparently, they forgot their umbrellas, too.

"I half expect Noah's Ark to go floating by," Silas said as he stood holding the door open for the hapless victims, soaked through to the bone as much as he was.

"Thanks, Professor Grey," the ladies said in unison.

"Don't mention it. Now, let's get to class before all three of us are marked tardy."

After wiping down his face and close-cropped hair in the bathroom, Silas walked into his awaiting hall and down to his podium to get on with his lecture. The class was "History of Religious Relics," one of the more popular courses at the home of the Tigers, and his personal favorite among his roster. He had made something of a name for himself in his young, blossoming career as one of the leading experts in relicology, the study of relics. Especially after the events earlier in the year allowed him to authenticate the veracity of the Shroud of Turin, the burial cloth of Jesus Christ, and scientifically prove he rose from the dead. Or at least prove something monumental happened in what is believed to be Christ's tomb, preserved within the Church of the Holy Sepulcher.

That seemed like another lifetime ago as he opened his laptop and arranged his notes on the podium. *Another life I'd just as soon forget about.*

Silas raked his hand over his damp hair and loosened his tie a bit to air out the sauna that had become the inside of his shirt. At least his tweed jacket was dry.

"Alright, class. Sorry I'm late."

"You were lucky, prof," a guy in baggy sweatpants and a dark blue Princeton hoodie said. "We were one minute away from exercising our student right to leave after a fifteen-minute no-show."

"That's fine because I would have exercised my *professorial* right to mark you absent. Sorry to burst your bubble, but that so-called *rule* is an old wives' tale. You better get more creative if you want to skip out on one of my classes."

A few in the class laughed. Baggy Sweatpants did not.

"I do sincerely apologize because my tardiness is disrespectful to your time and hard-earned tuition dollars. And, no, that doesn't mean you're getting a refund for the last fifteen minutes." A few more laughed, even from Baggy Sweatpants. "What it does mean is I'm going to bring my A-game today as we dive into the Passion relics of Christianity. Who knows what I'm talking about when I say Passion relics?"

The class averted their eyes in unison.

"Come on, nobody?"

"Does it, like, have something to do with Jesus?"

One of the ladies Silas opened the door for on the way in. Insightful. "You're getting warmer. And glad to see your hair has dried since our last encounter."

The coed blushed and slunk down in her seat slightly. The class murmured, turning into a wave of giggles.

Oh gosh! Now Silas blushed. "I didn't mean it like that! I opened the door for Ms. Simmons and her two friends as we walked in here. Late, might I add. And the rain and all, and then the wind..."

More murmuring, more giggles, more blushing. "Forget it," he said waving his hands before advancing to the next slide in his

PowerPoint presentation. "Passion refers to the Passion Week or Holy Week, the events leading up to Jesus' death. And there are a number of objects that many have venerated over the past centuries to preserve the memory of those crucial events, given their meaning and weight for Christians."

Silas advanced the slide again, coming to the first relic: the scourging post.

"Here we have a portion of the post at which Jesus was scourged. It's said to have been taken to Rome in 1223 by John Cardinal Colonna and is now kept in a small chapel in the Church of Saint Praxedes. Of course, by 'scourging' I mean the post that Jesus was tied to when he was beaten and whipped before his death."

The next slide held a passage from the Gospel of Matthew, chapter 27. He read it:

> Then the soldiers of the governor took Jesus into the
> governor's headquarters, and they gathered the
> whole cohort around him. They stripped him and
> put a scarlet robe on him, and after twisting some
> thorns into a crown, they put it on his head.
> They put a reed in his right hand and knelt
> before him and mocked him, saying, "Hail, King
> of the Jews!" They spat on him, and took the reed
> and struck him on the head. After mocking him,
> they stripped him of the robe and put his own
> clothes on him. Then they led him away to
> crucify him.

"As you can see, this is the account of Jesus' scourging from Matthew's Gospel. And I'm sure you can understand why this relic is so important to Christians. This passage also has another relic, the crown of thorns."

Silas changed slides, showing a picture of the wreath of thorn bushes wrapped in the shape of a crown. A few students whispered to one another in surprise.

"It is a bit frightening, isn't it? Three evangelists in their Gospels speak of this crown of thorns, but give no description of it. Now, when most Westerners think of 'crown of thorns,' they think of this picture. Except in the East, around the time and place of Jesus, crowns took the shape of a cap or helmet. Meaning, they covered the whole head. This theory is supported by this intriguing picture."

He changed the slide again, this time showing a yellowed piece of linen, commanded by severe burn marks on either side with the faint outline of a man's face. The Shroud of Turin.

The image brought back memories from earlier in the year when he was nearly killed in a mission to save it after teaming up with a little-known religious organization. He thought about the Order of Thaddeus, the ancient Church order dedicated to preserving the memory of the Christian faith. About Rowan Radcliffe, Master of the Order. Matt Gapinski and Zoe Corbino. And Celeste Bourne, director of operations for Project SEPIO, the special-ops team that executes the Order's protecting mission. He had reluctantly been dragged into another one of their missions over the summer preserving the apostle relics and true story of Christ while proving the Gospel of Judas a hoax—which his brother had almost conned him into authenticating.

I wonder how she's doing?

Silas realized he had been staring in silence. He glanced up from his notes and noticed several of his students slouching and beginning to doze off. He cleared his throat and changed slides. This should wake them up.

And it did. Several gasped at the sight: the Shroud had been enlarged and enhanced by a computer algorithm to accentuate the features of the imprinted image. One side showed the soft face of a dead, Middle Eastern man, with long hair and protruding nose lying in repose. The other side showed the back of his head with obvious, dark cut marks embedded in the man's matted head.

"What you're looking at," Silas continued, "is the image of Jesus Christ, seared into the burial cloth which held his body. Got your attention now?"

As if to say "Yes," many of the students sat straighter. A few nodded in response.

"We will cover the Shroud of Turin in a separate lecture later, but for now know that those marks on his head are from a crown of thorns in the shape of a cap, supporting this theory. This relic has been kept at various sites, after having been found in the Church of the Holy Sepulcher. Along with this."

He changed to yet another slide, showing the image of an ornate container holding a piece of wood.

"This is known as the Holy Cross or True Cross. In the year 326, Saint Helena, mother of Emperor Constantine, was sent to Jerusalem to recover the cross and other relics of the Passion. There are a few stories about how she came to be in possession of this Christian artifact, from rumors of clandestine missions to divine revelation. Whichever is correct, it is known Helena found the True Cross and that she and her son Constantine erected a magnificent basilica over the Holy Sepulcher with the exact place of discovery situated beneath the atrium."

Silas forwarded to the next slide of the Church of the Holy Sepulcher in Jerusalem, with its boxy shrine within the larger basilica housing the burial tomb of Christ. The one that was nearly destroyed in his mission with SEPIO while trying to protect the memory of Christ's resurrection.

"It is said that a portion of the cross was enclosed in a silver reliquary in this church, another piece was given to Constantine and enclosed in a statue of himself, and a sizable portion was brought to Rome and installed in yet another basilica named after the Holy Cross in Jerusalem. While it may seem farfetched to have been in possession of the actual cross of Christ, several early Church fathers assured members that the Church was in possession of it, from Cyril of Jerusalem to Saint Augustine. Relics of the cross of notable size are claimed by several churches, including the Notre Dame Cathedral in Paris."

Silas looked out at his audience. Sensing early morning restlessness, he checked his watch, then nodded. "Why don't we take fifteen?"

During the break, the sarcastic sophomore in baggy sweatpants approached him to have a chat. While addressing an issue with one of his recently graded papers, Silas noticed a woman had walked into the lecture hall from a door off to the side. She was carrying a large, black umbrella. Her long, dark hair was hanging loose and full down on her shoulders. She leaned against the wall and undid her raincoat, then smiled and waved.

Silas meant to smile back. Instead, his mouth fell open.

Celeste Bourne. What are you doing here?

CHAPTER 3

"Hello, Professor Grey."

Silas couldn't help but smile at her mentioning his name in perfectly polished British English. He greeted her by reaching in for an embrace, trying to hide his surprise. He asked the obvious: "What are you doing here?"

"What, can't a girl drop in on her former partner-in-crime? After all, we did almost get blown to bits in our last two encounters."

Silas chuckled. There certainly was something about hanging on the precipice of death that bonds two people. But this was unexpected. And suspect. He noticed the coeds he rescued from earlier in the morning glancing over, then giggling. He rolled his eyes, then motioned for them to step into the hallway.

Celeste led the way, taking her time walking in her long, black boots. Silas followed, trying not to stare at the figure in front of him. As a former MI6 agent and director of operations for SEPIO, she knew how to keep in shape. It showed. He glanced back over to the group of coeds. They smiled and giggled again. He removed his tie, feeling the heat rising again. Nothing about the morning was going as planned.

Silas closed the door to the lecture hall. "Nice seeing you, and all, but what's up? I told Radcliffe I wasn't interested. The first time and the seventh. Sending you isn't exactly the best way to plead his case. No offense or anything."

Celeste smiled slightly, her lips never parting, but nose flaring slightly. "None taken."

The tone of her British-laced words wasn't as frosty the first time he met her. But there was an edge to them. Silas raked his hand over his close-cropped hair and glanced up the hallway, then down at his watch.

"Seriously, what's the deal? I've got a class to get back to."

Celeste opened her mouth to say something, but then stopped herself. She folded her arms before saying, "Is there someplace we can talk?"

"We are talking."

She sighed. "I mean someplace private." She unfolded her arms and said in a lower voice, "Please, it's important."

Silas got the feeling he was being recruited for another hair-brained mission. Why else would Celeste be here? He shifted and glanced up the hall again.

"I've got, like, two minutes before I'm supposed to lecture more about the True Cross. Plus, I'm still paying my Dean for missing a week of lectures last time you used me for one of your operations during the semester."

"I seem to recall you benefited from that operation you speak so highly of. Besides, I'm sure your students won't mind getting let out early."

Silas stepped back, tilted his head backward, and squinted one eye. "What you got cooking this time?"

She just folded her arms again and smiled.

He looked at his watch again, looked at Celeste, then sighed. "Hold on."

Most of the room had already reassembled itself and sat ready for the last half of the lecture. Silas was sorry to disappoint. After explaining something had come up that he had to attend to, he dismissed the class for the morning until next week. He grabbed his raincoat and satchel, and met Celeste back out in the hallway.

Walking past her, he said, "This better be good."

"No need to fret. It is."

The rain had stopped, but a frigid breeze had replaced the mild temperatures. Since classes were still in session for another hour, the sidewalks were virtually empty, leaving Silas and Celeste to chat in peace.

"So," Silas started, hands in his coat and head down, "how've you been?"

Celeste grinned slightly, mildly amused at his attempt at pleasantries. "Oh, you know. Same ol' same ol'. And you? How's your brother?"

Silas appreciated her asking. On their mission to save the Shroud, he had shared their relationship had been strained ever since their father had passed, and he had found religion in the military. As a spiritual-but-not-religious former-Catholic agnostic, Sebastian strained to understand his life direction as a professor of Christian theology. Silas admitted he had played the proselytizing card too early, too often, and too hard, which contributed. He had only wanted to share with him what he himself had experienced. But it was too much. And then with Sebastian being caught up in their exploits, having been nearly kidnapped by the ancient enemy of the Order and Christian faith, Nous, and then betraying Silas's trust, the past few months had returned to a status quo they both seemed to have reconciled themselves to.

He looked over at her as they walked, nodding and smiling slightly. "Thanks for asking, but nothing's changed."

She turned to him and offered a sympathetic smile. "Sorry."

"It is what it is. At least we're still mostly on speaking terms."

Silas held the door open for Celeste when they reached his office building.

"How chivalrous of you, Dr. Grey," she said taking off her jacket. Silas nodded and led the way inside.

"Hello, Millie," Silas said when they reached his office. "This is my friend Celeste. You might remember her from my harrowing adventures the past few months."

"Why, yes!" She came out from around her desk and gave Celeste a hug. Which was quite the sight, seeing the five-foot-four Millie embrace the six-foot Celeste. "So good to meet you, Celeste. I've heard so much about you!" She winked at Silas and grinned widely before returning to her chair.

Silas rolled his eyes. "You'll have to excuse my administrative assistant. She had a concussion a few years back and is prone to alternative facts and misremembering things."

"Aren't we all?" she said, following Silas to his office.

"Professor, for whatever reason have you returned?"

"Hello to you, too, Miles. Miles meet Celeste. Celeste, Miles. He's my trusty sidekick."

"Celeste?" Miles said, turning to Silas. "As in, Celeste Bourne? That...lady?"

Silas frowned. "That is, he's *been* my trusty sidekick. But that could always change."

Celeste smiled and extended her hand. "Nice to meet you, Miles." He took it, and said, "Likewise." He turned to Silas, and said, "But why are you back, what, almost an hour early?"

Silas set his satchel down on a pile of papers on his desk then took off his coat. "Super-secret meeting for which we need our privacy." He nodded toward the door, eyebrows raised.

"Got it. Nice to meet you." Miles waved goodbye and left, closing the door behind him with a wink.

Celeste said goodbye and looked for a place to sit. The only two seats available were filled with stacks of books and manila folders full of papers, some spilling their contents. Between the shelves of thick, musty books, the Mr. Coffee full of day-old coffee on a mini-fridge in the corner, and a stack of records next to his desk, the cliché of the messy absentminded professor was perfectly formed.

"Sorry about that. Here, let me move those." Silas came out from behind his desk. She picked up one of his records as he tossed the contents of one of his chairs to the floor, then motioned for Celeste to have a seat.

"Miles Davis fan, are you?" she asked holding up the record.

"You know it. Here, have a seat."

She set down the record and took a seat. When she did, she gave a startled cry.

He turned around and frowned. "Barnabas!"

A slate-gray Persian cat had lunged for Celeste's lap and was making himself at home. She sat frozen with arms raised and eyes wide. "What do I do?"

Silas laughed and crossed his arms. "Am I to understand that Celeste Bourne has met her match in a *cat*?"

"Just get it off, would you?" she said waving her raised arms.

He laughed again, then came around the desk and grabbed the stout feline. "There, there, big fella. She takes a while warming up to you. I'd know."

Celeste scoffed and smacked his back with the backside of her hand as he plopped the gray furball outside his door.

"Didn't take you for a cat person," she said as Silas went back to his chair.

"Neither did I. Picked him up while serving with the Rangers during Operation Iraqi Freedom. He was just skin-and-bones when he wandered into camp looking for a handout. I'd always been a dog lover, but the poor fella played a number on my heart-strings, and that was that."

"Aww, what a fine chap you are. But I thought U.S. Central Command outlawed companion animals."

"They did, just before 9/11. But I was nearly finished with my tour, and it seemed like the right thing to do."

She cocked her head and smiled. "Barnabas…He was Paul's

companion on his missionary journeys, wasn't he? Means *'son of comfort,'* right?"

He nodded. "Sure was. And he's definitely lived up to his name. So, what brings you to my humble abode?"

She crossed her legs and leaned back in her chair. "Does the name Lucas Pryce mean anything to you?"

Silas snapped his head back and cocked it slightly. "Wow, haven't heard that name in a decade." He stopped and furrowed his brow. "But you already knew that, didn't you?"

The corner of Celeste's mouth curled upward. "Perhaps. So what can you tell me about him?"

Silas opened his bottom drawer in search of a clean coffee mug. "One of the leading archaeologists of our time. Expert in ancient, Near Eastern cultures, specifically ancient, Semitic culture, and especially Hebraic and the pre-Davidic dynastic eras."

"And you worked with him."

Having found a mug, albeit encrusted with a bit of stale coffee, he walked over to Mr. Coffee for a shot of brew. "And I worked with him, for a summer. It was an internship at one of his digs, Tell-es Sultan." Silas paused to fill up the mug from his alma mater Harvard with the tar-like substance leftover from earlier in the morning. Celeste grimaced as he did.

"That's the old Jericho site if you didn't know," he said, walking back to his desk.

"Yes, I did know, thanks. I have never understood how you Yanks could consume that sludge."

Silas picked up his mug and grinned. "What's this?" He took a swig, then grimaced himself. "It was better this morning. At any rate, he was one of my professors for an elective I took during my doctoral work at Harvard. The summer after the elective he had gone to the old Jericho site to oversee an expanded excavation of the southern section to test some theories he had regarding the city's destruction, and more importantly when that destruction took place. He invited me along for a front row seat. It was fascinating stuff."

"Did you discover anything of noteworthiness?"

He nodded. "We did. Not only did we discover identical rubble underneath two other layers of construction, indicating the same kind of sudden, cataclysmic destruction of the city as the previous excavations found. We also discovered that this portion was part of the royal quarters, which led to a most curious find."

Silas took another swig of his coffee, then leaned back in his chair and propped up his legs on his desk, pausing for dramatic effect.

Celeste raised her eyebrows and tilted her head. "And?"

One end of his mouth curled upward. "Preserved in a jar were scrolls that basically verified the story of the book of Joshua."

Celeste sat up straighter and scooted slightly to the edge of her seat. "The story of Joshua? Which one?"

"Which one? You're worse than my lapsed-Catholic brother."

Celeste rolled her eyes and sighed. "Just give it to me, prof. And without the cheek."

Silas held up his hands in surrender. "Alright. Didn't mean to hit a nerve. You know, the one about Joshua and the battle of Jericho. The prostitute Rahab and the two spies. The marches around the city with the Ark of the Covenant. The trumpet blasts—"

"Wait a minute," Celeste interrupted. "Did you say the Ark of the Covenant?"

"The one and only. Then on the seventh pass around the city, the people gave a shout and, 'The walls came tumbling down,'" he sang.

"Cute. Catholic school song or something?"

"Evangelical Vacation Bible School one summer. A friend brought me. Stuck with me ever since."

"Let's go back to the Ark. What role did it play?"

"George Lucas and Stephen Spielberg popularized it as some superpower weapon, but it wasn't like that. It was said to contain the power of God. Or, at least God's presence was with it as it circled around the city. It was his power and his presence that brought down the walls. Not the Ark."

"And Pryce discovered this verification in some sort of scroll you say?"

Silas squinted and tilted his head, the corner of his mouth curling up toward a smile. "What aren't you telling me, Celeste? Why all the interest in Pryce?"

Before Celeste could answer, there was a knock at the door. "Come in," Silas said. It was Miles.

"Professor, have you been on the internet?"

Silas brought his legs off his desk quickly and sat up in his chair, bringing his laptop to life. "No, what happened? Please don't tell me another bomb blast took out another one of my colleagues."

"No, no," Miles said waving his arms. "Nothing like that. It's your old professor, Lucas Pryce, from Harvard."

Celeste and Silas shot a wide-eyed look at each other. "Give me the 411."

"Apparently, he's found the Ark of the Covenant!"

CHAPTER 4

Silas and Celeste followed Miles out to the adjoining space where Miles kept his desk. It was a far cry from the cluttered mess of his boss.

Unlike Silas's, he kept his notes and books in neat piles, arranged on shelves. And there was an electric kettle of water boiling in the windowsill, with a half-drained cup of tea on his desk. He was the Yin to Silas's more messy, absent-minded professor Yang.

"What do you mean he's found the Ark of the Covenant?" Silas questioned as they shuffled over to Miles's desk.

"Well, not found, per se. More on the verge of finding. Just take a look." Miles angled his computer monitor so that Silas and Celeste could read the breaking-news article on CNN.com.

And what a fascinating read it was. Silas scrolled quickly as the two took in the almost surreal developments in biblical archaeology, undoubtedly one of the most monumental events of the millennia. As the article explained, Dr. Lucas Pryce was able to get the Imam of al-Aqsa Mosque and caretaker of the Dome of the Rock, and the Sephardic Chief Rabbi of the Jewish contingent of the ancient, holy city of Jerusalem to come together to open a new exploration for the Ark under the holy Temple Mount.

"This is unbelievable," Silas muttered as he continued reading, while Celeste looked on with less surprise.

The article continued to explain how Pryce had lobbied the two separately for nearly two years, outlining a case for the two religions to come together in the interest of peace and the world community to help unearth one of the most important relics for both religions. He apparently had offered new evidence for the location of the artifact and the genuine possibility of its unearthing, though Pryce withheld details for the sake of confidentiality.

"Did you know about this development?" Silas asked, looking up at Celeste while still leaning over Miles's desk.

Celeste folded her arms and hesitated. "We didn't know that it had come to this, to an impending unearthing of the most sought-after religious relic ever. Not to mention the forging of a bond between arguably two of the most important religious leaders in Islam and Judaism. But a SEPIO operative brought us intelligence indicating Pryce was on the verge of a major archaeological exploration of biblical proportions. Literally."

"I'd say. This is huge! And what's this ecumenical kumbaya? Doesn't make sense! Each of them has far more to lose than gain in joining forces. Something's not right."

"Sorry to interject," Miles said, "but there appears to be a live stream video attached to the article." Silas and Celeste broke off their conversation, looking on as Miles brought up the live feed.

"...of historic proportions, Wolf. You couldn't have scripted a better, more surprising reversal than the heads of two of the predominant religions in the world's most holy city coming together in this monumental show of solidarity and cooperation in order to explore, and, hopefully, discover, the world's most popular religious artifact."

"Indeed you couldn't!" Wolf Blitzer responded enthusiastically. "This is on the scale of James Rollins or Clive Cussler, isn't, Mara?"

Mara Mitchell chuckled. "Yes, it is, exactly. A made-for-block-buster twist, that's for sure. But hopefully not in the Dan Brown, religious conspiracy vein, Wolf."

"Hopefully not!" The man with thick, gray hair and round glasses pivoted from the reporter to the viewing public. "If you're just joining us, we are live from the Western Wall of the Temple Mount in Old City Jerusalem as there has been a stunning development in Israeli-Palestinian relations, or more specifically Jewish-Muslim relations as the head rabbi and imam in the Holy City have announced their partnership to, hopefully, discover the fabled Ark of the Covenant. Yes, you heard that right. And, no, such a partnership wasn't arranged by Dr. Jones, but rather a Dr. Lucas Pryce, chair of the Archaeology Department at Harvard University. Take a listen to a recap of a news conference that ended earlier today."

"Unreal," Miles said, voicing the collective sentiment in the room as the feed faded to a scene from earlier in the morning. It was a tight shot of Pryce, a tall, trim man in a loose-fitting, stone-colored linen suit sporting a scraggly, salt-and-pepper beard and bronzed skin from a lifetime of digs. Joining him was Chief Rabbi Shlomo Amar and Imam Muhammad Ahmad Hussein walking onto a stage, flanked by guards and surrounded by news cameras bearing all of the symbols of the world's news agencies.

The feed flashed again, forward to Pryce's announcement, given in a thick, but pleasant, Southern drawl: "Several years ago, I was on a dig in the heart of the West Bank, where I discovered an ancient manuscript from a forgotten civilization that stirred in me a passion for finding an ancient, religious artifact that has bedeviled archaeologists and historians for centuries."

"Hey, that was my dig!" Silas exclaimed.

"Shh," Celeste reprimanded. "Listen."

"And it sparked in me the possibility of not only finding the long-fabled Ark of the Covenant. But using the search to bring about a lasting peace between two interested parties who hold this artifact, this relic of the past, to be immensely important for their respective faiths. So, after hounding my new-found friends for several months," Pryce chuckled, turning to either side to acknowledge the rabbi and imam. They smiled in agreement. "After hounding them for nearly two years, imploring them to let me dig and explore a new passageway beneath the Temple Mount that runs through both Jewish and Muslim quarters, in the interest of peace and mutual, cultural understanding, they've agreed. And I must say, I couldn't be more pleased with the level of interest and empathy offered by both parties, Rabbi Amar and Imam Hussein."

Pryce turned in outstretched arms to acknowledge his new partners on either side, the audience clapping in recognition.

As Silas looked on, envy began creeping up his spine. For what Silas hadn't told Celeste was that he was the one who found the jars with the scrolls. It should have been his academic win. But since he was being supervised as a PhD student, legally and professionally, Lucas Pryce could claim it as his own. And since Pryce was the one who translated the royal court notations on the processions of the Israelites around the city of Jericho, perhaps he should be the one taking credit anyhow.

But, man...what he wouldn't have done to have been the one on that stage, getting credit for the original find. And for the Ark. What an achievement that would have been! Perhaps it would have compelled his Princeton colleagues to take him more seriously. Perhaps it would have compelled his brother to take his faith more seriously.

As Silas silently stewed, Pryce continued his press conference: "One hopes this new partnership in search of this lost, ancient relic that means a great deal to both religions will help build a bridge toward lasting peace in a way where others have tried and failed. I look forward to showing the world our findings very soon, resurrecting the Ark of the Covenant from hiding these many centuries."

The feed cut away from the press conference in Jerusalem and back to Wolf Blitzer at CNN's breaking-news headquarters. "That was Dr. Lucas Pryce of Harvard University announcing a stunning, monumental breakthrough between Israelis and Palestinians, Jews and Muslims. He announced earlier today a new effort to unearth the fabled Ark of the Covenant from apparently a recently discovered, hidden chamber using a passage that extends through both Jewish and Muslim territories in the holy city. We'll be sure to share further breaking developments in this fascinating story in the coming days."

The feed ended, then launched a commercial for the newest model of a Mercedes. The room was silent as it played its full thirty-seconds until cycling into an archived news item on the presidential campaigns.

Miles closed the laptop and looked at Silas for guidance. Silas broke eye contact and looked at Celeste.

"Miles, cancel my classes for the rest of the day. It seems Ms. Bourne and I need to have ourselves an extended conversation about my old professor."

CHAPTER 5

JERUSALEM, ISRAEL.

L ucas Pryce was a man who got things done. He was a
man of means who brought about ends to his liking.

For instance, when he was a young boy, he wanted a
Red Ryder. One of those slick wagons made of steel and painted
to a bright, polished red that zoomed down streets and strafed
corners like it was their business. Those things were made to fly.
And Pryce thought he was made to fly, too. But wagons don't grow
on trees, and neither does money.

Since his dad had been laid off for going on eleven months
after the local Chattanooga saw mill shuttered, Pops got him a
boomerang for his seventh birthday instead. He was so angry
with his cheap-wad-of-a-father that he broke the thing in half,
right then and there and stuffed the pieces in his birthday cake.

Lucas Pryce was a boy who got things done, gosh darn it. He
was a boy of means who brought about ends to his liking. So the
next day, after being sent to bed without supper for his tantrum,
he marched down to the local Five and Dime on Main Street,
shoved open the door without a care in the world for the little
tinkle-tinkle sound alerting the manager to his presence, grabbed
ahold of the handle of Mr. Thomson's last remaining Red Ryder,
and kept right on walking through the back storeroom and out

the door that serviced Mr. Thompson's smoking habit, who was completely unaware of the absconding. After all, who would suspect a seven-year-old boy, barely three feet tall and fifty pounds soaking wet, of robbing them blind?

Yes, sir. Lucas Pryce was a man who got things done. And today was no different.

After he finished giving his last interview of the morning, Pryce had headed straight for his hotel room. He was soaked through his white, linen dress shirt from the hot, sticky Middle Eastern morning. His stone-colored, linen suit was even starting to show wet marks in spots, and Pryce couldn't stand to let a good suit go stale. He had to look his tip-top best if he was to continue to delicately thread the fine needle between the two most contentious religions on the most volatile patch of land on God's green earth.

His long confidence game was about to come to an end. Finally. And he'd best be looking the part at the finish line, owning the prize and pissing on the religious losers. All three of them.

After stripping down to nothing but his birthday suit, Pryce opened the heavy, thin glass door and stepped into the shower of his well-appointed hotel room. He turned the right knob fully on, leaving the one on the left shut off.

For minutes he stood still under the cascading fountain of chilly water, his skin a coat of goose pimples. He needed every one of his senses drawn taut to their fullest alertness. The coming days called for DEFCON 1, and his little, pre-game ritual was just what the doctor ordered.

After a full thirty minutes under the arctic blast, Pryce shut off the water, stepped out of the shower, and slipped into a white, Egyptian-cotton robe hanging behind his bathroom door. He edged to his massive, king-size bed and flopped backward into its luxury.

Every fiber of his being was tingling. Not merely from the

cold shower, but from the adrenaline still coursing through him since he woke that morning.

After six-and-a-half years of painstaking preparation. After nearly two years fondling the egos and massaging the relationships of the rabbi and imam. After arranging all of the pieces on my board— it's within my grasp!

As he swam in the soft, billowy duvet of his bed, his mind buzzing with delight, he thought back to the day he discovered the golden ring. His *precious*, as he liked to call it. He had initially set out to disprove the historical veracity of the Bible's claims to the events surrounding the ancient city. Who in their right mind could believe in such a preposterous fable! Billions, apparently.

Including his pops. It's what he clung to when life went sour —when he lost his job, when he lost three kids to a house fire, and when he lost his wife giving birth to his youngest son Lucas James. Belief in God—even the kind of God who would level cities filled with women and children, who would take innocent kiddos in a residential inferno and a woman doing the most natural, God-given vocation on the planet—belief in this God centered Pops. It was his rock, his fortress. An ever-present help in times of trouble, as the good King David once wrote. Ditto for the parishioners of the small, country church that Pops had tried his hand at pastoring as a second career post-saw mill, the one Pops had been grooming him to take over when he turned twenty-one.

Yet, when push came to shove, that rock, that fortress, that ever-present-help couldn't stop the old man from blowing off the back of his head with a .22 Colt pistol. The crushing depression from a life of misery had finally dealt a hand the man couldn't beat, and God was nowhere to be found.

The worst part about it all was that Pops made him clean up the mess after he flew the coop to glory. It was always his messes that had needed cleaning.

What a Judas.

But Lucas Pryce was a man who got things done. And that bathroom wall never looked so spick-and-span! Even the toilet bowl and countertop never shined so well after Lucas Pryce was finished with them.

Pryce sighed at the memory. *Bastard.* Then another thought trailed that one: had it not been for Pops popping off his head— hey, he liked the ring of that. Pops popping. Anyway, had it turned out some other way, Pryce could very well be sitting in some parsonage with a wife and quiver full of kiddos and church flock to attend to.

A shiver shimmied up his spine, jolting him upright at the thought. He thanked the gods above and below for the full-ride scholarship that opened his eyes to the reality of faith, life, and everything in between and set sail his life down the path that had brought him to this crucial moment.

His mouth had gone dry from the day, so he sauntered over to the mini bar and grabbed the bottle of last night's champagne celebrating what was to transpire the next morning.

He poured himself half a glass, then poured some more just shy of the top.

Cheers, Dad. Thanks for the pop, Pops.

He began to take a sip, but giggled at the thought, the sudsy libation tickling his nose. He walked over to the large picture window facing the Old City and smiled, then took a sip. He swished it around slightly before swallowing.

Juniper and apricot. His favorite.

Lucas Pryce was a man who got things done. And he's only just begun.

CHAPTER 6

PRINCETON.

W asn't it enough for the Universe to take away from me the one professional goal I'd been striving for years to see realized, banking on for months? Now It had to rub salt into my professional wounds with Pryce's fame and academic glory? And all because of what I found half a decade ago?

The one-two punch left Silas deflated and defeated. He sat silent and fuming.

"What did you say?" Celeste asked, interrupting Silas's envious pity party.

"Huh?"

"Your lips were moving, but I couldn't hear what you were saying."

Silas blushed, then shook his head. "Nothing."

"Well, then, let's get to it. Tell me everything you can about Lucas Pryce, especially the dig you and he worked on, and that manuscript of the Ark he found."

Silas ran a hand over his head and sighed. "I'm not sure what there is to tell. The first semester of my second year at Harvard I took an elective from him on Semitic history and artifacts. It was interesting stuff. We worked through some of the material from the Old Testament, but mostly the Jewish Apocrypha and pseudepigrapha material, as well as several of the scrolls from the Dead Sea Scrolls cache from the mid-twentieth century. He was pretty skeptical of the historical significance of the readings, insisting they were stories generated by the community to preserve some sort of communal memory of oppression, rather than an actual historical record."

"So he was a religious skeptic, then?"

"You could say that," Silas paused. "Until the Jericho dig."

"Tell me about that."

"During the summer semester, Pryce took a few other students and me from the class to the dig site at Tell-es Sultan, the modern name for what many believe to be the biblical city of Jericho. Academics and archeologists first paid attention to it back in the 1800s when there was a surge of interest in the ancient history of the Middle East, particularly ancient Israel. The primary interest in the Holy Land was Jerusalem, but the second was the ancient, strategic site of Jericho. First, there was a British engineer who determined the large mounds were man-made castle-like structures. Then some Austrians and Germans unearthed a retaining wall circling the city that was meant to stop erosion. And in the 1930s, another British explorer applied more modern archaeological methods to the dig site, which unearthed a collapsed city wall on top of another wall, which was on top of that retaining wall. They also revealed evidence that the city was violently destroyed around 1400 BC, just like the Bible said."

"Fascinating historiography, professor, but what does this have to do with Pryce?"

"Hold on, I'm getting there."

Celeste held up her hands in surrender. "Carry on."

"The site languished for a while until our now-famous professor Lucas Pryce secured funding for another go at uncovering more of the city to see if there was anything else of interest."

"And was there?"

Silas rolled his eyes and chuckled. "You're worse than a

toddler at bedtime! And yes, there was. It was actually quite fascinating work. Pryce was able to secure use of LiDAR imaging equipment."

Celeste furrowed her brow and shook her head in confusion.

He explained, "LiDAR had been used during the Apollo 15 mission to map the surface of the moon and in large-scale terrestrial charting. But in the last decade, the resolution has significantly increased so that it can be used to unveil fine-scale archaeological features. Think of it as sonar for the ground."

Celeste nodded. "Got it."

"So we brought out this equipment and spent two days mapping some of the unexplored quadrants of the dig site. What we saw was incredible. Details of the implosion that hadn't been uncovered before showing fallen debris within the city walls, but also how the sections of the walls themselves had blown outward like a force had come down into the middle of the city from above, and then pushed the walls outward from the inside. It was pretty remarkable."

"Sounds like it."

"Then we used those images to carefully remove layers of earth surrounding buildings and some of the wall sections. It was a week of painstaking work, but what we found made even Pryce's jaw drop. The destruction was complete. Walls and floors were blackened by fire, and every room was filled with fallen bricks, timbers, and household utensils. In most rooms, the fallen debris was heavily burnt, but the collapsed walls of the eastern rooms seemed to have taken place before they were affected by the fire. Just like the book of Joshua said. The walls came down, then the Israelites destroyed the city."

"Remarkable."

"If that wasn't enough, we discovered jars of thousands-year-old grain that were burned to a crisp! The city had a full food supply at the time of destruction. Which is significant, because ancient siege techniques would cut the city off from its food supply, waiting them out until they ran out of food and starved to death. We found jars full of burned grain, telling us that the destruction of the city was sudden and total, probably happened at the completion of the harvest season. It also told us that the invading army didn't plunder its food supply. Again, just as the Bible reports."

"Incredible," Celeste whispered, but then hesitated.

"What?"

She smiled. "I appreciate the travelogue, but can we move along to the connection with Pryce and the Ark?"

Silas rolled his eyes again. "I'm getting to it. Sheesh. So we were pretty stoked at this point, having added significantly to the archaeological findings of the city and the historical record. But Pryce still wasn't buying that it supported the Bible's claim. Especially since previous carbon dating work had contradicted the claim from the one British explorer that the city was destroyed along the Bible's timeframe of 1400 BC. So, being the contrarian I am, I took another look at the LiDAR imaging data and noticed a large building with several chambers in the southern section we hadn't explored. It looked to contain lots of pots and other items. Pryce thought it was interesting, but was busy with the other findings. Since we had another week left, Pryce encouraged me to lead some of the crew and students in unearthing that portion."

"That was nice of him."

Silas smiled. "Well, I'm not sure about that. I think he didn't think anything would come of it that would bloat his fame more than what we had already found. But after a few days of careful, non-stop work, Pryce came to regret his decision."

Celeste's eyes widened. "The scrolls about the Ark?"

Silas grinned and said nothing.

"You found it?"

"Yep. It was part of a larger cache of proclamations and records belonging to the royalty class. And those were part of a larger set of structures that we discovered that were part of the royal courts and residential dwellings. After we peeled back several layers, I found six large pots sealed with clay, and what looked like some sort of royal insignia impressed upon the top marking it as part of the royal household. Naturally, I broke them open. And inside were scrolls. Between the sealed pots and layers of earth and environmental factors, they were perfectly preserved. I knew well enough not to do anything with them until I brought them to Pryce. So we carried the jars over to the main staging tent."

"I bet he went wild."

"Well, he was excited, but it wasn't until we unrolled them for translation that he got more interested in our work. In fact, he quickly took over, claiming credit for the find itself."

Silas huffed and shook his head, eyes narrowing at Celeste. She frowned and nodded, as if she understood his feelings of being sidelined and the envy he was now carrying in light of the CNN report.

"Anyway," he said shaking his head, "as much as we could figure, they were written by a scribe of the court. It must have been part of his daily duties to record matters of importance for the record of the kingdom. And that record described in detail the events surrounding what we find in Joshua chapter six. The scribe recorded the movements of the army of Israel over the course of six days, with particular attention paid to a large, golden box with two golden gods affixed to its top. He clearly thought it was some sort of spiritual weapon channeling the powers of the deities. Of course, there is no seventh pot with a seventh scroll, because he didn't have time to make one after the surprise that was in store for the city."

Silas paused. "Here, listen to some of it." He opened a drawer to his desk. He reached inside and brought out a well-worn leather book with red-stained edges. His old Bible.

Now Jericho was shut up inside and out because of the Israelites; no one came out, no one went in. The Lord said to Joshua, "See, I have handed Jericho over to you, along with its king and soldiers. You shall march around the city, all the warriors circling the city once. Thus you shall do for six days, with seven priests bearing seven trumpets of rams' horns before the ark. On the seventh day, you shall march around the city seven times, the priests blowing the trumpets. When they make a long blast with the ram's horn, as soon as you hear the sound of the trumpet, then all the people shall shout with a great shout; and the wall of the city will fall down flat, and all the people shall charge straight ahead." So Joshua son of Nun summoned the priests and said to them, "Take up the ark of the covenant, and have seven priests carry seven trumpets of rams' horns in front of the ark of the Lord." To the people, he said, "Go forward and march around the city; have the armed men pass on before the ark of the Lord."

Silas set it aside. "That manuscript I discovered five years ago is proof not only of the historicity of the city of Jericho and how it was destroyed. But of the Ark of the Covenant itself."

Silence fell between the two.

Silas finally broke it with a low hum, as if a memory had bubbled up to the surface.

"What's that?"

He shook his head. "Just something I remembered."

Celeste tilted her head, waiting for him to continue.

"What's interesting is that I remember Pryce was super interested in those scrolls. Which would make sense at some level. I mean, it was a major find. But it was different. He had them brought to his tent for the remaining two days we had left of our trip. And one time I caught him late one evening with the scrolls all unrolled and displayed around him. He was seated in the middle of them, and he was hovered over them just studying them. And there was this low muttering, and I could have sworn I heard him say something about the Ark."

"Peculiar."

"It was. And creepy. A few months after we returned, I asked him about the scrolls. Wanted to see whatever came of *my* find. He was very dismissive. Said they were nothing. That I shouldn't give them a second thought." He paused and shook his head. "But I know they sparked something in him. An obsession."

"And now, five years later, he's leading an exploration to uncover the hidden Ark of the Covenant."

Silas frowned and nodded.

Celeste sat forward, face determined. "You know what this means, don't you?"

Silas said nothing.

She stood. "We need to go pay your old friend a visit. You and me. Together."

CHAPTER 7

"No way, Celeste. No way!" Silas stood and walked over to the sludge left in Mr. Coffee, violating two of his cardinal rules: not more than one cup per hour after breakfast, and never waste the day on bad coffee. He frowned, shaking the pot slightly, but poured himself a second cup anyway.

"Hear me out," Celeste replied, having already returned to her seat for round two.

Silas returned to his desk, set down his mug, and flopped in his leather chair with a sigh. "I told Radcliffe I wasn't interested."

"You told Radcliffe you'd consider it."

"How do you know about that?"

Celeste cocked her head. "I know because Radcliffe sent me to fetch you."

Silas took another sip, grimacing, but pushing through considering the circumstances.

After his first mission and then again after he was dragged back into the Order's orbit against his will a few months ago, Rowan Radcliffe had revealed that SEPIO was tracking multiple Nous operatives and multiple developing scenarios within the secret society aimed at undermining the Church. He had asked

Silas to join them, stroking his ego by explaining they could use someone of his academic and military training, and dangling untold opportunity for research and academic discovery before his eyes.

Silas had demurred the first time and then a second, insisting he needed to return back to his students and work at the university. Secretly, he didn't think he could handle one more engagement that reminded him of his tours in Afghanistan and Iraq. And freezing again under enemy fire, as he had during the first operation, was not something he wanted to repeat. Especially under the gaze of Celeste.

"Well?"

Silas refocused on her, not having realized he had fallen silent. He took another sip of coffee. "Well, what?"

Celeste huffed. "Stop the dramatics. SEPIO needs your help figuring out what's going on with Pryce and the Israelis and Arabs across the pond. So are you going to man up, or what?"

Silas rolled his eyes. "You don't need me. You've got plenty of operatives who could suss that out. Shoot, you could woo the Indiana Jones wannabes yourself with your English charm and wit."

Celeste smiled slightly. "While you are probably right, it has to be you. You have the history with Pryce in a way that will cut down on the bridge-building. Besides, you can handle yourself if things...take a turn, and we need to use more kinetic means."

Silas grimaced at the euphemism for the kind of force that almost got him and his brother killed earlier in the year.

Celeste continued, "And don't you want in on one of the greatest discoveries in modern archaeology? Surely a good Ark-of-the-Covenant hunt should entice you to join. I can see the headline now: PRINCETON PROFESSOR FINDS ARK OF THE COVENANT."

Silas considered her ego stroking, draining his mug and setting it on the desk. He certainly would love to reclaim the honors of what his former professor had stolen out from under him. And he was always up for a good relic hunt. He sighed, propping his feet up on his desk and leaning back.

But was he up for another round? What if the panic attacks came back? What if he caused another operative to die? And what did it matter in the end, anyway, given his excellent life teaching and researching? What would happen to his current professional trajectory at the university if he bailed again?

As if reading his apprehension, Celeste sat forward to add one more thing. "Silas, I understand your apprehension. And I'm sorry to come at you like this again after last time. But there's another element I think you need to know about. We have a source embedded in Pryce's team who sent us some encrypted intel indicating there's something else going on with him and his Ark discovery. And then the day before last he went dark. Total silence."

"What do you mean? That there's something more going on? And what about this source?"

"We had a standard, mandatory check-in. And he missed it. He had been meeting every check-in since he was planted, and then the day before this big announcement, the guy goes dark."

That did sound suspicious. He remembered back to his days in Kandahar, and a similar situation going down with a local man who was recruited because of his personal connections with Afghan tribal leaders. Every week he had checked in like clockwork. Then one day nothing. His team chalked it up to a fluke, believing there was a good explanation for the miss. And there was. The next day they discovered why in the form of a convoy of suicide vehicles ramming their military installation. He was getting the feeling this could very well be that.

Silas brought his feet down off his desk, as if he was partly committing to Celeste and ready to follow. But she hadn't answered his other question. "You said your source said there was something more going on. Did he say what?"

She paused, looked down to the floor, then looked back at Silas. "The encryption had a phone number."

"A phone number?"

"Here." Celeste grabbed a yellow sticky note and a pen off his desk, and wrote down a series of numbers:

140-150-2119

Silas took the piece of paper from her and considered the intel.

"I assume you ran this number, checking with possible connections in Jerusalem."

"Zoe ran it with every international calling code and came up with several hits," she said, referring to the Order's resident techie, Zoe Corbino, who could run laps around the world's top researchers with her computer wizardry.

Silas tilted his head in anticipation. "And?"

"Nothing that made sense. Most were dead-end numbers that didn't connect to anything. A few were hits, but disconnected numbers. Then a few more hit either random businesses or residential numbers."

"And nothing?"

"No obvious connections."

"What about in Jerusalem or the broader Israeli-Palestine region?"

"That's the odd thing. The number didn't reflect anything landline or mobile."

"So nothing again?"

"Nothing. But we're sure something is there. Maybe some connection to those businesses, a shell corporation perhaps. Or a person at the other end of the residential or mobile numbers. We just don't have the manpower or resources to vet it all. Zoe is working on it, but it could take time. Time which I'm afraid we don't have."

Silas nodded in understanding, then fell silent, letting his mind drift to the numbers. A final phone number, left by a source planted by the Order to gain intel on Pryce. Or was it?

The synapses in his brain skipped to a favorite childhood pastime with his father and brother. At least twice a week his dad would pose a riddle at dinner to challenge him and Sebastian, stretching and working and honing their reasoning skills. Often it would be some sort of story riddle. But sometimes they involved numbers, either the problem-solving kind or—

"It's a cipher," he said confidently.

"A what?"

"A cipher. A relatively simple combination of numbers that connect to letters, forming words and sentences. My father challenged Sebastian and me to work through these kinds of puzzles as kids. That's what this is, I'd bet."

Celeste took the note from Silas and started working through the numbers from the perspective of a cipher. She set it on the desk. "You could be right. But how does this work out? Because there are two zeros in this string."

He shook his head as he looked at the numbers. "Not sure, but let's map it out." Silas wrote down the numbers on a piece of paper to start the decryption process.

"So 1-4-5-2-9," she said. "That's what we have to work with?"

"That. But also 14-15-21-11-19. We've got to account for all possible combinations."

"Which works out to..." Celeste paused, running the letters through her head. "A-D-E-B-I-N-O-U-K-U."

Silas wrote down the letters, sat back, and nodded. "That's right. And that's quite the set of letters."

The two sat quietly, working out the possible number-letter combinations. After ten minutes they had nothing. Nothing made sense.

"I give up," Celeste said throwing down her pen. "Certainly wasn't a cryptographer in another life."

"Yeah, I'm not getting anywhere either. Those two zeros are hanging me up. What do you make of those?"

Celeste shook her head, continuing to stare at the numbers and her attempt at translating them into meaningful, coded information.

Then it hit her.

"What if those zeros aren't anything at all."

"What do you mean?"

"What if they're blanks, meant to throw off anyone who might have intercepted the communication? So that they might have thought it was a phone number, but was something else entirely?"

Silas grinned and dropped back to his paper. That meant 1-4-0 could simply be 14. N. And 1-5-0 would be O. N-O.

"No..." Celeste said, looking on as Silas decoded. "No, what?"

Silas shook his head and continued with the remaining four. 2-1-1-9. B-A-A-I. That didn't make sense. 2-11-9. B-K-I. An airport code, perhaps? But again, didn't register.

"What about 21-1-9?" Celeste asked. Silas wrote it out: U-A-I. He set down his pencil and tilted his head, resting it on his closed fist. UAE was the United Arab Emirates, so maybe there was some connection there.

No. Wait.

He picked up his pencil, his heart quickening with an adrenaline surge.

Not 21-1-9. 21-19. U-S.

He wrote the two letters next to what they had deduced from translating the zeros as blanks. Celeste's jaw dropped when he did, and she looked at him with wide eyes.

N-O-U-S.

Nous.

CHAPTER 8

When Celeste first showed up at his class, Silas had a sinking suspicion that Nous was somehow responsible for her arrival. After all, Nous was the Order of Thaddeus's archrival, the Church's archenemy. And she was the head of a project within the religious order that had pledged itself to counter Nous's attempts to dismantle and destroy the memory of the Christian faith. Project SEPIO.

He had first learned about this ancient enemy of the Church and covert project earlier in the year after a terrorist attack had left his colleagues and one of his mentors dead. He was also the target and would have been taken out had it not been for the team of SEPIO operatives grabbing him before the other black-clad Nousati had. Once he was brought to the Order's operational headquarters hidden underneath the Washington National Cathedral in DC, Rowen Radcliffe had laid it all out for him.

As he had explained, the Order of Thaddeus was a religious order formed early in the life of the Church by one of Jesus' disciples and the early Church leader Thaddeus, or Saint Jude as he is often known. As the patron saint of lost causes, he was acutely aware of the forces already pressing in against the Church and the teachings of the faith, which he wrote about in a letter to

Christians living in Asia Minor. The heart of his epistle included in the canon of the New Testament reflected this urgency: "*Contend for the faith that was once for all entrusted to God's holy people.*" Not only for the faith itself, but the shared, collective memory of the faith. Thaddeus had already seen evidence for the need to preserve and protect this memory and worked toward institutionalizing this preservation effort with the ecclesiastical organization.

Around a decade ago, the Order realized it needed to make a more deliberate effort in contending for and preserving the memory of the faith. In the face of a number of threats from within and without, the Church was quickly coming to a precipice unless they took measures to deliberately preserve and protect the once-for-all faith and teaching tradition. Project SEPIO was launched to spearhead that movement, the full acronym being: *Sepio, Erudio, Pugno, Inviglio, Observo.*

Protect, Instruct, Fight For, Watch Over, Heed.

The meaning of the Latin word *sepio* itself captured the project's mission perfectly: "to surround with a hedge." In the case of the Order's project mission, surround the memory of the Christian faith with a hedge of protection. Not only the dogma and doctrine of the faith, but also the Church's objects and relics containing the memory of the faith, exploiting them to inform and nourish the faith of God's children—and keeping them safe from Nous.

Originally a Catholic religious order and Vatican-run initiative, the Order was now an ecumenical effort. Rowan Radcliffe was the Order Master, Celeste Bourne was the operational director of SEPIO. She had been recruited by Radcliffe after serving in the United Kingdom's military-intelligence arm, commonly known as MI6. With a background in Church history combined with her intelligence field work, she made for a steady, sturdy guide for the Order's memory-preservation efforts, as well as a formidable opponent to Nous. Which the

Order has been keeping at bay since the earliest days of Christianity.

The scourge of the Church, Nous, has manifested itself in various ways over the ages. At its heart is a teaching rooted in the original divine principle, the eye of reason for comprehending the divine, leading to higher knowledge and salvation. The essence of its worldview is ancient Gnosticism, the root of the Church's earliest heresies, teaching that salvation was reserved for the select few who could reach spiritual enlightenment and progress and push the human race forward through self-salvation. The central kernel of Gnostic and Nous teaching, *gnostikos*, begins with the basic assumption of the divinity of the individual, a God-consciousness and God-in-hiding that every person bears to greater or lesser degrees. There is no sovereign deity, but lesser spirit-deities. Pantheistic to the core, Nousati believe the Divine invades all things, living and non-living. And they assume that pre-historical humans enjoyed uninhibited access to the kind of spiritual truth that would bring about a humanistic salvation. Like Friedrich Nietzsche's Übermensch (Overman or Beyond Man) the individual has become like God— not only knowing good and evil, but deciding it and transcending it.

The Beyond Man, transcending this world and armed with the knowledge to determine good and evil, is the essential aim of the Nousati, to hammer and hone reality into the *imago homo*, the Image of Man, through brute force. The pursuit of spiritual power through ritual magic has been a constant theme throughout the history of the Church's archenemy. In fact, some of the highest-ranking Nazi officers were members of Nous. Joseph Goebbels, even Hitler himself, were Nousati. Heinrich Himmler himself was a Grand Master. Which makes sense because Gnosticism and the kind of occultism leveraged by Hitler's monsters are closely allied. The Shaman has a prominent place within the Nous occult system of spiritual enlightenment. Gnostikos and Nousati are governed by Guides, as they are known, who steward human knowledge in order to help the masses climb out from the pit of ignorance to achieve spiritual enlightenment and salvation.

Nous is the organizational embodiment of this ancient world-view—an organization that's laid hidden in the shadows of history, until now. There is a militancy about Nous that has always threatened the Church and the faith, but has resurfaced with a vengeance. Early in the life of the Church, Nous tried to undermine the essence of the Christian faith by destroying her teachings. Its power and influence has waxed and waned over the centuries and manifested in various ways. The Order and SEPIO have been following the organization for generations, keeping tabs on it and keeping it at bay to preserve and contend for the faith.

And stop it from destroying it.

"So give it to me. What's this got to do with Nous?" Silas asked.

They were speeding across the slick payment on their way to Newark airport for a flight out to Tel Aviv courtesy of the Order. Celeste had informed him that she was sent by Radcliffe to recruit Silas for an exploratory operation at the Pryce dig in Jerusalem. Given the significance of the Ark of the Covenant's possible discovery and unveiling, not only for Judaism and Islam, but also Christianity. Radcliffe wanted his own set of eyes and ears to gather as much intel as possible. And given Silas's previous connection with Pryce, he thought Silas would be the perfect candidate to create an opening for SEPIO. The team was going to be light: just Silas and Celeste.

"We don't have details. Only that cryptic string of numbers from the source."

Silas considered this, but continued pressing as he drove through the slick roads toward the airport, rain lashing the car. "There has to be something. The source didn't offer anything else in his intel reports that could point to some sort of connection between Nous and Pryce's dig?"

"There was one thing that may be connected. The source had overheard a conversation that mentioned something that seemed totally disconnected from the Ark, which was why he flagged it for us."

"What was it?"

"It was a word that kept coming up. *Helena.*"

Silas snapped his head to Celeste. A horn blared to his right as he began drifting into the other lane. He corrected and swerved back into his lane.

"Watch it!" she exclaimed, grabbing the handle above her window.

"Celeste, does that name mean anything to you?"

"No, why? What does it to you?"

"Helena is also known as Saint Helena."

Recognition washed over Celeste. She sank deep into her seat and stared out the window. "As in mother of Constantine, Emperor of Rome."

"Exactly."

"That doesn't make sense. Because Helena wasn't even around until nearly a thousand years after the Ark. What connection does she have to this ancient Hebrew artifact?"

Thunder rumbled in the distance as silence enveloped the SUV. "Helena..." he mumbled as he continued driving, deep in thought.

"What's that?" she asked.

"Huh?" He looked at her, veering slighting to the right again.

"Watch it, mate, before you anger another evening commuter."

Silas corrected again, the synapses in his brain making the connections between the revelation of Celeste's source.

"So, what did you say?"

"I said Helena."

Celeste turned toward Silas. "What are you thinking? You know something."

"What do you know about her, other than she was the mother of Constantine?"

Celeste smirked. "Alright, professor. Give it to me."

He looked at her and smiled. "After Emperor Constantine converted to Christianity, she became interested in the faith of her son and led a contingent of Roman officials and soldiers into the Judea-Palestine region to investigate all things Christian. Tradition has it that she found the original site of Jesus' resurrection, and buried inside were the other relics from his crucifixion. The scourging post, the crown of thorns, the nails, the shingle above him announcing he was the King of the Jews—"

"And the cross," Celeste said turning to Silas.

He looked at her and nodded, then fixed his eyes back on the road.

"But why was Helena referenced at a dig purporting to unearth the Ark of the Covenant in Jerusalem?" she wondered.

"Good question," Silas said as he pulled into the airport, following signs directing them to the terminal of their private plane. "But something tells me we're about to find out when we have a little chit-chat with my old buddy Lucas Pryce."

DAY II

CHAPTER 9

ROME, ITALY.

The man with the mustache and round, dark shades hadn't left his table for over two hours. Content to while away the mid-morning hours with a newspaper and several espressos.

Which made Gapinski annoyed.

His annoyance was amplified by his grumbling stomach, which hadn't seen a fresh fill of food since he and his partner started tracking the man earlier that morning.

"Was that your stomach?" Naomi Torres asked him.

"Sorry," he huffed. "But some of us can't live on buttered ciabatta bread and espresso alone."

"I told you, you should've taken those apples before we left the hotel."

"And I told you, I hate apples. Growing up, Ma took that old apple-a-day wives' tale literally. By the time I was ten I had eaten a whole orchard and vowed never to let another Newton or McIntosh see the inside of my stomach."

"Look where that's gotten you," she mumbled.

"I heard that," he replied, feigning offense. "And for the record, I'm big-boned, alright?"

"Whatever you say. It's your move by the way."

Gapinski eyed the chess board they had commandeered in the plaza across from the café where the man had perched himself for the morning, figuring they would blend in better if they were engaged in some kind of activity. He took out a pawn that had advanced a little too close for comfort with a rook from the other side of the board.

"And for the second record, I'm your superior on this mission. So, you know, show me a little of the R-E-S-P-E-C-T, would ya?"

She smiled wryly and nodded, returning her gaze to the mustachioed man across the street. Then took out his rook with her knight. "Check," she said.

"Thanks for that."

"No problem, chief."

Radcliffe had recruited Torres from, of all places, a treasure hunting outfit operating out of Miami, Florida. She had been a lead researcher at San Jose New World Salvage and Exploration, where she had earned a reputation for historical and archaeological acumen, as well as the hard-nosed negotiating chops to deal with corrupt governments and even more corrupt treasure-seeking pirates operating out of the Caribbean. Part historical and cultural preservation effort and part money-making venture, her uncle Juan Manuel Torres, from her father's side of the family, had made most of his money by exploiting oil drilling rights in Venezuela and Mexico. Tired of the corruption and boredom of that line of work, he took his earnings and put it to work trying to preserve his people's cultural heritage, while making a few pesos on the side. He hired his niece, Naomi Torres, after she finished dual master's degrees in Mesoamerican and pre-Columbian studies at UCLA to lead the research team.

Her first assignment had been to help a team of scientists and archaeologists seeking a lost, Spanish treasure fleet returning from the New World to Spain in 1715. After setting sail for the Old World on July 31, eleven of the twelve ships were lost in a hurricane near present-day Vero Beach, Florida. Also known as the

1715 Plate Fleet because it was carrying vast quantities of silver, the fleet had grabbed the imaginations of treasure hunters for a century. When her uncle was approached by a wealthy businessman acting on behalf of the Cuban government to find the crown jewel of the fleet, the Urca de Lima, he assigned his niece to handle the logistics and the recovery. Through her meticulous research of past fleet records, eyewitness accounts, weather patterns, and with the assistance of newer LiDAR technology, she found the sunken ship in a deep-sea valley, catapulting her uncle's salvage company to the top-tier of Miami outfits.

The find also put her on the radar of all the major exploration, salvage, and historical and archaeological societies. Including the Order of Thaddeus. Being acquainted with her grandfather from his time serving as a Jesuit archbishop in the Vatican's Congregation for the Doctrine of the Faith, Rowen Radcliffe had known about her deep faith and commitment to the Church. And having read about her archaeological exploits in the news and known about her experience with the Israeli Defense Force as the daughter of her ethnically Jewish mother, Radcliffe had contacted his old friend, who put him in touch with his granddaughter.

Initially, she was resistant, having devoted years of academic work and vocational energy to preserving the culture of her father's people. But after sitting down with him and Celeste, she had been intrigued by the idea of offering her talents for historical inquiry and anthropological preservation in service of the Church.

Within weeks she had left Miami and flown to Washington, DC, where she spent half a year training as an operative with SEPIO. She was a quick study of both the historical and theological aspects of the Order's work, as well as the tactical and physical demands of being on the front lines, though her experience with the IDF certainly helped. After the Shroud incident, the Order had stepped up its initiatives through SEPIO to protect and preserve the artifacts, manuscripts, and relics that contained the memory of the faith. This assignment with Gapinski was the fruits of that effort, her first.

Given the recent events with the Shroud of Turin and the Church of the Holy Sepulcher, and then the Gospel of Judas and apostle relics, it was clear Nous had launched a new phase of its attempts to undermine the Christian faith. Now, it seemed like all-out war, with their intent to destroy rather than merely debilitate. SEPIO had ramped up its intel operations in response, embedding agents in purported Nousati cells and tracking the whereabouts and conversations of known associates of the anti-Church organization.

One of those was finishing up his fourth espresso, after having set down his newspaper. Little was known about him, other than his name and origins. Marwan Farhad, from the central Iranian city of Yazd. He was thought to have a background in Zoroastrianism, the oldest spirituality known to that region stretching back to the Persian empire. But that hadn't been entirely confirmed.

All Gapinski and Torres knew was that the man was a cell leader within the upper echelons of Nous, and that he had booked a ticket from Berlin to Rome. When he did, Zoe had been notified by a C-level analyst in Munich monitoring Europe. That triggered an automatic re-route to Radcliffe's desk, where he ordered the two to immediately board a plane for Rome. With zero intel to go off of, other than the high-level nature of the man and the prospects for even higher-level activity, they were left having to track him using the mainstay of old-school intelligence gathering: patience and persistence, observation and tracking, and a lot of luck.

"What's with this guy?" Gapinski complained as he moved his queen to cover his king. "Not even a bathroom break?"

Torres looked over at the man again, who received a fresh cup of espresso.

"And that's gotta be his seventh or eighth cup of joe."

She moved the knight again, repositioning it to take the queen three moves out. "Fourth."

"Excuse me?" he said, moving his bishop to take out her knight.

"Fourth cup of joe. Or, rather, espresso."

"Whatever. The guy could do us the courtesy of taking a leak so I can take one myself."

"If you've got to hit the head, then by all means. I can cover him. I'm ready." She moved her queen diagonal of his king left vulnerable when he moved the bishop. "Check, by the way."

"Wait. He's moving." Gapinski stood and darted over to a large sycamore tree to block the Persian's line of sight

Mr. Mustache stood and stretched, then walked over to a bench near the road lined with bushes that covered its back. He sat, then leaned over. It looked like he was fishing for something underneath his seat. Then he sat up and stretched his legs outward, head down staring at his lap.

Gapinski was squinting and shielding his eyes from the late-morning sun. Torres joined him at the tree. He said to her, "Did he just take something from underneath the bench?"

"Looked that way."

"Crapola! What just happened? Was there some sort of drop that we missed?"

"Not that I saw. We had our eyes on him the whole time. Other than when you were complaining about food, of course. And getting whooped at chess."

Gapinski frowned. "From one smart-ass to another, now's not the time."

Torres nodded, then looked at the ground.

"Wait, he's reading something. No. Yeah, I think he's reading something. He's reading something, isn't he?"

Torres looked back up and strained forward. "I think you're

right. It looks like he's cradling something with his left arm, but he's being all casual about it."

"And what's that in his other hand? Did he just discard some type of box?"

She shook her head. "I don't know. Maybe some kind of package?"

"Sonofa...My first lead in, like, forever, and I blow it." Gapinski leaned against the tree with his left arm and shook his head.

"Looks like he's returning to his table," she said, "and maybe settling back in."

"I'm going to have to call this in. Maybe Zoe had a satellite or one of those new drone doodads on the guy."

"Why don't we get back to our game before he catches us peeping his way?"

"Always something," he grumbled as he set off back toward their table.

The two settled back into their benches. Gapinski phoned Radcliffe to report what they had witnessed, then asked for Zoe to check on any aerial intel gathering she may have had going to support them. She said there was nothing. Radcliffe told him not to worry, but to check in with him the minute anything else changed. It seemed clear there was a reason Farhad was in Rome, and if he had picked up something at a drop site, that meant there were more than just him waiting to act.

"Your move, big fella."

Gapinski raised an eyebrow, then took out her knight with his queen. She responded by taking out his queen with a bishop hidden at the back. He cursed under his breath, then moved his knight.

"Ahh, the Fibonacci move. Interesting."

He twisted his face. "Fibo-what? You made that up."

Torres smiled. "Sorry, my friend—"

"He's on the move."

Gapinski was already back at their observation tree by the

time Torres knew what was happening. She moved her queen forward, taking out his knight before she left.

She caught up to him before they crossed the street in pursuit, then said, "Checkmate."

He frowned as he looked both ways. "Alright, smarty-pants. Let's see if you can translate those mad chess skills into the real world."

He looked at her before they crossed. "Because it's about to get real."

CHAPTER 10

JERUSALEM.

The chartered flight provided by the Order of Thaddeus had taken Silas and Celeste from Newark Liberty International to Munich for a quick refueling stop before landing at Ben Gurion International in Tel Aviv. It was just before lunch when they arrived, so the two ate at a tapas bar before the hour drive to Jerusalem.

The day was bright and pleasant, reminding Silas of when he had first come to Jerusalem during a period of leave while serving in the military. It was after he had his conversion experience at an on-base Christian meeting, having come back to the faith after he had lapsed as a Catholic. The experience was a powerful one.

The chaplain had been reading from Saint Paul's letter to the Philippians, chapter three, when he described how he used to put his confidence in his "flesh," as he put it—his childhood faith, his adult religious zeal, his good works. But then he considered all of that a loss compared to intimately knowing God in a personal relationship. "I want to know Christ," Paul had written, "and the power of his resurrection and the sharing of his sufferings by becoming like him in his death, if somehow I may attain the resurrection from the dead."

Silas had wanted that too.

When the chaplain was describing the change that God works in the heart through faith in Christ, Silas felt his heart "strangely warmed," as the old English minister John Wesley had described. It was then, at that meeting on a base in southern Iraq, that Silas felt he did trust in Christ, Christ alone, for salvation. When he did, an assurance was given him that God had taken away all of his personal baggage, his sins and hurts and habits, he had been carrying around.

So he did the only thing he thought to do under the circumstances: he went on a religious pilgrimage, touring the well-known Christian sites of veneration, beginning with Israel. Five years later, after his commitment to the military was up, he left the Rangers and returned to join his professor on that fated archaeological dig at Tell-es Sultan. Where he had found historical proof of its biblical destruction and the Ark of the Covenant —right before the good professor took credit for his incredible find.

"What are you thinking about?" Celeste asked Silas as he drove through the Israeli countryside.

"What?" Silas said, startled from enjoying his personal memory.

"You've been silent since we left the airport. Lost in that head of yours. Wondered if anything was wrong."

Silas smiled. "Just enjoying a memory."

"Hope it's a pleasant one."

He looked at her. "Sweet and sour."

"Do tell."

"I was just thinking about the first time I was here. After I came back to the Church and gave my life to Christ, I had a window of leave from Iraq and went on a pilgrimage, touring the Christian religious sites, beginning with Jerusalem." He turned to her. "That was the sweet part. You can probably guess the sour part."

"Lucas Pryce."

He nodded.

"What happened with that anyway?"

"Just what I told you before. I had come to help him with the Jericho dig, and then I found the jars with the scrolls. Then he took credit."

Celeste shook her head. "And you haven't heard anything else from him about the parchments or the Ark since?"

"Nada. Until now I thought he thought the whole thing was nonsense. I guess I was wrong."

"I imagine we're about to discover a whole lot more in the coming day about Pryce and the Ark."

"Indeed."

AFTER ARRIVING, Silas and Celeste ditched their car in an overnight parking lot to the north of the Old City, opting to carry their overnight bags to a hostel inside the ancient city itself.

Four large tourist buses were dropping off their load as they approached the Damascus Gate. The tourist contingent seemed to be unusually high for this time of year. Most of the groups were obviously Christian, sporting brightly-colored t-shirts with Christian crosses and church names or tour-agency names like Maranatha Tours. Silas spotted a large group of men with the unmistakable long side locks and beard with the Shtreimel felt hat, Hasidic Jews come to pray at the Western Wall, he imagined.

"Check out the increased security," Celeste said, pointing toward the gate as they joined the queue waiting to enter the Holy City. Heavily armed Israeli Defense Force units wearing gray fatigues and stern-looking faces were checking bags and purses at the entrance.

"Guessing it has something to do with the impending Ark discoveries," Silas said. "Knowing how volatile the issue is for all three Abrahamic faiths, it makes sense to up the military presence to ward off any potential riots—or worse."

The two made it through security without incident, then made their way down Bey HaBad Street. Off to the right lay the Church of the Holy Sepulcher. The memories were still fresh from that experience earlier in the year when he had helped SEPIO battle the forces of Nous. Neither of them spoke about it as they passed the street leading to the church's side entrance where they stole inside under cover of darkness.

The smell of kabobs wafting from street vendors made Silas's stomach rumble in protest as they waded through the thick crowds. The two pushed past them, taking Chain Street to the rooms they booked at the Chain Gate Hostel. Sitting just 150 feet from the Dome of the Rock, the Western Wall, and the Holy Sepulcher, it was the perfect staging ground for their investigation into Pryce's archaeological project.

Constructed out of entirely Jerusalem stone, the hostel felt as old as the Temple itself. Bright, orange mandarins greeted them in a stone bowl at the entrance, as well as an assortment of left-over pieces of bread and cheeses from the morning continental breakfast. Silas took one of each. They weren't kabobs, but he knew he should eat since he didn't know when they might get a chance next. He tossed Celeste an orange as he walked up to the check-in counter. She smiled as she caught it, then immediately pealed it. Apparently, the kabobs had tempted her, too.

"Shalom, sir, madam," offered a short, pinched-faced woman wearing a wilting floral dress.

Silas replied, "Shalom. We've got two rooms booked under Grey."

She typed on a '90s-era desktop PC, then scowled and pulled out a single key.

"I sorry, but we have one room for you."

"There has to be a mistake," he said nervously, looking to Celeste and blushing before returning back to the hostess. "We specifically asked for two rooms. The Vatican arranged it."

"The Vatican?" the woman said in disbelief, eyeing him as she held tightly to the one key Silas wouldn't take. "We have one room for you. Not two. Very busy with the activity down below. You lucky you have one."

He sighed, then looked at Celeste again with a mixture of apology and resignation.

She shrugged her shoulders, then nodded toward the woman.

He held out his hand. "Thanks. We'll take it."

Working their way through a dimly-lit, narrow hallway on the top floor, they found their room. It was as spartan as he expected, although the bunk beds would work well for their needs.

Silas threw his bag up on the top bunk. "I call tops."

"Not fair! I've always fancied the top."

He smiled. "Better luck next time."

She huffed playfully, then threw her bag underneath the bottom bed. "Why don't we pay a visit to your old mate, Professor Pryce. Lots to learn about his dig and the Ark, and time is of the essence."

He sighed. "Do we have to?"

"Come on. It'll be fun."

Silas opened the door. He went to step into the hallway when he caught sight of someone darting away down the hall.

"What the—"

The figure was medium height and build, wearing loose, light-colored clothing meant to blend in. And running away from their room, as if Silas had interrupted him in progress.

"Hey!" he called after the mystery person.

"What's wrong?" Celeste asked, stepping into the hallway and looking in Silas's direction.

"Stay here," he commanded as he turned away in pursuit. "Go back inside and lock the door!"

He ran fast through the narrow, dimly-lit hallway, catching sight of the person a few yards down.

The man dodged around a small set of table and chairs, toppling them as a diversion to cover his escape.

Silas darted around the upturned table, but couldn't avoid a chair. His leg slid into the arm, and he tripped over it, twisting his ankle and sending him to the floor.

He cried out and cursed loudly, but got up quickly. His ankle screamed in pain, but he hopped it off and kept at his pursuit, running into a small, open-air courtyard. He heard hard footfalls up ahead, but he had to slow because of his ankle.

Silas continued forward back into the main lobby of the hostel, catching sight of the figure. He ran near a small beverage refrigerator, then pulled it out and toppled it over as he had the table and chairs to stave off any further pursuit. The man kept running and shoved through tall, green, wooden doors that led into the hostel, and out into the crowded, Old City streets.

Silas hobbled to the front desk, where the older woman was speaking in rapid Hebrew into a handset.

"Excuse me," he said breathing hard. "Did you get a look at the man?"

"I no see! I no see!" she said in broken English before returning to her phone conversation.

He turned back toward the door and mumbled a curse.

Have we been made?

CHAPTER 11

Shortly after the man made his escape, and Silas was given the brush off by the front desk woman, Celeste came up behind him in the lobby.

"What was that about?"

He winced as he turned around. "I thought I told you to stay put."

She paused. "Yes, you did. And I decided against it."

He nodded, then hobbled over to the open door, squinting for a look into the bright, Middle Eastern daylight and seeing nothing but a mass of people. He shook his head and cursed himself for losing the mysterious figure.

"What happened to your ankle? It doesn't look good."

He turned back inside and walked slowly back toward the front desk, favoring his right ankle, but forcing himself through the discomfort. "Had a run-in with an overturned chair. I'll be fine. But I am worried about who that was. And why it looked like they were at our door."

"Here," she said, handing Silas his Beretta.

He looked at it, then smiled. "Always prepared, aren't you?"

"For every possible contingency. Let's go have a chat with Pryce."

The walk down to the Western Wall Plaza where Pryce had staged his archaeological circus was a quick five minutes. It made Silas Grey both delighted and saddened to see the Western Wall of the Temple Mount area transformed by the flurry of activity that had come because of Lucas Pryce's archaeological project. Sad because the holy site had turned into a media carnival; delighted because a significant religious relic was about to be unearthed.

And a foremost expert on relicology and Church history was always interested in bringing the religious past to the surface. Even if it was because of a chump like Pryce.

The media from the day before were still stationed at the periphery of the Western Wall Plaza, cameras trained at the Wilson's Arch, the modern name for the still-visible, ancient, stone archway that had once supported a road into the Temple compound during the time of Jesus. Now it is supported against the northeast corner of Jerusalem's Western Wall so that it appears on the left to visitors facing the Wall. All the major news networks were represented. From CNN to MSNBC, the BBC to Sky, Al Jazeera to Russia Today, all were covering the most monumental archaeological, historical, religious, and political discovery of all time.

One large canvas tent and two smaller ones had been erected along the northeast corner of the Western Wall to the left of the Wilson's Arch. Generators hummed loudly to feed the academic activity occurring within. People dressed in light-colored shirts and shorts seemed to be competing in some sort of synchronized running activity as they worked to finalize the preparations for the unveiling.

"So what are you thinking?" Celeste asked as they walked past the row of cameras. "How should we approach Pryce?"

A man emerged from one of the smaller tents with a cohort of young, Indiana Jones wannabes. He looked to be of African descent, with a shiny, eight-ball head, so it wasn't Pryce. But the guy looked like he was in charge, as he was directing the swarm of worker bees.

"Follow my lead," Silas said.

He walked over to the man as he was dispensing instructions, then interrupted by tapping him on the shoulder. "Excuse me."

The African man stopped mid-sentence and turned around, mouth hanging open with rows of gleaming white teeth, clearly taken aback that someone had the nerve to interrupt him.

"Yes? Can I help you?" He said in polished, British English.

"Where can we find Lucas Pryce?"

The slight man with dark-chocolate skin and beady, little eyes set behind thick, round glasses eyed Silas with an equal mixture of confusion and appall.

"And who are you?" he said quickly.

Silas took a step back and huffed, as if offended. He folded his arms, tilted his head, and said, "Who am I? *Doctor* Silas Grey. Professor of religious studies and Christian history at *Princeton*. As in, the university in America."

The man's features softened a bit. His eyes darted to Celeste, then back to Silas again. He smiled weakly. "I am sorry, sir. I didn't recognize you. And I had not known you were coming. What brings you to our site?"

Silas was inching the man forward toward his desired outcome, but he wasn't going to go willingly.

"As you probably know, I'm one of the foremost experts on relicology in the world and thought it appropriate I come to lend my...expertise to this little project of yours. In fact, you could say I'm responsible for it, as I worked with Dr. Pryce closely on the archaeological dig at Tell-es Sultan a decade ago and was the one who found the scrolls referencing the Ark in the first place. Yes, me."

Playing the part of the pompous academic was a risk, but Silas wanted to throw the man off and force him to make a decision about him. Hopefully, the right one.

"I see," he said skeptically.

"So I thought I would come lend a helping hand to my former professor and colleague. And offer my congratulations and celebrations for the momentous day, of course."

"Is Professor Pryce expecting you?"

Silas sighed. "I'm sorry, I didn't catch your name."

The man said, "Oliver Tulu," before he quickly adding, "Doctor Tulu."

"Doctor? Really...from?"

"Oxford."

Silas snorted. "Figures. Now if you'll be good enough to take us to Lucas Pryce, I would be most appreciative. And I'm sure he will, too."

Tulu seemed thoroughly confused by the conversation and not at all sure how to proceed. He looked over to the large tent, giving away Pryce's location, as if deciding what to do.

Finally, he simply said, "Follow me."

Silas winked at Celeste as Tulu shuffled off toward the large tent commanding the base of the Wilson's Arch. Celeste smiled wryly as the two followed him forward.

The inside of the structure was surprisingly serene. It carried none of the hustle-and-bustle activity from outside, though this didn't surprise Silas. He remembered from his time with Pryce a decade ago how the man was militant about a policy of strict privacy and calm within his private tent, insisting he needed uninterrupted, peaceful space. This version of what he had back then certainly fit the bill.

It was cooler inside than the outside, and far less humid, the temperature and air being strictly controlled. Mainly because of the nature of the work handling manuscripts and artifacts and other potential ones that might emerge during the excavation required a climate-controlled space, which the state-of-the-art mobile facility provided. The lighting was dim, provided only by what sunlight filtered in through the tent's canvas and a few banker's desk lamps. And it smelled of old wood and tobacco, a sign of Pryce's continued taste for expensive cigars and even more expensive antique desks and cabinetry. His fellow grad students had joked that Pryce had been playing out his Indiana-Jones fantasies. When one of the students jokingly asked him about it one evening after a night of drinks, the good professor hadn't denied it, saying the items helped him channel the great archaeologists from the past. Like Howard Carter, the great British Egyptologist who discovered Tutankhamen's tomb, and the American explorer, writer, and diplomat John Lloyd Stephens who explored ancient Maya. He had collected some of their treasured possessions in order to channel their greatness. The desk was Carter's, the bookcases Stephens's.

Apparently, it had worked.

Pryce was hovering over a large wooden table, commanded by a slew of maps and manuscripts and other diagrams, still working on the stub of a cigar that looked as if he had lit it an hour ago. Tulu walked up to him and tapped him on his shoulder, then whispered something into his ear, causing Pryce to twist sharply to meet his visitors. For a brief second, Silas thought he caught a face of anger or fear, he couldn't tell which. But then a broad, toothy grin splayed across the man's scruffy face.

Pryce snuffed out his cigar in a glass jar then strode over to the pair.

"Professor Silas Grey," he said in the Southern drawl that had annoyed Silas from his grad-school days. "My eyes deceive me! What on earth are you doing here?"

CHAPTER 12

The two shook hands before embracing awkwardly.

Silas raked a hand over his close-cropped hair and offered a forced smile. He said, "I heard the news about your latest archaeological find and naturally wanted in on the action."

Pryce chuckled. "Ever an opportunist. That's the Silas Grey I remember."

Silas smiled and said nothing.

The man turned toward Celeste, smiling and taking her hand. "And who is this? Your wife?"

Celeste laughed. Silas quickly said, "No, no. This is Celeste Bourne." Neither of them had thought about how to introduce her to Pryce, which left him fishing for words. "She's a...a friend. Well, more like a colleague who is involved with the retrieval and cataloging of Church relics and other significant Christian manuscripts. She begged me to come along, said she couldn't miss such a monumental discovery by one of the leading archaeologists of our day. She's been a fan of yours for years. Tell him, Celeste." Silas thought the ego stroke would soften the way for what they needed to accomplish in the next few minutes: probing Pryce for information about his excavation.

"Right," she said looking from Silas to Pryce, readying her performance. She withdrew her hand and put a strand of stray hair back behind her ear, then smiled widely. "I'm a real fangirl, professor, having followed your work closely ever since your work on the Dead Sea Scrolls and then your remarkable work at the Jericho dig. I must say, it's quite the honor to be meeting you like this. And under such exciting circumstances!"

Silas stole a glance at an antique table that commanded the work area while Celeste continued laying on the compliments. A number of manuscripts and maps and opened Moleskine notebooks with Pryce's notations were scattered about. He couldn't make out any of his notes, but he did catch sight of a map of what looked like Old City Jerusalem, as well as the Temple Mount. Most likely Pryce was using them to chart the course for his excavation. He also saw an opened, ancient-looking book, with two paperweights at either end keeping it open.

He looked back at Pryce and smiled at Celeste as she ended her laudings, then glanced back at the book trying to make out the words. The characters weren't English, nor were they any modern language he could discern. They were clearly ancient and looked to be Semitic, but Silas was uncertain and confused.

That table, with that book and those maps and other manuscripts, would be another line of inquiry for the pair to follow up on. Just not in that moment. Which meant a return trip.

"My dear," Pryce said, moving closer to her and smiling. He took her hand. "Thank you, my dear. It is excitin' times. But you never said why you're here." The smile quickly faded as he turned back to Silas.

He replied, "Mostly to say congratulations and to celebrate my former professor. But also to get a front row seat to your work. You know," he cleared his throat, trying to swallow his pride, "after the scrolls were found when I joined you at Tell-es Sultan, I had always wondered whether or not you had followed up on the Ark of the Covenant. I recalled your skepticism of the Hebrew account, not only of Jericho, but also the Ark itself, believing it to be a mythical element devised to reinforce Israel's religious identity during exile. A talisman to root the nation during times of strife and uncertainty. What changed?"

Pryce smiled. "Yes, well, thanks to your little find that was pretty much put to rest, wasn't it?"

You're welcome, Silas wanted to say. Instead, he offered: "Well, it's a remarkable thing you are doing here, both for religion as much as for history. I suspect you'll join the ranks of the great archaeologists of our past and present!"

"Oh my, how kind," he said chuckling. "I'm not sure about that. And, well, I can't take all the credit anyway."

Really? You sure had no problem stealing my glory a decade ago.

Celeste playfully tapped Pryce's arm. "Oh, professor, surely you are being far too modest!"

He chuckled again, seeming to enjoy the pretty brunette's flirtation. "Not really. The original passageway was discovered in July of 1981 by the Chief Rabbi of the Western Wall and all holy places in Israel, a Rabbi Meir Yehuda Getz. They had been in the process of constructing a new synagogue beside the Western Wall that would face the Temple Mount when his workers rediscovered the lost Warren's Gate and the passage behind it quite by accident. Something about installing a Torah cabinet or something or other. Anyway, there was leaking water, so they traced it to its source and found our opening."

"The Warren's Gate?" Celeste said, turning to Silas for clarification.

"One of the original gates leading into the Temple Mount," Silas said. "The gate once led directly into the Temple courts and was used for bringing in wood, sacrifices, and other materials needed for the ancient sacred rites of the Jewish people when the Temple still stood and served the cultic needs of Israel."

Pryce had a satisfied look about him. "Sounds like you retained some of what I taught you."

"I had a good professor," Silas replied, leaving sarcasm for another day.

Pryce smiled, then continued: "For centuries the so-called Warren's Gate had been hidden away 150 feet into the Western Wall Tunnel, buried under centuries of build-up until it had been originally discovered more than a century ago by Charles Warren. By accident, he happened upon one of the four ancient entrances to the Temple during the first excavations underneath the Temple Mount. Remarkably, it was once used as an Arab latrine until 1967 and partially used as a water reservoir until the late twentieth century."

"Remarkable," Celeste said.

"Yes, it is remarkable. What's more remarkable, though, is that the good Rabbi thought he could excavate the passage in secret! Word got out, however, as it always does. And the border police and army intervened, shutting them down when Arab riots broke out, and there was the threat of violence."

"I can imagine a discovery of such religious magnitude didn't sit well with the Muslim authorities," Silas said.

"No, it did not. But no matter. Because afterward the Warren's Gate entrance was sealed and reinforced with steel, and a plaster wall was placed over it by the Ministry of Religious Affairs."

"And kept safe and sound for your little unveiling," Silas said. "How convenient."

Pryce grinned, but said nothing.

"But why is this gate so important?" Celeste asked, trying to probe for more information while Silas edged for a sword fight. "Aren't there others that lead into the Temple Mount complex?"

"True, there are," the professor continued, "But this one is the most important of all the gates because it is the nearest one to the former location of the Most Holy Place, the Holy of Holies."

"Which is where the Ark of the Covenant used to reside," she said.

"Precisely. Many scholars of the Semitic period believe that underneath this locale, King Solomon constructed a secret chamber to act as a secure vault for the temple treasures should the need arise to steal them away, perhaps even in the event of the Temple's destruction."

"And those treasures included the Ark."

"Including the Ark. And these biblical scholars believe the Ark was secreted away during a few possible instances with the intention of later returning it to its proper place within the Temple."

"During the reign of Manasseh and before the Babylonian invasion," Silas added, not to be outdone by Pryce.

He nodded. "You're right. Jewish tradition holds that the Ark continued to exist in hiding, and that it would be rediscovered and restored to Israel when the Messiah appeared. The longest of the Dead Sea Scrolls, known as the Temple Scroll, speaks of this very thing. It describes a new, future Temple that will eventually be built containing the Ark of the Covenant. If such a holy place were to be considered legitimate, it must include the Ark."

"Why?" Celeste asked.

"Because without it the glory of God cannot return to take its appointed place between the glorious wings of the cherubim. No Ark, no true Temple. And this same Jewish tradition tells of the Ark being hidden away safely and secretly. At least that's what the tradition tells us."

"So what's your interest in this, Pryce?" Silas asked. "I never took you to be a religious man. Certainly not a Jewish one."

He paused, then smirked. "Let's call it historical inquiry and academic progress."

Silas pressed further. "That's a lot of expense and hoopla for historical inquiry and academic progress. How benevolent of you."

Pryce said nothing.

"By the way, you never said where your funding came from for this venture."

"Didn't I? Well, I'm sure you can understand a number of benefactors and philanthropic organizations have a strong interest in seeing the Ark resurrected, so to speak."

Silas nodded and chose not to press the matter. That's one item they would have to uncover on their own. Follow the money, as they say.

"How exciting," Celeste piped in, trying to redirect the conversation. "Because you're the one who found the secret chamber!"

He beamed with pride. "Yes, I did."

"Do tell the bits of that discovery."

"Now this story demands another cigar!" He reached for a humidor sitting on top of his desk. "You don't mind, do you?"

The two waved off his concern.

"Excellent!" After snipping one end, he aimed the cigar over a lighter and puffed it to life. He took several puffs before continuing.

"Now, for confidentiality reasons, the details of the arrangement are sealed. But after we had secured permission to uncover the Warren's Gate once again, we opened it and discovered a giant hall shaped like the Wilson Arch, but with exit tunnels running this way and that."

"How positively thrilling!" Celeste said, encouraging him onward.

"It was! The hall was something like 75 feet long, with a set of stairs that went downward roughly 30 feet. But low and behold, it was filled with water and muck."

Celeste gasped. "No!"

"Yes, my dear. So we spent days pumping it away only to discover our first proof."

Celeste leaned in closer. "What was that?"

Pryce paused to take another puff of his cigar. "The imprint of an insect in the floor."

She leaned backward. "An *insect*?"

"An insect. And this insect verified it was the place opposite the Most Holy Place."

"How so?"

"Because," Silas interjected before Pryce could answer, "the Mishnah records in the Yoma tract that if the priest was found unclean, which rendered him unable to get out of the Most Holy Place, he was to release an insect that would go under the veil."

Pryce simply nodded. "Once we saw this marker, we knew we were on to something. From the place where we discovered the insect, we saw several openings. One of those entrances led to a passageway extending northeast. It was closed, but we managed to open it in due course. From there we've been excavating onward toward the direction of the Most Holy Place the past several months.

"Sounds like arduous work," she said.

He huffed and rolled his eyes. "Oh, goodness, has it ever been! Along the way, we found chambers filled with water, which we had to drain in order to progress onward. Then we came to a junction that suffered a severe collapse. Rocks and dirt everywhere. But they were cut rocks, having been shaped by precise, careful masonry. So we knew we were getting somewhere. For the past two months, we've undergone the careful, painstaking excavation of the tunnel, believing we were on to something, and not wanting to disturb the ancient passageway."

He paused, puffing his cigar back to life. He looked up as he puffed, then smiled. "And then we came upon it."

He let the revelation linger.

Silas didn't bite, but Celeste raised her eyebrows and widened her eyes, feigning surprise and playing into Pryce's showmanship. "What? What did you stumble upon?"

"A door."

Silas rolled his eyes at the dramatics. *Get on with it!*

"A door?" Celeste pressed. "What door? What was behind it?"

"The door. The door of all doors in the history of archaeology," he said, his voice rising with delight. He took another satisfied puff of his cigar, clearly reveling in another audience. "It's the kind of door you would expect if it was guarding something of significance. It isn't a large door, but there is heft to it, appearing to be made entirely out of bronze. It's the last piece of the puzzle, just waiting to unveil what it has been hiding all these years."

Silas felt a jolt of excitement and interest, though he was careful not to reveal his emotion. "And you believe that behind this door lay your temple treasures."

"I'm convinced of it."

"Why is that?" Celeste asked.

"Because etched into the bronze door is intricate artwork depicting two cherubim hovering above the double doors, and beneath it is a box that matches the description found in the Book of Exodus, as well as the golden lampstand, the golden table of showbread, and the golden altar of incense. It's all depicted, just as it would have been in the Temple!"

Silas said nothing, arms remaining folded and legs firmly planted in a mixture of irritation and envy.

"What a story, professor!" Celeste said, with a bit too much enthusiasm for Silas's taste. "And what a find."

Pryce chuckled. "Well, we haven't found anything yet. So keep your fingers crossed!"

"When's the big unveiling?" Silas asked.

"Tomorrow." Pryce puffed on his cigar. "We've got a few more things to work through in preparation. Then there's the media and the interviews and such. Hard work, you know, being in the limelight. The whole world is watching!"

I bet.

Pryce leaned against the table, and took three long puffs from his cigar, as if in thought. "You know, you should come along. The both of you."

"What, me?" Silas said, surprised at the gesture.

"Absolutely! After all, had it not been for your little find during our summer dig those years ago authenticating the historicity of the Ark, I might never have followed the trail in the first place."

Silas smiled. "That's very kind of you, professor. But we don't want to be a bother."

"Bullocks. It's no bother at all. Wait a minute."

Pryce motioned over a young man dressed in khakis holding a clipboard and said something to him. The young man hustled away, but returned a minute later with lanyards holding red plastic cards.

"Here you go. All-access passes."

"Wow," Silas said with genuine surprise as he put the pass around his neck. "That's very generous of you."

"The least I could do. Now, if you'll excuse me, I need to rush off to make some preparations for our big day. Be sure to find me in the morning. You should have a front row seat for the unveiling."

The two waved as he left.

"I'd say you earned your keep this trip," Celeste said, holding up her pass.

CHAPTER 13

ROME.

Farhad was moving casually, but deliberately. As if he was certain where he was heading, yet didn't want to draw attention to himself.

Torres had seen this kind of behavior before, during one of her stakeouts of a competitor salvage company tracking the sunken Spanish treasure galleon, the *San Juan*. Her uncle had been obsessed with the stories surrounding the sunken vessel, going so far as to name his newly formed company after the ship. When he had gotten wind that another, larger outfit out of Miami made a crucial discovery about its whereabouts, he had sent her to track down the intel that would lead him to it first.

She had followed a lead to a guy who knew a guy that was about to deliver a USB with PDF and JPEG images of schematics and nautical trade routes that had been discovered in Havana. For an afternoon she played shadow to the man who held her uncle's prized possession, and he had been evasive and noncommittal all afternoon, as if he had suspected he was being watched.

Just like this guy, Farhad.

The Persian stopped short at a shop with a large window displaying expensive-looking, Italian-made suites and designer dresses. The guy was checking himself out in the window, playing with his hair. But she knew better.

"Hold up," Gapinski said suddenly, putting his hand out to stop Torres. "He's checking to see if he has a tail. Act natural."

"I was until you nearly clocked me with your arm like a crossing guard."

Gapinski busied himself with his own window, filled with cakes and pies and other baked goods.

She sat down at a small table outside the café and played like she was tying her shoe.

This went on for another few minutes. Then the guy took off again.

Torres stood, and said, "Can we play like we're two normal people taking a stroll down a Roman road again, chief?"

"Sure. As we were."

They started shadowing Farhad on the other side of the road. He walked with his morning newspaper underneath one arm and looked straight ahead, rarely looking to his side, never looking behind him. Anyone would have thought him a local resident or a seasoned tourist.

This guy is good.

The late morning foot traffic started picking up the farther into the city they walked, and the closer they came to the typical tourist destinations. The Colosseum was in the general direction, as was Palatine Hill. There were several basilicas, but far too many to choose from.

"Where do you think he's heading?" she asked.

"Beats me. All I want to know is what he has in that newspaper. He's holding it funny under his arm, like it's stuffed with Lord-knows-what. I bet it's whatever he picked up at that bench drop site. And I hope he gets wherever he's going soon because my dogs are barking."

"Your...your dogs are barking?" she asked, not understanding what Gapinski was getting at.

He looked at her like she was from another planet. "Yeah. My dogs are barking."

They continued walking, Torres's eyebrows furrowed in confusion.

"As in, my feet are aching me. Never heard of the expression south of the border?"

She narrowed her eyes, not appreciating the condescension and ethnic innuendo.

"Actually, I'm from within your border. As in, a naturalized U.S. citizen. But thanks for the clarification." She walked faster to get a better view of Farhad, leaving him behind.

"Sorry, I didn't know!"

She was breathing hard, but tried to keep it together. Living as a Latina-American had never been easy. But she had learned to ignore the insinuations and the taunts. The demand for identification from cops at "routine" traffic stops. The second and third glances at retail stores. She understood Gapinski was a jokester, and he meant no harm. But being out of her elements surrounded by her books or researching the latest Mesoamerican find was getting to her. It was putting her on edge.

She did agree with the big beluga, that whatever was in that newspaper was suspect. What was he carrying? Where was he going?

What had she gotten herself into?

Farhad turned right down Via Giovanni Giolitti, pulling Torres back into the moment. She heard Gapinski behind her on the phone, apparently talking to SEPIO command.

"Yeah, we've just turned right onto Vie...Giovanni...Giol..li...titi something." He paused. "Yeah, that."

She slowed to catch up with her teammate. He smiled and nodded as if apologizing for before. She smiled back, then looked forward at the—

Where did he go?

"Do you know where the heck we are?"

Gapinski was oblivious to the disappearance. She looked behind her. A wall of people was pressing in from behind, old people and young people, families with kids and people with shopping bags and fanny packs.

But no Farhad.

She walked faster, leaving Gapinski behind.

"Hey, wait a minute, Zoe," she heard behind her. He called out, then started walking faster. "Naomi. Hey, wait up!"

She couldn't wait up. Not when Farhad had disappeared.

But she stopped, and Gapinski caught up, out of breath.

"Geez Louise, sister. Where's the 911?"

"Farhad. He's gone. That's the 911." She was curt, she knew it. But this guy was beginning to grate on her.

Gapinski looked around the street with a look of disbelief, phone still stuck to his ear.

"Uh oh," he said, then waited for a reply. "Zoe, can you see him with one of your doodads?" He paused. "Oh, yeah. That's right. No doodad. Well, do you know where he could possibly be?"

Torres frantically searched the area. People passed and glared at her with mixed looks of irritation and concern and confusion.

Wait. Across the way, a figure ran across the street in front of them and through an alley.

Wearing shades and a mustache.

She pulled at Gapinski's shirt to lead him forward.

"Hold on, where are we—"

"Over there, he ran into an alleyway. Either he knows we're on to him, or he's doing what either of us would do and play it safe with a mad dash."

He smiled at her, then followed her as she ran, Zoe still on the line.

They crept up to the side passage through the centuries-old Rome structures, Gapinski taking the lead. He leaned around the corner, then pulled back quickly.

"Did he see you?" she asked.

"I don't think so. No. I saw him exit out the other end."

She nodded. "Let's do it."

They both rounded the corner, then slowed. Nothing and no one there. They quickly ran across to the end of the ally, only to see a beautiful basilica and Farhad a block ahead of them.

"Come on," she said with urgency.

Farhad bypassed the basilica and slowed as they reached a piazza in front of it. He strolled across the well-manicured lawn, still holding the paper between his arms. Never diverting his attention from what was ahead.

"Talk to me, Zo. Where are we? What's—Wait a minute."

Farhad darted down another side street.

The pair ran after him. They reached the street, going against the traffic.

"There," Torres said, pointing to a nondescript, rust-colored chapel at the end of the street. Farhad entered through a small side entrance.

Horns honked at the pair as they weaved their way through the oncoming cars in chase.

"Yeah, right back atcha," he exclaimed, waving his arm in the air at a green Peugeot.

They reached the end of the street. He said into his earpiece, "Zoe, Radcliffe. Farhad's entered what looks like a chapel. We're going in."

He hung up on them, turned off his phone, and slipped off his earpiece. Then he turned to Torres. "Ready to earn your keep?"

CHAPTER 14

G apinski and Torres wasted no time following Farhad into the minor basilica.

"Come on," he said, leading the pair to the same door on the side of the rust-colored building Farhad had entered a few minutes ago.

A man sat next to the original, ninth-century facade, welcoming them in the name of the Father, Son, and Holy Spirit. Torres smiled and crossed herself. Gapinski did not, but nodded to the man in acknowledgment.

He flung open the wooden doors to the ancient church in pursuit. They thudded loudly inside the great hall beyond, echoing off its high ceilings. The two ran forward, only to stop short once they cleared the entrance and entered the nave, realizing their error.

They found themselves at the front of the massive, sacred space near the high altar, with all eyes of the congregants fixed on them. They had assumed it was empty, or sparsely occupied with a few tourists.

They were wrong.

Not only was it comfortably full, but they had interrupted a Eucharistic Celebration that had already commenced. A crowd of people had turned toward the sudden interruption, several of them gasping in surprise and disgust. The priest had stopped the ceremony and was staring at the couple, the host and cup prominently displayed on the altar.

Gapinski, shrugged and mouthed *Sorry*, then walked along the side of the sanctuary, scanning the large interior of the ancient space.

There he was.

Farhad was seated on the end of a pew next to one of six massive pillars. Gapinski glanced at the man as they passed him, who sat staring forward, newspaper resting next to him, bulky and proud.

What is in that thing?

Gapinski smiled slightly, feeling relief that they had caught up with the man and that he was within their sights once more.

Several people eyed them ruefully as they made their way around the interior of the ancient basilica across the colorful, hexagon tile work, past the giant, oak double-doors at the back of the nave and to the other side. They found an open spot for two at the end of a pew next to another one of the massive pillars holding up the ornately decorated ceiling. Gapinski motioned for Torres to sit next to a visibly irritated older woman, while he took the end.

As the priest resumed the sacred ceremony, Gapinski looked around the space, appreciating the architecture and holy ambiance that beckoned the worshipers heavenward. Six large windows at the top filtered in the bright sunshine down below. The ceiling was divided into four sections, each inlaid with gold bearing six inset panels of a sea of blue and a constellation of golden stars. It really was a sight to behold. A far cry from the clapboard country church of his childhood within the Deep South.

Having grown up a Southern Baptist, Gapinski had conflicting views about what was being performed at the front.

The more confrontational side of him wanted to stand up in the middle of the service and set them straight about the error of their transubstantiation ways—arguing the loaf was a loaf, not Jesus' actual body; the chalice held fermented grape juice, not the actual blood of Jesus.

That's what his grandpappy would have wanted him to do, at least, a dyed-in-the-wool SBC preacher. He recalled helping the man dutifully prepare the Lord's Supper celebration in their country church every three months as a kid. He was responsible for cutting the crust off the Wonder Bread slices, while Grandpappy poured thimble-size plastic cups full of watered-down grape juice. As a teenager, he was hoping for at least some Yellow Tail, but the old man was definitely the teetotaling type.

The other side of him was mesmerized by the ritual, as it connected with something within Gapinski that longed for the tangible, the experiential. Before Christ crawled up on those ancient Roman boards of execution, he had given thanks at a Passover gathering of his disciples for the simple table bread before he broke it. Then he said, "This is my body, which is for you; do this in remembrance of me." Then after supper he took the cup of Yellow Tail, saying, "This cup is the new covenant in my blood; do this, whenever you drink it, in remembrance of me."

At some level, the bread and wine were Christ, whether in symbol or representation or actualization. They were given to feed the faith of his children to nourish it and satisfy it and grow it.

Gapinski's faith was hungry. All the time.

He was transfixed on the priest's upheld arms, which raised the chalice heavenward in thanksgiving. His mouth was moving slightly as he uttered a soft prayer, the wine transforming into Christ's shed blood, as it was believed.

When the priest finished the blessing, the chalice exploded in his hands as a deafening gunshot rang out within the sacred space, pieces of the ritualistic vessel and the crimson liquid reigning down on the holy man. His mouth fell, his eyes widened. His face twisted with a mixture of surprise, fright, and disgust at what had happened as he stood behind the altar in stained garments.

Instinctively, Gapinski and Torres leaped out of their seats as the room collectively screamed and crouched for cover.

A collection of beige-clad gunmen wearing loose fitting clothes and scarves over their faces filtered into the nave from a single door at the center of the back of the church, firing semi-automatic weapons high and wide, shouting indecipherable commands.

"Always something," Gapinski cursed as he and Torres moved behind separate columns along the edge of the nave.

Women were screaming and crouching where they sat. The priest was cowering behind the altar, trying to soak up the spilled blood of Christ with his robe. Parents were screaming for their children to climb underneath the wooden benches. Men were yelling to protect their family and friends, and in protest at the intruders, not knowing how else to respond.

Mr. Mustache had gotten up from his seat, quickly making his way into what looked like a small chapel through dark-gray, marble columns directly to his right. The hostile invaders quickly ran along the east side of the nave, one of them dragging a large case behind him. Two of the hostiles joined Farhad, while two others stayed outside of the chapel entrance, guarding whatever was happening inside and spraying bullets across the sanctuary every few seconds. Again, high and wide, but enough to scare the crap out of everybody.

Gapinski noticed Farhad's newspaper was sprawled across the pew where he had sat. Which meant whatever it was Mr. Mustache had gotten in that drop-site package was now being used in that tiny room across the way.

"Over here," Gapinski ordered, running to another large,

square pillar directly across from the hostiles. Torres followed, attracting a spray of gunfire. It splintered into a wooden confessional booth, sending shards of wood into a family huddled behind them.

"What do you think is going on in there?" he asked Torres.

"My guess is the guy is after some relic. Only reason for all the firepower."

Across the way, Gapinski spotted Farhad and one of the other operatives dragging a dark, marble-looking object, spotted with white into the center near the dark, gray case. It looked like an oddly large chess piece.

His watch chimed. He'd received a text from Zoe. He looked down, twisting his face in confusion.

"What's Santa Prassede?" he said.

"What?"

"I just got a text from Zoe. She said we're at Santa Prassede."

"The Church of Saint Praxedes."

"Saint who?"

She paused, face dropping. "What a minute. Praxedes. The name isn't important. It's what it guards."

"And what's that?"

She looked at the chapel, trying to discern what was happening inside, her adrenaline beginning to gallop her forward for a fight.

He asked again, "What's inside?"

"One of the most important relics of the Passion of the Christ."

"Passion relics?"

She nodded, gaze fixed forward with purpose on the side chapel. "Objects that were part of the events of Jesus' crucifixion."

She paused, remembering what her grandfather had taught her as a little girl. She said, "In this case, the black, granite pillar where Jesus was beaten to a bloody pulp."

"Great. This is Notre Dame all over again!"

Suddenly, an explosion of violence and prolonged gunfire erupted from the chapel entrance, sending the congregants scurrying away toward their position in search of relief in the other small chapels behind them. Clearly the intent of the gunmen.

"That's it," Gapinski growled. "We've gotta end this. But we need a better angle of attack."

He motioned toward the final square pillar at the front of the nave near the high altar, then made a run for it, drawing weaker fire this time.

Maybe they're running out of steam.

He made it. Torres stayed put, giving them a double-angle advantage.

Gapinski aimed toward the gunmen guarding the entrance to the small chapel. He understood the oath he had taken when he joined SEPIO: seek to do no harm, use the minimum force necessary to execute the Order's missions. He agreed in theory. But in practice, with bullets of fire and fury whizzing this way and that, it was crap. The moment called for far more retaliatory measures, the kind that married gunpowder with cold, hard steel.

At minimum.

Three other operatives laid down more covering fire. Farhad emerged from the small room. One of his minions was dragging the large case behind him.

Sorry, dude. Not on my watch.

Gapinski waited for an opening through the crowd as it fled, then sent five rounds toward the hostiles. Two of the shots went wide. One of them lodged in a man's right leg. Another exploded into a marble urn above the entrance, sending heavy chunks to the ground around the gunmen.

Torres flashed him a look, then said, "I'm pretty sure that was a third-century marble urn you just destroyed."

Before he could respond, the gunmen had recovered and sprayed a hornet's nest of angry lead toward their position. They ducked behind the large, wide column as the bullets chewed chunks of ancient masonry to the ground.

Torres tried to steal a glance, but the assault was relentless. She relocated, crouching behind the splintered confessional, and when there was a reloading pause, she aimed her SIG Sauer with purpose and sent a barrage of her own, sending the hostile Gapinski had hit earlier to the floor clutching his other leg.

"Nice! But remember, I hit him first."

They didn't get long to revel in their scores. The wall behind them exploded in another round of semi-automatic gunfire, sending them back behind their column for cover, and giving Farhad and his man time to escape from the small relic chapel and down toward the back of the nave.

"They're moving," Torres yelled.

"I know, but I can't get a sight on them. Can you?"

The angle was wrong from both of their positions. Too far forward and too far off to the side from their route.

The gunfire seemed farther back now, so Gapinski stole a glance, bending around toward the high altar and then around toward the center of the sacred space.

They were slipping out the back door!

The nave had been cleared of civilians by now, all having either packed into the small chapels behind them for cover or exited out of the entrance to the left. So he let his gun rip, emptying his clip toward the exit at the back.

His bullets thudded uselessly into the set of hardwood doors as it closed behind the hostiles.

Gapinski cursed, then motioned toward the back. "Come on!"

Torres reached the exit first, positioning herself at the opening. Gapinski came up quickly and grabbed the handle. He looked at her, then nodded. He flung it open, and Torres inched through, arm outstretched with weapon at the ready.

They hustled into an open-air courtyard the size of a basketball court.

But no Farhad.

She inched forward, Gapinski close behind her. A door at the other end of the open space thudded shut. He ran forward, she followed closely, then opened the door for him.

Without looking, he ran through it, weapon pointed forward.

There was a long, dark passageway, made of old masonry work and stone flooring. Light at the end indicated an open door, and silhouetted inside the bright space was the outline of a man.

Instinctively he popped off three shots. He saw the man jerk forward, at least one of them connecting. Another silhouette appeared, answering his shots with twice the amount of power. He dove into a doorway along the passage, shielded by the ancient brickwork. Torres closed the door to the passage, protected behind its heavy, wooden weight.

The passageway darkened. Gapinski came out and ran forward, Torres joined him close behind.

Now or never.

He pushed through the door at the end with all of his six-foot-four weight and ran into a closed, wrought-iron gate. He tried opening it, but it was locked from the other side.

Speeding away was a black-panel van. He caught sight of the word *Vesta* and the image of a creepy-looking chick holding a bowl of fire.

He shook the bars in anger, but there was no give.

"Crapola!"

Torres came through the doors, finding her partner trapped. She was breathing hard, staring toward the end of the block as the van turned to join the city traffic.

"We need confirmation," Torres said, motioning back toward the inside of the church.

Sirens were screaming closer as the pair walked back through the corridor, through the courtyard, and back inside the church through the opened, wooden doors. The priest had come out from his hiding place. He was shaking as he slowly made his way down the steps of the elevated platform of the high altar, his garments stained crimson.

The two walked underneath the faded mosaics of the basilica and to the right toward where Farhad had staged his coup. A small sign indicated it was the Chapel of Saint Zeno, whoever that was.

The first thing Gapinski noticed was a small drill and a cordless power sheer lying on the ground in the center.

That settled what was in the newspaper.

Second, leaning against a small altar at the front under an icon of what he presumed was Saint Zeno was a perfectly removed panel of glass.

Third, to the right of the altar was a small alcove. Inside was an ornately decorated reliquary made of pure gold sitting on a marble pedestal, with four small columns supporting a domed roof.

It was empty, but for a three-foot, glass enclosure with the missing panel.

And a missing marble scourging pillar.

The one containing the memory of Jesus' suffering before bleeding out on the cross.

CHAPTER 15

JERUSALEM.

Lucas Pryce leaned back in his leather chair and put his feet up on his desk, puffing another cigar to life after pouring himself a tumbler of 30-year-old Macallan scotch. He let the spicy aroma of cedar and coriander drift into his nose, then lungs, before exhaling the smoke out of his mouth. He closed his eyes, walling off the world inside and outside of his tent, if only for a moment.

He was so close. So close to unveiling what history had hidden away for millennia. So close to achieving what countless religious saviors before him had failed to achieve.

The birth of a new End Times harmony, one that would progress the human race forward into a new era of existence long anticipated, yet so far unable to achieve by the brightest minds and most passionate hearts.

He puffed again on his cigar, eyes still closed, feet still propped on his desk as he contemplated what he was about to achieve.

And yet...there was a wrinkle.

Silas Grey.

He had been troubled by the two newcomers ever since they had left the tent.

His tent.

Two questions kept needling him through the afternoon: *Why are they here? What do they want?*

He hadn't seen Grey in nearly a decade, not since he had him as a student and Grey had joined him at the archaeological dig at Tell-es Sultan. And then made the brilliant parchment find authenticating not only the biblical story about Israel's battle against the city led by Joshua, but also the ancient, religious relic known as the Ark of the Covenant.

A giggle slipped from his mouth as he clenched the cigar, remembering how he had commandeered the scroll and took credit for the find. He felt slightly sorry for the fellow, knowing what that would have meant for his academic career. But then he thought about where that little find had led.

Had it not been for Silas, he wouldn't be sitting in a giant climate-controlled canvas tent in the Western Wall Plaza, puffing away on a cigar less than twenty-four hours before his unveiling.

A thick cloud of smoke had amassed above him during his contemplation. He pulled out his cigar and licked his lips. They tingled with nicotine and spice. He took a sip of the scotch that he had left unattended, then thought about what would transpire the day after tomorrow, when the real work began.

A buzzing sound beneath the maps of Old City Jerusalem and schematics of the Temple caught his attention.

He put his cigar back in his mouth, brought his feet down from his desk, then leaned forward to search for his phone. After retrieving it, he glanced at the screen.

Rudolf Borg.

What does he want?

He took a long swig of the caramel liquid then swallowed it in one hard gulp, enjoying the burn as it slid down into his empty stomach.

.   .   .

"Rudolph," the man on the other end of the phone said, sounding unconvincingly happy to hear from him.

There was that dreadful, Southern twang. How he hated the man from Chattanooga. "Dr. Pryce, how are you? I trust your preparations are coming along smoothly."

"Lord willing, and the creek don't rise."

What was he talking about? The man had a funny way about him, that's for sure. But he'd sure gotten results. Nous's resources had been well spent.

"I take it that means you are set for our little...unveiling tomorrow."

"Yes. Sorry, sir. Just a little expression us Southerners like to use. All is going according to plan. Remarkably so, if I might add."

"Good, good."

Borg paused, letting the silence linger before he laid into his reason for calling.

"I heard you had a visitor today."

He was met with silence at the other end. Which he expected. Pryce hadn't known of the amount of monitoring Nous had undertaken to ensure this phase of their operation went off without a hitch. One of his operatives had caught sight of Grey and the SEPIO operative known as Bourne entering into the Old City. He had followed them to a hostel, then to their room where he listened in on their conversation about approaching Pryce and learning about the excavation. After nearly getting caught, he reported back to Borg immediately.

"Yes..." Pryce said, fishing for words. "Yes, I've had many visitors today, as you might imagine."

"The two I'm referencing go by Silas Grey and Celeste Bourne. They paid you a visit a few hours ago. Isn't that right?"

The man hesitated, then said, "Yes, my former student and a colleague of his. They came to offer their congratulation. I must say, it was wholly unexpected. But then again, Silas had always angled to touch the hem of my garment."

"Then you don't know who they truly are."

"Truly are?" he replied, sounding confused. "I know Grey is a simple professor at Princeton, of historical theology and religious relics or something. The woman I had understood was a colleague of his."

"That's only partially true. Bourne is the director of operations for SEPIO, a special-ops entity of the Order of Thaddeus. Earlier this year, they had recruited Grey for a special operation to protect the Shroud of Turin, and then the Church of the Holy Sepulcher."

Borg's throat clenched with emotion for a moment as he recalled the disaster that was supposed to have thrust Nous into a new phase of religious resistance and spiritual enlightenment. The Church's insistence that Jesus of Nazareth had been raised from the dead had always been central to its teachings. He and the Council of Five and Thirteen believed that if they took out the Holy Shroud bearing the supposed image of the resurrected Christ, the tangible experience of the memory of the resurrection, then the Christian faith would begin to weaken. After all, nowadays it was the tangible, the concrete, the experiential that ruled the hearts and minds of the world.

Then there was Jacob Crowley, his dearest Jacob, who died at the hands of that wretched man. His childhood lover had sacrificed himself for the cause, and with nothing to show for it. Borg vowed Grey would pay.

"My, Lanta," was all that Pryce could offer.

"So you didn't know?"

"Know that my former student was an operative with a secret Vatican-run outfit supposedly stretching back to the time of the earliest founders of Christianity? What are you saying, Rudolf?"

"I'll take that as a no." Borg heard a crash, as if glass had broken.

"Heavens to Betsy!"

"You alright, professor?"

There was silence. And then, "I spilled my scotch, that's all."

Spilled or threw?

"At any rate," Borg continued, "I need to know what exactly you spoke of, and if they gave any indication of what they are planning."

"As I said, Grey said he came to offer his congratulations for my archaeological success. And get in on the action by offering his assistance, as he said, but I took that to be more jest than anything. We talked a bit about how we came about the passage and the chamber. Then I..."

Pryce drifted off, as if remembering something of importance.

"Then you what, Pryce?"

"Then I gave them all-access passes to the site so they could have a front row seat for the unveiling."

"You what?" Borg exclaimed. Imbecile. The man from Chattanooga would be the death of him.

"I had no idea they were ecclesiastical holy warriors, for Pete's sake! His arrival had taken me completely by surprise, I didn't know how to respond. He was a former student, as well as a reputable expert in his field. And since his original find a decade ago was partly responsible for the whole kit and caboodle to begin with, I thought it appropriate. Naturally, I'll cancel their passes at once."

"No. Don't do anything."

"Why? You said it yourself. They're dangerous. My head has been throbbing all afternoon wondering why he came here and what he wanted. Now I know he aims to cause us trouble."

"Not necessarily. I cannot imagine SEPIO is aware of our involvement. And frankly, your work would seem to support their agenda. Let them keep their passes. In fact, letting them have free reign will serve us well."

"Why?"

"As Sun Tzu said: 'Keep your friends close and your enemies closer.' We'll continue to monitor their movements and make you aware of any developments with them and the Order. And you keep me apprised of anything they might see or do. Understood?"

There was an audible sigh on the other end. "Understood. How is the second phase fairing?"

None of your business. Instead, Borg said, "We're making progress. I'll be in touch."

With that, he closed his sat-phone and started heading down to the crypt where the Council awaited his update.

Soon, a new epoch of enlightenment would be ushered in.

And the three Abrahamic faiths won't know what hit them.

CHAPTER 16

"They took what?" Silas exclaimed, sitting across from Celeste in the corner at a small café down the road from the Western Wall. After meeting with Pryce, the two decided they needed to regroup and figure out a strategy to get to the bottom of what he was after. It was clear from their conversation that something else lay beneath the surface. They had planned on going back to the dig site to leverage their all-access pass for all it was worth.

Until Radcliffe called to update them on the events in Rome.

"What happened?" Celeste asked.

"You knew about us dispatching Gapinski and the new recruit, Naomi Torres, to Rome. Ever since the Shroud and Holy Sepulcher incidents earlier in the year, and then the dreadful business with the apostle relics this summer, we have been tracking Nous cells throughout the world, but particularly hotspots of religious significance to the Christian faith. A few days ago, we had gotten word that a high-ranking Nous operative had left Berlin for Rome."

"How high?" she asked.

"One of the Thirteen. Marwan Farhad. "

Celeste whistled.

"Why's that so significant?" Silas asked.

"Apart from the Council of Five, the Thirteen is the group of highest-ranking associates of Nous that executes their missions. We know little about Farhad, other than he's a Persian who fled persecution from the Iranian Mullahs as a Zoroastrian prophet."

"Why was he in Rome?"

Radcliffe answered, "We hadn't fully understood the reason when we dispatched Gapinski and Torres. Their mission in Rome was meant to be a simple tracking exercise. We thought maybe he was meeting another associate, or perhaps an important informant. Maybe we would get a few opportunities to eavesdrop in on a conversation or two. Instead, they followed Farhad to a church. Before Zoe could explain where he was heading off to, we lost communication with them, and a team of Nousati stormed the church and took one of the Passion relics. The scourging pillar."

"All the markings of Nous, for sure," Celeste said.

Silas closed his eyes, pained by the revelation. He remembered well the black-and-white speckled marble when he visited the Chapel of Saint Zeno during his pilgrimage, imagining his Savior being torn apart like a slab of beef in a slaughtering house.

Before a crucifixion, guards would often flog their victims with a device called a flagrum, a wooden handle of several strips of leather with pieces of sharpened metal and hooks attached. Soldiers would whip their victims with the device, destroying their backs, ripping out chunks of their scalp and the side of their face—all while they were securely restrained against a stone or marble post.

Like the one contained in the reliquary at the Church of Saint Praxedis.

As tradition has it, Jesus was attached to that marble post, then flogged for hours. He was so physically incapable of carrying his cross beam to the site of his crucifixion after the experience that one of the guards pulled someone out of the crowd to force him to carry it for him.

Silas gritted his teeth. "So basically you're telling us that Gapinski lost one of the most important memory-markers of the Christian faith."

Celeste threw him a look, then said, "What are we doing about this, Radcliffe? Nous can't get away with this."

"We're already on it, Celeste. I have Zoe reviewing CCTV footage and images from nation-state and commercial satellite coverage of the area to locate the van. And Gapinski and Torres are already mobilizing. But..."

Radcliffe faded, going silent.

Celeste glanced at Silas, sharing a look of concern. "Radcliffe? You there?"

"Yes, I'm here."

Silas said, "Then what aren't you telling us?"

"There's been an explosion of chatter on all fronts. And then there have been unconfirmed reports coming out of Africa of attacks on some of the Orthodox churches there."

"Africa?" Silas said, twisting his face in confusion.

"Probably unrelated, as the region has been a hotbed of anti-Christian activity of late by Islamic extremists. It's all happening rather quickly. We'll let you know more, but I have to say that the timing of this is highly suspicious. What with Pryce's unveiling in the coming day."

Silas nodded at Celeste. He had to agree.

"Speaking of which, have you made progress on the Western Wall front?"

Celeste said, "We made contact with Pryce. He's...colorful."

Silas smiled. "That's generous. He was sure surprised to see me, and I think we did our best to cover our intentions. We did score all-access passes from the man. So I'd say that's a win."

"I must say," Celeste added, "that given the known Nous connection reported on by our embedded agent, God rest his soul. Or at least some sort of connection with Nous, I have to believe Pryce is going put together our connection with SEPIO and the Order. If he hasn't done so already."

"What're your next steps, then?" Radcliffe asked. "I assume with the pass you've been given access to the unveiling tomorrow?"

"Yes," she said, "we definitely plan to be at the unveiling."

"That's not enough," Silas interjected.

She turned to him. "What do you mean?"

"Given the activity at Saint Praxedis and the level of activity of Nous cells around the world, there is something bigger going on."

"What are you thinking, Silas?" Radcliffe asked.

"Not sure entirely, but among some ancient-looking maps and schematics for the city and Temple I saw a book open on Pryce's work table in the main tent when we were talking with him."

"A book? What kind? Did you get a read on it?"

"I only caught a glance and wasn't close enough to read. But I would say it's old. Maybe thirteenth or fourteenth century. I did see the typography, however, and it looked to be ancient Semitic."

"The ancient languages of the Middle East?"

"Exactly. I say we go back for a closer look. Maybe try and have a look around some of the workstations for some intel on Pryce's operation."

Celeste nodded in agreement. "No use sitting around until tomorrow. Given what SEPIO is tracking and given what just transpired in Rome, it's time we step up our engagement with the good professor's little project."

"What do you have in mind?" Silas asked.

"Why don't we rummage around the site for a while and see if there's anything we can hear or find? Surely these all-access passes are good for something."

He smiled. "I like the way you think."

"Me too," Radcliffe said. "But be careful. No use blowing your cover before the big day tomorrow."

"Agreed," Celeste said. "We're going dark with our communication until after the unveiling. This place has to be crawling with Nousati. And the fact our room at the hostel was almost broken into, I don't want to take any chances."

"Report back tomorrow, or the minute you've learned anything more. Godspeed, you two."

Celeste ended the call, then leaned back in her chair. "You ready for some more field work?"

Silas stood. "Bring it."

SILAS AND CELESTE left the café as the sun was slipping beneath the outer wall of the Old City, casting buckets of oranges, yellows, and reds across the clear, blue sky. They made their way back to the Western Wall Plaza, wading through crowds of people seemingly from all corners of the earth. No doubt drawn to Pryce's spectacle. Who could blame them? Discovering and unearthing the Ark would go down as a significant, historical achievement. Silas was not a little irritated it wasn't his doing.

As they pushed through the crowd, he wondered how they would take the unveiling. Surely those gathering inside the city were interested in the Ark for different reasons, all with differing agendas and religious commitments. He worried the stage was being set for an epic showdown, and bringing the Ark to light would be the match that set the whole region ablaze.

The media were out in full force, reporting live from the array of cameras splayed around the plaza. Tourists and other interested onlookers were milling about trying to catch a glimpse of the action. Others were simply the religiously devoted, there to pray as spiritual seekers.

Silas said a prayer of his own as they walked past the smaller tent of Pryce's staging grounds and toward the entrance to the larger one, crossing himself on instinct from his childhood Catholic faith.

They reached the entrance just as their good friend with the shiny, eight-ball head, Oliver Tulu, was coming out, head down and studying his clipboard, nearly running into the pair.

"Excuse me," the man said in irritation, then startled and stopped. He hugged his clipboard to his chest, and said, "Pardon me, *professor*. I didn't see you there. Miss," he said, nodding toward Celeste. "I trust you had a good and fruitful conversation with Professor Pryce earlier."

Silas said, "Oh yes. Very good. Very fruitful."

"Good, good." He stood in the entrance, his lanky figure towering over them and white teeth gleaming in a fixed, forced smile.

"In fact, we were just heading back to see him now."

"Oh, I am sorry, but the professor has left for the day and will not be returning until tomorrow's unveiling."

"That is disappointing."

He continued to stand in the doorway, immobile, immovable. "Is there anything else I can do for you?"

"No, thanks. We'll catch him at the ceremony tomorrow."

The two left back where they came. Silas glanced back as they rounded the smaller tent. Tulu was still eyeing them as they turned the corner.

"Well, that went nowhere fast," Celeste said.

"Come over here," he said, stopping at the corner of the tent. "I have an idea."

He walked along the thick canvas to the back where it met the old, sand-colored structures. There was enough of a gap between the building and the tent to fit through, so Silas stepped inside.

She glanced backward. Satisfied no one had seen them, she followed him through.

The temperature had to have been fifteen to twenty degrees warmer. Between the tightly enclosed space and the heat, Silas felt a panic attack setting in. Not having his little, blue pills, he focused on breathing as he moved through the gap, squeezing through the hot, cramped space of rock and canvas. He stopped suddenly, then stooped to the ground.

"Do you hear that?"

Celeste cocked her head to listen. "A generator?"

"Air conditioning unit. That might be our way inside. Come on."

He pressed forward, carefully squeezing through the gap so as not to attract attention from the other side.

They came to the end of the longest side of the small tent and found the beginning of Pryce's larger one. In between was a narrow, twelve-foot canvas tent hallway adjoining the two tents.

And there it was, humming away. A large unit embedded in the side of the canvas wall of Pryce's workspace, about half the size of a person.

Silas smiled in satisfaction and relief at coming out of the tight-squeeze space. He hustled over to inspect the air-conditioning unit, running his hands around the edges and to the bottom.

"There we go. What I suspected."

Celeste crouched, inspecting what he found. There was a Velcro slit at the bottom holding the canvas together around the unit to create a seal.

"We used these same types of tents in Iraq as mobile command centers. And the god-awful heat required the same kinds of air-conditioning units, embedded into the tent with Velcro."

"So we undo the Velcro and slip inside. Brilliant!"

Silas nodded. "That's the idea. Let's hope there's no one on the other side. Or else things are going to get real awkward real quick."

He crouched down to his belly and slid underneath the large unit sticking out of the tent. It was two feet off the ground and supported by a platform, with a horizontal strip of Velcro holding the tent together. He carefully undid the flap and slid a finger down the seal a few inches. Pulling it back, he peered inside.

From this angle, he could see the legs of several tables and chairs. A few people were standing on the other side of the vast interior around a large work table with a few more seated. Other than that, it looked mostly empty. Unfortunately, there wasn't any barrier between them and the rest of the room. Once they committed to slipping inside, it was do or die.

Just then his phone gave a slight, but audible, *ping.*

He quickly closed the flap, then slid back.

"What was that?" she asked.

He pulled out his phone, then frowned. "Battery indicator. Less than twenty percent left." He turned it off, then shoved it back in his pants.

No more room for error.

Then he got back on his stomach and slid back to the opening. He carefully peeled back the flap, checked the surroundings, then undid the rest of the Velcro seal. Celeste pulled back the two-foot flap as he slid inside. She quickly followed. When she did, the unit suddenly shut off.

Startled, Silas shuffled up off the ground, then pulled Celeste inside and up to her feet.

He felt exposed in the silence, as much as the wide-open space. To the side was a kitchenette with a large water cooler and a countertop with hot coffee. He quickly reached for the pot and a Styrofoam cup. Even though coffee was the last thing he wanted, he poured himself a cup, then handed one to Celeste.

He turned around and leaned against the countertop as she followed his lead, trying to act as if he had been there the whole time, dutifully preparing for the big day and needing a coffee break. The group around the large table across the way never looked over at them.

Suddenly, a man walked toward them, one of the young, Indiana Jones wannabes.

Have we been made?

He seemed to be picking up his pace. He was looking at Silas, then opened his phone. When the man came over, he nodded a greeting to Silas.

Silas smiled and nodded back, then took a swig of the thick, black brew. "Nectar of the gods," he said raising his cup.

The man offered a weak smile, then poured his own cup. He was jabbering in another language into his mobile. Celeste said hello, then took a sip herself. He nodded to her as he continued talking, doctoring his coffee with cream and way too much sugar. Then he hustled over to the group huddled in the back corner.

Silas closed his eyes, then sighed audibly. "That was close. A few seconds more and we would have been busted."

"Let's have a look at the professor's table," Celeste said, "Then let's get on our way."

She strolled over toward the center of the space where Pryce had set up shop. Holding her coffee with one hand, she slung the all-access pass around her neck and prominently displayed it in case anyone had questions. Silas did the same.

They reached Pryce's table, but there was nothing there. No maps, no schematics, no notebooks.

And no mysterious, ancient book with Semitic text.

"Are you kidding me?" Silas mumbled as he searched Pryce's desk, then bookcases. A few members of the group in the corner glanced their way, but he played like he belonged there, slowing down his search.

Celeste sat in Pryce's leather chair as Silas continued. He glanced over at the group in the corner as he worked. They were back to whatever it was they were so concerned with. He opened the middle drawer and rummaged through its contents. Mostly pens and paperclips and rubber bands. He brought out a small stack of papers, and something fell to the Persian rug.

Celeste got out of the chair and retrieved it. It was black and made of plastic, about the size of a credit card.

Or a keycard to a hotel room.

She smiled and quickly got up off the ground, then headed for the exit. He shoved the papers back into the drawer and followed after her back into the Western Wall Plaza.

Another score for SEPIO.

CHAPTER 17

Celeste half-expected Tulu to be standing guard outside the door. Thankfully, the coast was clear.

She continued walking across the plaza and the full length of the Western Wall to the other side, where she found two empty white chairs under an umbrella near a barrier roping off the resting area from the site of prayer. She hadn't even looked at the card until she knew they were safe, keeping it pressed against the palm of her hand inside her pocket.

Celeste sat in one chair, Silas in the other. She pulled out the card. It was charcoal gray with a black, paisley pattern and the unmistakable white 'WA' logo imprinted on the front.

Waldorf Astoria.

Silas scoffed. "Of course Pryce is staying at the Waldorf!"

Celeste raised an eyebrow. "Jealous, are we?"

He folded his arms and said nothing.

She smiled. "Here's the opportunity we need to figure out what Pryce has been up to. We use this to gain entrance into his room and have a look around."

He took the card from her and flipped it over, then frowned. "Except how do we know which room it is?"

She stared forward toward the large tent in thought. Then she took out her phone and placed a call. It answered on the first ring. "Zoe, it's Celeste. We found a keycard to a hotel in Jerusalem, but haven't a clue which room it opens. It looks to utilize a near-frequency chip, so I wondered if you could uplink to my phone and use the NFC embedded in it to read the card and figure out where it belongs."

Zoe said she could, and to give her a minute to connect.

"Impressive," he said.

"Once in a while."

Within a minute Zoe had reported back that she found the room. Third floor, room 323.

"Thanks, Zoe," Celeste said, then ended the call.

"Alright, what's the plan, chief?" Silas asked. "Because I'm not sure how comfortable I feel breaking and entering. Pretty sure the Bible has something to say about stealing and what not."

"We're not going to steal anything. Just have a look around. Hopefully he isn't there, and hopefully we learn something that will help us better understand what the bloody hell he's up to. And what it might mean for the Church."

"What could go wrong?"

The two took a cab out of the Old City and to the upscale hotel a fifteen-minute drive away. After paying the man, Celeste led them into the well-appointed building, where a doorman held the door of glass and bronze as they entered. Greeting them were vases of orange Israeli wildflowers, crystal chandeliers, English-tan leather couches, and a central seating area lit by the glow of the fading, evening sky through skylights in an expansive, covered atrium at the center.

They walked farther into the cream-colored lobby when Celeste stopped suddenly.

"There he is," she mumbled, turning away and slowing inching toward a marble archway. She leaned against it and pointed past a small, green indoor tree to a table near a railing. Seated were Pryce, sporting a dark-blue jacket and unbuttoned pressed, white shirt, and a dark-colored man in a cream-colored suit. Oliver Tulu.

Silas rubbed his hand over his close-cropped hair, adrenaline beginning to flow in anticipation of their next series of moves.

"At least we know Pryce isn't in his room."

"But for how much longer?" Celeste turned to him and handed him the keycard. "Take this and get going. No time to waste. I'll stay here and monitor him and Tulu. If they move, I'll text you, and you text back to indicate receipt. Sound good?"

Silas nodded. "Sounds good. Got it."

Silas stuffed the card in a pocket, then backed away to the central stairwell before turning toward it.

It's go time.

SILAS TOOK THE WHITE, marble stairs two by two, quickly ascending to the third floor.

Orange sconces and a full moon shining brightly through the skylight of the central atrium lit the way as the evening sunlight quickly gave way to purple, inky darkness. He passed a couple who were dressed to the nines, him in a crisp, black tuxedo and her in a floor-length, white, strapless gown. They eyed him wearily as he passed. It was then that he remembered he was wearing jeans and a polo, and covered in Palestine dust from the dig. Probably didn't smell too good, either. He chuckled to himself, then pressed forward to room 323.

He found his target at the end of the hallway, a double set of doors with a keycard pad on the wall. He glanced behind himself, then held the charcoal card against the pad. Within a second, a green indicator light went off with a soft *ping*, and he could hear the lock click open. He quickly pressed the handle down, then opened the door and slid inside, quietly shutting the door behind him.

So this is the life of a thieving academic.

Envy flooded him as he walked across the cherry, hardwood floor of the spacious room of luxury. A large, modern, impressionist painting of bright flowers hung on one of the walls. A Persian rug decorated in bright yellows and dark blues and pink swirls sat in the middle of the living quarter, commanded by two overstuffed, dark leather chairs and a long leather couch. A bedroom off to the right housed a king-size bed with soft, cream-colored bedding and the sister rug underneath.

He walked to the window, overlooking the Old City of David. Underneath it was a cherry-wood buffet table with an ice bucket and half-empty bottle of 30-year-old Macallan.

He picked it up and smiled. *Don't mind if do.*

He plunked two ice cubes into a glass, then poured himself three-fingers worth of the caramel-colored scotch. He took a long swig as he watched the sun make its final descent over the city. He sighed, letting the oaky liquid warm his belly. But then remembered why he was there. It definitely wasn't to drink 30-year scotch.

He took another mouthful, then set the glass down. He walked over to a desk. It was clean, not a paper or book on it. He opened the drawers. Nothing.

He frowned and put his hands on his hips. Then walked over to the couch and chairs, looking underneath each of them. Again, nothing. He opened all of the cupboards and drawers of the buffet, finding them empty. Same for the entryway closet and another small cabinet with a golden bowl of fruit on top.

Then he turned to the bedroom. It was slightly humid and warmer than the living room, as if Pryce had finished with a shower before he met his assistant for a drink. On his bed were the aged maps of the Old City and schematics of the Temple Mount he had seen earlier on Pryce's work table. He shuffled through them, looking them over for any clues as to his professor's intentions. They were interesting, but revealed nothing.

What are you hiding, Pryce?

He realized something was missing. The book.

He spun around to a large chest of drawers. He walked over and opened them, then rummaged through his clothes. Nothing there. He opened the drawers to two oval nightstands, which was another waste.

This was taking too long.

An armoire in the corner caught his attention. He shuffled over to it and opened its doors. He was greeted by several pressed shirts and pants. And an electronic safe.

Silas cursed. Of course. He took out the keycard, but no luck. There was a digital number panel on the front, with the user controlling the PIN number to lock the safe upon shutting the door. There was no way he was cracking that, especially not in the five or so minutes he had left.

But then he realized the safe was too small to fit the book anyway. Perhaps it was hidden away somewhere else. But where?

He turned around and faced the bedroom, scanning it for possible hiding places. He looked at the bed, then down where a cream-colored skirt reached the floor, obstructing his view. He quickly knelt on the floor and lifted the skirt.

Bingo.

He pulled out a package stuffed at the back near the center of the headboard. It looked like a red, woven mat of some sort. And there was something wrapped inside. His heart raced forward as he unfolded the package.

There it was. The mystery book, as well as a leather-bound journal tied tightly with a leather strap, dusty and well-traveled.

He instinctively looked toward the door and waited, literally holding his breath. Nothing.

He exhaled, then set aside the journal for now. He turned to the book, then carefully pulled back a thick, dark-colored cover and started flipping through it, its heavy, ancient pages whispering with each turn. Beautifully, richly colored marginal images of reds and blues and greens accented the text. It was definitely an ancient, foreign language, but struck him as familiar, like the Afroasiatic language family originating in the Middle East he saw while studying with Pryce at Tell-es Sultan. While he wasn't a linguist by any means, the script looked to be far older than even a few centuries ago.

He pulled out his phone to take some pictures of the book for later. He would send them to Zoe for analysis while he and Celeste—

It was off.

Panic settled quickly into his gut. He had forgotten he turned it off after the low-battery alert episode at the tent. What if Celeste had been trying to warn him?

He quickly pressed the power button, willing it to come back to life.

Come on, come on.

It did, the white screen with a black Apple logo indicating the startup process.

His heart was pounding in his ears, his breathing quick and panicked. It was now that he really needed his little, blue pills.

A screen appeared asking for his PIN number. He quickly typed it in, then he was brought to the home screen.

That's when a flood of texts came through from Celeste.

> *Pryce and Tulu paying.*
> *Tulu has left.*
> *Pryce finished paying, leaving the table.*
> *Silas, what's your ETA?*
> *Pryce is taking stairs.*
> *Why no reply? WHAT'S GOING ON??*

Not good. How long ago were these warnings?

No matter. He had moments to act. His phone's juice was just under twenty percent. And Pryce could come back any time. He switched his phone to camera mode, then started snapping pictures of the book. He had no idea what he was capturing, but figured Zoe could sort through the images later, translating what he took and finding more to fill in the gap, maybe even the book itself.

He looked back at the bedroom entryway, still no sound.

He tossed the book back on the red, woven cloth, then looked at his phone. It had been four minutes since the texts came flooding in. But he needed the contents of that journal. He huffed and grabbed it, then quickly unwound the leather strap and started flipping pages and taking pictures without even reading its contents. It was too full of notes and research to capture it all. He just fired at will and hoped he was catching something useful.

Alright, time to get the heck out of here.

He carefully wound the strap back around the journal, placed it on the mystery book in the center of the rectangular mat, then wrapped it and slid it back to its hiding place.

He stood, breathing hard and sweating.

There was a sound, muffled and knocking. At the door.

Pryce.

Within seconds, he would be inside.

Silas acted quickly to position himself for Pryce's entrance.

In one second, the outside keypad pinged softly, in another, the door opened and in stepped the tall, gangly Southern man, head down.

He closed the door and suddenly snapped his head toward one of the overstuffed leather chairs in the center of the room.

Where Silas was sitting, sipping a tumbler of 30-year-old scotch.

His eyes widened, but he didn't react like one would expect, with an adrenaline fight-or-flight, chest-clenching yell of surprise or anger.

Instead, he said ten words, slowly, deliberately: "Grey, what the hell are you doing in my room?"

CHAPTER 18

Silas swirled the caramel-colored liquid in the thick crystal tumbler with one hand, the ice no longer giving off the clinking sound after having melted. His mind was tripping over itself as it rushed forward to craft a believable story for why he was in the man's hotel room.

Not breaking eye contact with Pryce, he said, "I thought we needed to talk, face to face, before tomorrow."

He couldn't quite tell if Pryce was trying to suppress uncontrollable rage at Silas being in his room or was simply thoroughly shocked at finding someone in his room—much less enjoying his scotch.

The man slowly took off his jacket and slung it over the other overstuffed leather chair facing Grey. He took out his cufflinks one by one and set them on an end table, then walked over to the buffet underneath the window overlooking the city.

"What do you think we need to talk about?" he said flatly as he uncorked the bottle of Macallan. "And how the hell did you get into my room?"

Time to play this game carefully.

Silas took a long sip, then set down the heavy tumbler on a thick, marble coaster. "I sweet-talked one of the floor maids who had come in for the nighttime turndown service. Told her I was a long-lost friend who had come in town to surprise a guy who just made a monumental, history-changing discovery. Said the hotel front desk gave me his room number. Said he was told there might be someone upstairs for his turndown service and could let me in."

Pryce turned around and scoffed. "And she believed you?"

"Apparently."

"That's frightenin'." He finished pouring himself his own tumbler of scotch, minus the ice, then sat in the chair opposite Silas.

"Let's get down to it," he said, his voice bowing low, his accent thickening. "What the hell do you want?"

The question seemed multilayered, beyond just "What the hell do you want *right now*?" But more of a general question of want that covered Silas's entire reason for being in Jerusalem in the first place.

Does he know something about him and Celeste, more than he's let on?

Silas took another long sip, then took an even longer breath. He exhaled, and said, "When I heard you on CNN a few days ago, I have to admit, I was jealous. There was even a part of me that wanted to punch you in the face."

Pryce chuckled. So did Silas.

"Because you and I both know that your little project here is because of what I found back at Tell-es Sultan."

The grin on Pryce's face sunk. He narrowed his eyes and took a sip of his scotch, saying nothing.

Silas continued, "What you did, taking credit for my find, was wrong. But it also hurt. Because I had thought of you as a sort of a second uncle."

Pryce's face brightened slightly. "You had? Why?"

He hesitated, then said, "I don't think I had mentioned it, but my father was military. So we moved around a lot and didn't see our family too often. Then he died at the Pentagon on 9/11."

"My Lanta." Pryce set down his tumbler and crossed his legs. He said softly, "No, I didn't know."

Silas grew silent, then took another mouthful of his drink. "We seemed to click, both in the classroom and at the dig. And we worked well together. So when you—When you, betrayed me..."

Pryce frowned, then took his own mouthful. "I'm not sure that's fair. It was my dig, and I had right-of-custody of whatever came of our excavating work. You knew that when you signed up to join me."

Silas nodded. "I know. But I also wanted to tell you I'm fine now. And I'm thrilled with where it led, even if I didn't get any of the credit."

His goal at that moment was to mollify the man, and Silas certainly was neither fine nor thrilled when he went into the conversation. But for some inexplicable reason, at that moment, the cloud of envious tension that he had been carrying with him all these years and that he had dragged with him to the Holy City had lifted. In his former life, he would have blamed it on the scotch, a temporary reprieve thanks to the alcohol. But he felt as if the Spirit of God himself had slapped him upside the head and taken away his offense.

What did it matter, anyway, that Pryce had taken credit for his discovery? The good Lord had blessed his life despite the professional slight. And all carrying around a chip on his shoulder against Pryce had done over the years was give him a backache. Besides, as Jesus himself said in John's Gospel: *Let anyone among you who is without sin be the first to throw a stone.* He was the last person on God's green earth who had the right to throw stones, that's for sure. Not even at Pryce.

He breathed in deeply, took another sip of scotch, and offered a smile.

Pryce offered a weak smile back. "Well, thanks for that. But I do understand what you're saying. And I'm sorry for what happened and how it happened—truly. But look at what it led to! It gave me the inspiration and academic gumption to go down this road." He raised his glass. "So cheers to that."

Silas raised his glass. "Cheers. And cheers to your work. It really is a remarkable achievement."

They both drank. Then the two fell silent.

"Well, I should get out of your way." Silas drained his glass, then stood. "You've got a big day tomorrow, and I should let you go. Sorry for barging into your room unannounced."

Pryce stood and chuckled. "Thanks for stoppin' by, Professor Grey. I'll see you in the mornin'."

The two shook hands and Silas left, taking with him everything he needed to nail Pryce and uncover his true motives.

SILAS LOOKED BACK UP to the third level as he raced down the white, marble stairs. He reached the lobby and searched for Celeste. Not seeing her, he rushed into the atrium, scanning benches at the perimeter and the tables where Pryce had been earlier.

Where is she?

"Silas!"

He startled, then turned around. Relief flooded his face.

"Why the bloody hell have you been dark? What happened? I've been worried sick!"

"I'm so sorry," he said, leading her through the lobby and out the front door. The same doorman from earlier opened it for them. Silas nodded in thanks.

When they had reached the end of the block, he continued. "I had turned my phone off back at Pryce's tent after the low-battery alert sounded. Totally forgot to turn it back on."

"Goodness, Silas. You gave me quite the fright."

"I know. Bad move. Rookie move." He extended his arm to hail a cab. "I didn't see your texts until literally minutes before Pryce walked through his door."

Celeste grabbed his arm. He glanced down. She smiled, then pulled back. "What happened? What did he say? Did you find anything?"

"Relax, I'm an old pro at this SEPIO breaking-and-entering business by now." He grinned. She laughed. Then he reached into his pocket and held up his phone, his grin widening.

Her eyes widened, too. "You didn't!"

A cab pulled up to the curb. "Oh, I did." He opened the back-seat door, and Celeste got in. He slid in beside her. "Found that large, mystery book I had been looking for, as well as a notebook filled with Pryce's research."

"Where you go?" the cabbie barked in broken English.

"Old City. Chain Gate Hostel."

The man grunted an acknowledgment and took off.

"What did it say?" she asked. "What was the book?"

"Not sure what that book is, but it sure is old. And the text is vaguely familiar, probably ancient Semitic. Didn't get a chance to read the journal, but snapped as many pictures as I could."

"Let's have a look, then."

He took out his phone and opened it to his photos. He scrolled to the beginning, to those taken of the mystery book.

The first image was of the cover, black and scarred with age. The next few were blurry, but another of the title page bore a curious seal and large, Semitic characters. No other markings or notations, and no use at all.

"Any idea what this might be?" he asked.

Celeste shook her head. "Keep scrolling. Maybe something will pop up."

He did, encountering more blurry images from his rushed picture-taking, as well as some photos of the pages with beautiful marginal notes and more Semitic text. All indecipherable.

She said, "I haven't a clue what I'm looking at. Do you?"

He shook his head in silence. He continued scrolling, but encountered more of the same. Until they got the images to Zoe, they were a dead end. "Hopefully Zoe and her team can make sense of these ancient chicken scratches."

She gently punched his arm. "They aren't chicken scratches. It's obviously a holy book from an ancient culture. Be proper."

Silas felt foolish and raised both hands slightly in surrender. "Sorry. Meant no disrespect. Let's check out the journal entries."

The first several were another batch of blurry images caught in the heat of the moment. But he did make a mental note to get a new phone because Apple wasn't living up to its picture-taking claims.

The next one was more promising. "I remember this one," he said. "I thought it might be a hand-drawn map of some sort. Look." He pointed to a squiggly line running down the center of the page, a river perhaps. There was a single dot a quarter of the way down, unfortunately unlabeled, and then the line split into two separate ones and then rejoined near the bottom. The whole thing was flanked on the right by pencil shading.

"Where do you suppose this indicates?" she asked.

Silas shook his head. "Could be anything. But that shaded part on the right seems significant, narrowing the possibilities. A body of water perhaps."

Celeste sighed and shook her head, too. "Could be Egyptian, but could be Greek or Roman. Or even Indian. That shaded part could be the Sea of Galilee, or maybe the Dead Sea."

"I don't know...that would have to make the squiggly line a road of some sort. Which definitely could be the case. But then where? Jerusalem, maybe?"

The two sat in silence, trying to make out the map.

"Keep flipping through the pictures of the journal," she said. "Maybe something else will be of use."

Another few photos over, they landed on some promising

intel. At the top were two words: Shishak and Chartres. Shishak was circled several times over, as if Pryce had wanted to highlight it and emphasize it. Silas's heart beat faster at the revelation. He could taste the significance. He smiled at the find and possibility of gaining the upper hand on Pryce. Underneath were a number of notations he had made, but they were indecipherable from the image that was captured.

"What do you make of that word there?" Celeste asked pointing to the encircled *Shishak*.

"Not sure, but it's obviously significant."

"And what of the connection between a thirteenth-century French cathedral and the Ark?" She said, her face twisting in puzzlement at the mention of Chartres.

Silas said nothing.

"And look." She pointed at the screen, where there were two other words with no further explanation. Or rather two other names.

Bernard of Clairvaux and Wolfram von Eschenbach.

Silas leaned back and looked at Celeste with a mixture of confusion and surprise.

Clairvaux he knew. He had studied the eleventh- and twelfth-century Cistercian monk and mystic in graduate school, though he hadn't paid much attention to him. The other name looked German, but he hadn't heard of him before. Certainly hadn't heard of either of their connection to the ancient Hebrew relic.

A dread began churning within his belly that things were not as they seemed. It was clear from the beginning that Pryce was up to something. And these names, of books and cathedrals and people, indicated something way beyond a simple archaeological discovery.

These images changed everything about what they were investigating.

Suddenly, the car stopped. Silas looked up smiling at their

discovery. But it quickly faded, replaced with a scowl of confusion.

They were not at their hostel. They weren't even in the Old City.

As he looked at Celeste, panic turned into recognition, the driver pivoted around sharply holding a gun.

"Get out, Mr. Grey." He was training the weapon inches from Celeste's head. "Slowly. And don't do anything stupid."

Major fail, Grey!

Silas slid his phone into his pocket, then opened the door and slowly exited the vehicle, jaw locked with narrow eyes trained on the gunman.

The man opened his door, eyes trained on Silas, gun trained on Celeste.

"Now your turn, Ms. Bourne. Get out."

She looked at Silas, mouth slightly agape, chest rising and falling rapidly. He smiled slightly, then nodded. She opened the door and slid out, the gunman exiting in sync.

He waved the gun at Celeste, motioning her to join Silas. "Move over next to your partner. Both of you keep your hands where I can see them."

Neither of them could have done anything anyway since they both left their weapons safely stowed in their room.

"Now hand it over. Set the phone on the roof of the car, then walk back to the curb underneath that street lamp."

The man motioned toward Silas with his weapon. He didn't move. He kept his eyes trained on the man, hands at his side. "Who are you? You working for Pryce?"

The man scoffed. "Pryce is just one man in an ocean of ambition."

"So you're Nous."

The man's eyes flinched slightly, revealing a glimmer recognition. "Put the phone on the roof of the car, then walk backward.

Or I blow both of your heads off." He outstretched his weapon toward Celeste. "Beginning with this pretty little thing."

Celeste clenched her teeth and narrowed her eyes. "Do it," she whispered. "We saw what we needed. We'll take it from there."

He looked at her and sighed. Every fiber of his Ranger-trained being wanted to chuck it at the man and start a fight.

One he knew he'd lose.

Instead, he slowly stepped forward and reached over the passenger's side, placing the black device on the roof. Then he and Celeste backed up to the curb, as the man demanded.

The gunman inched forward, his weapon arm stiffly trained on the pair. He climbed on the edge of the opened driver's side door, then reached for the phone. When he did, Silas thought he caught glimpse of an unmistakable tattoo peeking underneath the man's coat sleeve as his pale arm stretched forward over the roof under the lamplight. Two intersecting lines bent at the corners. The Phoenix symbol of Nous.

The man grabbed the phone. He grinned with satisfaction, then hopped down and quickly jumped inside the cab. He started the car and drove away.

Silas cursed loudly. Celeste echoed him.

Score one for Nous.

DAY III

CHAPTER 19

JERUSALEM.

Lucas Pryce stood in a white, Egyptian-cotton bathrobe at the large window overlooking the Old City, contemplating the history he would be forging in the next few hours. The morning was bright, full of hope and expectation. Yet a wet blanket of uncertainty had been cast over the day's coming event from the night before.

Silas Grey.

The presence of the man sitting in his overstuffed leather chair drinking his bottle of 30-year Macallan nearly sent him into the same rage he channeled as a child. But he'd held it in check, preferring to see how the conversation would play itself out.

He hadn't believed for one second the man's pathetic, thinly veiled excuse for visiting his room. He wasn't there to speak about the past slight at Tell-es Sultan? Not there to talk about not receiving due credit for Pryce's professional achievements? Had no interest in pressing for more of the lime-light glory with the Ark?

Please!

He came fishing, sent by the Order and that miscreant Rowan Radcliffe to divine what it was that they were up to underneath the Temple Mount. He had fully planned to revoke their passes and teach that ingrate Grey a lesson in propriety and professional respect. But Borg intervened. He was probably right. It would be helpful to have operatives of SEPIO on hand to verify what he would uncover. The world wasn't ready for the discovery and would need a third party like the Order of Thaddeus to provide validity to his findings. But he still didn't like it, Grey poking around in his business and all.

A knock at the door woke him from his contemplation. It was the room service he had ordered a half hour ago, complete with cheddar-cheese eggs, thick bacon, wheat toast, red-skinned potatoes, pressed Ethiopian coffee, fresh-squeezed orange juice, and a small bottle of champagne. He tipped the server generously, then promptly uncorked the bottle and mixed himself a mimosa.

He walked back over to the window, then took a mouth full of the orange juice-champagne cocktail. He let the sweet, bubbly liquid sit in his mouth before swallowing it, smiling, and clucking his tongue with satisfaction.

This was really happening, finally, after so many months of plotting and planning and negotiating. Lucas Pryce was going to make history, the history he knew deep down he was destined to make.

Make. He grinned with more satisfaction than when he drank his mimosa at that thought. He liked the sound of that word. Same for *forge* and *form.* And *hammer, hone, shape.* That's exactly what he was doing. Making and forging his destiny. The destiny of the world.

The collective destinies of the Abrahamic faiths.

"WHAT A BLOODY DISASTER," Radcliffe growled from the other end of the line. While the sun was beginning to rise over Silas and Celeste's hostel above the Western Wall, the moon was still shining bright and strong in the dead of night in Radcliffe's world. And he was in a foul mood for it.

After the two had been mugged and left stranded in an unknown part of town by the Nous operative, they had used Celeste's phone to call another cab back to their hostel. When they arrived back at their room, they had phoned in the incident to SEPIO command, but were unable to debrief with Radcliffe until the early morning.

The two had called him with a report after grabbing a few items from the breakfast buffet in the lobby. Putting him on speaker, Celeste had relayed the day's events, from stealing into the tent at the dig site and finding the keycard, to Silas raiding Pryce's room and getting caught, to the theft of the phone with pictures during the cab ride back.

"Pretty sure the guy was Nousati," Silas said. "Certain I caught a glimpse of a tattoo when the man exposed his forearm grabbing the phone. The unmistakable black phoenix marking was peeking out from underneath his jacket. And then he flinched at the mention of Nous."

Radcliffe said, "And on that phone was a cache of images of whatever ancient book Pryce had been secreting away, as well as a journal notebook of his research and thoughts on the Ark? Am I to understand that correctly?"

Silas sighed. "You're correct."

"Bloody hell," Radcliffe cursed. "Well, did you catch a glimpse of anything memorable when you were taking the pictures? Anything at all that might give us a leg up on whatever it is that Pryce might be up to within the Temple Mount?"

"We were able to review some of the images before we were accosted," Celeste said.

Silas added, "Here's what we know. The mystery book seemed to be written in some ancient, Semitic language, but neither of us could decipher any of it, and nothing was translated in the margins. Does any of that ring any bells?"

Radcliffe said, "I'm sorry, but my familiarity with Ark lore is a bit rusty, I'm afraid. I haven't a clue how that book is associated with the fabled Jewish relic."

"Neither do we. But there was more. A hand-drawn map with what looked like either a river or a significant road, an ancient highway perhaps. There was what appeared to be a town along the route. Again, ring a bell?"

"No, but if you can reproduce it on your smartphone and send it through, I'll get Zoe on it."

"Perfect. And the town and river or road was near a large body of water, perhaps the Sea of Galilee or the Dead Sea. Hope that helps."

"That should narrow it a bit. Anything else?"

"Four more interesting, if not confusing items," Celeste said. "On a single side of the journal was a word circled in bold, *Shishak*, and the name *Chartres*, which we took as the cathedral, with some indecipherable notes underneath. Then the names *Bernard of Clairvaux* and *Wolfram von Eschenbach*. How about those names? Mean anything to you?"

"Obviously, Clairvaux is the medieval Cistercian mystic, and probably the most significant religious figure of his time. But I don't know why he would be connected with the Ark. Now, Shishak does sound a bit familiar, but I can't place a finger on it at the moment."

"What about Wolfram von Eschenbach?" Silas asked.

"Sure. Several years back I read his medieval German romance novel, *Parzival*. It's quite a rousing, Arthurian adventure story about a young lad searching for the Holy Grail."

Silas and Celeste looked up at each other on either side of the bed, confusion and curiosity registering on their faces.

"Wait a minute," Silas said first. "Did you say Grail? As in, like, *Indiana Jones and the Last Crusade*?"

Radcliffe chuckled. "That would be the one. But the literary work is much more of an exposition on the quest for spirituality than the quest for a supposed lost chalice of Christ's blood."

"But how on earth is it connected to the Ark of the Covenant?" she asked.

Radcliffe grunted his own confusion.

She continued, "So to recap: Pryce is bearing a mystery book written in what appears to be an ancient, Semitic language; there's a map of a river or road near a large body of water with reference to a town or city, but we haven't a clue where; and the words *Shishak* and *Chartres,* and names *Clairvaux* and *von Eschenbach.* But we haven't a clue how any of it is tied together or to Pryce and his motivations for his archaeological excavation, much less the Ark of the Covenant itself. That about the long and the short of it?"

"Indeed," Radcliffe said. "And I'm afraid we're not going to know the answer to that or any of our other questions until after that chamber is opened and the Ark is unveiled. But one way or another, I imagine we'll have some answers soon enough."

Silas looked at his watch. "Speaking of which, we should go. I believe the schedule called for a midmorning press conference, and then immediately afterward is the opening of the chamber. I imagine security will be a madhouse, and we need to make sure we're there for that unveiling."

"Then get along," Radcliffe urged. "I'll set Zoe to work on these items. And report back the minute you're free. I want to know what's in that chamber."

CHAPTER 20

P ryce was wrapping up the morning press conference when Silas and Celeste arrived at the Western Wall Plaza. He was flanked by the same Rabbi and Imam from the earlier one a few days ago. Security was tight, with the Israeli Defense Force out in full checking all baggage and instituting wanding procedures for every entrant, even on the other side of mobile, metal-detector units. It was also a strict off-limits zone for anyone other than those with proper credentials.

Lucky for them, they had all-access passes.

Silas half expected them to be rejected when they were scanned after the stunt he pulled the night before. But they worked, and they were waved through to join the rest of the high-profile visitors and dignitaries to witness history being made.

The two weaved their way through a gauntlet of media, keeping their heads down and trying to avoid the cameras. The last thing either of them needed was to be filmed, given the nature of their work with SEPIO. Especially his own work as a professor at Princeton. He doubted McIntyre or the rest of the tenure board would be all that understanding. Or forgiving.

"Oh no," Celeste said, pulling at his arm. "Looks like we've got company."

Oliver Tulu was heading toward them, bearing a clipboard and a look of irritation and indignation they had come to expect.

"Professor Grey, Ms. Bourne. Professor Pryce asked that I keep a look out for you two. He asked that I bring you to him personally, as he didn't want you getting lost on your way to the unveiling."

How nice of him.

Silas smiled. "Why that's very kind of the good doc. But I think we can manage."

He went to continue walking, but Tulu stepped in his path, a gleaming set of white teeth telling him to halt. "Please, I insist. If you would just come this way." He motioned toward the familiar staging area of canvas tents."

Silas looked at Celeste for confirmation. She nodded. He bowed his head at Tulu, and the man led them out of the crowded plaza and brought them into the climate-controlled tent of Pryce's personal study. He was hovering over his work table along with three others, a cloud of smoke hovering above.

"Professor," Tulu said. "Dr. Grey and Ms. Bourne have arrived."

Pryce spun around puffing a long, fat cigar. "Splendid!" he exclaimed holding out his hand. "Grey, are you ready for a front row seat to the forging of history?"

Any negative feelings from the previous night seemed to have dissipated, probably brought on by the euphoria of his impending, archaeological achievement. Silas smiled and shook the man's hand, saying, "Well, done. Seriously. Well done."

The man offered a wide grin, then took another few puffs of the cigar sticking out between his teeth. He spun back to his table, addressing a schematic of what looked like a series of tunnels under what Silas could only assume was the Temple Mount.

"Roland, here, my chief engineer, has told me we have encountered a slight setback for the morning. Apparently, there was a minor collapse, here," he said pointing at the schematics, "at this juncture leading toward the chamber entrance. Nothing to fret about, however. To be expected with the age of the tunnel and the amount of build on top. But we will need to sit tight a little longer before we can move forward while his men work. Feel free to make yourself at home while we wait. There's coffee over in the corner. But I do need you to stay here, inside the tent. We really can't have you traipsing all over the site today, given the media presence and sectarian frenzy, not to mention the work my team is undergoing to bring us to the finish line. I'm sure you understand."

The two nodded and excused themselves to grab some coffee while Roland and his men left to clear away the rubble and Pryce finished his own preparations.

It wasn't until an hour later that Roland returned. It looked like good news because Pryce slapped the man on his back and made a fist of victory. The two walked over from their chairs.

"Good news?" Silas asked.

"Good to go! We're going in now, assembling over at the Wilson's Arch entrance and will be embarking on the journey toward the entrance in the next ten minutes. Meet us there as I assemble the rest of the team."

"Here we go," Celeste said quietly as they walked toward the tunnel entrance.

Several minutes later, Pryce came rushing over with an entourage of staff and religious officials from both Judaism and Islam to mark the historic occasion. A camera crew with BBC was also on hand to film the momentous event.

Pryce said a few words marking the occasion, and then he led them forward. Silas and Celeste had positioned themselves near Pryce at the front so they could follow closely behind. They wanted to be sure they'd be some of the first inside the chamber once it was opened to view the ancient relics.

Orange lights embedded in the floor guided their way

through the main public tunnel. It was cool and dry, having been sealed and climate-controlled for years. The hum of generators was fed by cables running the length of the ceiling, which Pryce seemed to be following as he quickly led the team forward. They came to their first juncture, a rough-hewn square hole cut into the wall large enough for a single person to fit through. Silas assumed this had been the sealed section of the Warren Gate originally excavated in the '80s.

One by one, the group of eager on-lookers filed through the small opening into a large passageway that smelled like his childhood basement, carrying forward for another thirty meters. This section was taller and narrower than the Wilson's Arch tunnel, having acted as the subterranean passageway the anointed Jewish priests had used to transport the necessary cultic material for their sacred rituals deep inside Solomon's Temple.

Silas's heart began to gallop faster at the thought. A smile curled upward as he considered the reality that he was walking the same path countless Levites had walked bearing the sacrificial goats and bulls and sheep that would make atonement for the sins of the people.

That is until that fateful day in April, 33 AD when the final Sacrifice made atonement for the sins of the people once and for all. A favorite passage from the book of Hebrews raced through his mind:

> *For it is impossible for the blood of bulls and goats to*
> *take away sins. Consequently, when Christ came*
> *into the world, he said,*
> *"Sacrifices and offerings you have not desired,*
> *but a body you have prepared for me;*
> *in burnt offerings and sin offerings*
> *you have taken no pleasure.*
> *Then I said, 'See, God, I have come to do your will,*
> *O God'*

(in the scroll of the book it is written of me)."
And it is by God's will that we have been sanctified
through the offering of the body of Jesus Christ once
for all.

Silas's excitement for laying eyes on the ancient Ark relic was tempered by the realization that the cross made it completely moot. The object of wood and gold was no longer the channel for God's presence, redemption, and mediation. All of that was accomplished in the person of Jesus Christ on the butcher's block of the Roman cross.

As they continued forward, he meditated upon the meaning of this once-for-all sacrifice in light of the Ark. Jesus was God-made-flesh; the very presence of God himself walked around on the earth. He understands our life because he lived our life. Jesus was the Great High Priest because he offered his very self as the ultimate, final sacrifice upon those boards of execution; the cross was the altar, his broken body and shed blood the sacrifice. He paid our price in our place, paving the way for our forgiveness from sins and making peace with God. And as the exalted King who gave himself as a ransom payment to the Father, Jesus is the one mediator between God and man, interceding on our behalf.

So Silas knew that even if they discovered the Ark on the other side of those chamber doors—*when* they discovered the Ark on the other side of those chamber doors—it didn't matter anyway. At this point, it was a fascinating religious relic from ages past. A significant piece of history, no doubt, but no longer a channel of religious ritual or spiritual significance.

Although he did wonder what it might mean for the Christian faith if Judaism regained its central religious icon. How would that affect the Christian claim that the cross was all-sufficient to take away the sins of the world and make people perfect if God's former sacrificial altar was resurrected? What would its discovery mean for the claim, as Hebrews says, that Jesus was the once-for-all sacrifice for people's sins? That sacrifices were no longer needed—that the Ark itself was no longer needed?

Silas guessed they were about to find out.

Several men in bright yellow hard hats and boots had congregated up ahead, presumably the site of the minor collapse from the morning. Stone and piles of sand lay on either side of the floor, along with orange caution cones.

"Watch your steps, please," Pryce advised, his Southern-accented voice trembling from excitement. "It's just a little way farther." He hustled along faster, and before Silas and Celeste could contemplate where they were, the door appeared. It was just as Pryce had described, but more majestic than Silas could have anticipated.

The sealed burnished bronze doors stood firm, guarding their secrets behind an intricate design of vines and images depicting the sacrificial practices of Israel that provided redemption and reconciliation between them and Yahweh, the God of Israel.

Silas chanced walking up to the doors. He pressed both palms on them, their sacred coolness sending a jolt of electric excitement through his arms and down his spine. A drunken giggle escaped him, and he turned in embarrassment to Pryce who was standing at his right looking slightly annoyed. He looked behind him, finding the cohort of people staring at him. He blushed and stood back against the passage wall.

Pryce cleared his throat. "Thank you all for being here. And a big thanks to Rabbi Amar and Imam Hussein for their efforts in making this momentous discovery possible." He turned to Silas and grinned slightly. "And thank you, too, Dr. Grey, for pointing me in the right direction those years ago."

Silas was surprised by the acknowledgment. He felt his neck grow warm with embarrassment, but he nodded his thanks.

"I had a speech all prepared, but how about we skip the pleasantries and open the cotton pickin' thing!" The crowd chuckled approvingly.

He motioned toward two men in hard hats. One of them was holding a hydraulic prying machine. There were no handles nor any obvious way to open the doors, presumably having been sealed shut by some secure, secretive means. The two men carefully positioned the device in the sealed crack where the massive, heavy bronze doors met, then switched it to life. An air compressor sprang to life near Silas, enabling the jaws to begin their work.

At first, nothing happened. The compressor hummed away while the jaws didn't move. They seemed to have difficulty finding purchase. The men adjusted the position of the hydraulic device, moving it this way and that. This lasted for several minutes, frustration and concern registering on Pryce's face.

But then an ache escaped from the doors as the hinges began to give. A cheer erupted from the crowd, and Silas couldn't help but join in. Celeste squeezed his arm and smiled.

This was it.

The chamber entrance sighed from the sudden pressure differential after being sealed shut for centuries as the hydraulic jaws slowly cracked open the door panels a few inches. Which ratcheted up the crowd's enthusiasm even further. Silas was close enough to catch a whiff of the acrid air escaping the widening doors, smelling like the floor of a deep forest ravine filled with rot and musk and condensation and dirt. Silas strained to look around the working men trying to catch a glimpse of the inside, but it was still too dark to see anything.

The men stopped their work and switched to manually opening the chamber entrance, carefully tugging on the ancient doors. Pryce joined in, as well, a satisfying smile beaming across his face as he helped uncover the hidden Ark of the Covenant. The passageway was completely silent now, but for the faint protest of the doors' hinges. But soon enough the chamber was completely exposed.

Silas could feel his heart beating in his ears now, its pace matched by his heaving lungs. The feeling coursing through him was just as it was the first time he had experienced the thrill of a monumental archaeological find. Like at Tell-es Sultan when he discovered the original Ark scrolls. In the military, he had been drunk off his butt more times than he cared to admit, especially before he had become a Christian. But finding those scrolls was 100 proof better. A drug addict's high, really.

That archaeological ecstasy was nearing its climax as the huddled mass inside the Warren's Gate passageway stood at the precipice of the Temple treasures chamber where the Ark rested, waiting to be unveiled for all the world to see after all these years.

He strained again to catch a glimpse of the inside, the passageway light now illuminating the interior even more.

"Does it look to you that another level dips beneath this one?" Celeste whispered.

Silas nodded, standing on his tip-toes and continuing to crane his head ahead. "It does. And the chamber looks large. Large enough to accommodate the ritualistic artifacts of the Temple's inner chamber."

Nothing was visible beyond the threshold of the chamber, which meant the Temple treasures were probably hiding securely below the entrance level.

He smiled at her. She returned the grin, intoxicated by the nearness of the unveiling.

Pryce smiled at the crowd of onlookers and rubbed his hands as if he didn't know what to do.

"Shall we?" he finally said. He hesitated, seemingly apprehensive of what next to do. Then he stepped into the darkness.

Following closely behind him were the two workmen armed with LED headlamps and flashlights. Silas and Celeste squeezed themselves forward into the chamber entrance, edging past the rabbi and imam. Silas greedily took one of the flashlights from a workman and lunged forward to Pryce's side.

The chamber was indeed split between two levels, measuring

the size of a high school gymnasium. Two wide stairways sat at either side of the threshold platform. What looked like large wood torches still stood at the top and base of each set of stairs, complete with charred carbon ends, their fires having flickered out after the chamber had been sealed shut.

As others filed in behind him, their murmurs echoing around the ancient space, Silas quickly shined his LED light in the well of the chamber.

All he saw was an empty void of all-consuming blackness.

He held his breath, ears ringing with the pulse of his blood.

It can't be...

Empty?

No golden altar of incense. No table of shewbread. No lamp-stands of pure gold.

And definitely no Ark of the Covenant.

The murmurs grew louder, more confused. More indignant.

He looked at Celeste, whose face expressed the same what-on-earth dumbfoundedness everyone else was beginning to verbalize.

"This isn't right," she said.

He agreed.

He swung his lamp toward Pryce, eager to read his face.

Where he expected to find utter surprise and dismay, there was instead what appeared to be a moment of met expectations, relief even.

Then, with the flip of a switch, he seemed to turn on a performance of shock and disappointment and humiliation.

Did Lucas Pryce know the chamber was empty?

That the Ark of the Covenant wasn't underneath the Temple Mount?

That it had never even been there?

All along?

CHAPTER 21

ROME.

Gapinski and Torres had ended up with a whole lot of nothingburger nearly twenty-four hours after the scourging post was stolen from the Basilica of Saint Praxedes.

Zoe had been combing through CCTV footage in coordination with the Vatican and Rome police, searching for the black-panel van with the description Gapinski had given her.

Vesta and creepy-looking chick holding a bowl of fire.

She had discovered that the creepy-looking chick holding a bowl of fire was the Roman goddess Vesta, one of two ancient household deities. Vesta was a company that provided a range of household services, from cleaning to dry cleaning to food preparation. But that was as far as she was able to get.

When it came to tracking the van's location, she had come up empty. One win was that she had been able to get a clear shot of the vehicle and its license plate from a street cam, and discovered the van had been stolen a few days prior. The problem was that it was one in a fleet of Vesta service vehicles. The chance of finding the right one among a sea of other cars was impossible enough. But the prospect of finding the right car in a city the size of Rome, with all of the tourist traffic on top of the residential traffic was worse than nil.

Yet Gapinski drove onward, believing he could somehow stumble upon the rainbow-colored unicorn.

"So, Torres," he said, merging onto a major thoroughfare through the city. "What's your story? How'd you find yourself in our little outfit, anyway?"

Torres looked at him with a raised eyebrow. "That's not forward at all."

"Oh, come on. We're practically blood siblings by now after what we went through at the basilica. And besides, you got anything better to do while we drive around like crazy people?"

She shrugged.

"Come on. Spill it."

She rubbed her chin, then looked out her window at the passing traffic. How much should she share?

"Well, I'm sort of an ecclesial mutt. On top of being an ethnic mutt. My dad was Mexican, raised a strict Catholic. Mom was Jewish."

"Wow! How'd that happen?"

She chuckled. "They met in college. Fell in love. You know how that goes."

"So you were raised, what, like, a Catholic Jew? A Jewish Catholic, or something?"

"Mom was from Israel, so she was ethnically Jewish. But she was Messianic. She had believed Jesus was the long-awaited Messiah prophesied from the Hebrew Scriptures, and she put her faith in his death and resurrection. So she was a Christian like Dad was."

"Got it. But wait. Did you say, *was*?"

She smiled weakly, staring out at the passing cars. "Yeah. Mom and Dad died when I was young."

Gapinski whistled softly. "Sorry about that. Didn't mean to dredge up an old memory."

"It's fine."

"When was that, if you don't mind me asking?"

She continued staring at the quaint world slowly passing outside, a part of her longing for such a simple life again. She sighed, and said, "I was sixteen. Moved in with my uncle, who was an oil mogul in Mexico and Venezuela."

"Like the cartel?"

She shot him a look. "No. Not like the cartel. The cartel peddles in drugs. And violence and mayhem."

"Sorry," he quickly said.

"Anyway, so I lived with him a few years in Venezuela. Mostly on my own, since he had his hands tied up with his business. He'd never married, so I had the run of the place. It was nice."

She smiled, the memory of her uncle both sweet and sour, his generosity overshadowed by her betrayal.

"Sounds like it. So you had the run of some kick-ass mansion in the mountains of Venezuela. Then what?"

"Then, when I was eighteen, I joined the Israeli Defense Force. Wanted to discover my roots and all that. Served three years, then got out and moved to America."

"Wait. IDF? So are you, like, some Krav Maga ninja chick?"

She smiled and shook her head at the thought. "I wouldn't say that. But I've got some moves."

"Can't wait to see those!" He stopped short, blushing. "You know, in some confrontation with Nous or something."

She laughed. "I'll be sure to bring it next time we meet Farhad."

"So IDF to America."

"IDF to America. I enrolled in an accelerated program at UCLA studying Mesoamerican and pre-Columbian cultures."

"Meso-what?"

She smiled. "Mesoamerican. It was a region and cultural area in the Americas, extending from central Mexico down to northern Costa Rica.

"Like the Mayas and Aztecs?"

"Exactly. Basically, they were people groups who flourished before Columbus came and jacked everything up and the Spanish colonized the Americas in the 15th and 16th centuries."

"Ahh. Got it. So you were following the ancestor's trail, as you did with IDF?"

Torres furrowed her brow in thought. "You know, I hadn't really thought of it like that before. But...I guess I was sort of trying to connect with two parts of my family history."

She was taken aback by the man's insight. And she didn't like that he could put a finger on her psyche like that. She sank slightly in her seat at the thought. She was far too guarded to let someone figure her out.

"Alright, hoss," she quickly said. "Your turn. How'd you end up with this ecclesiastical street gang."

He snorted, then smiled. "Ecclesiastical street gang. Good one."

"Let's have it. What's your story with SEPIO? What's your interest in all of this?"

He gripped the steering wheel and took a breath. "You said you were an ecclesial and ethnic mutt. I'm the farthest thing from. Born and raised in the Deep South."

"Oh, yeah? How deep?"

"Like, Georgia deep. And my grandpappy was a Southern Baptist Minister."

"Ahh, that deep."

He chuckled. "Yep. I'm as American as apple pie and Johnny Cash."

"And I bet your church was, too."

"Pretty much. July Fourth had its own Sunday service alongside Christmas and Easter."

"But never Epiphany, Day of Ascension, or Feast of the Immaculate Conception."

"Hell no!"

They both laughed at the incredibly different ways they had been raised in the faith.

"But you're an operative within a Catholic Order," Torres pressed. "Well, I guess not Catholic anymore, since it's gone all ecumenical, from what I understand."

"Yeah, no more Popery, as the Reformers would say."

She scoffed at the mention of the Reformation.

Gapinski turned to her. "What, you're not down with the Reformation?"

She shrugged. "I'm agnostic about it."

"Nice."

"Anyway. Enough with my story. Back to you. Can't imagine your Southern Baptist grandpappy, as you said, was all that thrilled about his grandson working for a former Catholic order."

"Well..." Gapinski started, "he thinks I'm working for some super-secret government-like agency."

Torres turned in her seat to face him, feigning shock. "You lied to your Southern Baptist pastor grandpappy?"

"I didn't lie per se. I didn't say *government* agency. I said government-*like*. SEPIO is an agency. And it's super-secret. He just didn't need to know what kind of super-secret agency." He turned to her and grinned. "And actually, maybe you didn't get the memo, but that's the party line if any of your family asks."

"Yeah, I gathered from my orientation that the Order of Thaddeus wasn't too keen on the rest of the world knowing about our little side project."

"Not really. What's important is the memory we're protecting and preserving. Not how we go about doing it."

"Got it," she said. "But wait a minute. You never said how you came to be working for the Order and SEPIO."

Gapinski gave a deep, hearty laugh. "Now, that's a story." He turned down another street that was stopped with traffic. "For the love!"

"Stay calm, and spill the beans."

"Actually, I blame my Southern Baptist grandpappy."

"Really? Do tell."

"Don't get me wrong. I love the man. And he's taught me more about God and his love and his ways than anyone else on the planet. But growing up in the Baptist world that was drained of liturgy and a real, tangible connection to our collective spiritual past began to weigh on me."

"Interesting, but I don't follow. What do you mean?"

"Well, take Communion. Or what you Catholics call the Eucharist. You are Catholic, right? I guess I made a big assumption there, with you being from Mexico and all."

She paused and smiled. "You could say that."

"So growing up I used to help Grandpappy prep communion, cutting up the Wonder Bread and filling tiny plastic cups with grape juice."

"How cute."

"Oh, it was! But then we started using these little vacuum-sealed, grape-juice-filled cups with a stale, cardboard-tasting cracker thingy on top. Think Stouffer's TV dinners. Same fake, unfulfilling experience."

"Gosh. That seems sacrilegious to me."

"Tell me about it. No meaning, no communal connection. The farthest thing our Christian ancestors practiced when it came to following Jesus' command to remember his crucifixion. How does a pre-packaged, plastic cup of grape juice and vacuum-sealed, stale cracker serve as a remembrance of the slaughtered, broken, bloody body of our Savior? Might as well serve Kool-Aid and Twinkies!"

"So you're a Protestant-turned-Catholic, then?"

"I wouldn't say that. But I got super-burned by the shallowness of my childhood faith experience. Never lost sight of Jesus and the faith. But wanted more. Long story, but got connected to Radcliffe and he offered me a vision for fighting for what I'd been searching for. Figured why not become the change I wanted to see, as the saying goes."

He went silent and continued driving in search of the white-whale mystery van.

"Hey, look!" Gapinski exclaimed.

Torres searched outside through the windshield. "What? You see the van?"

"No a KFC. Guess American cuisine has colonized even the Eternal City."

Torres slugged her partner.

"Ouch! What was that for?"

"I thought you were pointing out something important," she said.

He pulled into the parking lot, finding a spot near the entrance. "KFC is important. I'm starved. Let's get some grub."

Torres rolled her eyes. "I guess I could use a bucket of Extra Crispy."

"Now you're talking!"

Gapinski held the door for Torres as they walked inside. She smiled at his chivalry.

"Was that your stomach?"

"You heard that?" he said as they got in line. "I'm way past due for a fill-up. And a whiff of that All-American goodness has got the gut fired up."

"I'd say."

They made their way to the front registered, far too slowly for the liking of Gapinski's stomach. When a register opened up, Gapinski took the lead.

"Howdy, partner. We'll take a bucket of Extra Crispy for the lady."

"I can't eat a whole bucket!" she exclaimed.

He smirked. "Lightweight. Alright, we'll share the bucket, but add some Extra Crispy tenders on the side. Then we'll have a tub of mashed potatoes and a couple sides of gravy. Might as well add a tub of green beans to balance it all out."

He turned to Torres. "You like mac and cheese?"

She tilted her head in thought. "I could go for mac and cheese."

"A tub of that, then. And...a box of biscuits. And make sure you add a handful of honey packets. Nothing like biscuits and honey."

"Goodness! It's just the two of us, man."

"What? Gotta take what you can get and fill up when you can. First rule of the stakeout. Never know when you'll get to eat again."

He handed the cashier his credit card. After paying, they stepped to the left side of the counter to wait for their food. It was taking longer than Gapinski's stomach could handle. He looked outside the drive-thru window to see a black van pulling away. It slowly moved past a large picture window on the other side of the restaurant and stopped, its driver stopping to inspect the contents of the bag.

On the side panel were the words "Vesta."

And the creepy lady holding the bowl of fire.

"What the..."

Gapinski ran to the final window panel as the van was pulling away to get a look at the driver. He startled.

He turned toward Torres, and yelled, "It's Mr. Mustache!"

All heads turned to her standing next to their newly arrived bags of food. She ran to the window to confirm as it stopped at the driveway exit just beyond the window.

Sunglasses and a mustache.

Had to be Farhad.

"Let's go," she said turning toward the exit.

"First things first," Gapinski said. He ran to the counter and grabbed their tub of fried chicken and bags of sides. "Now we're ready to roll."

CHAPTER 22

The soft hum of the Gulfstream coursing through the atmosphere at 982 kilometers per hour was the balm Lucas Pryce needed after months of careful planning and execution. So was the glass of scotch nestled in his cupped left hand resting on the soft, cream leather recliner, its oakiness lingering in his nostrils and on his tongue. A welcomed guest.

A wave of turbulence rumbled through the private plane, the ice cubes clinking in response. One of the flight attendants on point for his trip caught his attention, then motioned with his hands for Lucas to connect his seat belt. He rolled his eyes, sighed, and sat up straight, then obliged. He smiled weakly and nodded, then raised his glass and took another long drink, the half-diluted, caramel-colored alcohol still packing enough punch to delightfully burn his throat going down.

Lucas closed his eyes and thought about the rest of the journey ahead. A few more days and it would all be over. Yet there were still far too many moving parts, too many unknown variables.

Not the least of which was Silas Grey.

He wondered what the man had thought of the little shell game he was playing with the Ark of the Covenant. He grinned just thinking about the look on his face. Priceless. The man who had been single-handedly responsible for confirming the existence of the fabled Hebrew relic through extra-biblical means thought he would lay hands on it.

Poor guy. What a chump.

He assumed Silas had slunk back to Princeton since he had seen neither him nor his brunette co-conspirator after his press conference *mea culpa*. Hopefully, the empty chamber put to rest any suspicions concerning its whereabouts and Silas would leave the matter alone. But he couldn't be sure, especially after finding the man in his room. He had known the man to be resourceful. Just look at what he had discovered those years ago. No matter. His former student would be dealt with soon enough.

As far as the world was concerned, the Ark was still missing as it had been since the First Temple period. More importantly, it was no longer connected to the Temple, dispelling any Jewish End Times expectations the Ark would serve in a Third Temple period.

Just as Nous had wanted. And Lucas Pryce.

The rabbinic Judaism that had formed after the Second Temple period came to a close with the destruction of the Temple in AD 70 continued to believe firmly in the importance of the Temple treasures for the future of Israel and the Jewish faith. They had insisted that those vessels, especially the Ark of the Covenant, would be rediscovered and restored in the End Times with the final restoration of Israel. Jewish tradition had always maintained that the treasures of the Temple would remain hidden until the coming of the Messiah. Which is why the Holy City's Rabbi was so eager to help Lucas. He had seen Lucas's interest and his discoveries as a providential answer to prophecies concerning the restoration of Israel. Yet, the man's hopes had been dashed in upon the shoals of his brilliant conspiracy.

Shortly after his team had finally broken through the collapsed, hidden shaft leading to the chamber entrance, Pryce had hired an excavation outfit out of Miami, Florida. He'd heard about the successes of San Jose New World Salvage and Exploration in Cuba finding the fabled, lost Spanish fleet. Their LiDAR imaging technology had been lauded as a breakthrough in excavation techniques, revolutionizing how old goats like him went about the task of unearthing the past. An academic contact in America freelancing with Nous had put him in touch with Pryce, and the company had signed on to help confirm his suspicions about the Temple treasures.

Using their equipment, he was able to all but verify the chamber was empty. He couldn't be sure, because the images revealed the two levels they discovered upon entering. But he was nearly confident of the outcome before opening those bronze doors. He had paid off the team to manipulate the images to suggest the presence of artifacts. The doctored proof had clearly made the Holy City's Rabbi drunk with religious fervor.

For generations, Jewish activists who had tried to see those Messianic expectations realized by forcing the new eschatological era to the surface had insisted that the Ark would be returned to a new Temple. Such a return would usher in the long-awaited day where Yahweh would cause his Shekinah glory to dwell once again in the Third Temple, as the prophet Haggai had prophesied. Those zealots wanted to make all mankind worshipers of the One God in Jerusalem on the Holy Temple Mount, and finally resume the former glory of the Temple's primary function: the atonement sacrifices. Discovering the Ark of the Covenant was the final piece for making that a reality.

But with the clear proof, for all the world to see, that the Temple treasures were not where the zealots believed they were, those Jewish expectations had been dashed. Which set him up perfectly to foment sectarian violence and fervor at the missing religious treasures. Already there had been reports of rioting in both the Jewish and Muslim sectors of the Old City at the loss.

And yet that one accomplishment of revealing the complete

absence of the Temple treasures from the Temple Mount complex paled in comparison to the weight of significant religious revelation that was to come.

He smiled, pleased with himself for what he had accomplished for Nous.

And what he was about to accomplish for his religion.

Lucas felt a light tap on his left arm. He slowly opened his eyes. It was the flight attendant again.

"Yes?"

"Sorry to bother you, sir. But you have a phone call."

"A phone call? How? From whom?"

"Came in on our communications receiver. It's Mr. Borg, sir."

Lovely.

He unbuckled his seat belt, then crossed his legs, readying himself for the engagement. "Give it here."

The man handed the phone to Pryce, then topped off his scotch. He nodded and smiled. *Good man.*

"Rudolf. Good to hear from you. Is everything alright?"

"Everything is perfect. The Thirteen and Council of Five are most pleased with the progress you have made executing our interests. The Holy City is in chaos. The Messianic hopes of Judaism have been dashed. Sectarian violence has been sparked between Islam and Judaism. And so far Farhad is having the same kind of fortune, which bodes well for the greater scheme of things."

He sighed at the mention of Farhad and his stupid side project. He had thought from the beginning that running after the so-called Passion relics was a complete distraction from the vital mission of denying Judaism their most prized religious possession and unveiling the Ark in a way that served their more pressing sectarian and religious interests.

"Is there something wrong, Pryce?"

His eyes widened suddenly with panic. He must have sighed too loudly. "N—No, Rudolf. Nothing at all. I just...I just don't want Farhad's work to distract us from securing the Ark and—"

"It is not a distraction, Pryce," Borg interrupted. "Far from it. From the beginning, Nous has been very clear about our objectives. And your very tiny place within them."

Pryce's eyes narrowed. *Very tiny place? That's the way they viewed the most consequential religious find ever?*

Borg continued, "Billions of people believe that the shedding of blood can appease the wrath of a vengeful God. The one thinks it's the blood of bulls and goats. The other thinks the blood of a so-called Son of Man, a man-god. Nous knows better. It is time humanity finds release from the clutches of these primitive forms of spirituality and take hold of our destiny, the one Nietzsche prophesied would rise up out of the ashes of primitive religion.

"'Man is a rope, tied between beast and overman—a rope over an abyss...' Master Nietzsche said through his prophet Zarathustra. It's time we clip the rope, releasing humanity from religious bestiality in order to fully grasp the power of the Übermensch, the Overman who can rise above and beyond conventional Christian and religious morality to create and impose his own values through brute force of the inner, divine will, conjured from the divine mind. Before long, not only will we destroy the items that contain the memory of the Christian faith in the crucifixion of Jesus. We'll also undermine it and the effects of that singular event by sowing confusion through the Ark's revelation. And it's quite vexing to hear you speak in a way that seems to undermine that grand vision, Pryce."

He should have kept his mouth shut. They had parallel goals, though Lucas's was slightly different, far more personal. Now he felt his ability to act on that goal had been jeopardized by his careless mouth.

"I apologize if I have vexed you," he said quietly, cursing himself for the quiver in his voice.

"Oh, it is not only me you have vexed, but the entire committee and council. Isn't that right, brothers?"

Pryce trembled as he heard the grunting approval of Borg's disapproval. He must have been on speaker, his questioning of their goals plain for the upper echelon of Nous to hear. He quickly downed the rest of his scotch.

"Gentlemen...err, brothers," Pryce started. "I meant no disrespect. I am fully committed to your vision for the Ark. I will not fail you in the final phase of our operation."

"You better not."

The line went silent. Pryce set the handset on his table and looked out at the clouds drifting below, unnerved by the conversation. He had known of Nous's spiritual fervor when he had agreed to join their project after having been contacted by Borg himself. But he hadn't truly appreciated its scope until that conversation.

No matter. Their interests served his interests. He was close, so close. He only hoped Oliver Tulu could put together the final pieces he needed to confirm the final resting place of the Ark.

And that Silas Grey kept his big, fat nose out of his business.

CHAPTER 23

LUXOR, EGYPT.

S ilas kept his eyes closed while pockets of atmospheric speed bumps jostled the plane as they crossed the expanse of water below. He hated flying, and boating for that matter. Anything that took his two legs off of God's green earth. That's why he had joined the Army, rather than the Air Force or Navy or Marines.

His father had said if God meant for man to fly he'd have given him wings. Had he meant for him to float across the water, he'd have given him gills.

Dad had a point. So he had followed in his footsteps after that fateful 9/11 day by signing up at the Army recruitment center, and later with the Rangers after an instructor pulled him aside because of his exceptional marks.

The small private jet dipped suddenly, then evened out and shuddered. He gripped his armrest tighter, then instinctively reached inside his coat pocket searching for a little, blue pill. He sighed when he came up empty, as well as at his weakness.

Here we go again, he thought, reminiscing about his mission with SEPIO in Paris earlier in the year. *Back into the fray.*

After the team had exited the Temple's passageway empty-handed, feeling utterly dejected and distraught and confused by the massive miscalculation, Silas and Celeste had quickly moved out of the way to watch the circus unfold from a distance as Pryce addressed a bank of news cameras from around the world on a makeshift platform, flanked on either side by the representatives of Judaism and Islam.

His remarks had been curt and clipped: "I regret to inform the watching world that we apparently made a rather large miscalculation, and of historic proportions. We did indeed discover a chamber beneath the Holy of Holies of the Temple Mount. But it was empty."

A murmur had rippled through the Western Wall Plaza, from the news anchors to the onlookers to even the cameramen.

Pryce had expressed utter shock and dismay at the absence of the Temple treasures, not least of all the still-missing Ark of the Covenant. It was a career low...a professional humiliation...a cultural and religious disappointment...a loss for the Abrahamic faiths...and on and on.

Then he had ended the presser by saying, "I want to thank Rabbi Amar and Imam Hussein for their wholehearted belief in offering the world the benefit of the Ark's unveiling. We intend to regroup and double our efforts in the coming months to search for the hidden Ark of the Covenant for mutual religious edification and cultural appreciation. Thank you."

With that, he had walked off and through the crowd into an awaiting Mercedes, which whisked him away to safe harbor.

It had been a shocking experience for Silas and Celeste, standing in the empty chamber beneath the Most Holy Place, all the anticipation and buildup, the expectation and hope all deflating in one fell swoop.

And yet it hadn't been. After he had raided Pryce's hotel room and discovered the notes and intel, there was a part of Silas that had a niggling suspicion that the chamber would be empty.

Because things were not as they had seemed.

And there he was, on yet another private jet chartered by the

Order, off to another location of import to the Christian faith to get to the bottom of what had happened. More importantly: to get to the bottom of what Pryce was up to.

Not that he minded it. He was beginning to take a liking to the adventure that came from protecting, instructing, fighting for, watching over, and helping the Church heed the memory of the Christian faith—as the name of the Order's Project SEPIO explicitly meant. It beat grading papers and the looks and the complaints from a bunch of half-interested, self-indulgent college students. Some students were a joy, particularly when they took an interest in exploring their faith and spirituality, and he could walk with them through that journey, like Jordan Peeler from earlier in the year. That was the highlight of his job, for sure. But they were few and far between.

He sighed. His college students. Princeton University. The tenure board. Doc McIntyre. In the excitement of it all with Pryce and the Ark, his mind had locked away what was waiting for him back home.

Perhaps that should tell him something. That the part of him devoted to life as a professor was fading, that it was time for something new. But how could he let go of an identity he had spent a decade carefully crafting, hammering, and honing to professional perfection? He was on the verge of being Princeton's youngest tenured professor. That is if he could escape the wrath of McIntyre and make it through the gauntlet of Human Resource's STEPs program. Was he willing to throw that away? And for what, working behind the scenes to secure ancient relics that nobody gave two rats patooties about anymore anyway?

Jude 3. The Scripture reference was crisp and clear in his mind's eye.

Contend for the faith that was once for all entrusted to God's holy people.

He smiled, remembering the day he had given his life to Jesus one evening at that military base in southern Iraq. It was memorable not so much because he had offered Christ his soul. But because he had pledged him his entire life, his entire self. The chaplain had led the soldiers in the small Christian meeting through the singing of an old hymn that beckoned as much. He recalled the words as he drifted through the stratosphere, singing them quietly in his mind:

> *Take my life, and let it be*
> *Consecrated, Lord, to Thee;*
> *Take my moments and my days,*
> *Let them flow in ceaseless praise,*
> *Let them flow in ceaseless praise.*

He took a deep breath and sighed, smiling at the memory and humming quietly along. He silently meditated on the next several stanzas, reordering his hands, will, and love for the glory of God and the good of the world. Just as he had over ten years ago in the desert sands of Iraq.

For Silas, that moment's occasion when he passed over from death to life in coming to faith had included the offering of his intellect and will to Jesus, the product of his hands as well as his mind. So he had enrolled in graduate school to pursue historical theology, church history, and religious studies, vowing to do what Saint Jude, otherwise known as Saint Thaddeus, had urged him to do—using his classes and journal articles and conference presentations to contend for his faith.

Perhaps there was a calling to a more active role in contending for and preserving that faith. With the Order of Thaddeus, with SEPIO.

Celeste gently tapped him on his arm. He woke with a start and looked over at her.

She offered him a weak grin as she sat down next to him across the aisle. "Hello, sleepyhead. A few minutes to touchdown."

He smiled and nodded, then brought his seat upright and put his tray table in position for the landing. He glanced out of his window and watched a sea of blue receding into a body of pale, bone-dry land as the sun began receding below the horizon. Where on earth had Radcliffe sent them?

"And, here. This is for you." She handed him a large, brown shopping bag.

He turned toward her and raised an eyebrow in confusion as he took it. "What's this?"

"Apparently, Radcliffe left it for you. Thought it was appropriate for this next leg of our adventure."

He opened the mouth of the bag and looked inside. "What the..." he looked at her with a wry smile, then reached inside and brought out a deep-brown, leather fedora. He laughed and put it on, running his index finger and thumb around the brim as he fixed his gaze in a serious, Indiana Jones pose.

"Now, don't you look smart, Dr. Grey?"

"Don't you mean, Dr. Jones? And, what, no whip?" He looked back inside the bag, then folded it and set it next to him.

"I guess the Beretta will have to do." She handed him his weapon of choice. He took it and shoved it in his waist. "Thanks. And remind me to thank the chief for the hat." He buckled himself in and prepared for the landing.

She fastened her own buckle, and said, "Seems appropriate given our Ark escapades. Besides, it looks better on you than that other Yank, anyway."

"I just hope it doesn't mean we're heading to Tanis, Egypt, or else we're in a load of trouble!"

After the two had exited the Temple passageway and once they had cleared the Western Wall Plaza, Celeste had immediately dialed Radcliffe to inform him of the developments. Pryce had instructed the small group to embargo any communication until he had made a statement to the press, but she had ignored the protocol given the gravity of what had happened.

Radcliffe had been gobsmacked, but not entirely surprised, given the archaeological project's and Pryce's apparent connection to Nous. But that meant the stakes were even higher for the historical letdown. Something had happened to the Ark. And Nous was up to something. While the Order concerned itself with relics that contained the memory of the Christian faith, the Ark was a vital part of that memory, if only tangentially. SEPIO had work to do, which meant Silas and Celeste had work to do.

Without giving much detail, Radcliffe had ordered the pair to head straight for Ben Gurion Airport and board an awaiting SEPIO Gulfstream that would take them to their next destination. Something had checked out with the images Silas had captured, giving them one of their first and only leads: the encircled word *Shishak*. He didn't want to get into it over the phone, given the turn of events and given Nous's apparent involvement, and Zoe was still doing a work-up on their assignment brief. They would get the full scope of the mission once they landed, which was in about thirty seconds.

Silas closed his eyes and held his breath, the sensation of the small bird suspended between the ether and the earth, strumming a mean song on his gut before it landed with a bounce and came to an abrupt halt at the end of a runway under a cloudless evening sky nestled in the flat, bone-dry desert next to a stretch of lush greenery that snaked for miles in both directions. Outside his window, he could see a banner in the distance welcoming them to Luxor International Airport.

"Luxor?" Silas said, turning to Celeste with a twisted face. "As in Luxor, Egypt?"

She shrugged. "I guess so. And I guess Radcliffe made a good call on the fedora."

He scoffed and turned back toward the window. "I've got a bad feeling about this."

After taxiing to a private hangar, they were met with a Land Rover, a set of keys, and an encrypted satphone. Silas took the keys and handed the satphone to Celeste. She dialed into SEPIO command under the Washington National Cathedral as Silas started the SUV and began driving out of the hangar and into whatever it was Radcliffe had gotten them into.

"I trust you made it safely to the Gift of the Nile," Radcliffe said through the SUV's speakerphone. "And that you got my welcome gift, Silas."

He turned to Celeste and smiled. "Yes, I did. Thanks, Radcliffe. I think. But please don't tell me we're about to reenact my favorite childhood flick. I hate snakes."

"Not to worry, Doctor Jones." Radcliffe snorted. "Sorry about that. I had visions of you shimmying up a sandstone pillar in that silly hat I gave you." He sorted again, then continued, "Anyway, Tanis isn't your destination. However, the Valley of the Kings is."

Celeste punched *Valley of the Kings* into the Land Rover's GPS system, then said, "Alright, give it to us, Radcliffe. What did you find?" They would arrive in less than an hour.

"It isn't what I found, but what you found, Silas. And Zoe. I mentioned when you called in Jerusalem that one of the words you discovered was flagged as a match."

"Shishak, right?" Silas said as he turned left onto route 75 out of the airport.

"Exactly, Shishak. As in, king of Egypt."

"King Shishak?" Celeste asked turning to Silas. He shook his head and kept driving.

Radcliffe continued, "Also known as Shoshenq I, pharaoh of ancient Egypt and the founder of the twenty-second dynasty. Here, let me read it to you." There was a rustling of pages as Radcliffe found his place in a book. "Listen to this, from I Kings chapter fourteen:

> *In the fifth year of King Rehoboam, Shishak king of*
> *Egypt attacked Jerusalem. He carried off the*
> *treasures of the temple of the Lord and the*

treasures of the royal palace. He took everything, including all the gold shields Solomon had made. So King Rehoboam made bronze shields to replace them and assigned these to the commanders of the guard on duty at the entrance to the royal palace. Whenever the king went to the Lord's temple, the guards bore the shields, and afterward they returned them to the guardroom.

Silas whistled. "So this Shishak or Shoshenq, or whoever he was, is said to have carried off the temple treasures, and during the ninth-century BC after invading the southern kingdom of Judah, including the Ark of the Covenant. Do I have that right?"

"Indeed. After the death of Solomon, Israel divided into the two kingdoms. The Kingdom of Israel in the north and the Kingdom of Judah in the south, containing Jerusalem. This southern kingdom was led by his son Rehoboam, and around 926 BC it was invaded by Shishak of the Egyptians, as I just read from 1 Kings. As the biblical text quite clearly states, the king came up and attacked, and then not only carted off the treasures of the royal household, but 'carried off the treasures of the temple of the Lord.'"

"Fascinating," Celeste said. "And we can corroborate that the Ark of the Covenant itself was part of that treasure trove?"

"Not exactly," Radcliffe replied. "However, the temple of Karnak in Luxor contains the pharaoh's own account of his triumph over Jerusalem, and in it we learned that he offered the spoils of his campaign to the god Amun. What's more is that in 1939, Shishak's tomb was discovered in Tanis, and both Shishak's sarcophagus and mummy were adorned with gold, presumably from the gold shields Solomon had made."

"Or from the temple treasures," Celeste added.

"Perhaps. But many scholars believe the account discovered in the temple of Karnak combined with the discoveries in

Shishak's tomb is evidence that the Ark was indeed brought to Egypt. Now, there are certainly detractors. Some have maintained that Shishak never entered Jerusalem, since it wasn't among his own list of captured cities. Others believe those Temple treasures were merely the items stored in the treasury outside the Temple, not the sacred ones from the inner sanctuary."

"Like the Ark of the Covenant in the Holy of Holies," she said.

"Exactly."

"And then there's 2 Chronicles 13:11 and 35:3," Silas said as he turned onto the Luxor Bridge to Al Maris.

"Well, look at you," she said, "all Bible Answerman, and all."

He smirked. "Thanks."

"So what does it say?"

"That the altar of incense, the menorah, and the table of showbread were still in use in the temple. And then Josiah directed the Levites to put the sacred Ark in the Temple that Solomon made. Which would seem to pose a problem for the theory."

"Yes, except for the hidden room in the burial chamber of King Tutankhamun."

"King Tut?" the two exclaimed in unison.

Silas took off his fedora and tossed it to Celeste, then said. "Please tell me you're joking."

"Not at all. There has been a resurgent interest in the pharaoh of the eighteenth dynasty who lived four hundred years before Shishak and coincidentally restored Amun worship to the kingdom. As I mentioned, King Shishak apparently had presented the Temple treasures as an offering to the god in the temple just across the river from the good Tut's tomb. And apparently scientists are investigating whether there are hidden chambers behind the walls of King Tut's tomb."

"I do seem to recall something about a radar specialist finding evidence for hidden doorways on the north and west walls," Celeste said.

"And that's good enough evidence to send us traipsing across the Red Sea and Egyptian desert?" Silas said with no small amount of irritation. "Seems like a stretch, and a waste of time considering the stakes."

Radcliffe added, "That, and the private jet bearing the signature of Pryce's aircraft left Tel Aviv for Luxor shortly before you did."

Silas whistled again. "OK, now I'm intrigued."

"You're saying Pryce left Jerusalem for Luxor?" Celeste said.

"It appears that way."

"Which means he's got a leg up on us, again. Great."

She turned to him, and said, "But it also means the man must also believe there's a degree of truth to the possibility that the Ark was taken from Jerusalem by this Shishak fellow. Why else would he traipse across the Red Sea and Egyptian desert, as you said?"

Silas nodded. "True. That makes sense enough." He took his fedora back and put it on his head as he pulled into the deserted parking lot to the Valley of the Kings. "Looks like we've got a genuine *Raiders of the Lost Ark* remake on our hands."

"That's what the hat is for," Radcliffe deadpanned.

CHAPTER 24

The sun was still several hours away from slipping beneath the horizon as they exited the Land Rover near the park entrance, giving them plenty of time to investigate whether or not there really was something to the Shishak theory surrounding the Ark's disappearance. Fortunate for them, the usual hustle-and-bustle of tourists was nixed by a national Egyptian holiday. Only a few cars and pickup trucks sat near the park entrance.

Silas smiled as he craned his neck skyward, letting the dry, Egyptian sun warm his face. But his smile began to fade as he took in the sight of the dead parking lot, piled high with mounds of pale, packed desert sand. A shudder ran from head to toe as memories from what seemed like a lifetime ago began clawing back to the surface for attention.

Memories of social rote and mayhem wrought by a cadre of governments who didn't know what the hell they were doing or why they were doing it. Memories of the smells that turned his stomach even then, smells of burned sulfur from discharged weapons and of burned flesh from exploded ordnances, of discharged bowels from tortured suspects and frightened citizens alike. Memories of the taste of breakfast, lunch, and dinner coming back up after a particularly fierce firefight. And of course the memory of half his best buddy landing on him after a roadside IED ripped apart their Humvee, and that face staring up at him with a mixture of relief and fear before the life inside snuffed out like a candlewick.

He could feel his chest tightening as he continued standing and reliving the piles of memories as he stared at the piles of sand encircling the near-empty lot. He put his hands on his hips and stood still, closing his eyes and beginning a countdown coping mechanism he had developed for such times.

999, 998, 997, 996...

He kept counting down from a thousand, willing and praying away the kind of panic attacks that he had been wrestling to the ground ever since Iraq and Afghanistan—which was settling upon him in that moment.

981, 980, 979, 978...

Breath in, breath out. Stand still, don't move.

He continued the counting as the attack's iron grip held firm. He continued the breathing ritual, but it was as if a coffee stir stick was strapped to his lips. He was struggling for breath.

He felt a gentle touch on his shoulder. In an instant, the iron grip loosened, and he could feel it fall away. His body shuddered slightly, but then it relaxed. His chest opened up, and he could breathe again.

Celeste.

Silas let his arms fall to his side, and he opened his eyes and took a deep breath.

"You alright, partner?" Her hand was still resting on his right shoulder while she stood next to him, her face a mixture of compassion and concern.

An embarrassing heat began working its way up his neck. He clenched his jaw and narrowed his eyes briefly, then relaxed and offered a struggling smile. "I'm fine," is all he said, turning away toward the trunk of the Land Rover.

He opened it, but found it empty.

"Looking for this?" She held up a large, black gear bag Radcliffe had left them for Tut's tomb.

He smirked and closed the door, then locked their ride with a chirp of the key fob.

"We best get going," he said shoving past her.

But she placed a hand on his shoulder again, this time grabbing it more firmly.

"Seriously, are you alright?"

He stopped and scowled at her hand, then at her. She wouldn't let go.

"I said, I'm fine."

"You didn't look fine. It happened again, didn't it?"

He huffed in irritation and put his hands on his hips. *No, need to act like a jerk, Grey. She's got a right to know.*

His face softened. Then he said quietly, "It's this place. The sky and air, the piles of sand." He breathed in deeply. "Bringing back old memories, that's all. But I can handle it."

"You sure?" she said, her head dipping slightly and face probing. "Because if—"

"It's passed," he interrupted. "Seriously. And thanks to you."

Her hand slid off his shoulder and face seemed to brighten at the suggestion. "What do you mean?"

"You touched my shoulder and...I don't know. The attack just fell away. Never happened like that before. So, thanks." He offered her a smile of gratitude, then felt foolish and let it drop.

She smiled back, then pushed her bangs behind her ear and turned away. "We should move along. Time is tight."

"Wait. We forgot something?"

She stopped short and held up the gear bag in confusion.

He unlocked the driver's side door, grabbed his fedora, and carefully positioned it on his head with one hand.

"Now we're ready." He took the black bag from her, dipped his head, and led the way.

She chuckled. "Alright, Doctor Jones. Let's get this party started."

Radcliffe had arranged for a pair of official-looking badges indicating the two were research archaeologists from something called The Institute for Archaeological Advancement. It was a shell organization SEPIO used from time to time in order to conceal their exploits. Apparently, Zoe had even hacked into the registrar of the Supreme Council of Antiquities so that their work appeared to be sanctioned by the Egyptian government itself. The badges were in the bag, as was their necessary equipment: a ground-penetrating radar device to search Tutankhamun's tomb.

As Silas lugged the bag through the parking lot, passing a few men and women in khaki shorts and short sleeve shirts on their way out of the park, he wondered what on earth they were doing. Did Radcliffe really think the Ark was stowed away in some secret chamber in Tut's tomb? Seemed like a wild goose chase to him, even if Pryce himself was racing to confirm the theory himself.

Speaking of which...Silas scanned the parking lot, but there were no signs of the man. Only a few beat-up German and Japanese imports, caked with dust. True archaeologist vehicles. And the exiting people he passed, fellow researchers he presumed. But no sign of Pryce.

Celeste pointed up ahead as they reached the main area within the park. Silas could see the famed entrance to Tut's tomb poking up out of the barren land. As well as a guy with a clipboard waving goodbye to a few other men with the same khaki getup. Silas was encountering far too many clipboards of late. But he pressed on, following Celeste to the man.

"Hello, sir?"

The man looked up, young and eager and tanned, with shaggy, black hair dusted with Egyptian sand wearing thick, black glasses and...khaki. Silas was beginning to feel out of place with his faded jeans and a white polo.

"Can I help you?" he said hugging the clipboard to his chest.

"Yes, we hope you can. I'm...Celeste Bourne. Doctor Bourne. And this is—"

"Doctor Silas Grey," the young man said excitedly. "I've been waiting to meet you!"

Silas smiled weakly and looked to Celeste, then back at the young man. "You have?"

"Absolutely! When I saw the authorization for your test of Tutankhamun's tomb, I was super excited about having followed your work with the Shroud of Turin."

Silas smiled more widely and looked at Celeste with a measure of satisfaction at having garnered a new fan. She rolled her eyes and looked away. "Why thank you, Mister..."

"Abboud. Aziz Abboud."

"Alright, Aziz. Thanks for your help."

"It's an honor, sir."

"Well, then, lead the way."

Aziz led them across packed, pale desert sand straight to the tomb, its opening rising from the ground without much fanfare. Discovered in 1922 by Howard Carter, the remarkable find received worldwide press coverage and sparked a renewed public interest in ancient Egypt, for which Tutankhamun's mask, now in the Egyptian Museum, remains the popular symbol.

"Watch your step," he said as he led them down a set of wooden stairs, leading into a well-lit passageway of the same pale sand as above. But where Silas expected smooth, if not pock-marked walls, hieroglyphs filled them from top to bottom. His heart leaped at the sight. He inched closer to a wall and went to lay his hand on the ancient surface.

"No, no, no!" Aziz exclaimed before hustling over and gently pushing Silas's hand away. "Sorry, Dr. Grey. The glyphs are off limits to the public."

Silas frowned, but nodded. "Alright, my friend. Let's see King Tut."

The passageway led them to an antechamber, which brought them to the brightly lit tomb of the famed pharaoh.

Silas slung the black bag down to the floor. Celeste stooped down and opened it, taking out the parts of the GPR device while Silas took in the surrounding images of life-size portraits of the man depicting his afterlife journey set against a mustard-yellow backdrop, as well as various gods and goddesses to accompany him on his journey.

"Hey, Doctor Jones."

Silas snapped his head toward Celeste, who was still crouched on the ground, with brow raised and hands pointing to the radar device. "Care to lend a helping hand?"

"Sorry." He grabbed the pieces of the GPR and started fastening them together, recalling how the unit fit from when he used a similar model at Tell-es Sultan. Several minutes later, the unit was assembled and ready for action.

"If you don't mind," Aziz said, "I'd like to watch. Doubt you'll find anything since three other such tests have found nada, zip, zilch. But, one can always hope."

Silas turned to the young man, frowning. "Watch and learn, my friend."

The young man put his hands up in mock surrender, then leaned against a wall as Silas began scanning one of them for a possible hidden chamber—hiding the hidden Ark of the Covenant.

The process was laborious, requiring Silas and Celeste to work together to man-handle the unit. They slowly, deliberately traced the wall from top to bottom, back and forth to penetrate the wall with the radar unit and discern what, if anything, was on the other side.

An hour later, the two mapped the north wall, but came up empty. So they got to work on the only other possible wall. Another hour gave the same result.

They rested the unit on the ground, and Silas gave it a gentle punch in irritation. "Why do I get the feeling this was a big, fat red herring that—"

"Shh. Quiet," Celeste commanded, crouching behind Tut's tomb and pulling out her SIG Sauer.

The unmistakable soft *psht* of a silencer pistol echoed down into the chamber, and poor Aziz's head snapped backward, a geyser of blood and matter spraying on the mustard-colored walls.

CHAPTER 25

Suddenly, Silas's vision narrowed. His ears started ringing. His chest tightened and breathing became difficult.

This was MIT all over again. And Mosul.

He looked on, horrified as the young man's body crumpled to the floor. He dropped with it, taking cover behind the sarcophagus along with Celeste.

"Don't you dare flake out on me, Grey. I need you!"

Silas turned toward his partner, his eyes wide and face red and wet with sweat. Her voice had the same effect as her touch earlier. It was the breadcrumbs he needed to claw his way back to reality. He swallowed hard and nodded.

In an instant the lights cut out, plunging the cramped space into total and utter blackness.

Nous. And he knew what the darkness meant.

Years of Ranger know-how and enemy combat experience clicked him into autopilot. Without thinking, he reached into Celeste's back pocket and fished for her phone. She gave a short protest, but when he found it, he quickly crawled around Tut's bulky dwelling of last repose toward the entrance just as the crunch of footfalls echoed closer down through the antechamber and toward the burial chamber.

Silas inched toward the entrance and waited for the moment when—

There.

He brought out the phone, flicked it to life, then selected the flashlight icon and shoved it outward toward his assailant. Praying he was right.

He was.

The man yelled in protest, blinded by the white LED being magnified a thousand-fold through his night-vision goggles.

Silas launched for the man, but not before the hostile popped off a few wild shots. They narrowly missed Silas and thudded into the ancient sandstone walls behind him.

He whipped the butt of his Beretta around and smashed it into the assailant's face. Then again, and one more time until the man went limp.

Three shots sounded to his right, causing him to recoil back into the burial chamber for safety. Then five more. *Rat-tat-tat-tat-tat.*

The man was met with a healthy response. Seven rounds, all eaten by the mawing darkness around the corner.

Celeste to his rescue. As always.

Then silence.

White light from the phone flooded the space from the floor as the two waited for the man to show himself. He looked back toward Tut's sarcophagus, searching for Celeste.

She appeared around the front, padding forward with weapon outstretched. She nodded toward the antechamber, motioning for him to join her.

He scurried off the sandy floor and picked up Celeste's phone, glancing down at the first Nousati for a look.

The man from the hostel.

One down, one to go. Hopefully.

He held out the phone with one hand and gripped his Beretta with the other, resting it on his forearm. He padded forward as

Celeste neared the opening to the passageway stretching toward the stairs up to the surface.

Whoever it was who had shot them had retreated to safer ground. But they were definitely not out of the woods yet. The other hostile had higher-ground advantage.

Not good.

Celeste glanced back at him as he came up close. She nodded toward the other side of the entrance, then looked back at him. He nodded in recognition. He could see her take a deep breath, then wait a beat before slipping across to the other side of the darkened mouth.

No gunfire. No nothing.

Silas stepped close to the left side of the entrance, hugging the wall and shining his light toward the opening. He looked at her for orders.

With one hand, she trained her SIG Sauer at the entrance. With the other, she motioned for him to crouch to the ground on three, phone and weapon trained forward. She would come around up top.

He nodded. She counted off.

One. Two. Three.

They held their breaths, and in one motion they moved to their positions to engage.

Again, nothing.

They waited, the silence of the passageway was deafening.

Without looking back, Celeste started inching forward. When she cleared the threshold, Silas stood and followed. The phone light bobbed as he moved, the walls closing in on them with the way the white LED light was playing with the shadows.

The passageway stretched forward and narrowed to the set of stairs. It seemed empty.

They continued forward, inching toward the stairwell. Silas's heart thudded in his ears, his breath hot and heavy as he chugged ahead.

There it was, the stairs illuminated by the high, Egyptian sun like Jacob's Ladder emerging from Heaven.

Suddenly, Celeste halted and held up her hand.

Silas took a sharp breath and adjusted his grip, then came up to her side.

"What is it?" he asked.

"Nothing. That's the point. There's a shoot-out and then silence. Doesn't make sense."

"He's biding his time. He knows he has to wait us out. Unfortunately, there's nowhere else to go."

"Well, I don't like it."

"Got a better idea than to press forward and hope for the best?"

She looked at him with flat lips. "I don't know about Uncle Sam, but 'press forward and hope for the best' wasn't in Her Majesty's playbook."

"It is now, partner."

A noise up the well of stairs caught their attention.

The unmistakable sound of something bouncing, metallic and menacing.

Clink.

Clonk.

Clunk.

They looked at each other, then immediately ran forward, both intimately familiar with what was coming down from above.

Grenade.

They took the stairs by twos and started shooting, wildly and with abandon.

Then an explosion of force and fire, dust and debris catapulted them upward.

They hit the stairs hard. Celeste lost her weapon. Silas hit his head; it blossomed in a shower of stars and pain.

The passageway below collapsed in an angry show of fire and fury. Sealing any escape below.

But no time to cry about it. Bullets were flying again.

He answered back as Celeste scrambled to recover her SIG Sauer.

The raining lead from above stopped briefly with the reply.

But then Silas clicked empty. He reached for his spare, but came up dry. Must have lost it in the explosion.

Luckily she recovered her own weapon—and just in time.

Another flurry of bullets pinged off the stairs and chunks of stone scattered about from the explosion and the collapsed entrance below. One of them grazed past Silas's forearm. He yelled, not so much from the pain, but from the surprise. But it had seared a mark that was bubbling with blood. He'd live to fight another day.

Celeste stood defiantly, arm outstretched, sending one-two-three-four bullets toward the hostile.

And it worked.

There was a cry of pain. And then something stumbled down the stairs.

Not the Nousati.

The Nousati's Glock pistol.

Glock, really? Figures.

Silas retrieved the weapon and shoved it in his waist as Celeste scrambled up the stairs. He followed close behind, emerging into the hot, dry Egyptian afternoon.

A figure was crawling across the packed path of desert sand, crimson trailing him in his wake.

Silas ran over to him and pressed his boot against his shoulder, kicking him over onto his back. He quickly trained his Beretta on the man, then narrowed his eyes with recognition.

"You..." he growled.

Celeste came up next to him and looked from Silas to the man. "The thieving cabbie, from Jerusalem."

"Search him. See if he's got my phone."

She crouched to the ground and reached inside his front

pants pockets. Finding nothing, she turned him over and searched the back.

She stood back up, handing a black rectangle of glass and plastic to Silas, but frowning. "This what you were looking for?"

He smiled, and said, "That would be the one." But it quickly faded when he turned over the unit.

Cracked screen. Bullet hole dead center.

The man on the ground groaned, then had a coughing fit. Blood splattered on his chest. A hole in his gut was oozing more blood. He would be a goner in a few minutes.

He offered a short, weak chuckle and smiled as blood trickled down his chin.

Silas clenched his jaw. "You got something to say?"

"Phone," he wheezed. "Kaput." The man took several short breaths, then grinned with satisfaction, white teeth stained with blood.

"Maybe Zoe can crack it," Celeste offered.

"Doubtful." Silas huffed and stuffed the phone in his back pocket. He went to interrogate the man, but he was gone.

A distant sound sliced through the valley, unmistakable in its authoritative whine. The Egyptian police must have been tipped off about the explosion at one of their most important, and lucrative, national treasures.

"We'd better get going," Silas said, taking off toward the parking lot.

"Radcliffe's not going to be happy about this one," Celeste said as they reached the Land Rover.

He opened his door. "Yeah, especially since I lost his fedora."

CHAPTER 26

Another jet, another destination. This time Paris, France. A place Silas would just as soon forget about, given what happened earlier in the year.

After the ambush at Luxor, Silas and Celeste narrowly escaped the valley and headed straight back to Luxor International Airport, passing several frantic Egyptian police units along the way. Even the military was racing toward the scene. Which made sense given all the terrorism the country has experienced since the fall of Hosni Mubarak during the Arab Spring and rise of the Muslim Brotherhood.

Given what Silas had discovered, one of their only solid leads was the Chartres Cathedral. So off to France they went. In the meantime, Zoe and her team would continue parsing out the intel and trying to make connections. Unfortunately, Silas's phone was indeed toast. So no luck there. But another one was waiting for him when they arrived. Hopefully, something else would turn up soon, because their first lead was exactly as Silas called it: a total-bust red herring. Whether Pryce had deliberately planted the false, encircled Shishak lead was uncertain. Near as he and Celeste could figure, Nous had commandeered Pryce's jet as a ruse in order to throw the Order off his trail. And then take out their two headaches—Silas and Celeste—once and for all.

By the grace of God, the plan didn't work. But unfortunately, that meant Pryce was who-knew-where. And they were left with nothing.

After touching down near evening at Orly Airport just south of Paris, the two convened in a conference room being held for them off the private hanger. Radcliffe had an update on their research.

"Trust the flight was uneventful after your latest brush with death," Radcliffe said.

Silas scoffed. "I've traveled better roads in wore-torn Iraq and Afghanistan than the ride we had. And sorry, but your hat is MIA."

"How unfortunate. But better to have saved your skin."

Celeste nodded, and asked, "Radcliffe, any word from Zoe and her team?"

"Yes. Zoe was able to make an important confirmation from the intel you relayed, Silas. The mystery book is what is known as the *Kebra Nagast*. And it appears Pryce had a copy."

"*Kebra Nagast*? What is that? Why does Pryce think it's relevant to his hunt for the Ark?"

"It's entirely relevant," Radcliffe chuckled. "And I must confess a measure of ignorance surrounding the book. Apparently, it is a text revered in the Ethiopian Orthodox Church."

Silas turned to Celeste. "Ethiopia?" She shrugged her shoulders. "What does Ethiopia have to do with the Ark?"

"A lot. *Kebra Nagast* is a thirteenth-century manuscript. It's greatly revered among the Ethiopian people and written, as you pointed out Silas, in an ancient Semitic language, called Ge'ez, a dialect originating in the Horn of Africa, which later became the official language of the Kingdom of Aksum and Ethiopian imperial court."

"Interesting," Silas said.

"The religious text contains the earliest surviving version of an ancient story surrounding the Ark that's...how shall I put it? Well, some have gently suggested at best it's a far-fetched legend meant to inspire Ethiopian nationalism and religious devotion. At worst, a politico-religious lie meant to undermine one political opponent and exalt the rights of another as the rightful heir to the throne of Ethiopia."

"And the legend?" Celeste asked.

"The legend centers on the relationship between King Solomon of Israel and Queen of Sheba. Of course, 1 Kings of the Hebrew Scriptures tells the story of when the queen visited Solomon after hearing about his fame and relationship with Yahweh, the God of Israel. She brought him a large caravan carrying spices and gold and precious stones, as well as tested him with hard questions to discern his wisdom. After an extended conversation, Solomon gave the good queen all that she desired and asked for, aside from what he had already given her out of his royal bounty. Then she left and returned to her own country. Now, what the Bible does not say, but the *Kebra Nagast* suggests is that King Solomon gave the queen something else."

Radcliffe paused. Silas asked, "And what was that?"

"A son."

"A son?" Silas and Celeste said in unison.

"Named Menelik. And this ancient manuscript you stumbled upon, Silas, tells this story about the birth of their son, as well as something else."

Radcliffe paused again. He seemed to be relishing the role of the wise sage.

"Don't tell me," Celeste said, "the Ark of the Covenant."

"As the legend goes," Radcliffe continued, "Menelik abducted the Ark from the First Temple in Jerusalem and brought it to Aksum."

"Remarkable," Silas whispered. "Is there any validity to the claim?"

"Well, the Ethiopian people sure believe the account. It is highly revered, almost in the same way the Holy Scriptures are, believing it tells the whole truth and nothing but the truth about the ancient Israelite relic. Without question, the Ethiopian people believe they possess the Ark of the Covenant."

"But?" Celeste said, anticipating a reply.

"But there are problems with the account."

"Such as?"

"Such as the ethnic identity of the Queen of Sheba, for one. There's doubt that she really had been an Ethiopian. Another is a question surrounding the advancement of the Ethiopian civilization. Not to smack of Western ethnocentrism or anything, but many doubt whether it could have been a sufficiently 'high' enough civilization to have engaged in direct diplomatic contact with ancient Israel. Then there is the issue of Aksum itself."

"Why's that?" Silas asked.

"It wasn't even in existence during Solomon's time. Therefore, the legend of the Ark having been brought to the city simply isn't possible."

"Well, that's disappointing. I was hoping we finally had a *Raiders of the Lost Ark* remake on our hands. So you're saying the legend can't be true. That the Ark isn't in Ethiopia."

Radcliffe cleared his throat. "I'm saying it's highly improbable. From where the evidence stands, at least."

"Well, someone sure thinks there's a connection! Both Pryce and Nous. Why else would he have a copy hidden away in his hotel room? Unless it's another red herring, like with him high-lighting Shishak with that big, fat circle."

Silence fell between the three.

"Wait a minute," Celeste interjected. "Didn't you tell us earlier yesterday that there have been a number of unconfirmed reports of an increase in persecution among African churches?"

"That's right," Silas said. "What's that about?"

"Indeed. And now there have been several confirmed thefts of sacred objects throughout several Ethiopian churches in particular. Something called a *tabot*."

"A what?"

"Every Ethiopian church has its own supposed replica of the Ark that is kept in the sanctuary chapel of the Church of Saint Mary of Zion in Aksum. It's called a *tabot*. Apparently, some are made of wood, but most are made of stone. Again, I'm embarrassed at my lack of familiarity with this branch of the Church, and even the Order's ignorance, given that we've pledged ourselves as protectors of the Church's sacred relics and memory vessels. Anyway, that's something we need to explore."

"I wonder..." Celeste said.

"Wonder what?" Silas asked.

She turned to him. "I wonder if Pryce knew all along that the Ark wasn't in the Temple complex, in the chamber beneath the Holy of Holies. I mean, did you see his face when it looked like the wool was pulled over his eyes?"

Silas nodded. "Sure did."

"It's like opening the chamber only confirmed what he had already suspected, or already knew."

"And didn't it seem like he was almost relieved to see them absent?"

"Absolutely. Relief. That's a good way of putting it."

"Why relieved?" Radcliffe wondered, adding to the discussion. "From what? Or, rather, *for* what?"

Silas shook his head. So did Celeste.

"That's what we need to figure out," Celeste said. "Because why deliberately...basically, stage an exhumation when you know the body has already gone missing?"

"Unless you're trying to make a point."

"But what is that point? That there is no Ark?"

Silas shook his head. "Can't be that. My discovery a decade ago proved there was. Or, at the very least, convinced Pryce that it was real and worthy to put his professional reputation on the line in pursuit of it. So I don't think this is about proving the Ark isn't real. Especially if he's already making connections with a possible alternative location. Because if Luxor taught us anything, it's that Nous wants us off the trail of the hunt for the real location. That means Pryce and Nous must still want it. And want to expose it."

Silence again flooded the room, accompanied by a low-grade dread.

Radcliffe finally spoke. "You two better get off to Chartres, the day is already growing late, and the cathedral will close in a few hours. Zoe and her team will continue their research. But I have a sneaking suspicion that the solution to this riddle will come from boots on more ground."

Given their last success, that's what Silas was afraid of.

CHAPTER 27

CHARTRES, FRANCE.

W ithin an hour, Silas and Celeste had driven from the airport to Chartres Cathedral, causing not a small amount of déjà vu.

Also known as the Cathedral of Our Lady of Chartres, the majestic Gothic Catholic cathedral was mostly constructed between 1194 and 1220. Around the same time the location from their last ill-fated mission was built, the Notre Dame Cathedral. Similar to Notre Dame, the sacred structure's floor plan is cruciform in style, forming a Latin cross with a long nave crossed by a transept.

The gloomy, overcast sky set the tone for their arrival. As did the flying buttresses, sad-looking stone darkened by the passage of time, and the entrance through the western facade. Dominated by two spires soaring upward toward the heavens and centered by the dual-rose, stained glass window of The Last Judgment and central portal of The End Times, Silas and Celeste were invited to contemplate their eternal destiny as they entered through the bulky, walnut doors.

Out of habit, Silas crossed himself. As a former Catholic-turned-Protestant, some of his former practices still came naturally on impulse and were part of his spirituality. One of those being his practice of sacred rituals, like crossing and the divine prayer hours. The other being an appreciation for sacred architecture—soaring ceilings, enchanting stained glass, flying buttresses and all. That's where Protestants missed the mark.

Inside was as he expected, mirroring what he experienced at Notre Dame earlier in the year, yet more magnificent. Thanks to a multibillion-dollar renovation almost a decade ago, the interior creamy-white masonry, with *trompe l'oeil* marbling and gilded detailing; the 176 stained glass windows lining the nave depicting various apostles, saints, and stories from Scripture; and the high-vaulted ceiling all joined hands in creating a space that beckoned its parishioners to taste and see that the Lord is good through the beauty of the fruits of his co-creators' labor.

The two walked far into the nave, their footfalls echoing off the ancient stone. They craned their heads in wonder toward the impressive vaulting and stained glass above feeling closer to the divine than before they entered. They stopped at the back row of wooden chairs, where there would have been benches originally.

Silas sighed as he took in the sight, smiling slightly as he glanced from stained glass to stained glass, the apprehension of his heart being slowly softened.

"So where should we begin?" Celeste asked interrupting his contemplation.

"Why don't we split up? Seems we would cover more ground that way trying to find our needle in the cathedral haystack."

She put her hands on her hips and searched the nave. "And what are we looking for? There is still no sense about it."

Silas sighed heavily in agreement. "Hard to say. Could be a stained glass window or a mosaic or a relief. Anything that's even remotely connected with the Ark. Pryce is no dummy. There must be something that drew his attention here."

A sound pierced the sacred silence. A few visitors near them in the back sitting in quiet contemplation turned toward him in poorly veiled irritation.

Silas's phone.

He quickly silenced it, then brought it out. The display read: *Sebastian.*

He furrowed his brow, then showed it to Celeste, who matched his confusion and shrugged.

"I better answer this," he whispered.

"I'll go have a look at the place. Text me if you find anything useful."

He gave her a thumbs up as he swiped his phone to life.

"Sebastian. Hey, brother. Long time no chat."

"You got that right!"

Silas smiled and sighed. Sebastian was the only family he had left, their mother having died at their birth and father during 9/11. Grandparents had passed, and both parents were only children. He was never calling Seba enough. And his brother reminded him of it often. But since his betrayal during the summer, he hadn't had the stomach for it anyway.

"What's up?" Trying to regain some fraternal ground he added: "How are you feeling? Keeping at your physical therapy?"

"I'm getting along. The physical therapy post-shooting has done wonders. Feel back to my tip-top shape."

Earlier in the year, Silas had convinced his brother to join him on a mission to prove that Jesus had risen from the dead, as the Gospel accounts had recorded and the Church had insisted for almost 2,000 years. Initially, Sebastian balked. But after Silas played the family card, he had no choice: going back to the death of their father, if either one of them needed the other, they could call on each other to help, no matter what. Silas was desperate, so he brought him to the Church of the Holy Sepulcher to use him for a machine he had devised as a professor of physics.

Only it didn't end so well for his brother.

Regret replayed his gut like a fiddle, the string of guilt playing its familiar, sad tune. "Sorry again about all that," he said softly. "I never meant for you to get hurt."

"Oh stop the dramatics. I'm over it. I only wish you weren't so absent."

Silas said nothing, pacing around the narthex. He needed to get to work. What was this about?

"So...where are you?" Sebastian asked.

Silas paused mid-pace, confused by the question. "Where am I? What do you mean?"

Sebastian huffed. "Can I not see what my brother is up to without twenty questions?"

He sighed. He didn't want a fight. He quickly said, "Chartres Cathedral."

"France again? My, my, my. I got into the wrong line of work. Princeton must pay a boatload more than George Washington University. And for *religious* professors, no less."

His nose flared at the slight emphasis he put on "religious." It sounded like he was making air quotes, as if Silas wasn't a true-blue professor because he wasn't STEM-approved.

Silas let it go. "Not with the university."

"Then the Order of...what the hell was it, again?"

"Thaddeus. The Order of Thaddeus."

"Yes, right. And that Navy SEALs for Jesus outfit, with that cheeky brunette in tight, black leather. Now, what was her name, her name, her name..."

Silas's neck was growing warmer by the second. He had started pacing again. "Celeste," he said through gritted teeth.

"Ahh, right. Celeste Bourne. Named after that godawful Ludlum character. And the director of S-E-P-I-O."

"Was there a point to this conversation?" he exclaimed, annoyed and impatient.

"Goodness, Silas. We don't talk for months after I nearly died saving your ass," Sebastian scoffed, "and you can't even take my phone call?"

Silas ran his hand over his crew-cut hair and took a breath. The impulse to strangle the guy with one of his trademark bow ties was growing by the nanosecond. "I did take the phone call. Now I'm confused what we're talking about, and I have to get on with something."

"Oh yeah? What could possibly have drawn you to the Chartres that you have to scurry off to?"

It almost slipped, but he thought better of it. Silas closed his mouth. Then said, "Can't say. And I have to go."

"Can't? Or won't?"

Something about his tone unsettled Silas. Why was he trying to get after his reason for being at Chartres? He left it alone. Probably his brother being his typical, neurotic self. "I really need to go. I'll call you soon, alright?"

There was silence.

Silas checked his connection. It was fine. "Sebastian? Alright?"

"Fine," he said quickly. "Talk later."

He rolled his eyes and ended the call, then quickly stowed the phone in his pants pocket.

What a weird conversation.

Silas decided to start at the beginning, so he walked out of the narthex entrance and back outside to the west-facade portico reliefs. He started with the left entrance examining the carvings, but found nothing. Then he moved on to the center one, where he had just exited. Still nothing. He shuffled to the left and searched more of the relief carvings depicting various saints and religious scenes, coming up equally empty. He headed back inside.

His phone buzzed gently in his pocket. *Not again.*

He pulled it out. It was Celeste. She had texted, *"Any luck?"*

He texted back, *"No. Stuck on the phone with my bro. Weird convo. Checked west facade. Empty. You?"*

He walked back through the nave along the southern wall.

Another gentle buzz. *"Nope. Nothing in the nave. High altar empty too. Checking small chapels. Why don't u check N/S porches?"*

Good idea. He made his way to the South Porch, imbibing the ancient space's numinous atmosphere. He passed the labyrinth, which had helped metaphorically guide the spiritual journeys of countless souls. The soaring walls, built by architects with purpose and precision reminded Silas of God's own handiwork with creation. He smiled at the graceful beauty bestowed by a loving God to the world through his own careful planning, in the way those craftsmen bestowed their own measure of magnificence to him at that moment.

And to the group of college students on independent study. He waded through the crowd of maps and cameras and parkas, then exited through the South Porch, thinking about his own students. He wondered how they were getting along, the burden of his absence and his pedagogical responsibility weighing on him more than he realized.

However, his responsibilities to the Church weighed heavier. The lingering feeling that maybe there was a place for him at the Order returned. Perhaps even at SEPIO by taking more kinetic actions to safeguard the deposit of the Christian faith's memory.

A soft drizzle had overtaken the late afternoon, making the ancient stonework slick and dark. A few tables across the street outside a brasserie sat empty, but the scent of their wares was drifting up toward the cathedral, the earthly meeting and mingling with the heavenly.

Before turning to face the southern facade, the restaurant's baby-blue signage caught his attention.

La Reine de Saba.

Silas furrowed his brow. That sounded oddly like *Sheba*.

He started toward the cathedral, but glanced back, wondering about the name. He checked his watch. It was already dinner time. But Celeste would kill him if he ate without her. He turned back toward the brasserie, his stomach grumbling in protest, begging its master to succumb to the frying meat and potatoes.

All part of the investigative process, right?

He carefully made his way down the slick stairs and jogged over to the little bar, shoving through the glass door, the humid scent of food hitting him hard. The place was still humming with activity, a line forming to the right of the cashier five patrons deep. He took his place in line and stood looking at the menu, then prepared to order. The line moved quickly, and within a few minutes, he was ordering a ham sandwich with potatoes and a beer.

"Your name," Silas said nodding toward the entrance. "It's an interesting one."

"Is it?" the man wearing a saggy face and even saggier apron grunted, his silvery comb-over flapping in sync with his response.

"Why was it chosen?"

Saggy Face pointed over to the South Porch. "Because of the statue. Over there. The one of Queen Sheba."

Silas caught his breath and grinned. He could hardly believe it and laughed out loud in shock at the revelation. "Perfect."

"Hey! You not pay!"

He ignored the man and his meal and ran out of the shop, saying a silent prayer of thanks to God for his providential direction. He quickly ascended the stairs, nearly slipping half-way up. He decided to take his near-death experience as a good sign and stood still in the middle of the stairs, looking from entrance to entrance, right to center to left. But the rain-soaked stone obscured his vision.

The guide.

He took it out and flipped to the diagram of the cathedral, which mapped each porch and labeled each relief. He traced his finger down the page, droplets of water keeping pace.

There it was. The guidebook read:

The inner archivolt of the outer arch has twenty-eight statuettes of kings and queens of the Old Testament: we recognize David with his harp, Solomon with a scepter, and the Queen of Sheba holding a flower in her left hand. At the top, the four major prophets, bearded, talk with the four minor prophets who are cleanly shaven.

Interestingly, the entire south porch had been built during the first quarter of the thirteenth century. The same time period when *Kebra Nagast* had been written concerning the Queen and Solomon, and their son.

He shuffled toward the location, keeping a finger in the book. There she was, the Queen of Sheba. He looked around, half expecting a Nous operative to jump out through the door, ready to take note of the figure and make sure Silas didn't make it out alive knowing the fact.

But nothing happened.

He smiled at the thought, then looked at the relief of the queen. Nothing special about it. No markings or insignias. No phrasing or letters. Nothing that would seem to remotely connect it with the Ark. He spent several more minutes examining the statue and the surrounding reliefs for any sign of any connection with the fabled, sacred Jewish relic.

Nothing.

He glanced back at the guidebook, wondering what went wrong. He read further, then he saw something unusual.

There was another statue of the queen, a second one at the North Porch.

Apparently, it, too, had been built during the same time *Kebra Nagast* had been written. The entrance featured extensive portrayals of Old Testament men and women and themes.

An image caught his attention in the book diagramming the porch. An inscription beneath one of the sculpture pieces in one of the bays. There was a larger grouping of words etched into the stonework, but the angle of the picture accentuated two of them, isolating them in his attention field.

ARCHA CEDERIS.

From his Latin training, he knew the first word without even thinking about it.

Ark.

CHAPTER 28

ROME.

"How does that even happen?" Torres said

Gapinski shrugged. "Most of the time with this gig we're running on a buck and a prayer." He fist-bumped the SUV ceiling. "So thank the Big Guy Upstairs."

"That's a mighty big answer to prayer. I mean, what are the odds?"

He smiled. "God works in mysterious ways, as they say. Seriously, though, I've seen him lend a helping hand more times than my toes and fingers can count. I'll take whatever way he wants to offer up. In this line of work, you learn to take whatever lead you can get. Like a big, fat black panel van falling out of Heaven itself in KFC's drive-thru."

Torres chuckled, wondering what she had gotten herself into when she signed up for the new gig. Papa had said it would be like her old job, only more spiritual. More worthwhile.

Not that there was anything wrong with the secular. Studying extinct Mesoamerican and pre-Columbian cultures was worthwhile in its own right. There was still so much to learn about how they lived and why they died off. And it was just as worthy of study as the sacred work uncovering the archaeological truth behind the Bible and the history of the Christian Church.

Yet there was something special about putting her talents to work in service of the Church and her faith. After all, it was a fascination with the ancient world of the Bible that got her interested in ancient history and ancient cultures in the first place.

When she was a kid, she had been entranced by a VHS, animated series, called "The Greatest Adventure: Stories from the Bible." Two protagonists, young archaeologists, and their sidekick, stumbled across an ancient door into Bibleland, where they met famous Bible heroes like Noah, Moses, and David. As a little girl, she had play-acted going on the same adventures as the girl in the video.

One of her favorite episodes was the epic story about Joshua and the battle of Jericho. The one where an army of Israel marched around the walled city, blowing trumpets and giving a loud shout, eventually bringing the walls crumbling down. Noah and his Ark filled with animals made for another spectacular story, especially when she watched a documentary from a '90s network show, called "Unsolved Mysteries," investigating the possibility that the story may not just be a legend, but that the gigantic ship may have been real, resting somewhere on a mountaintop in Turkey.

She had intended to devote her life to finding such biblical relics and proving the Bible's history, but her stint in the IDF had soured her to religion. After experiencing up close and personal the plot of land known for all that Bible history, religion, and the faith springing from that land seemed to offer nothing more than violence and discord. Whether Christian or Jewish or Muslim. She still had her faith, but it was more private and separate from the rest of her life. Certainly not something that would ever mingle with her work as a historian and cultural anthropologist.

But when Rowan Radcliffe had contacted her, she jumped at the chance. Why not return to her first love, the history and culture of the Bible? But she wasn't going to lie either: the money was pretty good, and she missed some of the action she'd had while serving in the IDF. And when things started going sour with her uncle's operation, she thought why not put her services to good use for the Church? Besides, she could use the fresh start.

Dodging bullets and tracking down religious terrorists, however, wasn't in the job description. So she was beginning to seriously second-guess her vocational switch. Those dues had been paid long past with the IDF. And she had left that life behind when she joined her uncle. What she hadn't told Gapinski, or Radcliffe for that matter, was that leaving his salvage company hadn't been entirely voluntary.

It had started innocently enough. A few small pieces here and there from the collections she had discovered. The coins and figurines and pottery were worth hardly anything to anybody anyway. And with all the business she had been providing her uncle with her reputation and expertise, she figured he owed her.

But when she had made a return trip to the Urca de Lima and had taken some of the more elaborate gold pieces from the cache, that's when things went south.

Her first mistake had been taking them in the first place. Especially since it had been a government-sponsored salvage. The uncovering of the sizable Spanish fleet had been a boon for the Cuban culture, not to mention the economy and political climate. And their attention to the site was more than she had expected.

Her second mistake was trying to sell the items on the black market. She still couldn't say why she went that route. Other than bald-faced greed, she couldn't say why she had betrayed her cultural heritage by trying to sell to the highest bidder. But the INTERPOL sting had done what they had set out to do. Too bad they thought they'd caught a whale-shark dealer when in reality they'd caught a minnow-of-a-researcher who had made a terrible choice.

Her final mistake was the familial betrayal. It was nearly too much for her uncle to bear. The Cuban government fined him and his company, given that they were the custodians of the excavation. They severed their relationship with him and his company, which had a rippling effect across his other business relationships. Thankfully, he had been able to hold onto and maintain those contracts, but not before the damage had been done to his reputation.

Her act had especially stung because he had taken her in as a teenager when her parents had been tragically killed by a drunk driver. She was family, which made the betrayal all the worse.

Torres realized a tear had rolled down her cheek without her sensing it. She wiped it away and glanced at Gapinski. It looked like he hadn't noticed. She returned to staring out the window.

A fresh start was just what Naomi Torres needed, and she hoped the Church could provide the reset. In more ways than one.

"Crapola!"

She startled back to the present moment. "What happened?"

"I lost the van."

She sat up straighter and looked out the front windshield. "You lost the van?" She looked out her window and around out Gapinski's window before glancing out the rear. "How could you lose the van? It was right there!"

"I don't know, alright? I was following it a few cars back, and that big, fat truck got in the way. I thought I was following it a few blocks later when the thing turned, but then it vanished."

She dialed Zoe. Unbelievable.

"Zoe, we lost the van. Have you been following us with a drone or CCTV?"

"Negatory, Naomi. It's been all you. I can try and tap into area surveillance packages and backtrack the footage. But there's no guarantee."

Gapinski turned suddenly down a side road. "What'd she say? Do we have a read?"

"Sorry, pal."

"Double crapola," he growled.

"Zoe's going to try and tap into CCTV footage and maybe some government surveillance vehicles, but don't hold your breath."

He turned right again, seemingly getting himself further lost by her account.

"I feel like we should stop and wait for Zoe," she said. "I'm sure something will turn up if we let her work. I doubt winding our way farther through Rome is going to get us anywhere."

He jerked the wheel again, this time left. "No, we gotta keep going and find that bastard. I've got a good feeling about where we're heading."

What have I gotten myself—

The window to her right shattered, spilling glass all over her as the world toppled upside down with a deafening crash.

They'd been hit. They were no longer on all fours but sprawled on the side.

Her head lanced with pain. She raised a trembling hand to her temple; it was bleeding.

She looked over to her left at Gapinski. He was unconscious, resting against the pavement through his own shattered window.

The world was dimming, going in and out of focus.

More shooting pain, mostly her right side. Where the van had hit them.

Van. Black van. Vesta. Creepy lady holding the bowl of fire.

Nous.

An arm reached into her window, the glint of a blade catching her attention as her eyes lifted and closed, lifted and closed. She watched it lazily as it sliced through her belt.

She tried pushing it away, but the hands were too powerful, and her resolve had been short-circuited by the concussive crash.

She felt a small pinprick at the base of her neck. Hands grabbed her. She was rising out of her seat.

Then her world went dark.

CHAPTER 29

CHARTRES.

S ilas raced through the transept connecting the south and north porches, stumbling through an empty row of wooden chairs to the other side. The sky was growing dark from the thickening clouds and setting sun, and the cathedral would be closing soon. The center entrance doors were open, so he quickly went through them and down the stairs, a foot slipping before he recovered, then turned around to survey the landscape.

He went back up the stairs to the left bay of statues and started examining them. One was of the Virgin Mary holding the infant Christ child. Joining her were Isaiah and Daniel. Moral tales were also depicted, where Virtues triumphed over Vices. Another portrayed the beatitudes of the body and soul, which Silas knew to have been described by the twelfth-century mystic monk Bernard of Clairvaux, an interesting connection, to be sure, given he was one of the names in Pryce's journal.

Finding nothing of interest, he moved on to the central portico, which was dominated by ancient Hebrew patriarchs and prophets from the Old Testament. What caught Silas's attention was the figure of Melchizedek, described in Genesis 14 as the mysterious priest-king of Salem and traditionally identified with

Jerusalem. He was surrounded by more ancient Jewish figures: Abraham, Moses, Samuel, David, and Elisha, as well as Peter from the New Testament Christian Scriptures. A relief depicted the Garden of Eden, with its four rivers, and a crowned Virgin Mary seated beside Jesus in Heaven.

Where was the Queen of Sheba?

He shuffled over to the final portico, and there she was. The Queen herself. But this time, she wasn't some obscure statue on an arch, as she was at the South Porch. Instead, she dominated the bay as a full-size statue and positioned next to Solomon. What caught his eye, though, was that she was standing on a crouching African. He furrowed his brow, then flipped to his guidebook, where it described him as her Ethiopian servant.

He looked back at the statue and smiled. *An Ethiopian servant?*

To Silas, the depiction meant that the Queen was understood to be Ethiopian. Just as *Kebra Nagast* itself said. And that the sculptors who worked on the North Porch at Chartres in the thirteenth century believed her to be African, placing her in an obvious Ethiopian context. Which meant they could have been familiar with the tradition surrounding her in the legend. Why else put a pagan ruler in such a sacred Christian building if there weren't a critical religious memory attached to her?

Like the Ark of the Covenant.

Silas stood back, brow furrowed and stroking his chin in thought. *But how could such a story have filtered into northern France, and during the late twelfth and early thirteenth centuries?*

As he contemplated the piece of revelation, Silas saw something on a column between the central and right-hand columns. The carving of Latin he had seen in the photo in his guidebook.

ARCHA CEDERIS.

He smiled and crouched down to get a closer look. Though the stonework had not aged well, having been damaged and eroded with time, he could still make out a miniaturized depiction of a box or some sort of chest of a sacred nature etched into the stonework being transported on an oxcart. Beneath it were those Latin letters. To its right was a man who looked as though he was stooping over the chest, with another set of Latin letters, though a little difficult to make out:

HIC AMICITUR ARCHA CEDERIS.

He checked his guidebook, but it had rendered it differently: *HIC AMITITUR ARCHA CEDERIS.* He looked at the etchings again, noticing that some of the letters could be perceived in different ways. Either way, *ARCHA* seemed clear: *chest* or *ark*. But what of the other words? Was this sculpture depicting the Ark being transported on an oxcart? The scale seemed right, as described in Exodus, and given that it was positioned close to the Queen of Sheba it appeared the builders of Chartres knew something, perhaps being influenced by the *Kebra Nagast* legend itself.

Then he noticed something else: the chest/Ark object was smack-dab between Melchizedek and the Queen of Sheba. As he studied it further, he realized the chest/Ark resting on its oxcart was positioned *away* from Melchizedek and toward the Queen of Sheba.

He stepped back, considering this depiction. A crucial question rose to the surface, an almost farcical one: Did this portico contain an echo of the legend, as found in a thirteenth-century Ethiopian text, that the Ark of the Covenant had been transported away from ancient Israel and to Ethiopia?

Silas went back to the Queen, again noting the African figure on which she was standing. Then he went over to Melchizedek. He studied him more, looking for clues to the puzzle his mind was beginning to piece together. Dangling beneath the priest's right hand was a censer, the kind that holds incense and the kind priests in the Most Holy Place would have used to cloud their vision and prevent them from laying eyes upon the Ark, requiring their death if they ever did catch its glimpse. In his other hand was another curious object: a long-stemmed chalice or cup, holding a round object of sorts, rather than liquid.

Silas opened his guidebook again, searching for answers. One caption read that Melchizedek was meant to be a sort of Christ figure, where the chalice and the object represented "the bread and the wine, symbols of Eucharist."

Another photo with caption actually compelled him to draw his face closer to the book:

Melchizedek bearing the Grail cup out of which comes the Stone. With this, we may connect the poem of Wolfram von Eschenbach, who is said to have been a Templar—though there is no proof of this—for whom the Grail is a Stone.

He startled audibly, dropping his jaw and the hand holding his guidebook to his side and raising his other to his forehead.

"Are you kidding me?"

There was the other name. Wolfram von Eschenbach. And Grail and Templars? What the heck?

His mind was reeling, trying to make connections between all of what he had discovered. But one thing was certain, he couldn't deny that a connection had been made eight hundred years ago that seemed to have considerable bearing now.

There he was, Solomon and the Queen of Sheba, and standing on an African holding an orb-like chalice. Melchizedek, the Priest of Salem, holding the same orb-like chalice. A cart with what could reasonably be considered a sacred box. Like the Ark. And it was positioned directly between Melchizedek and Sheba. And it was moving away from the one and toward the other.

Away from the Priest-King Melchizedek and toward the Queen of Sheba; away from Jerusalem and toward Ethiopia.

Maybe there really was something to the Kebra Nagast legend.

He raised his phone and started taking a few pictures of the statues and the sacred object upon the cart, and then the carved letters beneath it.

But the world suddenly burst into stars, and then went dark.

CELESTE SAW it happen in slow motion from inside the cathedral. It didn't make sense. A man came up behind Silas, with chocolate-colored skin and a shiny, eight-ball head.

Oliver Tulu.

He loomed over Silas quietly. And then suddenly, he hit him on the back of the head. He went down like a sack of potatoes, flopping to the ground in one heap.

She froze, taken aback by what was happening. It was all so sudden, so unexpected.

Several tourists joined Celeste in her confusion and appall, screaming and scattering.

Two men suddenly joined Tulu and began dragging Silas away from the entrance and down the wet, cobble stairway.

That's when she sprang into action.

She grabbed her SIG Sauer from behind her waist and ran out of the South Porch entrance yelling.

"Tulu! What the bloody hell do you think you're doing?"

Tulu froze, as well as the two men. The look on his face made it clear he wasn't expecting to be recognized or have company. His companions reminded her of a few of the young men she'd seen hanging on Tulu's clipboard around the dig site. They held Silas steady, tightening their grip, their faces unflinching.

Whatever they were doing at Chartres and whatever they were planning to do with Silas was over. No way were they going to get away with it!

She kept her weapon trained on Tulu. She narrowed her eyes and glanced at the other two men to make sure they knew she was in charge. A few tourists behind them eyed her with concern, mobile phones at their ears.

"Please. Put the weapon down," Tulu said, his voice smooth and commanding.

"Not a chance. Put down my partner."

"You don't know what you are doing. What you are mixing yourself up in. You've made a massive miscalculation."

"Are you mad? You accost my partner and try to kidnap him, and you have the gall to suggest I've made a mistake? No, sir, you're the one who's made the massive miscalculation. Did Nous send you? Here to clean up your boss's mess after having lost the Ark? Trying to divine an alternative location of the Ark?"

Tulu said nothing, his face hard and unmoving.

"What is this all about, anyway? This business with the Ark? Clearly, Pryce knew it wasn't in the chamber. So this has to be more than just an archaeological fishing expedition aimed at bolstering his academic credentials and byline in the history books. And what is your play in all of this?"

The man said nothing for several seconds. Then he narrowed his eyes and lowered his head, and said, "The Order of Thaddeus would be wise to leave this alone. You, too, Bourne. Put the gun down and walk away."

Bourne? She hadn't remembered sharing her name with either Tulu or Pryce. She gripped her weapon tighter.

"The Order pledges to preserve and protect religious artifacts," she said. "Like the Ark. You would be wise to come clean and lay your play out for the world to see."

Silas began to stir while slumped over by each arm between his two kidnappers. Sirens started sounding, their wail distant, but growing closer. Tulu glanced at his men.

Good. A few more minutes and this will all be over.

Tulu took a step forward.

Celeste gripped the gun tighter and leveled it at his chest. "I said stay where you are."

His face was set like flint, eyes narrow and haunting.

In one movement, his two associates hoisted Silas upright between them, causing her to switch her attention and her aim to their distraction.

It worked.

They shoved Silas forward at her, and bolted across the street, causing her to drop her aim in order to catch him. They both went down, her gun skittered across the cobblestone stairs.

Tulu lunged for the weapon. Celeste gently pushed Silas off of her and laid him on the cobblestone stairs, then side-kicked Tulu in his hip while he was reaching for the SIG Sauer, sending him to the ground.

But only after laying hold of it.

He fumbled with the weapon, managing to get off two shots. Both went wide into the surrounding buildings, sending onlookers screaming for cover.

Celeste launched a roundhouse kick at the man's arm, sending the gun flying once again, several yards away. But she received an equal reply.

Tulu's right foot smashed into the left side of her face, the force of it jerking her neck and sending her across the pavement in front of the cathedral stairs.

Pain blossomed on the side of her face, but that wasn't important. What was, was stopping this madman from doing any more damage and protecting the Ark. She recovered and positioned herself to engage her opponent once again.

But the man fled down a small path between the buildings across the road bordering the cathedral grounds.

She huffed and went after him.

When she reached the road, a car sitting in an alleyway burst out of its den to the right, its tires screeching on the wet pavement and stopping feet from her, forcing her to stumble back to narrowly escape its front end.

Tulu flung open the rear door and dove into the back seat.

The rust-colored Peugeot floored it south, just as the police began arriving at the north end.

Bloody hell.

Celeste was breathing hard, the left side of her face tender and bruising. She hobbled back to where Silas was lying in front of the cathedral. A few onlookers rushed over to see if they could help, speaking in rushed German. She waved them away. Silas was moaning and stirring and trying to push himself off of the ground.

"Silas? It's Celeste. You've been attacked."

He sat upright, clutching the back of his head. There didn't appear to be any blood, thank God. But a sizable goose egg had already formed.

"What...What happened?" he moaned.

"It was Tulu. He hit you from behind. I saw him from inside the cathedral. A few of his men tried to carry you off."

He looked up into her eyes. "That's twice now you've saved my life. I'm not liking this pattern."

She smiled. "Here, maybe you should sit against this stone barrier."

"Nonsense," he said slowly trying to stand, but stumbling from the beating. "We've found the missing clues."

"What do you mean? What did you find?"

She helped him to his feet, and up the stairs. He showed her what he had discovered. She wasn't entirely convinced, but thought it was enough to keep pursuing the line of inquiry. She called Radcliffe to inform him of their developments.

"I want you two to report back to the Order's Paris operation," Radcliffe instructed. "The extensive on-site library should help you make sense of these new pieces of revelation."

"What about support?" she asked. "There's a lot to work through here and not a lot of time."

"Zoe is putting together a dossier of her own research and will conference with you in the morning."

He paused, clearing his throat. "On a side note, I've got unfortunate news out of Rome."

Celeste looked at Silas, who looked at the phone. "Gapinski?"

"No, his partner. Naomi Torres. She's been captured."

"No..." Celeste said.

"What happened?" Silas asked.

"I don't want to get into it other than they were tracking a lead on the stolen Passion relic. And things went off the rails. Greer has been dispatched as back up for Gapinski, and an all-out effort at finding her is underway."

Celeste and Silas said nothing.

"The gears of Nous's plot are slowly turning into place," Radcliffe continued. "Yet the picture is far from clear. Which means you need to figure out what is really going on. And fast."

DAY IV

CHAPTER 30

ROME.

Torres was floating in a darkened pool of unconsciousness, the sensation black and cold, all sound and smell muffled by the state.

All at once, she sensed herself coming back into an awareness of reality, like a REM cycle drawing to a close and bringing wakeful bliss.

Except this entrance back into consciousness was anything but blissful.

Her mind was a fog of pain, head pulsating in protest. She tried flickering her eyes open, but the distant light was a supernova of overwhelm.

Where am I? What happened?

It all came back in rapid-succession recognition.

The Order of Thaddeus. SEPIO. Gapinski. The scourging post. The SUV. The black van. Vesta. Creepy lady holding the bowl of fire. The crash. Then the hands, the knife, the pinprick, and rising through her window into black nothingness.

Her heart started beating rapidly, pulse pounding in her head as the gravity of her situation crashed into her. She had been drugged and kidnapped by terrorists. She was the prisoner of Marwan Farhad, a Member of the Thirteen, an operative of Nous.

An enemy of the Church.

She pried her eyes open, ignoring the severe strain it put on her aching head. The darkness was all consuming but for a small amount of light in the distance fighting for survival. The ground was hard and gray. The air was cool yet heavy. Perhaps they were underground. And it smelled of wet concrete and mildew and bodily fluids, as if the room had been used before as someone else's prison.

She tried moving, but the effects of the drug made movement stiff and slow. She craned her neck, catching sight of her environment, which was more expansive than she had initially realized.

The space was warehouse-like, and she was at one end with a light source at the other. The kind she used to use on her digs with her uncle's excavation company. She could make out a group of three or four people. Probably the men who took her. They were huddled around a table next to the light source. A few feet away was another table, and something stood on top, a cylinder rising about a meter.

The scourging pillar of Christ.

She craned her neck, taking in her surroundings. To the right was a door, not more than ten feet away. Instinctively, she moved toward it, but was jerked back by a heavy chain. She fell hard against the cement floor. It was then that she realized her hands were bound behind her. She immediately stilled herself on the ground, hoping her rashness hadn't drawn their attention. She let a few minutes tick by, then slowly opened her eyes. They hadn't so much as looked up from their table. They were deep in conversation. Looked to be deep in planning, the way their ringleader was motioning.

She raised herself slightly and repositioned herself, straining to hear what they were discussing. Words and fragmented sentences were rising and falling around her in a language she didn't understand.

Wait. What was that?

She heard it again. More clearly this time.

Santa Croce in Gerusalemme.

Her heart started beating faster. For she knew exactly what that meant.

Holy Cross in Jerusalem. As in the basilica that stood a twenty-minute walk from the site of their first excursion into the city at the Basilica of Saint Praxedes.

A story came rushing from the depths of her childhood.

"Tell me a story, Abuelo," young Naomi said.

"A story?" Abuelo Torres said, putting his hands on his hips. "A story? I will tell you something better than a story. I will tell you hi-story."

"History? What's that?"

"A reminder of a future not yet attained."

She wrinkled her nose, not understanding what her Abuelo meant. But if he liked...history, then so did she!

"OK. Then tell me a hi-story."

He chuckled and sat down in his well-worn, brown threadbare chair. "Alright, mi nieta. Up, up, up!"

She grinned, then climbed up on his lap.

"Once there was a very old queen who went on a very long journey for her very powerful son. The Emperor of Rome. She traveled from the land of the Seven Hills to what was once known as the Promised Land. For years it had been a land of war. But because of a group of brave, young soldiers, the land once again saw peace."

Little Naomi loved to sit on her abuelo's lap, nestled in his large, long arms staring up into his wrinkly face. Especially when he told her stories. He was the best storyteller she knew.

"You see, her mighty son had a grande piggy bank. And he said she could have as many pesos as she needed to retrieve five very special objects. The five most special objects on the planet that were very special treasures to the Church!"

"What were they mi Abuelo? And why were they special?"

"They were special because they were special treasures of the Church that had the power to bring to anyone who looked upon them the memory of Jesus' death on the cross."

"Cooool," she said.

He chuckled softly. "Yes. They were cooool. So our queen—"

"Wait. Papa."

"Yes, Naomi?"

"You didn't tell me the queen's naaaame!"

He slapped his forehead with the palm of his hand. "Yo olvidé!"

Little Naomi giggled.

"Helena. Queen Helena. But now, we call her Saint Helena."

"Cooool."

"So Queen Helena left her home country and sailed across the seas, and traveled across the deserts, and rode through the forests until she reached the magnificent city of Jerusalem."

"Isn't that where Jesus lived?"

"Yes, Naomi! It is. He taught there. Performed miracles there. Died there. And then rose from the dead there. And when Queen Helena arrived, she got to work protecting the memory of Jesus' life. So she built two churches, the Church of the Nativity in Bethlehem, and the Church of Eleona on the Mount of Olives. The two places where Jesus was born and where he flew into the sky. She also got to work digging in the dirt."

"Why did she do that?"

"Because that's where the five special treasures were! One by one she found them. The first special treasure was the pillar of granite where Jesus was beaten and bruised. The second was a piece of the crown of thorns that the soldiers pushed on Jesus' head and that he wore when he died. The third one was one of the nails that held Jesus to the cross. Fourth was the board above Jesus' head announcing that he was the King of the Jews. And the fifth and final special treasure was a piece of the True Cross, the very cross that Jesus was crucified and died on."

"No way!"

"Yes way, mi nieta! Do you know what those special treasures mean for you?"

"What?"

"Jesus was an innocent man. He never did anything wrong. He never hurt anybody. He never said a bad thing to anyone. He never hurt anyone's feelings. But that's not the case with me or you, is it?"

Little Naomi looked away and frowned. "No, it isn't."

"We all do bad things. Even Papa."

"You do?" she asked, brightening a little.

"I do. Which is why I need a sacrifice, and so do you. Because as the Bible says, the wages of sin is death. The cost for doing all of those bad things is separation from others and from God. But the good news is that the Bible also says God's gift to us is eternal life through Jesus Christ. Jesus paid the price for all of the bad things we do. He died so that we can be healed and be with God forever! Now, what do you think about that?"

"I think that's so cooool!"

He smiled and nodded. "It is, so cooool." Then he tickled little Naomi.

"No, wait Papa!" she squealed as he continued tickling her. "What happened to the queen?"

"Oh yes. I almost forgot! When she returned to her home country, she built a big, beautiful church to keep her special treasures safe. We call those special treasures the Passion relics because they are from Christ's Passion. And they are in a Basilica. Can you say that? Basilica?"

"Bas-li-ci-ca."

He smiled and chuckled. "Close enough. The Basílica de la Santa Cruz en Jerusalén. And one day you are going to grow up to be big and strong and find the special treasures of Christ's Church and keep them safe. Just like Queen Helena."

Little Naomi smiled and yawned, believing what Papa said was true.

"Alright, now let's say our prayers."

Little Naomi got down from her abuelo's lap. The two of them knelt at her small bed, a candle flickering gently on her nightstand. They folded their hands, then said the prayer the Lord Jesus himself had taught his disciples to pray. The Lord's Prayer.

"Padre nuestro," they said together, "que estás en el cielo.

"Santificado sea tu nombre. Venga tu reino.

"Hágase tu voluntad en la tierra como en el cielo.

"Danos hoy nuestro pan de cada día.

"Perdona nuestras ofensas, como también nosotros perdonamos a los que nos ofenden.

"No nos dejes caer en tentación y líbranos del mal."

"Amén," Abuelo Torres said.

"Amén," little Naomi echoed, yawning long and loud.

He chuckled softly, then picked her up and set her in her bed. He brought the sheets up over her shoulders and tucked them gently around her. She was already sleeping when he gave her a kiss on her cheek.

"Buenas noches, mi Naomi."

A TEAR SLID down her cheek at the memory. Then she smiled, knowing that it was Papa who had led her into this mess. She wasn't angry or resentful, but grateful for his guidance during a difficult time in her life.

The men were talking again. The man in the middle gestured at the scourging pillar, then pointed at something on the table.

She knew exactly what they were planning to steal. The four remaining special treasures of her childhood faith.

The crown of thorns. A holy nail. The plaque above Jesus' cross announcing the crucifixion of the "King of the Jews." And a portion of the boards of execution that held the limp, lifeless body of Jesus Christ.

A piece of the True Cross of Christ.

CHAPTER 31

VERSAILLES, FRANCE.

Silas awoke to the smell of fresh-baked bread, frying hardwood bacon, melting cheese, and strong coffee. The sensation was only outmatched by the restful sleep he had enjoyed in his tiny, abbey bedroom.

It was already well past early morning by the time he had climbed out of bed. He had crashed hard the night before. He needed it after what they had been through the past few days uncovering the Nous plot. Now that they were closer to solving the mystery, he needed every ounce of energy he could get. So he took full advantage that night, which did his body good.

The sun was already up and at work, waking the rest of the world below his small window. He stood and stretched, said his morning prayers, then went in search of the hot meal that had rudely awaken his deep slumber.

After the revelations and connections at Chartres, and the incident with Tulu and his men, Radcliffe had sent them to the Order's Paris operations, the old Port-Royal des Champs Abbey complex southwest of Paris and just outside of Versailles. Silas and Celeste were to use the Order's extensive library and research tools to solve the mysteries surrounding the Ark of the Covenant, as well as Nous's plot against the Church.

Originally a Cistercian, female monastery built in the heart of the Chevreuse Valley in 1204 in the lineage of the Abbey of Clairvaux, the Port-Royal Abby launched a number of culturally important institutions, most notably the *Little Schools of Port-Royal*, which became famous for the high quality of the education they offered. Most people forget that the Church was the center of learning and knowledge during the so-called Dark Ages, a misnomer to be sure. And the abbey played their part in preserving the best knowledge Europe had to offer at the time through their pivotal education reforms.

Eventually, most of the complex was razed to the ground at the start of the eighteenth century following a series of papal bulls after it was caught up in a controversial, Catholic religious-reform movement primarily directed at the Jesuits. The Order of Thaddeus eventually reclaimed the property and rebuilt the abbey for their intellectual and theological pursuits.

Silas followed his nose to a large hall, where a hearty breakfast awaited him. The center was commanded by rows of heavy wooden tables. Hanging from the ceiling were large wrought iron chandeliers with modern light fixtures instead of the candles they had once borne. Celeste was halfway through a plate of bacon and cheese eggs when he sat down.

"Good morning, sunshine," she said, taking a sip of her tea. "How did you sleep?"

"Like a rock. You?"

"Same. Which is good, because we have lots of ground to cover. So grab yourself a plate and fill up. The library awaits."

He smiled at the thought of getting his hands dirty with a hardcore research project. Most of his days were spent teaching a load of classes and then dealing with his students' complaints, squeezing out precious research and writing time. He grabbed a plate, filled it with the goodness he had smelled from his room, filled a large mug of coffee, then sat down to enjoy his food before the day of research.

It had taken two decades to restore the original abbey complex to its former glory as a working monastery, but the complex was a sight to behold. Outside a large window, Silas could see an expanse of rolling, green hills punctuated by apple orchards and vineyards that were eventually pressed into apple cider and fermented into wine. Three stories of rooms housed the ecumenical coterie of scholars and students dedicated to retrieving and preserving the vintage Christian faith. A large chapel held the daily prayer services, for both the abbey itself as well as the surrounding village community. The largest of the buildings was an original one, which later served as a national museum: the library, which they headed to after breakfast.

The familiar smell of old paper and ink was dizzying, sending Silas into a drug-addict high that only bibliophiles could appreciate. The dark, walnut-lined walls and bookcases, and burnished-bronze light fixtures primed the senses even further. He thought about all that these walls had witnessed with the attempts at reforming the Church to bring it back in line with a historical understanding of the once-for-all faith entrusted to the saints.

"May I help you?" an aged, hunch-backed man with a kind smile and even kinder eyes said as he slowly approached the pair.

"Yes, thank you," Celeste said. "We're with the Order. Here on a temporary research assignment, having arrived yesterday."

"Ahh, welcome. Welcome! And you are?"

"Celeste Bourne," she said extending her hand. The man took it.

"And Professor Grey. Silas Grey."

"Ahh, professor. Nice to have you both. I'm Brother Rémy, caretaker of this wonderful, literary establishment," the man said, waving his arms around the lobby.

"And quite the establishment it is," Silas said. "How many books do you have in this library?"

"Half a million housed inside, with nearly as many more in climate-controlled vaults beneath."

Silas whistled and craned his head down one of the hallways trying to get a glimpse of the literary wonderland.

The man chuckled, then cocked his head. "You wouldn't happen to be the fellows Rowen Radcliffe sent, would you?"

She glanced at Silas, then smiled. "We are. Did he contact you about our arrival?"

"He did. I've made arrangements for you to use one of our larger research spaces. You should have all the privacy and resources you need. Come."

The man hobbled along with a cane, leading them down a hallway narrowed by bookcases on either side. Silas hungrily eyed the books, trying to catch a glimpse of the Church thinkers he had fallen in love with over the years. They rounded a corner into a large, spacious room with high ceilings that took up the three floors of the building. At one end a fire cracked away in a stone fireplace the size of a person, tendrils of smoke escaping and mingling with the scent of the old tomes.

Silas stopped short. "Wait. Is that..." He quickly walked over to a table with an aged book opened, its pages stained with blue, red, and green marginals and text barely registering the script of its ancient knowledge. He whispered, "It is."

"What's that?" Celeste asked.

"The *Summa Theologica*," Brother Rémy said. "The best-known work of Thomas Aquinas. One of the original reproductions, actually. Normally, it's housed in the chambers beneath the library. But on occasion we let it roam free."

"Can I touch it?" Silas asked, as if approaching a rare animal. The man nodded. He grinned and carefully caressed the page with an index finger, running it down the side and across the text. "Magical," he whispered.

Celeste pulled at his arm gently, then nodded toward another hallway. "Shall we? We haven't much time."

He frowned slightly, then nodded. "Let's see that research space, Brother Rémy."

The old man took them to a modest room with large windows overlooking the vineyard. The sun was bright and cheery, which would serve them well as they pored over texts for the next several hours in search of answers. A computer terminal with a large monitor sat at one end of the room. Next to it was a cart with hot water and tea bags and a large carafe of coffee, as well as a platter of pastries. In the center of the table sat a large Bible and two e-ink tablets, with an assortment of notebooks and pens.

They sure did know how to treat their visiting researchers.

"Well, I'll leave you to it. Tea and coffee and some fuel for the research race ahead are yours to enjoy. As you can see, we've stepped into the twenty-first century, with the computer terminal and the full-sized e-readers. The computer gives you access to a catalog of everything we have housed in our facility. The e-readers give you access to an expanded billion-book catalog of books. You can even send articles from the terminal to the e-reader tablets. Feel free to use the notebooks and pens, which are provided for your convenience. Shout if you need anything."

The two thanked the man, then got to work.

Celeste sank into a chair and Silas walked over to the computer terminal. "Let's see what this thing can do."

He logged onto the powerful Boolean search engine to cross-search databases from hundreds of research institutions around the world, including the Vatican's own secure, digital records. He typed in the first obvious search string: *the disappearance of the Ark*.

"Right," Celeste said as she filled her mug with steaming water. "So what do we know so far?"

Silas walked over to the coffee to pour himself his own cup of research fuel while the search engine finished working its magic. "That the Ark isn't under the Temple Mount?"

She threw him a look of amusement as she added a lump of sugar to her cup, then walked back to the table and picked up an e-reader.

He walked back to the terminal. Predictably, it registered a number of entries. First on the list caught his attention, as it was titled, "The Disappearance of the Ark," by a Dr. M. Haran of Hebrew University in Jerusalem.

"Might as well start there," he mumbled. He selected the article and sent it to the e-reader tablets.

The two opened the article and began reading. Silas skipped to the end, learning from his experience as an academic to save time by just reading the conclusion. It read:

To sum up: Shishak and Jehoash did no more than empty the Temple treasures. It was Manasseh who set up vessels for Baal and Asherah in the outer sanctum and introduced the image of Asherah into the inner sanctum of the Temple. And it was probably through him that the Ark was removed. When Josiah cleansed the Temple, the ark was no longer there. Many decades after the 'sin of Manasseh,' Nebuchadnezzar entered the outer sanctum of the Temple and 'cut in pieces' its vessels (also plundering the Temple treasuries). Thus when the fateful moment of final destruction arrived, eleven years after the exile of Jehoiachin, the Temple was already deprived of most of its interior accessories.

"Well, that explains why the Ark wasn't in the Temple," he said, setting down the tablet.

Celeste finished the article, as well. "Right. Insightful historical and biblical overview of the Ark, but where did it go?"

Good question.

"Wait," Silas said turning to Celeste. "Did you read the whole article?"

"Of course, didn't you?"

He mumbled, "I skipped to the conclusion."

She shrugged. "What can I say? I'm a speed reader."

He smirked. "Show off." He returned to the article. "Haran's conclusions pretty much mirror the tradition surrounding at least one of the possibilities of the Ark's disappearance."

"What are the other traditions?" she asked blowing on her tea.

"Well, we know the one about Shishak is bunk after our jaunt to Luxor."

"Bunk?" she said, raising her brow and smiling. "Is that the technical term?"

"After what we went through, yes. Now, much of the legend surrounding the Ark's disappearance has held that it and all of the Temple treasures were placed in a chamber underneath the Temple. Some have insisted the priests moved the sacred articles during the reign of Manasseh, as this article suggests."

"Why Manasseh?" she asked, taking a sip of her tea.

"Because he corrupted the temple with pagan idols and altars. But there's some confusion over whether or not the treasures were indeed moved based on an account in 2 Chronicles."

"And what does it say?"

He reached for the Bible, then turned to the passage in chapter thirty-five and read it: "He said to the Levites who taught all Israel and who were holy to the Lord, 'Put the holy ark in the house that Solomon son of David, king of Israel, built; you need no longer carry it on your shoulders. Now serve the Lord your God and his people Israel.'"

He closed it and set it back in the center of the table. "The account seems to indicate the priests had the Ark in their posses-sion, which means Manasseh hadn't destroyed the Ark. Then they returned the Ark to the purified Temple, per King Josiah's instructions. So the alternative theory is that the Ark and the treasures were removed either during or just before the Baby-lonian invasion between 605 and 586 BC. Some believe the Babylonians themselves removed the Ark from the Temple along with the other vessels when they looted it, carrying them back to Babylon. Others suspect the Ark was destroyed when the Temple itself was destroyed during the invasion."

"But not all scholars agree?"

He shook his head. "Not at all. The main issue comes from the biblical text itself. The recorded lists of captured Temple articles in 2 Kings 25 never mention the Ark. And, actually, they don't mention the capture of any of the Temple treasures from the inner sanctuary. Most people who have spent any time researching the Ark, myself included, believe the scriptural silence on the issue is a significant statement against the Ark having been taken by the Babylonians. And the fact that the Persians later returned all of the vessels taken by the Babylonians, yet the Bible doesn't mention the most famous one of them all in the list in Ezra 1, pretty much seals the deal."

Celeste took another sip of her tea. "So then the Ark was removed from the Temple before the Babylonian invasion. Is that right?"

"That's what many biblical historians believe. If the Ark wasn't stolen or destroyed by the Babylonians, then it must have already been removed before they invaded Jerusalem and destroyed the Temple. The Levites could have moved it secretly at any time before that invasion. And, fearing more invasions of their sacred space and the potential for their central religious object falling into the hands of the pagans, they could have kept it hidden for a future time of unveiling."

"Of course, the million-dollar question is where."

"Sure is." He yawned loudly and rubbed his face with his hands. "But I don't think we're any closer to finding the blasted thing!"

Celeste set down her tea and playfully punched him in his left shoulder. "Cheer up, Charlie. You forget we've got a powerful, secret weapon at our disposal."

She drained her tea and stood, then walked over to the cart of hot water to pour herself a fresh cup.

He smirked, both amused and taken aback by her playfulness. "Oh yeah? And what's that?"

She returned, handing Silas a fresh mug of coffee, and said smiling, "Why, us, of course."

He took the mug and smiled, liking the sound of that. He raised it toward her and replied, "To us...the secret weapon to finding the Ark."

They clinked mugs, then got down to business.

CHAPTER 32

WEWELSBURG, GERMANY.

T he blood was pooling at the bottom of the ceremonial bowl, squirting in spastic bursts through the long, clear tube in sync with each pump of Rudolf Borg's heart. He imagined the organ squeezing and constricting, squeezing and constricting, the life-force flowing through his body and then out through the needle he had inserted in a large vein protruding from his forearm.

A small amount had seeped out around the needle. He scooped it up with a finger from his free hand, then brought it to his nose. The distinct smell of copper filled his head with dizzy delight. He opened his mouth, then wiped his finger on his tongue, smearing the red life-force around his mouth. His skin tingled with goose pimples as his mouth was filled with the taste of a thousand pennies.

He caught his breath, then sighed with more delight as he thought about the chaos he would be unleashing upon the faith of his pathetic parents when the week was through.

As good German Catholics, they dutifully went to Mass each week, dragging their only son along with them. He had never been able to engage with the service fully. Perhaps it was the guilt at having not confessed enough or trusted God enough or performed the necessary religious duties enough. And yet...

As a child, he knew there was something different about him. The boys in his German, working-class neighborhood were the rough-and-tumble type who battled dragons with stick-swords and played endless games of football and rugby. Not him. He preferred independent play and reading.

But it was more than that. It was as if he were blocked, like a force field within him repelled the teachings of the Church and her practices. The blockage was especially acute when he was brought to the front to receive the Eucharist at Holy Mass. His body started vibrating, his face started sweating, his hands went cold. One Sunday morning, he ran from the railing at the high altar just as the priest administered the blessing, launching an inquisition that rivaled the Middle Ages.

Perhaps the blockage was nurtured by the German philosophers he had read as a teenager—Nietzsche, Kant, Hegel. Or the growing fascination with the ancient *völkisch* Ario-Germanic religion, folklore, and pagan mythology of his distant ancestors.

They also awakened within himself an evil spark his parents had tried unsuccessfully to exorcise. Literally. After his mother had stumbled upon him stabbing a screwdriver into a large rodent in their backyard, she and Dad took him to see Father Grunwald the next morning. When it happened again, this time after they had found a cat with its throat slit, they sought the help of an exorcist the priest had recommended.

To this day, Borg didn't remember much about the sacred ceremony, except something happened that startled the exorcist so badly that he stopped and sent him and his parents on their way. Something that he himself had done while restrained by his parents beneath the priest's brass cross. Something his parents had refused to talk about, other than claiming it was sheer evil.

Whatever the exorcist had done had worked. The impulses to maim and torture and kill had subsided. Until he met Jacob.

He thought about Jacob Crowley, his companion from the orphanage he was sent to when his parents had had enough of him. The one who awoke within him feelings both primal and pagan. The one who had introduced his heart to the meaning of true love. The one who had been killed in the Nous operation gone wrong earlier in the year thanks to their newest member of the Order of Thaddeus's SEPIO project.

Silas Grey.

Borg squeezed his hand into a fist, the tubing recoiling like a snake at the fresh supply of blood pushed through its rubber.

Jacob had seen within Borg's soul a small, burning ember waiting to be fanned into a passionate flame. Nascent embers of interest that would eventually grow when nurtured by the ancient Order of Nous, consuming him with a cause worthy of his entire life. Through that nurturing, he would rise within the ranks to Grand Master of the Council of Five and trigger the moment that had been welling up for countless generations, like magma silently flowing under the earth's crust, waiting to burst forth in fantastic, finalizing destruction.

The demise of the Church and destruction of the Christian faith.

He looked at the crimson liquid in the stoneware basin, considering what Nous was about to soon accomplish. Then he looked out of the window from the third story of the weather-worn castle of stone and iron that had served as the base of Heinrich Himmler's völk-mysticism and occult practices during the Third Reich, now serving as the headquarters for Nous. Catching a glimpse of the small spire of his childhood village church peeking out behind the swaying trees, a scowl of revulsion began to work its way across his mouth. He thought about all of those services as a child and that crucifix hanging behind the altar, and all that it represented for those pathetic, mousy masses.

Blood. Death. Crucifixion.

The Passion of the Christ.

His body reacted with a spasmic shudder to the thought of those pathetic, haunting eyes of that golden Christ-figure staring down at him from those wooden, Roman boards of execution. He hated that artifact of the Christian religion most of all. He thought of all the reasons why as the blood continued to flow.

Exhibit A, Jesus' words to his disciples: "If any want to become my followers, let them deny themselves and take up their cross and follow me. For those who want to save their life will lose it, and those who lose their life for my sake will find it."

No, Jesus. Death is death is death! You find your life in naming it and claiming it. In grabbing it by the neck and wrestling it to the ground. Not by denying it!

Exhibit B, the cross itself. Utterly foolish to imagine that a dead god could save. As far as Borg was concerned, in his book a dead so-called Messiah was a failed so-called Messiah. The cross was the sign of ultimate weakness under might and power.

And exhibit C, the Eucharist. The continued, tangible practice of eating Christ's body and drinking Christ's blood, as if that superstitious practice could do anything for anybody. No wonder the Romans accused the early Christians of cannibalism!

The memory of that pathetic event of Christ's blood-letting on the cross was everything that was wrong with that pathetic faith. It was not the shedding of blood from some God-Man that would save humanity, but the brute, blood-shedding efforts of the man-god rising to meet the demands of his own salvation that truly moved mountains.

A quote from the great German Friedrich Nietzsche sprang to his mind as he finished the bloodletting into the basin. He had read it as a teenager, and that's when it clicked for Borg that Christianity was nothing but a little kiddie's bedtime story whose believability had long passed.

He removed the tube from his arm, then squeezed the crimson liquid through the tube, taking care not to waste a drop of it. After he was satisfied, he had gotten it all, he licked his fingers and gently placed the tube back into its granite case for later use. He got up from his leather armchair and headed to a ceiling-to-floor bookcase at one end of his study. He searched its shelves for the book with the childhood memory.

There it was, Nietzsche's *Human, all too Human*. The smell of the old paper brought him back to the day he discovered the German prophet as a thirteen-year-old boy. His words were pornographic, filling him with a forbidden tingle that felt at once dirty and delightful.

He flipped through its pages until he found the passage he was looking for:

> When we hear the ancient bells growling on a Sunday morning, we ask ourselves: Is it really possible! This, for a jew, crucified two thousand years ago, who said he was God's son? The proof of such a claim is lacking. Certainly, the Christian religion is an antiquity projected into our times from remote prehistory; and the fact that the claim is believed—whereas one is otherwise so strict in examining pretensions—is perhaps the most ancient piece of this heritage. A god who begets children with a mortal woman; a sage who bids men work no more, have no more courts, but look for the signs of the impending end of the world; a justice that accepts the innocent as a vicarious sacrifice; someone who orders his disciples to drink his blood; prayers for miraculous interventions; sins perpetrated against a god, atoned for by a god; fear of a beyond to which death is the portal; the form of the cross as a symbol in a time that no longer knows the function and ignominy of the cross—how ghoulishly all this touches us, as if from the tomb of a primeval past! Can one believe that such things are still believed?

Indeed. *Can one believe that such things are still believed?*

Fear and shame. Weakness and gullibility. Loser. That was what the cross meant to Borg.

Speaking of which...

Borg's phone was dancing to the tune of an incoming call on his desk. He picked it up and scowled, then swiped it to life.

"I expected you to check in yesterday. The Council has been anxious to hear from you. What happened?"

"There was a...wrinkle."

"A wrinkle?"

"A wrinkle by the name of Thaddeus."

Borg tore the phone away from his face, gripping it tightly. He breathed deeply, then brought it back to his ear. "Don't tell me you failed, Farhad."

"We secured the first relic. But we ran into SEPIO operatives. Don't worry. We took care of it."

"Took care of it how?"

There was silence.

"Farhad?" Borg growled.

"We were being followed, so we disabled their vehicle and managed to capture one them, left the other one for dead. A Latina, by the looks of it."

Borg nearly exploded at the mishap. The last thing they needed at a time like this was to be distracted by a captive hostile, much less provoke the Order.

But then he wondered if she might be useful. Nous knew precious little about the Order and its inner workings. With the Council unfolding a number of carefully-laid plans in the coming months, perhaps Farhad could persuade her to divulge information helpful to their cause.

"She will not be an issue," Farhad said, his normally steely voice shaking slightly. "If you're concerned. We're still on track to claim the remaining four Passion relics."

"I'm not *that* concerned. Pryce is readying to claim the Ark and execute on his end of the mission. And you better deliver on yours. Those relics are vital to the Council's plan. We will not be disappointed."

Farhad said he understood, and Borg told him what he wanted him to do with the woman.

One way or another, she would serve Nous's interests.

CHAPTER 33

VERSAILLES.

S ilas and Celeste had spent the morning scouring the library for resources that would help them unravel the mystery of the Ark. Undoubtedly, there was something in those ancient tomes that would give some indication of its where-abouts—a rumor, a tradition, a legend passed through the ages that offered hints at its location.

They returned an hour later with an armful of books, including Wolfram von Eschenbach's *Parzival* and books with teachings by Bernard of Clairvaux, which had been mentioned in Pryce's journal. There hadn't been a copy of the *Kebra Nagast*, which Silas thought was a long shot anyway. But they had an ebook version.

As they settled in to continue their research, the twirling ring of an incoming call interrupted them. It was coming from a large monitor on the wall opposite the windows. On it was the face of Zoe wearing bright blue glasses and a headset. Below her picture were green and red buttons, labeled "Accept" and "Decline."

Silas walked over to the screen, then pressed the green button. The screen came to life.

"Hi, guys," Zoe said waving to Silas and Celeste from the Order's Washington, DC headquarters underneath the Washington National Cathedral. "How are you settling in? I've heard the facility is amaze-balls for research."

The two raised their eyebrows at each other. Amaze-balls?

Silas said, "It sure is...whatever you said it is. We've only just started our research. How has it been coming along on your end? Have you been able to look into the *Kebra Nagast* and its claims? Anything there that can help us unravel this mystery?"

Zoe frowned. "It was sort of a bust."

He frowned and looked at Celeste. She frowned, as well, and said, "What do you mean? Surely there has to be something to the legend?"

"Well, the people of Ethiopia certainly believe it's legit. No doubt about that. But most of the academic experts we've consulted say *Kebra Nagast* is a remarkable piece of sacred literature, but that it should be taken with a very large grain of salt."

Silas shook his head. "Why's that?"

"For one, there doesn't seem to be any justification for its audacious claim that the Queen of Sheba had been an Ethiopian. The historical record doesn't suggest she started her journey in ancient Abyssinia, which is now Ethiopia. Likewise, it's pretty unlikely the culture was advanced enough to have even had contact with Solomon and Israel. Then there's the existence of her son Menelik, which is made of pretty thin evidence. Historians consider the supposed founder of Ethiopia's 'Solomonic' dynasty to be a purely legendary figure."

"Well, that sucks." Silas sighed heavily and leaned back in his chair. "I thought we had something there with that book."

Celeste said, "So then *Kebra Nagast's* claims about Solomon, about the Queen of Sheba and their supposed son Menelik, none of it can literally be true, is that right?"

"From my research, that's right. It can't."

She looked at Silas, who looked frustrated. He looked out the window and put both hands behind his head. "What if the legend served more like some sort of complex metaphor for an underlying truth?"

"What do you mean?" Celeste asked.

He looked at her. "It seems, both from the biblical and historical record, that the Ark of the Covenant couldn't have gone to Ethiopia during the time of Solomon, as the legend claims. But it seems plausible that it could have been brought there several centuries later, either right before Solomon's temple was destroyed by the Babylonians or some other time before. Maybe the story was some sort of fictional structure built on a foundation of historical truth."

Silence fell at the thought of the possibility. Zoe responded, "I'd say it definitely seems plausible, if not totally possible. Certainly, the legend has been preserved for nearly eight hundred years. And we know that it's not under the Temple, which the majority of scholars claimed. So it has to be somewhere. Because a golden box with two angels stuck on top doesn't just disappear into thin air."

"Right," Celeste said, "Good point."

Silas sat up and turned back toward the table, leaning on it with his elbow. "But we're sure it's Ethiopia? And being guarded by Ethiopian Orthodox Christians? For what purpose? We've got one shot at this. The window of opportunity is closing, and we're short on manpower."

Celeste leaned forward. "Zoe, have you been able to track down the whereabouts of Lucas Pryce? His plane or his person?"

"Unfortunately, no. It's as if he vanished into thin air."

"I guess that means I need to continue following the research trail and see where it leads," he said.

"Thanks, Zoe. Silas and I will take it from here."

They disconnected the feed, then both leaned back in their chairs in silence for several minutes.

"Now what?" Silas finally asked, sounding dejected.

Celeste opened up one of the notebooks and wrote down

three words: *Chartres, Clairvaux, Eschenbach*. "Right. So we know Pryce was interested in these three ideas. The cathedral, the mystic, the book *Parzival*."

"Yeah, but why?"

"That's what we need to figure out. What connects them? And how do they relate to the Ark?"

Silas sat forward and grabbed his own notebook, then took out his phone. He remembered the inscription he had photographed beneath what appeared to be some sacred box on an oxcart, possibly the Ark of the Covenant. He wrote down the Latin letters etched in the stonework:

HIC AMITITUR ARCHA CEDERIS

He remembered his guidebook had rendered ARCHA CEDERIS as *"You are to work through the Ark"* and HIC AMITITUR ARCHA CEDERIS as *"Here things take their course; you are to work through the Ark."*

But was that right?

Celeste leaned in closer. "What's that?"

"The Latin letters under that oxcart in the sculpture at Chartres. That's the interpretation the guidebook gave, but I'm not sure..."

"Why not?"

"Because the Latin etchings seemed a bit corrupted. Look." He began writing alternatives to the etchings. "ARCHA definitely meant *ark* or *chest*. But I wonder if CEDERIS could be a corruption of FOEDERIS. *Covenant*. That would mean the etching ARCHA CEDERIS would obviously instead translate as *'Ark of the Covenant.'* Which I admit is a little too on-the-nose. Or maybe it was CEDERIS, a form of the verb CEDERE, which can be translated as *'to give up'* or *'to go away.'* The verb tense isn't exactly true to form, but could be translated *'the Ark that you will give up'* or *'the Ark that you will send away.'*"

"Interesting."

He set down his pen and nodded. "Definitely."

"What about the longer inscription?"

"That one's more challenging," Silas said, picking his pen back up. "The fourth letter of the second word is obscured. My guidebook had presumed it to be a single 'T.' Except I'm pretty sure there isn't a Latin word AMITITUR with a single 'T.' Maybe the etcher had shortened it to one T to fit it all in. If that was the case, then the phrase would read something like *'Here it is let go, the Ark that you will yield.'* You could also translate it as *'Here it is let go, Oh Ark, you are yielded.'* If CEDERIS was a corruption of FOEDERIS, then it would be *'Here it is let go, the Ark of the Covenant.'* Then again, the fourth letter of the second word looks sort of like a 'C.' If so, then the phrase becomes *'Here is hidden the Ark of the Covenant,'* or *'Here is hidden the Ark that you will give up'* or *'send away.'*"

Silas set down his pen with a satisfied *plunk*, then folded his arms and leaned back in his chair, pleased he still had some Latin chops left.

"Cracking good work," Celeste said with surprise. "And with the way that the cart seemed to be leaving Melchizedek and heading toward Sheba, then perhaps the North Porch of the Chartres was some sort of a cryptic map to one of the greatest spiritual relics ever. That the Ark really had been given up or sent away from Jerusalem on to Ethiopia!"

Silas's head was spinning with the possibility, being carried away by Celeste's enthusiasm. "I mean, it seems so, despite what Zoe found. But then again, the Bible is silent on its location, suggesting it was hidden."

They went silent, both contemplating the significance of what the North Porch might be telling them.

Celeste leaned forward toward her notebook and circled Clairvaux and Eschenbach. "We've still got two more leads to check out."

Silas picked up Wolfram von Eschenbach's *Parzival* and tossed it to her.

"Since you're such a speed-demon reader, why don't you tackle von Eschenbach? I'll go back to the terminal and poke around."

She picked up the book and fanned its pages. "Challenge met."

For the next hour, they worked independently: Celeste underlining and dog-earring the pages of von Eschenbach's book on the Grail; Silas reading some of the articles he found, but not making any headway beyond what they already had figured out.

"Let's try something different," he mumbled. He typed into the search bar *Bernard of Clairvaux and Ark of the Covenant*, then hit enter. Several articles returned.

He clicked on one of them: *"Sir Thomas Malory, Bernard of Clairvaux, and the Quest for the Holy Grail."*

Of course, Sir Thomas Malory was the greatest English writer of Arthurian Romances, the culmination of those tales was *Le Morte D'Arthur*. The article was a scholarly examination of Malory's treatment of the sacred object as a 'vessel of gold,' which he claimed had been an idealized Christianized account of the true quest for spirituality. A process that had been undertaken by the Cistercian monastic order, and under the influence of Clairvaux. Apparently, other such writings had followed a pattern from generations of Christians who had associated the vessel of Christ, especially of his blood, with one person.

The Blessed Virgin Mary.

"*Mary Theotokos...*" Silas whispered.

"What's that?" Celeste said, looking up from her book.

"Huh?" He whipped his head toward Celeste confused after being lost in his research.

"I thought you said something." She set down *Parzival* and yawned, then rubbed her eyes.

"I just said Mary Theotokos, based on something I was reading in this journal article."

She cocked her head slightly. "Theotokos...God-bearer."

He smiled, appreciating her theological knowledge. "Good one. Yes, God-bearer. The sacred vessel as the one who contained the God-made-flesh Son of God. And get this, the article I'm reading says Clairvaux had explicitly compared Mary to the Ark of the Covenant in numerous writings and sermons. Listen to this:

Clairvaux, like other influential church fathers before him, had allegorized the significance of Mary: As the Ark of the Hebrew people of God contained hidden within its vessel the form of the Old Covenant, written on tablets of stone, so too had Mary carried, hidden within herself, the form of the New Covenant, personified in the person of Jesus, his very blood shed, his body broken in sacrificial death.

Silas said, "The article goes on to suggest this perspective had been woven into subsequent generations of Christians. For instance, it points to a Dominican church in Israel dedicated *A la Vièrge Marie Arche d'alliance.* 'To the Virgin Mary Ark of the Covenant.' One of the senior church officials, a Sister Raphaela Mikhail, was quoted saying: 'We compare Mary to a living Ark. Mary was the mother of Jesus, who was the master of the Law and of the Covenant. The tablets of stone with the Ten Commandments of the Law were placed inside the Ark by Moses; so also God placed Jesus in the womb of Mary. So she is the living Ark.'"

"So Mary was a living Ark and a living Grail!" Celeste exclaimed.

"That's the suggestion. Clairvaux's even."

Suddenly, Silas remembered something. He shuffled over to the table and grabbed his phone. He sat down next to Celeste and swiped it to life, opened his photo app, then started scrolling.

"There it is." He showed Celeste the picture on his phone from Chartres.

"What does that look like to you?"

She studied the statue holding something in his hands. "An orb. Or maybe..."

"A cup? A chalice?"

"The Grail!"

"That's what many experts believe. And some say inside is a stone."

Celeste's eyes widened. "A stone?"

He cocked his head slightly, noticing the change. "Yes...why?"

She stood and opened her copy of *Parzival*, furiously searching its pages. After several seconds, she found what she was searching for. She handed the book to Silas and pointed with a satisfied smile splayed across her face.

"There. Read that."

He took and read a section she had underlined:

However ill a mortal man may be, from the day on which he sees the Stone he cannot die for that week, nor does he lose his color. For if anyone, maid or man, were to look at the Gral for two hundred years, you would have to admit that his color was as fresh as in his early prime ... Such powers does the Stone confer on mortal men that their flesh and bones are soon made young again. This Stone is called 'The Gral.'

Silas's mouth went dry. *The Stone is called The Gral.*

He stood up and said slowly, "Didn't Radcliffe say every Ethiopian Orthodox church has a replica of the Ark? What did he call it?"

"A, umm, *tabot*, I believe."

"Yes," he said snapping his fingers. "A *tabot*. And didn't he say that these relic replicas are made of—"

"Stone!" she exclaimed standing to face Silas. "My God. And think of the references in the Bible to Jesus Christ as a stone!"

"Exactly. The Messianic prophecy in Isaiah comes to mind: 'He will become a sanctuary, a stone one strikes against; for both houses of Israel he will become a rock one stumbles over—a trap and a snare for the inhabitants of Jerusalem.'"

Celeste added, "And then Jesus himself quoted the Hebrew poem, Psalm 118: 'The stone that the builders rejected has become the chief cornerstone. This is the Lord's doing; it is marvelous in our eyes.' He was anticipating his rejection by Israel and his vindication through the resurrection as the cornerstone of a new covenant. One that would transcend and replace the old covenant."

"Which the Ark contained and even bore witness to!" Silas could feel the momentum of the research steaming forward, each discovery building on top of the other one. He lived for these kinds of revelatory experiences. He was drunk on discovery—and thrilled to be imbibing with the woman now standing face-to-face with him.

He continued, "And then the early disciples used this exact language to describe Jesus. In fact, Peter quoted this exact language when he confronted the Jewish religious leaders in the Sanhedrin. Jesus is 'the stone that was rejected by you, the builders; it has become the cornerstone. There is salvation in no one else, for there is no other name under Heaven given among mortals by which we must be saved.'"

Celeste added, "And then the apostle Paul quoted the Jewish prophecy concerning the new covenant in Isaiah to rebuke their unbelief: 'See, I am laying in Zion a stone that will make people stumble, a rock that will make them fall, and whoever believes in him will not be put to shame.'"

"So did Peter," she reminded him, "but for different reasons, saying that for those who believe in Jesus, he is a cornerstone. But those who don't, he is a *stumbling stone.*"

"And don't forget he called Jesus a *Living* Stone!"

Celeste grabbed both of Silas's arm in excitement. "That's right!"

Time froze, the atmosphere was taut with the excitement of their mutual discovery and shared revelations. The magnetism of the moment was compelling an attraction. For a few beats neither of them moved.

"Oh my," Celeste finally said, breathing deeply before letting go. She smiled embarrassingly and made a face. "Sorry. I don't know what came over me."

She backed away, then sat down, pushing her bangs behind her ears and trying to shield her reddening face.

He smiled and sat down, as well, then brushed his hand over his close-cropped hair and simply leaned back, not knowing what to say.

"We're so close," he finally said. "I can feel it."

She smiled and nodded.

He checked his watch, then yawned. He stood up and stretched his back, then went to the carafe to pour himself a cup of black brew, but only a few drops came out.

"Be right back," he said walking toward the door with the empty carafe. "Going to go find our helpful librarian to see if I can get some more research fuel."

"Good luck."

When he left the room, he breathed deeply, then sighed. His heart was pounding. Until that moment he hadn't realized how attracted he was to Celeste. But there was clearly magic percolating between them in that room. A woman with a big brain was his kryptonite; his willpower had clearly been depleted.

Hold steady, Grey!

Fifteen minutes later he returned, hesitating to open the door. He smiled to himself at the junior-high antics, then plunged back inside. "Brought you back a carafe of hot water. Figured you might need a refill, too. Though I'm not sure if that British stuff qualifies."

She giggled, then walked over to pour herself a fresh cup of tea and sat back down with her e-reader.

He poured himself a cup of coffee, then walked back over to the workstation and logged onto the search engine and looked over the results, searching for the missing link to make it all fall into place. One entry caught his attention.

"Islamic Tradition and the Ark of the Covenant."

There was a tradition of the Ark within *Islam*? Silas hadn't known of any connection between the fabled Hebrew relic and the Muslim religion. He clicked the link.

"Article has been removed at the request of the publisher."

He furrowed his brow. *Are you kidding me?* He went back to the results, then clicked the link again, this time harder and longer, thinking that maybe it would respond to the strength of force.

Nothing. Same weird message.

However, an abstract was listed, as well as the authors' names:

ABSTRACT: While the Hebrew Scriptures offer a detailed, historical chronology of the Ark of the Covenant, its formation and cultic use, as well as its place and history within Islam remains mostly unknown. However, there does exist a deep Islamic tradition surrounding the Ark, one that both transcends and intersects the Hebrew accounts. It also plays a vital role in Muslim eschatology, for it is a harbinger of the al-Mahdi, the prophesied eschatological, End Times redeemer of Islam.

AUTHORS: Emile de Saulcy, University of Paris; L. James Pryce, Harvard University.

"Holy cow..." he whispered.

Celeste looked up from her e-reader and over to Silas. "Find something interesting?"

"You could say that."

He turned to her, eyes wide and a drunken grin playing across his face.

She set her tablet down on the table, then shook her head "What did you find?"

"The mother lode."

She walked over to the screen to take a look herself.

"Bloody hell..." she said. "L. James Pryce. Any chance there's a connection to Lucas Pryce? Perhaps he used his middle name as a sort of pseudonym?"

"I'd bet my bottom dollar he did. But what's crazy is that the article is missing."

"Missing?" she said turning back toward the screen.

"Something about the article being withdrawn at the publisher's request."

"That seems unusual."

Silas nodded. "But we do have another name, and a location just north of here. A professor Saulcy, at the University of Paris. Care for a little mid-afternoon jaunt to the City of Lights?"

She smiled. "Don't mind if I do."

CHAPTER 34

ROME.

Marwan Farhad carefully smoothed his mustache as he leaned over the table in the dark warehouse. Darkened windows high above the expansive space gave them the privacy they needed. But combined with the gathering storm clouds outside, it didn't make for a helpful planning environment.

He adjusted one of the halogen lamps on the dual-head, tripod work lamp to give himself more light as he went over the floor plan one more time in preparation for tomorrow's mission. He traced the route to the room holding the sacred objects, plotting all the possible outcomes, making contingencies. Tulu had assured him the basilica would be empty, lying barren until the next day for the morning Mass. He hoped that the man was correct in his information, but he was ready for anything.

He moved the map to the side, making room for images of the four objects they were tasked with retrieving, encased in elaborate gold and silver reliquaries: part of a panel said to have been nailed to Christ's cross, bearing his designation as King of the Jews; two thorns taken from the crown placed on Christ's head by the Roman soldiers; one of the nails hammered into either Christ's wrists or feet, holding him to the cross; and three small wooden fragments of the True Cross, the object upon which the Christian Savior hung, bled, died.

As a member of the Thirteen, the Council of Five had tasked him with retrieving five of the holy Passion relics for Nous. They had wanted to time their theft and later destruction to coincide with the revelation of the Ark, in order to permanently destroy the tangible objects preserving the memory of Jesus' death, while sowing spiritual confusion and chaos with the Ark's unveiling.

A member of his team brought him a cup of steaming chai tea thickened with milk. Farhad smiled curtly and took it. Then he stood back from the table and took a sip, his eyes transfixed on those relics, his mind's eye transfixed on the memory they represented.

Atonement. Redemption. Salvation.

From the very first upright steps that Homo Sapiens took upon the earth, salvation from death and the bliss of an afterlife paradise has been the longing of the collective consciousness. The mystery has always been the *how*. How can one experience such salvation? Especially once humans started behaving badly, amassing a pile of sins stretching into the heavens—while reaping untold consequences.

Genocide, rape, murder, wars of attrition, environmental destruction, slavery, child abuse. And those were just the systemic sins perpetuated from generation to generation. Farhad himself had experienced such systemic injustice in Iran, as the Islamic republic had persecuted his people for years. Then there were the personal sins of the heart: adultery, thievery, cheating, lying, gossip, rage, malice, pride, envy, jealousy, and on and on. Every one of them he himself had committed in one way or another.

Farhad knew what everyone else knew deep down in their most honest moments: we're both brilliant and bad. Brilliant, because we're capable of achieving great good and offering greater love. Yet rotten to the core, because of all the bad we're capable of achieving. And, when we're also honest with ourselves, we feel guilt and shame for sins great and small, carrying with such deep, inner feelings the sneaking suspicion that such acts have harmed not only individual people, but the Universe itself. Something or Someone high above that has set the pace for how one should act in the first place.

Farhad took another sip of tea, letting its warm, spicy heaviness sit in his mouth and stimulate his taste buds. But the question he pondered as he swallowed the liquid, continuing to stare at the photos, the one that has haunted every person from the Stone Age to the Digital Age has been how such a pile of rotten trash can be swept away. How can the gods, or *the* God, or the Universe or whatever be appeased?

He knew the history of atoning for such sins. It started small, with people and families and tribes offering grain or fruit, then precious metals or stones. But was that enough? Were the gods/God/Universe pleased? Was all that communal and individual badness atoned for, somehow made right?

Did the offerings *work*?

Since no one could be sure, such offerings morphed into blood sacrifices, starting small with birds before escalating to lambs and goats and bulls.

But again, was *that* enough? Were the gods/God/Universe satisfied?

Did *those* sacrifices work?

Such questions continued to hang over humanity, leading to an escalation of even greater sacrifices until the ultimate ones, whether from battle or communal games or slavery.

People. Adults who were unfortunate enough to lose wars.

And then the greatest of all: children who were unfortunate enough to be born.

Yet the shedding of human blood never laid to rest those pesky ultimate questions that kept people up at night. Which is why the Christians had devised the greatest scheme ever.

God himself would die.

Farhad took another sip of tea, the warmth having escaped into the coolness of the warehouse. A smile escaped his mouth as he continued contemplating the significance of those relic photos. The relics that contained the innovation of the Christian claim that in Jesus Christ, God had paid the price for all of those sins in place of humanity, doing what they had tried for 10,000 years to accomplish on their own, but were never really sure they had achieved what they knew deep down they needed.

Atonement for sins, leading to forgiveness of sins, leading to salvation from divine judgment, ending in blissful eternal life.

A noise caught his attention. It was far back in the shadows. He saw it slink away, trying not to be seen.

That's right. The SEPIO prisoner. He'd almost forgotten about her, and Borg's insistence on interrogation. Now was as good as time as any. Besides, there was a strong chance she had seen or overheard something that could derail his carefully laid plans.

He walked over to a bench and grabbed something. He caught the attention of one of his associates, then motioned over to the woman.

Time to appease the gods once again.

TORRES HAD BEEN WORKING on her bindings, trying to slide her wrist out of the chain. She had been carefully working at them since she awoke early in the morning, keeping the door and promise of escape as her motivation.

But it wasn't working.

In frustration she whipped the chain tethered to her arms against the concrete, filling her corner of the warehouse with a deafening clang.

Did they notice?

The man with the mustache had looked her way, then turned around.

She sighed heavily. Great. Attention was definitely not what she—

Wait. The man was walking toward her with one of the other goons. She breathed in quickly. Her heart started firing on all cylinders.

Was there something in his hand?

It was too dark to make it out as they strode across the empty space, the soles of their feet echoing with purpose.

She instinctively backed up against the wall, seeking comfort and protection among the shadows. She strained against her bindings again, trying to loosen them. It was of no use. The men were almost there.

And holding some sort of weapon.

Her breathing quickened. The dark room felt like it was swirling in a muddy palette of grays and browns, blacks and blues.

This was not what she had signed up for.

The non-mustached man was built like one of the Latin Kings she'd seen prowling around her neighborhood growing up. Thick neck, thicker arms, and an even thicker head that was useful for one thing: inflicting pain.

He suddenly grabbed her by the shoulders and pushed her against the wall, raising her as high as her bindings straining against the floor beneath would allow.

"We haven't been formally introduced," the man with the mustache said, his voice pleasant and welcoming, friendly even, and smelling faintly of spices. "My name is Marwan Farhad. This here is Hamid. That's it. Just Hamid. There is nothing else you need to know about him. I, however, am someone you do need to know about."

She was standing on her toes, her jaw held firm by forearms of steel, head digging into the concrete wall. She could feel herself shaking. Rivulets of sweat were beginning to mat her long, dark hair to her forehead, winding down her face and neck.

"I am part of a multi-national organization your Order has grown to know as Nous. I am a member of the Thirteen, and next in line for the Council of Five. You know of such a hierarchy?"

She didn't understand why he was telling her this, but she nodded quickly.

He smiled widely, the pleasant smell of spices returning. "Good. Then you also know that such members have a...how do you say? A ruthless tenacity, yes that is how you say it. A ruthless tenacity when it comes to slowly suffocating your pathetic religion, draining the life out of it until it snuffs itself out like a candle wick."

Where was this conversation going?

He stepped toward her, raising his right arm slightly. Her eyes went wide as she caught sight of the weapon. Which was actually a drill.

Light from somewhere up above glinted off the wide head of the long bit sticking out of the drill's mouth, the kind used to carve wide-diameter holes in two-by-fours.

Her breathing quickened through her nostrils. She thought she was going to pass out.

"Let her rest on her feet," he said sympathetically.

Hamid let her down gently. She felt weak and tried slumping against the wall, but the steel arm held her firm.

Farhad stepped close to her so that she could feel his warm breath against her cool face. Now it smelled like stale tea leaves, the original, pleasant spiciness turning acrid. She thought she was going to wretch. She wished she would, all over that smug Persian man's face.

"We have set into motion plans that I have been waiting to reap fruit from for several years. There is no room for error. And I will not allow an operative of the Order of Thaddeus to meddle."

He brought the drill up to her face. She flinched, closing her eyes.

"You will tell me what I want to know."

"I don't know anything!" She said in a panic, her face scrunching up in fear. "I...I...I'm green. Brand new to the unit. I'm a nobody. There's nothing I can tell you!"

He started the drill, it's electric whine ricocheting off the walls. With a sudden, forceful motion he gritted his teeth and thrust it into the wall behind her.

She screamed, high and long, then short puffs of guttural responses. Her body started convulsing under the weight of the impending agony.

Chunks of concrete and dust flew into her hair and eyebrows, up her nose, and down to the floor.

As the sound of the drill wound down, another sound replaced its whine.

An explosion. Back from where Farhad and Hamid had emerged. Then gunfire, in rapid succession.

At once Farhad turned around. Hamid craned his neck, not knowing whether to hold on or let go.

When one of their associates dropped after more gunfire, he let go.

Torres slid to the ground, then scurried to make herself small against the wall, not understanding what was happening and wanting to get out of the range of a firefight.

The large man quickly withdrew a large weapon from his side and sent four rounds toward the gunfire, all of them going high and wide.

Farhad said something to him in Arabic, then put his hands over his head and crouched when more gunfire erupted. Six rapid rounds toward the other remaining Nous operative, sounding like they came from two separate people.

Torres could see that the main entrance had been blown open. The smoke had cleared, and two figures were near it, crouched behind a massive concrete column. One of the men was black and built like a tank. The other man was equally tall, but built more like an oversized elephant.

Gapinski!

Her heart leaped. Help had arrived.

They were driven back behind the column out of sight by more gunfire, from Hamid. Farhad joined in, laying down covering fire for their trapped comrade. The man ran for their location, spats of return fire coming from Gapinski and his backup, but not doing any damage. She hoped they would stop firing before they landed some metal her way.

Farhad and Hamid were successful. The man arrived unscathed. Farhad ran to an exit near her, then inserted a key.

Finding a window, the SEPIO operatives returned fire, all of it directed toward the door. The concrete exploded in little puffs of acquiescence.

Hamid and the other man drew close to their boss, crouching on their knees while he worked the lock. They offered a forceful response—until both guns clicked empty.

Torres sat up in hope, wondering how the next few seconds would play out. She could see one of the SEPIO agents advance forward, using the tables Farhad had been hovering over earlier for cover. Then Gapinski moved in behind him, sliding behind the granite pillar.

Was he using Jesus' scourging post as cover? What was the big beluga thinking?

Farhad clicked the lock open, then pushed through the door. Hamid and the other man had reloaded and offered a storm of metal coverage, their rounds splintering the wooden tables and pinging off the granite hiding place Gapinski had commandeered.

Within seconds her captors were out the door and into freedom. She sighed heavily and spread out on the concrete floor in exhaustion.

The air was thick with gunpowder and tension. It settled within seconds, and the two SEPIO men slowly emerged from their places of cover.

"Torres? You alive?"

She smiled. It was indeed Gapinski.

"Yeah, you big lug. I'm alive. Now would you help a sister out?"

The two men rushed over to her.

"Thank the good Lord," the one man said, helping her up. Gapinski's companion made quick work of her bindings and released her chain with a pair of bolt cutters he had found in a tool chest.

She massaged her wrists, then tried to stand before faltering.

"Whoa there. Take a load off. Greer, give me some of that water."

The large man gave him a canteen. He twisted off the lid, then lowered it for Torres. She took several sips, the cool water doing quick work to revive her.

"Thanks. That feels good." She took several breaths, then outstretched her hand and nodded for Gapinski to help her up.

He reached for her and pulled her to her feet.

Torres ran her hands over her head and face, dusting off the bits of concrete from Farhad's drilling. Then she dusted off her clothes and stretched her back.

She was free.

"You came for me."

Gapinski scoffed. "Of course we did. Never leave a man behind. Or woman, in your case. That's, like, basic."

"But how? I thought you were dead after the crash."

"What? Me? Takes more than a broadside to a crappy rental to take me out."

She laughed quietly to herself, thankful to be reunited with her partner, as annoying as he could sometimes be. She started toward the other end of the warehouse, eager to check on the status of the scourging post and whatever intel might have been left behind. She faltered, but Gapinski steadied her. She smiled, then continued.

"So you recover, then what? Because this place doesn't seem all that easy to find."

"Not at all. In fact, we would have been here sooner had Greer not passed it, what…" he glanced behind to his partner, "Like three, four times?"

"It was twice, Gapinski," the man corrected with a deep, baritone voice. "But your eagle eyes weren't much help neither."

Gapinski frowned, mumbling, "Whatever. Anyway, so after some little old lady revived me, and then fire and rescue hauled my ass out of that van, obviously, I called Radcliffe about what happened. Zoe got on the line and immediately started canvassing the area with her digital doodads. Took a while, but she was able to piece together a string of CCTV and satellite images to your location."

Torres kept walking, taking the steps slowly, marveling at the sophistication of the organization she had joined. She was also thankful for the dedication they had to their people, something she hadn't experienced in her last gig.

"Well, tell her thanks for me. And thanks to you, too. I owe you both."

"Naw, it's not like that. You would have done the same for me."

She looked at him and smiled slightly. She wasn't so sure she would have. Something she vowed to change.

They reached the other side of the warehouse. It was a disaster zone. Bits of concrete and paper and shards of wood were scattered about the floor. Torres shuffled over to the ancient relic. It had been clearly damaged from the gunfight, but was mostly fine. Probably deserved the beating considering the beating that had been dolled out on its granite surface two thousand years ago.

"Check this out," Greer said, hunched over the floor.

Torres and Gapinski joined him.

"What is it? A map?"

"Basilica di Santa Croce in Gerusalemme," she said.

They both turned to her, brows raised.

"The Basilica of the Holy Cross in Jerusalem. This ain't over, gentlemen."

"Sonofa—"

"Gapinski..." Greer interrupted standing up. "Not in front of the lady. Now, what do you mean this ain't over?"

She nodded back toward where she had been kept chained up. "Heard them planning their next moves from my prison at the other end. At least the name of the basilica. But I know what they're up to."

"Yeah? And what's that?"

"That short, granite pillar over there was only a trial run for a bigger operation. They're planning to steal four other Passion relics. Jesus' crown of thorns, a nail that held him to the cross, the sign hanging above him describing him as the King of the Jews, and a piece of the cross itself."

Gapinski sighed. "Always something. And when is this little pow-wow supposed to go down?"

"Sometime tonight into tomorrow morning, before the basilica opens for morning Mass."

Greer started gathering the papers lying on the floor. "Let's bring this back to the Order's Rome headquarters and touch base with Radcliffe. He's gonna wanna weigh in on our next moves."

"Which probably means another ass-kicking in some old, musty church," Gapinski complained.

Greer nodded toward Torres. "At least we've got one more on our side this time. She looks like she can handle herself."

Torres smiled slightly and could feel herself blushing as she gathered the images of the relics Farhad had been looking at earlier, feeling a sense of purpose that was different from the important cultural and historical work from her previous life.

She was beginning to think that stopping Nous and protecting the memory of Christ's sacrifice wasn't such a bad gig.

CHAPTER 35

"Hi, there," Silas said to the short, pudgy woman with gray hair swept into a bun that meant business. "We're looking for Professor Emile de Saulcy. Can you direct us to his office?"

She peered over a set of narrow lipstick-red glasses resting on the bridge of her nose, one eye twitching with suspicion between him and Celeste. "And *why* do you need to see the professor?"

"Is he here, in his office?" he replied, side-stepping her question. "I understood this to be his office hours."

The twitch was growing faster with skepticism. "He is. But what is the nature of your visit?"

"Forgive me, madam." Silas chuckled, playing the part of the absentminded professor. "My name is Silas Grey, professor of religious studies and Christian history from Princeton University."

"Princeton? From America?"

He smiled, glancing at Celeste. "That's the one. You see, I'm working on an urgent...academic matter, really an archaeological matter that I believe the good professor could help me with. I also believe it is in his own best interest."

"Really? In what way?"

Silas held his grin. She was far too nosy for her own good.

"It's a private matter, but concerns the professor's own academic and archaeological interests. So if you wouldn't mind directing my colleague and me to his office, we would be much appreciative."

Her face sagged, having been denied some juicy, institutional gossip. But she rose from her chair without a word and waddled toward a doorway. "Follow me."

Silas and Celeste glanced at each other, then followed the woman to the end of a long hallway. She stopped at a door and held up her hand, instructing them to wait at a distance from the entrance while she announced them to the professor. After a few minutes, she returned. "He's meeting with a student, but will see you when he is finished."

Silas smiled. "Thank you, madam. We appreciate your help."

She smiled curtly, then waddled back to her desk. In a few minutes, a young man emerged clutching a paper and a scowl. Apparently, his appeal hadn't gone very well.

Good for you, Professor.

He loathed open hours when students would barge into his quiet space and demand a passing grade or an adjustment of a half letter-grade, simply because they tried their best or spent all night studying or they weren't feeling well the day of the test or whatever other reason they gave. The worst was when parents came riding in on their helicopters to save the day. While he generally could keep his cool with students, it was those conversations with parents that he prayed for an extra ounce of the good Lord's mercy and patience.

"Professor Grey," said the squat man in an ill-fitting suit coat with saggy jowls and shaggy, gray hair. He rose from his chair and extended his hand. "Pleasure meeting you. Your reputation precedes you."

Silas gripped Saulcy's hand. "That's very kind of you to say. I hadn't known my work made its way across the pond."

Saulcy smiled. "When you're in our line of work, the pond separating us is more like a puddle. Sit, sit. And who might this be?"

"Forgive me," he said motioning to Celeste. "This is my... research assistant. Celeste Bourne."

She smiled wryly at Silas, then extended her hand. "A pleasure, Professor."

"The pleasure is all mine." He held her hand a beat too long before Celeste gently withdrew her arm.

"So, Professor Grey, my executive assistant mentioned some sort of academic and archaeological crisis you needed me to help come to the rescue and solve?"

He laughed. "My goodness, she has quite the imagination. I'm not sure I put it in those terms. There's certainly no *crisis*. But it does concern a bit of research I've been undertaking. Concerning the Ark of the Covenant."

The man's caterpillar eyebrows wiggled with recognition, then rested again. "Oh, really? And what's the nature of this...bit of research?"

Silas and Celeste both shifted in their seats, glancing at one another. Silas said, "I'm not sure if you've been following the events in Israel, at the Western Wall with Lucas Pryce."

"Yes, yes. Most unfortunate. I had hoped Pryce could have pulled off the greatest archaeological coup the world had ever seen, especially after he found proof of the Ark's existence in the first place at Tell-es Sultan."

After he found proof of the Ark's existence at Tell-es Sultan?

Heat began rising up Silas's neck. So was his blood pressure. Celeste gently touched his leg, as if understanding the annoyance at having to relive the professional slight.

"I believe you were there, weren't you? Pryce mentioned a bright up-and-comer assisting him way back when who found himself teaching at rival Princeton."

Silas smiled weakly at the man. "Yes. I was...assisting, as you say. Anyway, as you know, the Ark and other Temple treasures were not in the chamber beneath the Temple Mount after all. But, given my experience at Tell-es Sultan, I myself have been fascinated with finding the Ark and have been working on a sort of side project, trying to discern the possible location of the fabled, lost relic. That's when I came across an article you co-authored with our good friend Lucas Pryce. Or L. James Pryce, as he pseudonymously wrote under."

"Ahh, yes. *'Islamic Tradition and the Ark of the Covenant.'* That was quite the eye-opening endeavor."

Silas shifted in his seat. "Well, that's what we hoped you could help us with. Because during our research, while we located the article, we couldn't view it anywhere. It seems to have gone missing."

Saulcy smiled curtly. "That's because Pryce wanted the article pulled several years ago."

Silas glanced at Celeste, furrowing his brow. She said, "Why was that? Seemed like an important contribution to scholarship to simply pull it and stuff it in a sack."

"It was. And I was furious at the suggestion. But..." Saulcy folded his hands on his desk and stared down at them. "Pryce can be persuasive."

Silas noted that seemed to be a few years after he had made his discovery of the Ark scrolls. Was Pryce trying to hide any evidence connected to the Ark even back then? Burying any trace of its possible locations?

"Alright, so what did your article say?" Silas asked.

Saulcy turned toward a bookshelf behind his desk, then ran his fingers along a series of journals. "Ahh, here it is." He pulled one out and handed it to Silas. "Read for yourself."

Silas flipped to the article and started reading the abstract.

"Can you give us the bird's-eye view, professor?" Celeste asked as Silas read.

"Certainly, madam," he said winking. "In Islamic theology, the

Ark of the Covenant is the name of a treasure chest given by Allah himself from Heaven and used as a weapon of war by the Prophets. This included Moses, Aaron, David, Solomon. And many Islamic scholars also believe by their holy prophet Muhammad.

Saulcy leaned back heavily in his chair, resting his hands on his belly, then continued. "For Muslims, the Ark is a sign given to them by their prophet. As the Qur'an says in al-Baquarah, 'And their prophet said to them, Truly the sign of his sovereignty shall be that the Tabut come to you bearing tranquility from your Lord and a remnant left by the House of Moses and the House of Aaron, borne by the angels. Truly in that is a sign for you, if you are believers.'"

"Excuse me," Silas interrupted, "did you say *Tabut*?"

"Yes. It's Arabic for 'Ark.'"

He nodded with recognition, noting how similar their word for Ark was to the Ethiopian *tabot*, the supposed replicas of the Ark used in Ethiopian churches. "Sorry for interrupting, professor. Continue."

"One Islamic commentary explains that this Ark contained the Covenant, the Sakina, of the Islamic people. This covenant assured divine help and victory over the infidels with the prophetic relics contained in the Ark. These relics were connected to the rulership of God on earth as channeled by his prophets and messengers. And as such, the Sakina assured unfathomable and unrivaled powers to whoever possessed the Ark."

Sounded a lot like what the Nazi's had sought in George Lucas's hit flick. He could understand why Pryce would want such an object. And Nous for that matter.

"According to Islamic lore," Saulcy continued, "the Ark of the Covenant was actually from the era of Adam, not from the time of the wilderness experience post-exodus as it is according to the Judeo-Christian understanding. It was brought from Heaven down to earth. With the Ark, Adam was empowered as the Viceroy of Allah, and it contained the Black Stone in Mecca's Grand Mosque known as the Hajar al Aswad, the Staff of Moses, the Ring of Solomon, and the Sword of Prophet Muhammad called Zulfiqar, among other relics. The Ark was passed from Adam to Seth, and then to Thoth where it was moved to Egypt."

"Thoth? As in the Egyptian and Greek god?" Silas asked.

"Yes. Hermes Trismegistus, to be more exact, is a representation of the syncretic combination of the Greek god Hermes and the Egyptian god Thoth that's also important to Islamic tradition as Arab genealogists believe Muhammad to be a direct descendant of Hermes Trismegistus. But this is a digression."

"Sorry. Proceed."

"It is said that the Ark continued to be guarded by Adamite prophets who ruled in Egypt until the marriage of Hagar to Abraham and the birth of Ishmael, who is said to have inherited the Ark from his mother under the supervision of his father. The children of Ishmael, the Arabs, continued to possess the Ark, and it was moved to Al Khazneh in Petra, the treasury of the Pharaoh. According to this tradition, the Ark was eventually inherited by the Prophet Shuaib, whose daughter Safura married Moses. He was eventually given guardianship of the Ark of the Covenant and blessed to go free the children of Israel. Through the blessings of the Ark, they were freed, and Pharaoh was destroyed."

Silas asked, "So that's how the Israelites came to be in possession of the Ark, according to Islamic tradition?"

"Exactly. The Ark stayed with Israel, and in it they placed the relics of Moses and Aaron, the ones the Hebrew Scriptures describe. Then, when the children of Israel rebelled against Moses, the Ark was taken from them and hidden during the era of the Babylonian King Nebuchadnezzar. Eventually, they got the Ark back when Saul retrieved it. The Qur'an states that David inherited the Ark and the kingdom from Saul when he killed Goliath. Then Solomon inherited the Ark of the Covenant from

David and thereby became king. He rebuilt the Baitul Maqdis in Jerusalem, also known as the al-Aqsa mosque. King Solomon married Queen Sheba, and from her had a son, Menelik I. He gave the Ark's guardianship to his son, who carried it to Ethiopia after the death of Solomon, which was kept in secret for centuries."

Silas and Celeste looked at each other. This closely followed the legend of *Kebra Nagast*. Another connection with the Queen of Sheba and Ethiopia. More confirmation that it was likely the hidden location. Had to be.

Celeste asked, "So does Islamic tradition still hold that the Ark is in Ethiopia?"

Saulcy shrugged. "At this point, the tradition is unclear, as the location has remained a secret sworn to the Twelve Imams, and known only by the Mahdi."

"Islam's End Times savior," Silas said.

"Yes, the prophesied redeemer of Islam who will rule for a various number of years, depending on the interpretation, before the Day of Judgment and will rid the world of evil. According to the Sunni hadith, there will be a return to a governance system along the pattern of spiritual and secular monarchial governance mentioned in the Qur'an. Al Mahdi is said to be from the blood-line of the prophet Muhammad and from the descendants of Abraham and Ishmael. He will rule as a king over the Ishmaelites with the Ark in his possession."

"The Ark is important, then, to this End Times savior?"

"It is everything to the fulfillment of those eschatological prophecies." Saulcy retrieved the journal from Silas, who had closed it as he listened. He searched for a page, then began reading:

In one Hadith, the reports and traditions of Mohammed's teachings given after his death, the importance of the Ark and the Mahdi are clear: "The reason he will be known as the Mahdi is that he will show the way to a hidden thing. He will bring the Ark to light from a place called Antioch."

Similarly, Sulaiman ibn Isa states: "I was informed that the Ark of the Covenant will emerge from the Tabariyya Sea through the efforts of Imam al-Mahdi. It will be placed before him at the Sacred House. When the descendants of Judah see this Tabut, all except a few will embrace Islam."

The Qur'an itself reveals that the Ark is "a sign" for faithful believers, and some understand it to signal the identity of the Mahdi and the sovereignty of Allah he bears when it is found, evidencing his dominion and ushering in an era of moral purity and tranquility: "Truly the sign of his sovereignty shall be that the ark comes to you bearing tranquility from your Lord and a remnant left by the House of Moses and the House of Aaron, borne by angels. Truly that is a sign for you, if you are believers" (al-Baqarah; 2:248).

He closed the journal and set it on his desk. "It is unclear where the sacred house refers, either the Temple Mount in Jerusalem or the Ka'aba in Mecca, but the link between this End Times prophet and the Ark of the Covenant is clear. It is vitally important for the fulfillment of their End of Days prophecies."

"So according to Islamic tradition," Celeste said, "the Ark of the Covenant will be revealed by the Mahdi, a descendant of both Abraham and the bloodline of Muhammad, ushering in the final Day of Judgment and an epoch of Islamic rule. All will view this retrieval of the Ark as a sign, embracing Islam in response, even Jews. Is that right?"

"You're right, madam. After revealing this sacred, prophetic treasure, the Mahdi will be coroneted king of the Kingdom of God, ruling as both sacred and secular monarch."

Silas sighed, taking in the gravity of this Islamic connection with the Ark. This was huge, for the Ark's unveiling meant fulfilling Islamic End Times prophecy, which would usher in their own messianic, salvific era—and usher in the eschatological era of Islamic rule. But he was confused by Pryce's interest in the tradition.

"What did Pryce think about your findings?"

Saulcy breathed in deeply, then leaned forward in his chair and rested a thick arm against its armrest, staring at his desk as if searching for the words. "*Titillated* is the word I would use."

Silas coughed. "Excuse me?"

"It excited him, but in a way that went way beyond the bounds of academic inquiry. Frankly, he became obsessed with the idea of the Ark-eschatological savior connection and began exploring them on his own after we completed our co-authorship. But that didn't surprise me."

"Why not?"

"Why, because Lucas is Muslim?"

CHAPTER 36

He said it so matter-of-factly that it took Silas a few beats to realize the gravity of what he had just revealed. He snapped his head toward Celeste, trying to hide his shock. This changed everything.

Celeste moved to the edge of her seat. "Wait a minute, Pryce is Muslim?"

"You didn't know?"

"We weren't all that close," Silas demurred. "And the impression he gave in class was of an agnostic. Someone not really all that convinced either way about the prospects of religion, particularly the Judeo-Christian variety. His fascination with Palestine seemed more academic than personal or spiritual. Certainly not religious. At least that was the impression I got."

Saulcy nodded. "That was my impression, as well, when we began the project together. As a Reform Jew myself, I found the writing project a fascinating exercise in academic dialogue with an opposing religious partner that had staked its own claims on the Temple and the artifacts my people had claimed since the Exodus. But for Pryce...the interest seemed far deeper. I never really discovered why, other than him having a personal encounter of sorts that made him convert."

Silas sat back in his chair, not knowing how to process the turn of events. Then he smiled and sat up. It was time to get to work, no time to waste. They had their answer, at least a sizable piece of the emerging puzzle.

He stood, Celeste joined him. "Professor Saulcy, thank you for your time. You've been a great help with our research."

"Alright. Good, but I'm not sure how."

Silas shook the man's hand, then said goodbye, not wanting him to ask more questions.

The two cleared the hallway, hustled past the nosey executive assistant, and burst through the doors of the academic hall.

"My goodness!" Celeste exclaimed. "Pryce is Muslim."

"No wonder he was so intent on getting his hands on the Ark. I never took the man for a religious zealot, but I guess it's true. People really do change."

They walked quickly across the quad, then stopped midway in the shady relief of a large oak tree.

"But what does it all mean?" he whispered pacing.

"Near as I can figure," Celeste said, "he must be trying to undermine Judaism. What better way to completely undermine the faith than to show the world that the prized Temple treasures they've been waiting for generations to usher in the Third Temple period are completely gone? That there is no possible way for them to reclaim their religious and spiritual heritage because there no longer is an Ark."

Silas kept pacing, working through in his mind the significance of the past several days. The missing Ark. What they discovered at Chartres and the connections they made at the abbey library. The revelations from Saulcy, about the Islamic faith and the Ark and Pryce.

He stopped suddenly, then whispered, "No it's more."

"What?"

He spun around toward Celeste. "It's more than just about the Jewish faith. It's about Islam. He's trying to usher in the Muslim eschatological age, to bring about their End Times! He must have known, or at least had a pretty strong suspicion that the chamber was empty. Remember the look on his face?"

"Met expectation. Relief."

He snapped his fingers. "Exactly. He was glad the chamber was empty. That there were no Temple treasures. Tarnished his reputation, but that wasn't the end game to begin with. It was dashing the Jewish Messianic hopes. And what I discovered in his journal at his room must have been preliminary research for what he believed about the Ark's true resting place."

"In Ethiopia."

"Exactly. He probably had an idea that it was there, but needed confirmation. So he sent Tulu and his thugs to confirm Chartres. He spent time with *Kebra Nagast*, analyzing its narrative, figuring out its historical veracity, which we know he had in his possession. And then I can imagine he spent similar time with Wolfram Von Eschenbach's *Parzival*, trying to make similar connections, finding out what we ourselves discovered. All so that he could find it, steal it, then reveal it to serve his own religious ends."

"And right now he's in Ethiopia," Celeste said, taking out her phone. "Has to be."

Silas nodded as she dialed SEPIO command.

"Radcliffe," she said, putting the phone on speaker. "We discovered quite a revelation about Pryce. Apparently, he's Muslim."

Radcliffe audibly gasped. "That is revealing!"

Silas added, "Which means he has a vested interest in revealing the Ark. We guess that he wants to discover its final resting place, but for far different reasons than academic and professional. This is personal and surprisingly spiritual, religious even. Which, frankly, I can't believe knowing what I thought I knew about the man."

"So he intends to steal it, you think?"

"Steal it, then reveal it, according to the prophecies of Islam in order to fulfill their eschatological, End of Days expectations for their savior, al Mahdi, and usher in their own era of Islamic hope and salvation and the End Times and whatever."

"But what about Nous?" Celeste asked.

"What about them?" Silas responded.

"Clearly, Pryce had help. Major financing and major backing, which we know is Nous. Surely they can't be all that thrilled with one of the world's major religions finding prophetic fulfillment and End Times salvation. After all, they're transtheistic and transreligious."

"I'm glad you rang, then," Radcliffe interjected. "Because I think I have your answer."

The two looked at each other and turned toward the phone.

"First off, we have Torres," Radcliffe announced.

"Thank the Lord!" Celeste exclaimed.

"Yes, thanks be to God."

"With Zoe's support, and not a little help from the Lord himself, Gapinski and Greer were able to locate and extract her. She's doing well. A bit shaken, as you can image, but she's a tough one, that girl. She'll go far with us."

"Glad to hear," Celeste said. "Was she able to glean any intel while captive?"

"She was. And I think she may have discovered the missing piece to this whole Nous puzzle. You remember that two days ago operatives stole one of the Passion relics, Christ's scourging post."

"We do," she said.

"That was a dry run for their ultimate mission."

Recognition dawned on Celeste's face. "The Basilica of the Holy Cross in Jerusalem."

"Right you are. By all accounts, it appears Nous is after the remaining Passion relics."

"Wow," Silas added. "That makes this whole Ark disappearing act way bigger."

"Absolutely," Radcliffe said. "Earlier in the year, Nous had set out to undermine and destroy the memory of Christ's resurrection. Now it's the death of Christ. By laying hold of these Passion relics, it's clear Nous wants to remove these memory markers connected with Jesus' atoning death."

Celeste said, "What's the game plan? I assume the Vatican has been notified, as it's within their jurisdiction. And that SEPIO is taking point on this?"

"Yes, that's the plan. Gapinski, Greer, and Torres will execute a protective operation at the basilica."

Silas shook his head. "I don't know, Rowen. This sounds like the Church of the Holy Sepulcher all over again. Shouldn't the Rome police be involved and take point?"

"No," Celeste answered flatly. "For now, anything connected with Nous is being strictly quarantined under the auspices of SEPIO. There are too many unknowns to involve local authorities in terms of Nous's scope and ultimate mission. And if Farhad is involved, it will be vital to capture him, given he is a high-ranking member of the Thirteen."

"You're exactly right," Radcliffe confirmed. "And with their move to expose the Ark as some sort of prophetic manifestation of the Islamic eschatological era, the spiritual confusion they will sow regarding how sins are atoned is far too vital of a crisis to turn over to the secular authorities. Jews will go crazy, thinking they have an opportunity to reinstitute the Temple sacrificial system to appease God's wrath and provide forgiveness for sins. Christians who aren't grounded will wonder whether the cross actually worked if the former altar of atonement is rediscovered and put to use again to pay for the sins of mankind. And Muslims will be emboldened with the final, prophetic marker for their own salvation revealed."

"Which means it may not be such a good idea to unveil the ancient relic after all," Celeste said.

"Indeed, it may not," Radcliffe agreed.

"I doubt Pryce knows how he's being used," Silas added.

"Probably not. But given their plans against the Passion relics, it seems Nous is using his personal interest in seeing the Ark used to benefit the Islamic faith to help them undermine Christian belief in the sufficiency of Christ's death on the cross. This is no longer some Hollywood blockbuster unveiling or about some fascinating historical artifact. Souls are on the line! With the Ark back in service, clarity on the nature of salvation and how one is made right with God is on the line."

"What a disaster this could be," Silas said solemnly.

"Indeed. Which means you know what you need to do."

Celeste looked at Silas and nodded. "Aksum, here we come."

DAY V

CHAPTER 37

AKSUM, ETHIOPIA.

The burnt-orange tendrils of the Ethiopian sun were just beginning to curl up over the horizon in the deep, blue sky. Lucas Pryce carefully unrolled the red Persian rug on the floor of his hotel room, for he needed to perform the ritual before the sun began making its trek across the sky.

He had purchased the rug a decade ago after he had converted to the ancient religion when his life was falling apart. His wife left him for another man. Both his daughter and son sided with Mom, blaming him for breaking up the family. He had been temporarily denied tenure for lack of professional ambition, which meant he hadn't bolstered the name of Harvard with enough journal articles or critical archaeological discoveries. He fell into a deep depression and was searching for something, anything that would give his life meaning and direction. Something that he could use to put the pieces of his life back together again.

He had always been religiously curious, even as a child. Though raised Presbyterian, he had visited different denominations with his friends in Junior High and High School. The Baptists were too right-wing. The Pentecostal gatherings were interesting, far livelier than the frozen-chosen Presbyterians he had grown up with. But they were also too weird. Same for the Catholics, with the whole body-and-blood-of-Jesus bit. In college, he had dabbled in a bit of Hinduism and Buddhism. That's what everyone was doing in the '60s and '70s—and with a little bit of ganja on the side to heighten the spiritual experience. But neither had hit the mark. Too woo-woo for his taste.

He ended up leaving behind faith altogether. His life seemed perfectly fine without the trappings and guilt of religion. He had fallen in love. He had sailed through university and then into a PhD program that led to a prestigious professorship at one of America's premier universities. They'd had the 2.5 kids required of middle-class living; one girl, one boy, and a fixed mutt-of-a-dog. Eventually, they grew up, moved out of the house, then on to equally prestigious careers in law and medicine. Life was great.

Until it wasn't.

A close colleague of his knew of his troubles and tried to help. They weren't close, but friendly. Enough so that the Muslim gave him a copy of a Qur'an, said it had the answers his life needed.

At the time, he laughed inside at the quaint, proselytizing gesture. But he thought, Why not? He had spent enough time with the world religions to know they were basically the same. What harm could come from engaging with one more? He considered it an academic exercise, boning up on Islam just when the world had grown far more interested and aware in the religion thanks to the jihadist lunatics. But reading the sacred book struck him in a way that others hadn't, connecting with his own spiritual convictions.

He started reading pages in the Qur'an each day, and he stumbled upon a striking passage:

> Truly God alters not what is in a people until they alter
> what is in themselves.

In other words: Allah helps those who help themselves.

As a teenager and later as a college student, it had always struck him as ridiculous that a god would offer the promise of personal meaning and the removal of inner angst for free. Grace, the Christians called it. Unmerited favor. Pryce knew that nothing in life was free, yet Christianity offered salvation as a gift for the taking. Not of works, so no one can boast, one of their early missionary teachers wrote.

Preposterous!

Even Judaism required people to get their hands dirty with the blood of slaughtered animals for their sins, shoving their affront and offense against their god in their face. And their laws were thought to be the maintenance work needed to stay in the good graces of that god.

Islam was different. Their doctrines were rational and straightforward. It was a practical religion that promised personal inner peace, salvation even for aligning one's life with the laws of Allah. The Qur'an expects a person to help himself by changing their own attitude and behavior before Allah will come to their aid. The principle is the same as that in Aesop's proverb: those who expect divine help must first get the ball rolling themselves. And it offered a structure for a person like Pryce to save himself by pulling himself up by his own existential bootstrap. While he still remained secret about his spirituality, over time he grew to understand his chosen faith, falling in love with its worldview that empowered the individual to rise above themselves—ultimately saving themselves.

Pryce had discovered that everyone is a ball of divine potential that is blinded by ignorance. The gravitational attraction of worldly pleasures draws people toward the depths of the material world, and they know not what they are doing. As a result, they fall and become degenerate. Selfishness and temptation become embodied in individuals until it coalesces into civilization-wide catastrophe. Isn't that what happened to his family, and what had been happening increasingly in the West for generations?

The solution wasn't the blood of dead animals or the blood of a dead God-Man. What we need is a lifting of the veil of ignorance, an unveiling of divine knowledge. Secret knowledge that will empower individuals to rise to the challenge of living to their best, divine potential by living up to Allah's divine standard. That's what the chaos of the world needs most. Guidance. A Way. A new epoch of spiritual enlightenment. Which he was about to provide.

And all thanks to Silas Grey.

Pryce's archaeological career had mostly consisted of rehashing Holy Land dig sites that first-wave Europeans had uncovered during the century of fevered exploration in the Middle East. But finding the Ark scrolls had established him as a bona fide archaeologist and liberal guardian of culture.

Those scrolls were a talisman of good luck that righted his career, and life—his wife and kids be damned. Between the scroll and the Qur'an, things had never been better. The Qur'an gave his life structure and a way to make his life right. The scroll gave him purpose and meaning, sending him down a path that led to a celebrated journal article on the connection between Islam and the Ark of the Covenant. Which led to a fortuitous encounter with Rudolf Borg, who became the benefactor that eventually led him to standing in an Ethiopian hotel.

Pryce stood in the center and smiled at his fortune, at having been chosen by Allah for such a time as this. He raised both hands up to his ears, palms facing the direction of Mecca, and repeated his religion's mantra three times: "Allahu Akbar."

God is the greatest.

He lowered his arms then closed his eyes, relaxing his body and breathing deliberately. Then he brought his arms up to his chest, placing the right hand on top of the left hand.

"Audhu billahi," he intoned, "min ashshayta nirrajeem."

I seek God's shelter from Satan, the condemned.

He took a breath, then continued. The prayer of his chosen

religion had been burned into Pryce's consciousness over the years:

> *In the name of God, the Most Gracious, Most Merciful.*
> *All praise is due to God, Lord of the Worlds, The*
> *Most Gracious, the Most Merciful, Master of the*
> *Day of Judgment, You alone we worship and You*
> *alone we ask for assistance. Guide us along the*
> *straight path. The path of those upon whom You*
> *have bestowed Your blessings, not the path of those*
> *with whom You are angry nor the path of those*
> *who have gone astray.*

"Aameen."

Keeping his eyes closed, he recited a selection from the Holy Qur'an, the Chapter Of Sincerity, chapter twelve: *In the name of God, the Most Kind, Most Merciful say, "He is God, the One, God the Eternal, dependent upon nothing, yet everything is dependent upon Him, He does not give birth, nor was He born, and there is nothing like unto Him."*

"Allahu Akbar." He bent over, his back and legs perpendicular to each other, and recited three times, "Subhana rabbiyal azeem."

Glory be to my Lord, the Almighty.

Retreating to the standing position of the first prayer, he said, "Sami'allaahu liman hamidah."

God hears those who praise Him.

"Rabbana wa lakal hamd."

Our Lord, praise be to You.

A flash of excitement pinged his gut at the thought of all that had transpired the past few days. As well as all that would transpire in the days ahead. He smiled briefly, then cursed himself for allowing self-centered thoughts to invade this holy space.

"Allahu Akbar," he quickly said, reorienting his heart and continuing the sacred ritual.

He bent down. While prostrating himself on the well-worn red mat, he said three times, "Subhana rubbiyal a'ala."

Glory be to my Lord, the Most High.

He bent his torso backward, saying, "Allaahu Akbar." Then he sat for a moment, breathing deeply and centering himself around the will of Allah for the day ahead. "Allaahu Akbar."

He prostrated himself again and repeated the prayer: "Subhana rubbiyal a'ala."

He stood back up and repeated the process, ending in the same prostrated posture before reciting: *Salutations, all good things, and all prayers are for God. The peace and mercy of God be upon you, O Muhammad. Peace be upon all of us, and upon His righteous servants. I bear witness that there is no God except God and I bear witness that Muhammad is the Messenger of God.*

He paused, eyes closed and holding his position. He took a deep breath and continued: *O God bestow honor upon Muhammad and upon his family just as You have bestowed honor upon Abraham and his family. And O God, bestow Your blessings upon Muhammad and his family just as You have bestowed Your blessings upon Abraham and his family. In all of the worlds, You are the most praised and the most glorious.*

Pryce breathed inward slowly, feeling the power of the ancient religion coursing through him, his will becoming one with Allah's.

He stood back up, keeping his feet close together and back straight, then carefully repeated all of the necessary steps again. Islam was demanding, exacting. Yet it anchored his life and empowered him in a way Christianity never had.

Having repeated the entire ritual of postures and prayers, Pryce turned to face the right, and said, "Assalamu alaykum wa rahma tullaah."

May the Peace and mercy of God be upon you.

Then he turned his face to the left, concluding, "Assalamu alaykum wa rahma tullaah."

May the Peace and mercy of God be on you.

The sun had risen over the horizon, a bright orb in a clear sky of possibility. A good omen for Pryce and the work Nous would accomplish that day.

He breathed deeply and smiled. With the blessings of Allah at his back, he was ready to retrieve the sacred relic, the hidden covenant, bringing to light the necessary piece for the redeemer of Islam to emerge.

And usher in the Islamic End Times—a new epoch of spiritual enlightenment, guidance, and rule.

CHAPTER 38

ROME.

"Stakeouts bite," Gapinski complained as he shifted in the front driver's seat. "Hand me another energy bar, would you?"

"Sorry, brotha," Greer said from the back of their parked van. "You've hit your quota."

"Quota? Who died and made you the energy-bar police?"

Torres let a giggle slip, then covered her mouth.

Gapinski threw her a look. "Not funny, Torres. I'm starving. And cold."

"And cranky," Greer said quietly, his deep voice rumbling in the van.

He turned around and tried to slug the man one, but he couldn't reach. He scowled and turned back toward the front, and folded his arms in a huff.

Gapinski, Torres, and Greer had been parked within sight of the Basilica of the Holy Cross in Jerusalem under cover of darkness for the better part of seven hours. After rescuing Torres from the warehouse, the three had debriefed with Radcliffe. Gapinski went over the operational outcomes. Torres described what she had heard, and where she believed they would strike next, the basilica, in search of the remaining Passion relics.

To say that Radcliffe was troubled was an understatement. He was fuming. The thought that Nous would go after some of the most sacred of Christian relics tied to the faith's most titular event, the death and sacrifice of Christ on the cross, lit a blazing fire underneath him. He had wanted to call in reinforcements from the Vatican police, combined with Italian military, but Gapinski and Greer talked him out of it. They thought it was best for a small, surgical strike team to go in and disrupt Nous's operation. They figured only three were operational at this point, given the men who were able to escape the warehouse. Radcliffe relented and instructed them to immediately stake out the basilica when it closed at eight. They had been sitting in their van ever since.

"I gotta go pee," Gapinski complained, unbuckling his seat belt.

"What, now?" Torres asked. "What if someone rolls up on us while you're out there, and we have to move on them?"

"When a man's gotta go, he's gotta go. Besides, it's been seven hours since we've been sitting here and we've got bupkis. Doubt the worm's gonna turn in the two minutes it takes for me to walk over to those bushes, unzip, and relieve myself."

"Jeez, Gapinski," Greer complained. "Thanks for the mental picture."

He opened his door and stepped out.

"Hey, wait. Don't forget this." Torres tossed him a radio. "Never know."

He nodded his thanks, then closed the door.

Gapinski walked a few yards away from the van to an outcropping of bushes. He glanced around, looking back toward the van and then toward the basilica. Satisfied no one was looking, he unzipped his pants then took care of business.

Then lights came on bright and sudden.

"Sonofa—"

Without zipping, he dove into the bushes to evade being seen as they flashed across the tree line and then across the lawn toward the basilica parking lot.

A dark van rolled up quickly to the front entrance. Three men got out and moved immediately toward the set of doors.

Gapinski stayed put, zipping up his pants as he watched them from his hiding spot.

"Where are you, Gapinski?" his radio crackled, slicing through the midnight air.

Crapola!

He quickly turned down the volume, then held his breath to see if he had been heard. A few seconds went by, but no one came around the van and looked in his direction.

"I'm in an island of bushes, Greer," he said lowly into his radio. "Probably poison ivy, knowing my luck."

"Well, get your ass back to the van! Looks like they already made it inside, thanks to your two-minute potty break."

"Always something," he grumbled, then climbed out of the bushes.

Torres and Greer met him at the back of their van. Greer was assembling their infiltration packages, complete with side arms, flash grenades, and assault rifles. He handed Gapinski his trio, then turned to Torres to arm her.

"Just a sidearm for me, thanks," she said.

Greer shook his head. "Sorry, no can do. The order was we arm up. That means side arms and flashbangs and a rifle."

She frowned, but took the additional firepower. "Seems like overkill to me."

"Look, sweet pea," Gapinski said. "I understand you're new and all, but you don't know Nous like we do. These are highly trained operatives, usually ex-military who know how to use a weapon and are usually carrying at least eleven of them. I don't know about you, but I'm not ready to meet Saint Pete at the pearly gates, if you know what I mean. Let's move out."

He and Greer started moving across the lawn, Torres rolled

her eyes and quickly followed. They hit the pavement, then carefully padded to the side of the Nous van.

Gapinski took point, moving toward the rear. He stopped, then peered around toward the entrance.

Empty.

He could see the basilica entrance was slightly ajar. The lock had probably been broken or picked by the Nousati hostiles.

Crap, that was quick.

He moved forward, motioning the other two to follow, SIG Sauer outstretched and ready.

Greer moved to the right side of the ajar door, standing ready to open it.

Gapinski stood at the small gap, aiming and ready to enter. Torres was close behind as back up. He positioned himself, then took a breath and nodded to Greer. The man opened the door, Gapinski and Torres quickly moved inside the atrium, then Greer followed.

It was dark, except for the pale moonlight shining in through the large windows and entrance on the front facade. Gapinski caught glimpse of ornately painted frescos with bright colors of gold and red and blue. Neither the darkness nor the urgency of the moment gave them any chance to enjoy their beauty. He shook his head and pressed forward.

The three quickly fanned outward, checking the immediate interior for any sign of the Nousati. It was completely empty. They padded forward, weapons drawn and all senses straining for any sign of the intruders.

There were none. It was dark, it was quiet.

Gapinski put his sidearm in his waist and padded forward slowly, bringing his assault rifle around from his shoulder and positioning it ahead. The atmosphere was too weird for his taste. It was like they vanished.

Greer and Torres came up behind him. They moved farther inside, passing into the nave and toward the high altar.

"What do you make of this?" Greer said, his deep voice soft and low.

Gapinski shook his head. "I don't know. It's like they went all Big Foot on us, disappearing into the darkness. They clearly knew what they were doing. And where they were going."

Torres shushed the two men. "Listen."

They craned their necks, searching for any sign of life.

"Did you hear that? It's faint, but there. In the background."

Gapinski turned around to his right. Then stopped.

There it was. The faint sound of a drill or saw.

He whipped around to his left, facing a small, open door to a larger entrance built into the stonework of the basilica. A set of stairs led upward, apparently to a chapel according to a wooden sign they passed. He padded forward, following his senses.

Greer and Torres followed, hearing the same sound once they entered through the doorway and started ascending the stairs.

Gapinski glanced back at them and grinned, then pointed forward. The trace, distinct smell of working power tools convinced him he was on the right trail. The set of stairs brought them to a landing that opened up to a larger staircase to the right, a hallway flanked by the Stations of the Cross, the journey upward to the chapel meant to symbolize Christ's journey to Calvary.

The sound grew louder, more urgent. Surely the Nous operatives were getting close.

Gapinski motioned them forward and quickly padded to the top.

At once the work stopped. Then the sound of rubble being cleared away echoed around the sacred space, mostly the tinkle of glass like sweeping up after a car crash on a busy, four-lane highway.

Voices echoed toward them from around the corner. The same voices he and Greer had heard back in the warehouse last afternoon. There were three of them.

Three on three. Good odds by Gapinski's estimation.

But he couldn't mess this one up. Not like the Church of Saint Praxedes when the scourging post was stolen.

They had one shot. And now was as good as any.

He glanced back at Greer and Torres, nodded, then moved forward into the outer room before the relic chapel. Light from inside filtered through openings of glassless bronze panes embedded in the walls on either side of the chapel entrance. He stopped at the threshold, positioning himself to the left.

Gapinski hesitated, taking in the lay of the land beyond the room, confirming three hostiles and a floor-to-ceiling encasement made of brown marble commanding the rear of the space. Inside the massive case, three small reliquaries of silver and gold sat at the top, two medium-sized, silver reliquaries rested at the bottom, and one large golden cross was in the middle.

And its glass completely removed, shattered on the floor.

One man started reaching for the large golden cross, the big guy who had been holding Torres up against the wall. The other one was opening a large, black case beneath him.

Man number three was wearing a mustache. Then an expression of utter shock after catching a glimpse of Gapinski staring at him through the narrow entrance.

His hesitation had cost them.

Crapola!

"Farhad," Gapinski yelled, trying to regain command of the situation, "forget the relics and drop on the ground! It's over."

Not according to the Nousati gunfire.

It was instant and fierce. Flying through the entrance and shattering an icon of Jesus Christ to the right of the entrance.

So not right.

Greer had shoved himself against the left-most wall, giving him direct aim into the chapel through the openings in the bronze window panes. Torres had come up next to Gapinski on the right side of the entrance into the chapel, using the wide, marble threshold as coverage.

The bullets were relentless, burrowing into the marble at the back of the outer room and chewing the edges of the marble threshold, trying their best to find purchase through to Gapinski.

Thankfully, the threshold was winning.

Gapinski was stuck in his position, trying to squeeze his bulky, six-foot-four frame out of range. Greer launched several rounds into the room, but found it difficult to find any success given how the operatives had positioned themselves behind several wide, brown pillars inside.

Torres, however, could take the necessary shot.

It was the skinny one on the right, leaning against the brown column and spraying round after round after round with his rifle.

She had perfect aim, the perfect opportunity to take him down.

"Take the shot," Gapinski ordered, seeing the clear opening.

Why wasn't she taking the shot?

She glanced at him, gripped her weapon tighter, then aimed to take the shot.

Except the man behind the brown column had pivoted back toward her position, spraying more bullets through Jesus' face, and splintering what remained of the sacred icon.

Gapinski took the opportunity and pressed at will.

Got him.

A round barely caught the man in the back, but it was enough to send him staggering, where two more rounds from Greer sent him to the ground.

He got a healthy response from Farhad and the large man from the warehouse.

Greer yelled in protest, faltering backward from his position to the floor.

Gapinski looked down at him, he was cradling his hand quickly soaking with blood.

"Got me good. But I'll live."

Anger welled within him. This was not going well. He could not afford another mess like last time.

He pivoted to Greer's position and caught Farhad crouching behind a low, marble separation wall in front of the relics. He fired four rounds, sending the man to the floor for cover. The larger man twisted away from his column, aiming straight toward Gapinski.

He pressed his trigger to offer a reply, but it clicked empty. He slung the useless rifle around his back and pulled out his SIG Sauer.

Always something!

There was nowhere he could go from his position. His massive frame was too exposed in front of the open, bronze window.

Three shots echoed around him as he reached for a magazine to reload. He hit the floor, trying to evade the rounds. But saw the other large man behind the column slump hard to the floor.

He looked from him to his right. Torres had taken the shot after all! She nodded at him and was reloading herself. He smiled in return.

Just like that, a silence opened up after the man fell. The worm had turned.

"It's over, Farhad," Gapinski said, slowly standing with his weapon at the ready. "You've got nowhere to go. Both of your men are down. There are three of us out here ready to put the hurt on you. I'm guessing more is on the way after your little surgical operation of that glass case. So do yourself a favor and toss your weapons our way."

Farhad said nothing.

Gapinski looked over at Torres, then nodded.

Then dim light from the outer room glinted off an object as it slid across the floor into their room. It barely registered except for the echoing clink it made as it bounced off the wall behind them and back to the floor.

Grenade!

In one motion, Gapinski gave it a power kick with his massive leg, sending it sailing down the stairwell.

It exploded with deafening power down below, the narrow passage channeling its fire and fury, dust and debris toward them.

Instinctively, they dove for cover, but not before hearing another explosion of less intensity from the relic chapel.

Gapinski assessed the damage from his side of the divide: Torres had hit the deck, too, and was crouched in a ball—she seemed a bit shell-shocked; Greer laid motionless on the floor, blood clinging to the side of his head and his hand.

Double crapola!

He pulled himself along the floor toward the chapel entrance, dust choking his vision of what was happening inside. He moved back to his original position at the marble threshold of the opening, then took a breath and decided to go for it.

He padded through with his weapon raised and ready. Movement caught his attention high and to the left.

Farhad.

He had shattered a large, stained glass window and hoisted himself up onto its ledge. That must have been the minor explosion they'd just heard.

"Farhad, stop! I've got you in my sights."

The man wiggled himself farther inside the window bay. Gapinski took aim and fired two rounds to stop him.

But it was too late. Farhad plunged through the opening and to the world outside.

"Sonofa..." Gapinski mumbled.

He ran over to the window and hopped up on top of a large, black case to try and catch the man, but it was no use. Farhad was gone, and there was no way he was gonna hoist his fanny up and through the window even if he wanted to. Then he remembered.

The relics!

He shuffled toward the encasement in the chapel wall, panic gripping him.

Please, please, please let there be six of them.

He first saw the two medium-sized relics lying scattered on the floor beneath the case. The three smaller ones were still inside at the top.

Where was the gold cross? The one that held pieces of the True Cross of Christ, the ancient boards of execution that held his limp, lifeless body as he bled out for the world?

Torres had stumbled inside the chapel to join him. "Where's Farhad?"

"Jumped," he said in a panic. "Through the window." He continued searching the space for the sacred objects of veneration.

She ran over to try and catch a glimpse, but couldn't reach the ledge either.

"The cross is missing," he said with panic.

"What?"

"The relic of the cross, the golden thingamabob with pieces of the True Cross. It's gone."

"You think Farhad took it when he jumped? That thing had to have been fifty pounds."

He kept searching the room, kicking away the rubble with his feet in a panicked search.

Come on. Not again!

"Gapinski."

He turned around to see Torres standing over the large, black case beneath the window.

That's right! He shuffled over to her side and looked inside. There it was. Nestled in a bed of black foam, safe and secure.

He sighed heavily, then plopped down to the floor in exhaustion and smiled at Torres, giving her two thumbs up.

"Not bad for your first rodeo. Not bad at all, Torres."

CHAPTER 39

AKSUM.

S ilas and Celeste had arrived at Aksum, Ethiopia, mid-morning after hopscotching from Paris to Cairo to Addis Ababa and then to the original capital of the empire. What would have been ten hours by commercial airline was over fifteen with the Order-issued private jet thanks refueling stops. The Order's private travel had its perks; length of time wasn't one of them.

After landing, they had received word from Radcliffe that the Passion relics had been secured. Unfortunately, Farhad had escaped, location unknown. The two felt relief at the news, but knew they weren't out of the woods yet. They had their own work to do.

They secured a vehicle and headed to the Church of Our Lady Mary of Zion, the most important church in Ethiopia, and where the Ark of the Covenant was claimed to reside. The original church was believed to have been built during the fourth century by the first Christian ruler of the Kingdom of Aksum and has been rebuilt several times since.

After rumbling down a road that had probably never seen a good day in its life, they veered off onto a narrow, barely-visible path toward the ancient structure. Compared to the churches and cathedrals Silas was used to visiting with his research, which was mostly focused around the Mediterranean, it was wholly unimpressive.

The rectangular, beige building looked like a sad loaf of bread nestled within a small ring of hills. The trees looked like they hadn't seen water in a year, the grass in a generation. The windows were a painted patchwork of Ethiopian greens, reds, and whites. Little, yellow crosses sat underneath the windows, looking as if they had been painted by children. Certainly didn't look like a place that would house one of the world's most magnificent hidden relics! A newer building surrounded by an iron fence sat several yards toward the back of the property, farther north and east.

Silas parked the car underneath a cluster of better-leafed trees, butting against a row of bushes several yards away. It would conceal their presence as they scoped out the grounds to determine whether Pryce was there yet or not.

A cloud of dust followed the pair as they made their way to the church. If Pryce was around, he'd sure know it by now. Nothing they could do about it. They moved to the lawn, walking around the perimeter like they were two tourists taking in the Ethiopian sights, the grass crunching underneath their feet like uncooked spaghetti.

Not a trace of Pryce or anyone else. The morning was dead, but for some buzzards circling overhead and squawking to one another. They circled the ancient building once, then Celeste directed them toward the entrance.

It was locked tight. Silas tugged hard. Nothing gave.

"Either Pryce is already inside, and was able to secure the door behind him, or there's no going in."

Celeste put her hands on her hips, then turned around, taking in the surrounding area.

"I don't get it. I thought he'd have been here by now. Do we wait and see if—"

"Hold on." Silas pressed into the doorway and guided Celeste to do the same with his arm. "There." He nodded up the dirt road the opposite way they had come.

A white man with silver hair and a black man with a shiny head were getting out of a black SUV near a building a hundred yards from the church. Two other men followed them, dressed for action.

Pryce and Tulu.

Silas cursed under his breath. "We are way too exposed." At least they knew they were in the right place; apparently, their research had paid off. And this thing would end soon enough.

One way or another.

Silas and Celeste pressed against the entrance, hoping they would go unnoticed by Pryce and his entourage. Thankfully, the sun was low enough so that a dark shadow was cast against the side of the building.

The group walked toward the newer building at the back, seemingly oblivious of the two.

"That's right," he mumbled.

"What's right?"

He whispered, "I remember reading something about a separate chapel having been built for the Ark next to the old church, the Chapel of the Tablet. Apparently, it was moved there after some sort of a mysterious, mystical heat within the inner sanctuary of the church cracked the stones of its previous sanctum. It was claimed that it was a divine heat emanating from the Ark. Emperor Haile Selassie's wife was said to have paid for the construction of the new chapel personally. Anyway, that's where we should have headed."

They watched the group look around then casually walk toward the entrance of the chapel.

Celeste said, "Then let's go."

. . .

THE PAIR quickly inched around the building and made their way back to their car, using the foliage for cover. Then they followed behind the men back several yards as the group walked toward the chapel. A calm and peace permeated the surrounding area, the community not having stirred yet during the lazy weekend morning.

The two men guarding Pryce and Tulu forced themselves through the tall, iron fence surrounding the chapel. Pryce and Tulu walked past them down a path and toward its entrance.

"Let's wait here," Celeste instructed, motioning them behind a tall sycamore.

The chapel looked no happier or holier than the church. Its stout, square structure of pale stone was modest and unimpressive. The large entryway was covered with a deep crimson curtain, mirroring the protection the original Jewish Temple offered the chamber that housed the Ark, the Holy of Holies. Pryce parted the curtain, but couldn't move forward. He was stopped by a large door. He struggled with the handle, then seemed to be working out how to get inside.

Silas looked at Celeste. "I doubt Pryce or Tulu have any fight in them, but those other two look like a different story."

She nodded. "Yes, I imagine they're going to be a problem."

"I know the Order has an aversion to using violence to secure its interests. But it's two against four. Or at least two against two well-trained operatives. How about we bend the rules a bit?"

She looked back at the men, then at Silas. "Let's move to take out the two muscle heads. But this isn't a shoot-to-kill operation, alright?"

He nodded. "I'll get the one on the left. You take out the right."

"Fine."

Once decided, they quickly moved out of their covering spot. Each of them withdrew their weapons, Silas his Beretta and Celeste her SIG Sauer, then padded carefully toward the open gate.

While Pryce and Tulu worked the door with their backs turned at the entrance, the other two men stood facing out on the stairs, eyeing the surroundings.

They had one chance to surprise them and take them down. The only problem was the surrounding lawn wasn't very forgiving when it came to coverage. Just a short wall of bricks and mud offered them any relief. They took it, crouching low and waiting for a window to act.

Pryce and Tulu continued their work a hundred yards out. Content no one was looking and bored with their role, the other two abandoned their guard duty for a moment for a look at their progress, turning their backs on the path leading up to the chapel entrance.

There it was. The window.

Silas gave a quick glance to his partner for confirmation. She nodded, then quickly led them forward, weapons outstretched. He regulated his breathing until they reached the gate.

In one motion, the two crouched and aimed.

Silas held his breath, then sent three shots toward the man on the left. The first one exploded into the muddy stone wall next to the man's head. The second slammed into his left shoulder. And the third caught the man in his left butt cheek.

He screamed in protest, faltering to the ground in agony.

Celeste had the same luck, sending her man to the ground in one shot, rendering him harmless, as well.

They quickly ran up the path toward Pryce and Tulu, weapons drawn.

Except the other two were equally armed. And quick on the draw.

At the sound of the gunfire, the two had instinctively twisted around and removed their concealed firearms, aiming them straight at the two intruders.

It was a four-way draw: Silas was aiming at Pryce, Pryce at Silas; Celeste was aiming at Tulu, Tulu at Celeste.

Stalemate.

"It's over, Pryce," Silas growled. "You've lost, you're not going anywhere."

Pryce said nothing, his eyes narrow with resolve, his arm steady with equal intent.

"And I don't know about you, Celeste, but I can stand here all day. All year if I have to."

She tightened her grip. "Me too."

"What's the point, Grey?" Pryce said, his Southern accent echoing around the courtyard with foreign misplacement. "Why are you here?"

Silas flexed his fingers, considering the question, searching for an answer. Then he had it.

"'But when Christ came as a high priest of the good things that have come,'" he quoted, "'then through the greater and perfect tent (not made with hands, that is, not of this creation), he entered once for all into the Holy Place, not with the blood of goats and calves, but with his own blood, thus obtaining eternal redemption.'"

"What the hell are you talking about, son?"

Silas continued: "'For if the blood of goats and bulls, with the sprinkling of the ashes of a heifer, sanctifies those who have been defiled so that their flesh is purified, how much more will the blood of Christ, who through the eternal Spirit offered himself without blemish to God, purify our conscience from dead works to worship the living God!'"

Pryce stepped forward, tightening his grip and aiming directly at Silas's face, becoming visibly angry. "I swear to God if you don't shut up—"

"'For this reason,'" Silas continued quoting, face set like flint, growing louder and more intense, "'Christ is the mediator of a new covenant, so that those who are called may receive the promised eternal inheritance, because a death has occurred that redeems them from the transgressions under the first covenant.'"

Pryce was breathing hard, his eyes fanatical, as if the very words of the Bible had set his mind on fire.

"The Book of Hebrews, chapter nine," Silas finally explained. "That's why I'm here, Pryce. Because God has forged a new relationship, written a new covenant with humanity in the blood of Jesus. Which, by the way, those Passion relics in Rome you tried to steal, as well, all bear witness to. Yeah, we know all about your little plot, which SEPIO foiled. The memory of Christ's sacrificial death is safe."

Pryce's eyes widened in surprise, then narrowed at the revelation. "I didn't have anything to do with that! That was Farhad."

"Doesn't matter. And you're not getting away with this either. If the Ark has been replaced by the cross of Christ as the altar upon which the sins of humanity have been atoned, that means no more sacrifice is needed! I admit, when I heard about your project, I was envious and wanted in on the action. After all, it was me and my find that verified it and set you off on this path in the first place. I wanted to reveal it, too. And try and take credit. But that can't happen, whether the Ark really is behind those doors or not."

Pryce scoffed, rolling his eyes. "And why not?"

"Because revealing the Ark would create spiritual confusion. Jews would think that the terms of the old covenant still applied, with all of the regulations for Temple sacrifices to atone for people's sins and the shedding of animal blood to provide for forgiveness. Christians might wonder if the means of the new covenant, the shed blood of Jesus Christ on the cross, really worked to take away the sins of the world.

"After all, if the former method for atonement under the old covenant disappeared through God's divine direction, if he himself created the circumstances of the hidden Ark, perhaps that was God's way of saying how to find atonement for sins and salvation—completely apart from the Ark and the old covenant. I know that now. And frankly, I think the Ethiopian Orthodox

Church and the likes of Clairvaux and von Eschenbach did too. That's why the Ark has been depicted as a Stone. They recognize the old covenant has been replaced by the new one. That the Living Stone has replaced the Ark of wood and gold."

"Nothing but children's fairy tales!" Pryce roared, his face a shaking, sweaty, crimson mess of rage.

"You want to talk about fairy tales. How about the one about the revelation of the Ark ushering in the Islamic End of Days eschatological age?"

Pryce's face startled, falling and draining of color. "What do you mean?"

"Drop the act. I found your little article with Professor Saulcy, though you did a great job of covering it up once you were onto the Ark. In fact, we had a little chat with the man. Discovered your conversion to Islam and your obsession with the Ark's connection to the faith. You asked why I was here. I know why you're here: to bring about the Mahdi. The supposed redeemer of Islam."

The man's outstretched arm started shaking. His jaw was quivering, then settled into an otherworldly grimace. A voice arose from it that sounded as equally otherworldly—slow, low, and guttural: "You're not going to stop me."

An electric shock of fear rippled down Silas's spine at the sound. It was pure evil. He recovered, and said, "We already have. But I don't get it. A man such as yourself. Why Islam? Why concern yourself with the Mahdi?"

"It's the perfect religion for our day," he said, his voice returning to a Southern drawl. "The world has become unhinged. Governments, societies, cultures, whole economies are in chaos. People have become weak. People are becoming unmoored from any kind of spiritual rigor. Islam offers the kind of guidance and salvation people are longing for."

"The kind people provide all on their own?"

"Yes!"

"But how could we possibly think any of us could do enough or perform enough or work enough to save ourselves, to curry favor with God? Because that's what Islam, and for that matter every other religion besides Christianity claims. That somehow we can tip the scale in our favor. Only one problem: you'll never know if you've done enough to tip the scale in your favor until it's too late. That's the magic, the beauty of the Christian faith: God offered himself to do what we couldn't do ourselves. We can know that we are right with him. Right now, today. In this life."

"Enough! I'm through with you, Grey. This is over."

"No, Pryce." Silas took a step forward and gripped his weapon tighter. "Put down your gun. Let Celeste go, Tulu. Then both of you walk away, out that gate, back to your car and drive. It's that easy. You're right: it's over. But on our terms."

Pryce held his eyes, his glare hard and unwavering. "No, it's not, Grey. Not by a long shot."

He started lowering his arm, as if resigning to the turn of events, causing Silas to lower his guard.

Then in one movement he adjusted his aim and pulled the trigger.

His arm jerked back. Almost in response, so did Celeste's body. She startled backward, pushed by the force of the bullet ripping through her upper thigh as much as by the surprise of his move.

"No!" Silas shouted. He dropped his weapon, then quickly went to Celeste's side, catching her before she fell. Blood was seeping out of a dime-sized wound.

He looked up at his former professor. "You bastard!"

Tulu quickly ran down the steps and gathered up the two weapons dropped in the chaos.

Pryce quickly trained his weapon on Grey as Celeste's body slumped against him. "I'd say she has about an hour to live based on where my shot landed, the trajectory of the bullet, and—" He looked down at the woman who was clutching her leg wet with blood. "And the rate of blood loss. If you want to see your woman live, then get through those doors and secure the Ark yourself. She's collateral. I will not be denied."

Pryce stepped forward, pressing the barrel against Celeste's temple. "If I am denied my treasure…"

He looked down at the woman and grinned. "…then so will you."

CHAPTER 40

Silas eased Celeste to the hard stone stairs, then stood. He stared up at Pryce, jaw clenched, eyes narrowed. He remained still, his legs like cedars. Heavy, planted, unmovable.

"Run along, Grey. Time is running out."

He looked down at Celeste. Pryce was right, time was running out. He quickly walked up the stairs, taking them by twos. Pryce eyed him skeptically, training his weapon on him with each step.

Silas parted the thick, heavy, crimson curtain in front of the entrance, but was confronted by an even heavier wooden door, solid and constructed with care. He tried the iron handle. Nothing.

"We already tried that," Pryce said.

Silas sighed. "Hand me my gun."

"Excuse me?"

"My gun. To blow the lock."

"Do you take me for an idiot, Grey?"

"Time is running out!" Silas yelled. "Look, I'm not going to try anything. Scout's honor. Put a gun to my head if you want, but the only way I'm getting through there and securing your precious Ark is if I blow it open."

Pryce looked at Tulu and nodded. The man handed Silas back his weapon, then the two trained their guns at his head. He snatched it, then aimed for the door lock. He pressed the trigger three times. The sound was deafening, but it worked. The bullets chewed through the wood, and the iron handle fell off inside. There was a reason why the Beretta remained his weapon of choice.

Silas looked back at Pryce, his hand was outstretched. He handed his weapon back, parted the curtain, then pushed through the heavy wooden barrier to the other side.

Just beyond the door laid a small antechamber, the width of the square building and about ten feet in. The air was stale and still. Two sconces on either side of the entrance provided dim, orange light in the windowless room. The room was heavy with heat and humidity, the cramped space suffocating and closing in on him.

Before proceeding, he quickly brought out his phone and texted a mayday to Radcliffe: *Pryce/Tulu showed up, with shootout. Celeste hit and bleeding. Need extraction ASAP!* An extraction team was at least an hour out, but he breathed a short sigh of relief knowing the cavalry would arrive soon, and it would all be over.

But would he succeed in time to save Celeste?

The thought made him suck in heavy, rapid breaths for support. He felt a wave of suffocating panic begin to crest over him, but he closed his eyes and shook his head.

Get it together, Grey!

Standing between him and the rest of the space was another curtain. Silas approached it and stretched out his hands, laying them upon the heavy, fine linen woven with strands of indigo, violet, and crimson yarn, adorned with cherubim. He caressed it carefully, reverently. It was as if the room beyond hummed with a magnetic power that both repelled him and drew him inward.

He took a breath, then parted the heavy curtain, separating the outer entrance from the inner, sacred chamber.

The air inside hung thickly with incense. He could taste the spices in his mouth, a miasma that symbolized the Lord's presence. He started trembling slightly, his stomach a knot of butterflies with the realization that he was standing in a complete replica of what was once the Holy of Holies in Yahweh's Temple. He stood in awe of the massive inner sanctuary that stretched as long as the Solomon Temple itself had been wide, formed to its exact specifications from the Bible. There was barely enough light to make out the inside, an original feature intentionally designed to prevent people from looking upon the glory of the Lord as it hovered over the object of their pursuit. What little light existed came from twelve struggling candlesticks, symbolizing the twelve original tribes of Israel. The inside shimmered in undulating waves as the light ebbed and flowed over the twenty-three tons of beautiful gold overlaid upon its walls.

Commanding the room were sculptured cherubim, large and imposing, with wings outstretched and overlaid with more fine gold. One of the wings of the cherubim was seven-and-a-half feet and touched the inner wall, while its other wing touched the second cherubim's wing; the other cherubim had a similar wingspan and touched the first winged creature and the other temple wall. Their entire wings spanned thirty feet, and they faced inward, toward Silas and the object that lay below.

The Ark of the Covenant, the box of acacia wood overlaid with pure gold, both inside and outside, and decorated with molded gold.

His pulse quickened, his breath caught in his throat. There it was.

It was real.

It wasn't a large box, measuring less than four feet long and just over two feet wide and high. If it was indeed the Ark, it contained the sacred objects associated with God's presence with Israel in the desert, and serving as witnesses to future generations of the Lord's relationship with his people: the essential element of the covenant God forged with Israel, the pair of stone tablets with the Ten Commandments inscribed by Yahweh; the almond-wood staff of Aaron the high priest, which had miraculously budded and led to Israel's defining, redemptive event, the exodus; and a golden pot containing the last traces of the mysterious manna that fell from Heaven to sustain the Israelites during their forty-year desert journey before reaching the Promised Land.

Draping it was what appeared to be a thick, blue cloth, embroidered with an emblem. He couldn't quite make it out in the dim light, but it looked to be a dove. He recalled that in Wolfram's *Parzival* the dove had also been the emblem of the Grail.

Silas instinctively started toward it, drawn to it by some holy power, but movement out of the corner of his eye made him stop short.

"Who's there?" he called out, squinting through the incense fog, struggling to see in the dim light.

"I should ask of you the same thing, perhaps."

An older man emerged, his skin was dark and weathered. He was tall and lanky with a thick, gray beard down to his chest and wearing a gold-embroidered, pure white robe. His arms were folded in front of him, and he made no movement.

The Guardian Monk.

Silas stumbled for words, not knowing what to say. "For— Forgive me for invading your sacred space. I am a professor of Christian theology and religion. A Christian man myself, actually. I teach people about the memory of Christ and his Church. Anyway, my friend..." He turned toward the curtain, motioning toward the world beyond. "You see, my friend...she's been shot. And taken captive—"

"By men who would seek the hidden covenant," the man interrupted.

"Yes. I was told to secure it so that it could be retrieved and then exposed for the world to see. To give up its life for hers."

The old man said nothing.

"Tell me." He continued, taking a step forward. He hesitated, looking down at the floor, feeling foolish for even entertaining the question, but then he looked up and said, "Is it real? Is...Is it truly the Ark of the Covenant?"

The man continued looking at him saying nothing for the longest time, the silence of the moment filled by a sort of holy hum. Then he took a breath, and said, "What think you?"

Silas hesitated, looking from the man to the blue-draped, rectangular box. "I'm not sure. There is so much mystery surrounding it. So many different signs are pointing in several possible directions. But still leading here."

The man smiled, bright teeth gleaming in the barely lit darkness. "Ethiopians know that if you wish to hide a tree, then place it in a forest."

He understood the analogy. "Show me the tree. Tell me the story."

The old man stared back with weary eyes, as if he had been carrying a tiresome burden for half a century. "The story I will tell you, knowing a holy man you are, a servant of the Church you are. But with you, and you alone, the secret must remain."

Silas quickly nodded, his mouth going dry from the adrenaline surge of anticipation, his eyes wide and transfixed on the man. "I understand. The story is safe with me."

The tall man sat down and crossed his legs. He motioned for Silas to do the same. He hesitated, but dropped to his bottom. Then the man started:

"At the heart of the forest of clues and signs lies the golden Ark, which God directed Moses to build at the foot of Mount Sinai, the vessel of Yahweh's covenant carried through the wilderness and across the river Jordan. The one that brought Yahweh's people their victories in their struggle to win the Promised Land, and then was taken by King David up to Jerusalem and deposited by Solomon in the Holy of Holies of the First Temple."

To Silas, none of this was disputed. He sensed the true story of the Ark about to emerge.

"Some three hundred years later, the vessel of Yahweh's covenant was removed by faithful priests who wished to preserve it from pollution at the hands of the wicked, pagan king Manasseh. Hide it away in safety on the far-off Egyptian island of Elephantine they did, along the mighty Nile. There, a new temple was built to house Yahweh's hidden covenant, one that lasted for two hundred more years."

He recalled the crude drawing in Pryce's journal, the one with the line snaking down the center with what looked like a body of water to the east. Now he knew that wasn't a road, as they had thought, but a river. And the dot wasn't Luxor, but another Egyptian city, Elephantine. The Ark had gone west, not east to Babylon—not to mention down beneath the Temple, as most had assumed.

"Eventually," the Guardian Monk continued, "those Jews destroyed this temple. And wandering with this sacred vessel, resumed carrying it southward into the Kingdom of Aksum they did, a land crisscrossed by rivers. Having left one island, the Ark was brought to another one, Tana Kirkos, where it was installed in a simple tabernacle based on the design from the Torah in the Hebrew Scriptures, and worshiped there according to the customs. For the next eight hundred years, the hidden covenant stood at the center of a large Jewish religious system, the ancestors of all Ethiopian Jews today they are."

"Fascinating," Silas whispered. A verse came to mind, from one of the minor prophets, Zephaniah: "From beyond the rivers of Cush my worshipers, my scattered people, will bring me offerings." Cush was the entire Nile Valley, south of Egypt, including Nubia and Abyssinia—modern Ethiopia!

"It was in the fourth century that Christianity came to our lands. Abba Salama, the Ethiopian name for Friumentius the bishop of Syria, had led King Evan and the entire Kingdom of

Aksum to faith in the death and resurrection of Jesus Christ. Shortly after that, they seized the Ark for themselves and took it to Aksum, placing it in the great church that they had built there, a church dedicated to Saint Mary the Mother of Christ.

"As the weary centuries passed, the story of the memory of how the Ark had come to the people of Ethiopia dimmed. Legends begat more legends to account for how the Aksumite people had acquired the most significant religious relic in the history of the world, seemingly selected by God himself to hide away the memory of his old covenant. These legends were codified in the *Kebra Nagast*, a bedrock of history and truth concealed beneath layers of myth and magic."

Silas nodded with understanding. It was as he said to Celeste: a kernel of truth wrapped in myth.

"That truth, however, was recognized by the Poor Fellow-Soldiers of Christ and of the Temple of Solomon—"

"Excuse me," he interrupted, "did you mean the Knights Templar? They pursued and discovered the Ark?"

"Indeed, sir."

Silas thought of Wolfram von Eschenbach's *Parzival* story, where the Holy Grail served as a cryptogram for the Ark of the Covenant. In his story, the heathen Flegetanis revealed that there was indeed "a thing called the Gral." He revealed that it was guarded by a Christian progeny bred to a pure life, perhaps the lineage of Guardians of which this man was apart. Eschenbach concluded with these words: "Those humans who are summoned to the Gral are ever worthy."

So too were those who were summoned to hide the Ark, the vessel of God's covenantal relationship with his people. For Ark and Grail are one and the same.

Silas wondered if he was worthy enough.

He recalled the description of the sacred object from his research: the 40 cm square *tabot* of stone. "Why," he questioned, "has every Ethiopian church kept a copy of this relic? The *tabot*, you call it. And shaped as a stone slab? Why is it so important to your people to have a connection to the Ark in this way?"

The man smiled again. "What do the Holy Scriptures tell us about the two covenants between God known to mankind?"

The prophetic word from Jeremiah quoted by the writer of the Book of Hebrews came to mind. He recited it from chapter 31:

> *The days are surely coming, says the Lord, when I will*
> *make a new covenant with the house of Israel and*
> *the house of Judah. It will not be like the covenant*
> *that I made with their ancestors when I took them*
> *by the hand to bring them out of the land of Egypt*
> *—a covenant that they broke, though I was their*
> *husband, says the Lord. But this is the covenant*
> *that I will make with the house of Israel after those*
> *days, says the Lord: I will put my law within them,*
> *and I will write it on their hearts; and I will be*
> *their God, and they shall be my people. No longer*
> *shall they teach one another, or say to each other,*
> *"Know the Lord," for they shall all know me, from*
> *the least of them to the greatest, says the Lord; for I*
> *will forgive their iniquity, and remember their sin*
> *no more.*

"You are correct. A new covenant, authored by the Living Stone. The tabot is meant to serve as a reminder that the old covenant, written on tablets of stone has been done away, and that a new covenant, written on the hearts of men has been established through Jesus Christ. The one who casts his eyes upon it is invited to either believe in this Stone, trusting it as a cornerstone to their relationship with God and to life itself, never to be put to shame. Or they can disbelieve it, stumbling over it as a rock to make them fall into eternal destruction."

Silas nodded in recognition, marveling at the true depths of this metaphor for the sacredness of Jesus' death, and offer of new life through the cross.

Suddenly, he heard a sound, like the rushing of the wind or a tidal wave coming into shore. It sounded like the chanting and shouting of a mob of people.

And it seemed they were heading straight toward the chapel.

"Go. Old Grey Hair and his African companion are about to be paid in full. Generations of church deacons have guarded our treasure, using strength when necessary. They are here to make sure the relic of the old covenant stays hidden."

Silas got up to leave, but the man held up a hand. "I must caution you: do not share what you have witnessed, what we have discussed."

He nodded, then started toward the chamber exit. Several pops of gunfire stopped him cold. His heart sank. He looked at the old man, face stricken with panic.

The Guardian Monk looked toward the heavy curtain and nodded knowingly. "Go. Your redemption awaits."

CHAPTER 41

"Stand back, all of you!"

Silas emerged from behind the heavy, crimson curtain to a mob of men and women, their dark faces set starkly against their white robes. The Guardian Deacons, come to preserve the memory of their faith.

Both of Pryce's arms were outstretched, brandishing his and Silas's confiscated weapons. Tulu was standing off to the side, his face registering a mixture of fear and apprehension at engaging the mob. Celeste was on the ground between both of their feet, leg bloodied, face ashen, barely stirring.

He glanced backward when Silas emerged, shouting," Grey, you better do something about this crowd! Get them to back off if you want to see your woman alive. And get me my Ark!"

The scene made his pulse race forward, looking down at Celeste caused his stomach to sink.

He moved closer to Pryce, putting a hand on his shoulder. He said gently, but firmly, "It's over. Let's put the weapons down and leave. All they want is for us to leave their relic alone."

"Damned if I leave," he growled, waving his arms back and forth in front of the crowd. He glanced back at Silas. His face was frantic, twisted with fear and failure. He stammered, "Did you see it? The Ark? Is...Is it really here? Is it real?"

Silas didn't know how much to share, especially after the Guardian's warning.

"It's not what you think. And it's not going anywhere."

Pryce pivoted his right arm toward Silas, aiming it at his face. He kept his left directed at the crowd. "Like hell it ain't."

There was the moment. Now or never.

With an open palm, Silas punched his right hand upward with quick force into Pryce's forearm. The gun discharged, but then went soaring into the air before skittering across the base of the chapel.

Shock transformed into rage. Pryce swung the arm with the other gun around and lunged for Silas, catching him off guard. The two stumbled back against the facade of the chapel, Pryce pressing against Silas, breathing hard with nostrils flared.

Before Pryce could recover and raise his weapon, Silas kneed him in the groin. The man groaned and stumbled back, then raised his gun and fired twice. The shots exploded into the wall above Silas's head.

The crowd reacted to the shots by gasping and taking a few steps backward, content to let the two white men fight, not knowing which side they were on.

"Give it up, Pryce. The privilege of the Ark's mystery was never yours anyway."

"What the hell are you talking about? This was all my work. *Mine!*"

"Thanks to *my* find. You would never have made it this far, to begin with, had it not been for me," Silas said, goading the man. "That's right. Without that Ark scrolls, none of this would have happened. And now you have nothing to show for it. Not in Jerusalem, and definitely not here. Your goal of trying to launch the Islamic End Times and undermine the story of Christ's sacrifice is finished. You failed, Pryce!"

The man screamed with the passion of a zealot and lunged for Silas again. But this time he was ready.

He stepped to the side and used Pryce's momentum to plow him into the side of the chapel, head first. Pryce squeezed off two shots in the frantic change of circumstances, but lost the weapon when Silas grabbed his left arm and slammed it against his leg, breaking it in one fell swoop.

Pryce cried out and recoiled in pain, stumbling back. He righted himself then took a step back, but had miscalculated his position.

The man wobbled, then tumbled backward down the stairs to the base of the chapel. And at the feet of Guardian Deacons.

At once a pure white tidal wave came crashing forward into Pryce's fallen body. It coagulated around him, consuming him with force, and kicking him into submission. Pryce was screaming, as much in agony and fear as he was in defeat. The crowd then picked the man up and carried him down the dirt pathway off the chapel grounds and out of sight.

Keeping the mystery of the Ark and the sacredness of the new covenant intact.

SILAS RACED to Celeste's side. Her leg was wet with blood. She had gone ashen gray from the blood loss. Her breathing was labored.

He immediately stripped his shirt off, then he bunched it up and pressed it against her thigh. He held it firm to stanch the flow of blood.

"Stay with me, Celeste. Everything's going to be alright. Help is on the way." He lifted her body onto his lap, cradling her in his arms.

This felt like Iraq all over again when his buddy Colton was blown to smithereens by a roadside bomb. He had landed on Silas after his left side was blown off. He had similarly cradled the man as he breathed his last breaths, reassuring him that everything would be fine. That help was on the way. It had eventually come, but it was too late; he was far too gone to save.

No way was this situation going to be that situation. Celeste Bourne was not going to die.

He was having trouble breathing, his lungs feeling as if they were like water-logged sponges. His heart was pounding, his head filling with dizzying panic.

Where was the damn SEPIO extraction team?

She smiled at him weakly. "I guess today's the day I get to cash in my chips from having twice saved your life."

He chuckled, his throat catching with emotion. "Now we're even."

She swallowed hard and tried taking a breath, her face betraying her pain.

"It's alright," he reassured her. "You're going to be alright. Just hold on a few more minutes."

"Silas," she interrupted. "I need you to promise me something."

His eyes widened, his stomach dropped. Those were the word's Colton used right before he passed. He made Silas swear on the life of his future kids that he wouldn't quit until every one of the terrorists responsible for 9/11 were hunted down and gunned down. He hadn't known what to say, so he agreed. The man grinned with delight, before coughing up a handful of blood and passing on. It was the last memory he had of his wartime friend.

"Alright," he said softly, his voice shaking from the memory and the moment.

"Promise me you'll take my place." She coughed, then winced with pain.

Thankfully there was no blood.

"What...what are you talking about?"

"If I die," she said, struggling for breath. "If I die, take over my post. Lead SEPIO forward as director of operations."

Celeste's ask was preposterous on so many levels, not least of which was the thought of her dying in his arms

"Celeste," he said, his voice low and cracking. "Don't say that. Don't even think about that. You're not—"

"Listen to me!" Her strength of tone seemed to startle her as much as Silas. "Nous is growing in power and ambition. Rowan Radcliffe is a steady hand, but SEPIO is going to need someone with your passion for the vintage Christian faith, your special-ops know-how, and your academic chops with all things theological and historical and philosophical." She stopped to catch a breath, then looked straight into Silas's eyes. "The Project won't survive unless you take over for me. I need to know it's in good hands. Promise me, Silas. Promise me that if I...Promise me that you'll take over for me..."

He had looked away as she was talking, then looked back at her when she trailed off. Her head had rolled back. Eyes were closed, mouth agape.

Fear gripped Silas's belly like a vice.

No!

"Celeste?" Silas gently slapper her cheeks. "Celeste wake up." He turned his ear toward her mouth.

Thank God she was still breathing! But she wasn't going to hold on much longer.

Heavy thumping blades of a helicopter caught Silas's attention. He looked up at the sky. Within a minute, the bird descended and landed on the front lawn, dust and leaves flying high.

Within minutes, three SEPIO operatives had run up the stairs to the chapel. One carrying an automatic rifle, the two others a yellow, plastic stretcher.

"What happened?" one of the medics asked.

"Shot in the leg. About an hour ago. She's been losing blood all that time. My guess is it nicked the femoral artery. She's been in and out of consciousness."

He stepped to the side as they began to work on her. They immediately placed an oxygen mask around her face and hooked a set of wires to her chest. One of the men tore open a packet of some sort of solution. He removed Silas's shirt, now soaking with blood. Then he poured the packet of powder on her thigh. He took a fist-full of gauze and shoved it on the wound, then made quick work wrapping it with tape. The other man positioned the rescue stretcher near Celeste, then the other one grabbed her legs, and the two placed her in the plastic bed.

Silas stood to leave as the two operatives picked up Celeste.

The operative with the rifle said, "Sorry, buddy. But there isn't any more room on the chopper."

"Like hell there's not! I'm not leaving her, I'm coming with."

He started forward before the man pressed his hand firmly against his chest.

"No. You're not. You did good, soldier. But now it's our turn. A separate unit is on its way to extract you. Radcliffe can bring you up to speed on her condition if he chooses."

Silas sighed and placed both hands on his head, trying to hold back the dam of emotion wanting to burst through as he watched Celeste being carried down the steps and into the chopper.

Lord Jesus Christ, Son of God, you better keep her alive!

CHAPTER 42

ADDIS ABABA, ETHIOPIA. THE NEXT DAY.

The gentle hissing of the oxygen machine kept Silas awake all night standing watch in the Intensive Care Unit of Saint Paul's Hospital in Addis Ababa. As if he needed an excuse to stay awake, anyway.

Snaking out of Celeste's nose and mouth, arms and chest were wires and tubes of oxygen and fluids. Earlier that morning she had been downgraded from 'extremely critical' to 'critical, but stable.' It was a significant milestone in her recovery from the gunshot wound and loss of blood, but she wasn't out of the woods yet.

When they had left the Church of Our Lady Mary of Zion, the SEPIO medical operatives were able to staunch the flow of blood and give her the oxygen she needed to stabilize her vitals. They flew her to the second largest hospital in Ethiopia where surgeons were able to find the bullet and extract it, but her femur wasn't as lucky. The bullet had fractured it, requiring a rod to stabilize it and fuse it back into position. She was weak from the blood loss. Not critical, but enough that the doctors were concerned, keeping her sedated to allow her body to heal and replenish itself.

Not waiting for the extraction team, Silas had returned to

their car and sped toward the Aksum airport once the chopper had lifted. When he eventually made it to the hospital after catching a flight to the city, he practically tore off his shirt to give blood, as amazingly he was a match. He had tried to push his way into the surgery room to check on her condition, but was forcefully told to remain in the waiting room with everyone else.

Hours ticked by as they worked to repair her body, but he remained in vigil for his fallen comrade. Four hours later, a nurse came out to get him, telling him the surgery was a success and she was stable, but still in critical condition. He had been at her bedside ever since.

Lord Jesus Christ, Son of God, Silas mumbled, praying a prayer he had memorized in Catholic primary school, *You invite all who are burdened to come to you. Allow Your healing Hand to heal Celeste. Touch her soul with Your compassion for others; touch her heart with Your courage and infinite Love for all; touch her mind with Your Wisdom. I reach out to You with all her needs, asking for you to heal her. May my mouth always proclaim Your praise, may I help lead others to You by my example.*

Most loving Heart of Jesus, bring her health in body and spirit that we both may continue serving You with all our strength. Touch gently her life which you have created, now and forever.

"Amen," he said as the door gently opened.

A nurse slipped in, short and stout and wearing a kind smile.

"Sorry. I didn't mean to bother you."

He smiled and sat back. "No problem. How is she?"

"Sure is a fighter." She went through a routine of checking the wires and tubes, making sure nothing had become detached or blocked; checking the computers attached, ensuring all was in order; gently moving her limbs to ensure they were best positioned.

She smiled as she left, shutting the door gently behind her.

He sat forward and sighed. "What am I going to do without you, Celeste?"

The thought caught him by surprise so that he leaned back in his chair to consider what he had just said. What did he mean, what would he do without her? He had never needed anybody, much less a romantic companion.

It had always been difficult for him to form bonds with people. Women had been no different. As near he had figured, it stemmed from some sort of subconscious abandonment issue going back to his mother's death after giving birth to his brother Sebastian and him. And with being a military brat and moving around the world with his dad, he had always had to defend himself against the townie kids and stationed families who had far deeper roots than he had ever had. That rootlessness created a tough, outer shell and aversion toward connection. Even with women.

But there was something about Celeste that had struck him differently than any other relationship he'd encountered, something that had drawn him toward her, rather than compelled him to turtle inside his shell and look out for himself.

Maybe it was the self-assured demeanor that came from running operations for high-level governmental and ecclesial organizations. Maybe it was the way she carried herself: stand-offish, yet present; reserved, yet bearing a degree of openness; a woman of faith, yet earthly; physical, yet intelligent.

He rubbed his eyes with both hands, and then his face. This was silly. He had barely known her a year. He was allowing himself to be carried away like a runaway stagecoach. Care for her, yes, her health and healing and outcome. But as a person, not as a woman.

Yet, as he continued to sit next to her eyes-closed, still form, watching her chest gently rise and fall with each breath, listening to the machines around her as they monitored her vital signs, something was stirring within him. Something he sensed had been slowly emerging since the spring when she had dragged him from the ruins of Georgetown University's chapel, and then when they had fought alongside one another for the memory of Christ's resurrection. Then he recalled her showing up at his lecture hall earlier in the week. He thought his heart literally skipped a beat when he saw her standing there, holding that umbrella and wearing that nice-fitting raincoat. He was actually happy to see her. Thrilled, even.

She was a remarkable woman. But what did she matter to him?

What did she *mean* for him?

He was cut off by the vibration of his phone, paired with an audible ping letting him know a text had arrived. Probably his brother checking in on him again.

He reluctantly brought out his phone. Instead, it was an email.

From Dean Brown, Princeton.

He sucked in a chest-full of air, chased by his elevating pulse. He swiped his phone to life, summoning the email in the process. He scanned it quickly.

Not good.

Professor Silas Grey,

We, the Committee on Tenure at Princeton University, and I, as Academic Dean, are writing to inform you of the suspension of the recent proceedings to reinstate your tenure, voting unanimously to deny you a tenured, full-professorial position at Princeton University.

Your willful neglect of your pedagogical responsibilities, notwithstanding your unprofessional conduct, is unbecoming of the legacy of Princeton University and duty as an instructor.

Furthermore, you are hereby suspended without pay forthwith until a hearing of your peers, later to be established, evaluating your academic and fraternal competency to continue teaching at this hallowed institution.

Please submit your response to Dean McIntyre post haste.

Sincerely,

Michael Brown

Dean, Academics

Princeton University

Silas sat in stunned silence, the whiplash-change of professional events too remarkable to even register a reaction.

Had he just been fired?

He reread the email, grinding his teeth in anger and agony, trying to control his heavy breathing through his nose.

What a load of crap.

A feeling of rejection crashed inside of him. Everything he had been working for the past decade had just become unraveled in one email.

They have no idea what they are doing. They have no idea what I just did! What I uncovered. What I discovered. What I accomplished.

His throat caught itself as he tried to swallow, emotion begging for release.

"Knock, knock."

Silas's head jerked up, caught off guard by the sudden interruption to his rage.

Rowen Radcliffe furrowed his brow and raised a hand in regret. "Sorry. Didn't mean to disturb you."

"No, you're fine." He smiled weakly, happy to see a friendly face after such a painful blow. He motioned for him to come in.

He looked down at Silas's phone as he entered, taking a seat in a chair across from him. "Anything interesting going on in the interwebs?"

Silas smirked, then turned off his phone and stuffed it back in his pants pocket. "Just a Dear John letter."

"Dear me. Trouble on the home front?"

He sighed. "You could say that." He looked at the floor, not really wanting to talk about it. "It looks like I've got a fight on my hands back at Princeton when I leave here. Probably going to be fired. Seems like they're not too happy with my little...side project." He glanced at Radcliffe and smiled. "And other things, probably mostly my own doing."

Radcliffe nodded. "I see. Hope the Order hasn't caused you too much trouble."

Silas said nothing. He hadn't regretted helping SEPIO, both in the spring and over the summer, and then the past week. But it certainly was coming to bite him in the butt.

The silence was punctuated by the continued sigh of the ventilation machine and the occasional beeps from the other machines monitoring Celeste's vitals. Radcliffe looked from Silas to her, his face sagging at the sight of all the provisions of modern medicine guarding her life and helping her heal.

"Were you able to get everything back in order in Aksum when we left?" Silas asked.

"For the most part. As you can imagine, the Ethiopian Orthodox Church is none too happy with the attempt on their relic. Whatever it may be they're storing in that stuffy stone square of theirs. Speaking of which," he leaned forward toward Silas. "What did you see inside? Did you catch a glimpse of anything, anything at all?"

Silas considered his question, then simply smiled. "Nothing I can talk about."

Radcliffe nodded slowly in recognition. "You know, that's what's interesting about this line of work. Not only does what we do go mostly unnoticed by the outside world; we've designed it that way. Most of what we do and see goes unspoken, as well. Very different than the academy, that's for sure."

Silas sat in silence, wondering what Radcliffe was getting at and still brooding over the email. It seemed life was about to take a radical turn.

"What about Pryce?"

Radcliffe turned from Celeste to him. "Pryce?"

"Last I saw he was being dragged and beaten by a mob. Any word on his final fate?"

Radcliffe frowned and shook his head. "No. Which doesn't surprise me. The Ethiopian Orthodox Church has had a way of dealing with people over the years who've come seeking their relic in unholy ways."

"But nothing on his whereabouts?"

"We've gotten unconfirmed reports of his death. Someone else thought he saw the man in Yemen, though that seems unlikely. Either way, he won't be causing the Order any trouble soon. And once again, the memory of the Christian faith is safe from Nous. For now."

Silas caught his subtle emphasis on *for now*, as if suggesting it might not be safe from Nous in the immediate future, which would require someone at the helm of SEPIO.

He remembered Celeste's ask before she faded.

Promise me you'll take my place.

He swallowed hard, his eyes darting to the strong woman whose body was fighting to survive. *Lord, the Great Physician, hear our prayers.*

Radcliffe said, "So what are your plans, in the coming weeks and months?"

Silas turned toward the man. "My plans? You mean if Celeste doesn't survive?" His response had a sharper edge than he had intended.

Radcliffe sighed, then said softly, "I didn't mean it like that.

Celeste spoke very highly of you after the mission to rescue the Shroud and secure the Holy Sepulcher, and then again after the apostolic relics debacle this summer."

"She did?" Silas asked eagerly.

Radcliffe smiled. "She did. She jokingly made me promise that if she was ever taken out that I should move mountains to get you to take her place." He looked back over at the bed. "I never thought I would have to follow through on that request."

Silas considered this. Never would he have planned his life this way, being forced out of the one profession he had wanted since he was a kid and the only life that fulfilled his ambitions to make his mark on the world. Joining the Army after 9/11 was just an angsty way of dealing with his father's death. Through it, he had dealt with his demons and picked up some more. But God also used the experience to draw him back to himself, rekindling a faith that had burned down to cold embers. It was that ignition that had propelled him forward to pursue his studies in theology and religion, and a profession in making a difference in both areas.

But if he was honest with himself, the motivations were far more surface than substance. He wanted the prestige that came from publishing and public speaking, from discovering and uncovering.

So what would be his motivation for joining the Order and signing on to Project SEPIO?

Sebastian.

The word came out of nowhere, a divine name-drop from Heaven itself that was immediate and compelling.

His brother's agnosticism or atheism or spiritual-but-not-religious state had been a motivating factor for much of his study and academic pursuits. And the world was filled with plenty more who were just like him, not to mention his own backyard in the U. S. of A.

Nones they call them, a rapidly growing body of people who claim no religious affiliation, many who are former Christians who became disillusioned with and doubtful of their faith. Twenty-five percent who don't hold to a particular religious creed or go to a regular religious worship service or have any particular interest in God. They've turned away from, and in many ways against, Christianity and are increasingly hardened toward religion generally.

Just like his brother.

If there was one motivating factor to join the Order and make SEPIO his own project, it was him. Perhaps the Lord had prepared him for such a time as this through his military and academic training.

He breathed in deeply, then looked at Radcliffe. "I can't promise anything right now. I've got to go back and mop up the mess I've made and figure some things out."

Radcliffe raised his head, his eyes twinkling with hope. "Certainly. I understand."

"And I'm not sure what the heck I'm getting myself into..." Silas looked at Celeste, thinking about the promise he hadn't voiced to her, but had secretly made in his heart. "But let's talk in a few weeks."

Radcliffe smiled and nodded. "Sounds good." He got up from his chair and touched Silas's shoulder. "And, Silas." He turned toward the man. Radcliffe continued, "She's a fighter. She'll be fine."

Silas smiled weakly and nodded. Then Radcliffe patted him on the shoulder and left.

Leaving him alone with Celeste, with his thoughts, and with his future.

AUTHOR'S NOTE

THE HISTORY BEHIND THE STORY...

Let's face it: any religious conspiracy thriller writer worth their salt can't *not* write about the Ark of the Covenant. I mean...come on! So, here we are, another tome to add to the shelves of Ark lore. And yet this one is a bit of a departure from the Indiana Jones variety. So what's the history behind the story?

First of all, yes, the main antagonist's name is a not-so-subtle nod to the Grand Master of Ark stories. Lucas Pryce borrows his name from both George Lucas and one of the primary source authors I relied on, Randall Price. Both his *In Search of Temple Treasures* and *Searching for the Ark of the Covenant* were indispensable resources to help inform the possible locations of the Ark.

I also relied on one of the more popular narrative nonfiction sources that directly connected the Ark to the Ethiopian legend, Graham Hancock's *The Sign and the Seal*. A few elements from his own journey inspired some of the plot elements.

So where is the Ark of the Covenant if, as the explosive middle turning point indicates, it isn't hidden away underneath the Temple Mount itself? Here is some of the research I discovered that made its way into the book that informed some of Silas's and Celeste's adventures.

Shishak and Egypt

As recorded in 1 Kings 14, around 926 BC the southern kingdom was indeed invaded by Shishak of the Egyptians, also known as Sheshonk. As the biblical text clearly states, the king not only carted off the treasures of the royal household but "carried off the treasures of the temple of the Lord." Apparently, the temple of Karnak in Luxor confirms this account, recording that Shishak offered the spoils of his campaign to the god Amun. And in 1939 Shishak's tomb was discovered in Tanis, where his sarcophagus and mummy were adorned with gold, presumably from the Temple treasures. This account serves as the backdrop for George Lucas's *Raiders of the Lost Ark* blockbuster, which centered around Tanis.

However, there are good reasons why the Ark probably never made its way to Egypt. Some have maintained that Shishak never entered Jerusalem since it wasn't among his own list of captured cities. Others believe those temple treasures were merely the gold and other valuables stored in the treasury outside the Temple, not the sacred ones from the inner sanctuary. And as Silas said, there's 2 Chronicles 13:11, which says the altar of incense, the menorah, and the table of showbread were still in use in the temple. Further, 2 Chronicles 35:3 shows the Ark itself was still being used as late as Josiah's reign. He instructed the Levites, "Put the sacred ark in the temple that Solomon son of David king of Israel built," clearly posing a big problem for this theory.

The connection I made in chapters 23 and 24 with the famed King Tut was pure fabrication on my part. I found it convenient that there was a resurgent effort in the last year to apply ground penetrating radar to his tomb in search of hidden chambers. And when I discovered his dynasty pre-dated Shishak's by a few hundred years and then he reinstituted worship of Amun, the god to which Shishak was reported to have offered the temple treasures, I thought it an all-too-perfect plot device.

Menelik and Kebra Negast

The *Kebra Nagast* is a genuine thirteenth-century manuscript, greatly revered among the Ethiopian people and written, as Silas pointed out, in an ancient Semitic language, called Ge'ez, a dialect originating in the Horn of Africa, which later became the official language of the Kingdom of Aksum and Ethiopian imperial court. As explained, the legend centers on the relationship between King Solomon of Israel and Queen of Sheba. 1 Kings of the Hebrew Scriptures tells of this story when the queen visited Solomon. Now, what the Bible does not say, but the *Kebra Nagast* suggests is that King Solomon gave the Queen something else, a son named Menelik. This ancient manuscript tells this story about the birth of their son, as well as the legend of Menelik abducting the Ark from the First Temple in Jerusalem and bringing it to Aksum in Ethiopia.

Ethiopia and the Ark

Without question, the Ethiopian people believe they possess the Ark of the Covenant. The account from the Guardian Monk in chapter 40 mirrors some of the elements of the legend of how the Ark eventually ended up in modern Ethiopia. It is said that the Ark was taken and hidden away in safety on the far-off Egyptian island of Elephantine along the mighty Nile. There, a new temple was built to house Yahweh's hidden covenant, one that lasted for two hundred more years, until it was carried southward into the Kingdom of Aksum to Tana Kirkos. There it was installed in a simple tabernacle based on the design from the Torah in the Hebrew Scriptures, and worshiped there according to Jewish customs. For the next eight hundred years, the hidden covenant stood at the center of a large Jewish religious system in the Kingdom of Aksum, the ancestors of all Ethiopian Jews today.

When in the fourth century Christianity came to their lands,

King Evan and the entire Kingdom of Aksum came to faith in the death and resurrection of Jesus Christ. According to the legend, shortly after that, they seized the Ark for themselves and took it to Aksum, placing it in the great church dedicated to Saint Mary the Mother of Christ.

But there are problems with the account, not the least of which is there is no such record in the biblical and extrabiblical Jewish sources. There are doubts that the Queen of Sheba had been an Ethiopian. Many question whether the Ethiopian civilization could have been advanced enough to have engaged with ancient Israel. Then there is the issue of Aksum itself since it wasn't even in existence during Solomon's time. Therefore, most believe the legend of the Ark having been brought to Aksum simply isn't possible. However, every Ethiopian church does indeed have its own replica of the Ark, called a *tabot*. Some are made of wood, but most are made of stone.

When I read about this legend in my research, and then encountered the journey of Graham Hancock tracing the evidence to the Ethiopian city of Aksum, I found the legend to be an interesting story that would serve the broader plot, nothing more. That's why I used it, purely for the intrigue, mystery, and thrill—not to advocate for its location. Particularly the points of connection between the stone *tabot* replicas of the vessel of the old covenant and the biblical references to the vessel of the new covenant being a Living Stone and Cornerstone, Jesus Christ. The description of the interior of the chapel in chapter 40 is fictional insofar as no one has ever given an account of the interior of the chapel! However, it does mirror the description of the interior of the original Temple built by King Solomon.

Chartres, Clarivox, von Eschenbach, and the Ark

Hancock's *The Sign and the Seal* was a treasure trove of inspiration for this story. I was particularly fascinated by the connections he made between the Chartres Cathedral, Bernard of Clairvaux and Wolfram von Eschenbach's *Parzival*—believing the gothic architecture, the Cistercian monk, and Arthurian myth all held some sort of secret coded information for the Ark's location. However, I only used these as devices in my story because I thought they were an interesting connection for some of the later inspiration I wanted to offer.

What you discover in chapters 27, 29, 31 and 33 about the cathedral, the monk, and the book mirror much of the conclusions Hancock himself drew. I used them to push the story along and draw some conclusions of my own concerning the Ark and its ultimate role in the world—and why a Christian church and monk may have included the legend of the Ark in its architecture and theology.

One of those theological points, which I draw on at the end, mirrors the association that Clairvaux and others have made. Clairvaux had explicitly compared Mary to the Ark of the Covenant in numerous writings and sermons, allegorizing the significance of Mary as the *Theotokos*, the God-bearer. As the Ark of the Hebrew people of God contained hidden within its vessel the form of the Old Covenant, written on tablets of stone, so too had Mary carried, hidden within herself, the form of the New Covenant, the person of Jesus. His very blood and body shed and broken in sacrificial death would usher in this new covenant.

Islam and the Ark

For Muslims, the Ark is a sign given to them by their prophet. One Islamic commentary explains that this Ark contained the Covenant, the Sakina, of the Islamic people. This covenant assured divine help and victory over the infidels with the prophetic relics contained in the Ark. These relics were connected to the rulership of God on earth as channeled by his prophets and messengers. And as such, the Sakina assured unfathomable and unrivaled powers to whoever possessed the Ark. Chapters 35 and 36 reflect the Islamic tradition concerning the history of the Ark of the Covenant. I was particularly intrigued (and not a little excited!) about the tradition of Solomon marrying Queen Sheba and having Menelik, who then later carried the Ark to Ethiopia.

The connection between the Ark and the Mahdi was an important link in the story, the prophesied redeemer of Islam who will rule during the End Times before the Day of Judgment and will rid the world of evil. Al Mahdi is said to be from the bloodline of the prophet Muhammad and from the descendants of Abraham and Ishmael. He will rule as a king over the Ishmaelites with the Ark in his possession. According to a tradition within Islam, the Ark is everything to the fulfillment of those eschatological prophecies. The reports offered in the fake journal article between Saulcy and Pryce are genuine accounts.

In one Hadith, the importance of the Ark and the Mahdi are clear: "The reason he will be known as the Mahdi is that he will show the way to a hidden thing. He will bring the Ark to light from a place called Antioch." What's more, the Qur'an itself reveals that the Ark is "a sign" for faithful believers, and some understand it to signal the identity of the Mahdi and the sovereignty of Allah he bears when it is found, evidencing his dominion and ushering in an era of moral purity and tranquility: "Truly the sign of his sovereignty shall be that the ark comes to you bearing tranquility from your Lord...Truly that is a sign for you, if you are believers" (al-Baqarah; 2:248).

The Real Location of the Ark

So where is the Ark? Your guess is as good as mine! Aside from my little reveal that a rumored chamber beneath the former Holy of Holies underneath the Temple Mount is completely empty, Randall Price represents a number of people who seem to think that's exactly where the Ark of the Covenant lays hidden. The story Lucas Pryce recounts in chapter 12 mirrors one from several decades ago when the original passageway he and his team used was discovered in July of 1981 by the Chief Rabbi of the Western Wall, rediscovering the lost Warren's Gate and a passage behind it quite by accident.

The Warren's Gate was one of the original gates leading into the Temple Mount directly into the Temple courts and was used for bringing in wood, sacrifices, and other materials needed for the ancient sacred rites of the Jewish people in the Temple. Those who have considered the location of the Temple treasures agree this gate is the most important of all because it is the nearest one to the former location of the Most Holy Place where the Ark of the Covenant used to reside. Many scholars of the Semitic period believe that underneath this locale King Solomon constructed a secret chamber to act as a secure vault for the Temple treasures should the need arise to steal them away, perhaps even in the event of the Temple's destruction. And these biblical scholars believe the Ark was secreted away during a few possible instances with the intention of later returning it to its proper place within the Temple—during the reign of Manasseh and before the Babylonian invasion.

Jewish tradition holds that the Ark has continued to exist in hiding and that it would be rediscovered and restored to Israel when the Messiah appeared. The longest of the Dead Sea Scrolls, known as the Temple Scroll, speaks of this very thing. It describes a new future Temple that will eventually be built containing the Ark of the Covenant. If such a holy place was to be considered legitimate, it must include the Ark, for without it the glory of God cannot return to take its appointed place between the glorious wings of the cherubim. No Ark, no true Temple. And this same Jewish tradition tells of the Ark being hidden away safely and secretly—which is why the city's Rabbi would have been all-too-eager to help Pryce locate it!

Fictional story aside, is the Ark under the Temple Mount? "The historical accounts support the tradition that the Ark is presently hidden beneath the Temple Mount," Randall Price insists. "If it was indeed stored away in the past—and has not yet been removed from its hiding place—then it must still remain under the Temple Mount today" (149). After several intriguing chapters in *Searching for the Ark of the Covenant*, he concludes with this: "No conclusive evidence exists for the existence of the Ark, nor can its hiding place be definitively located. Yet our survey of the biblical, historical, and traditional sources provide sufficient warrant for us to conclude that the Ark still exists and could be discovered" (207).

Perhaps the hidden Ark will one day be revealed!

Does the Ark Still Matter?

As you might suspect, this book about the Ark of the Covenant really isn't a book about the Ark of the Covenant. It's a much bigger story about the nature of our rescue as humans by a God who cares deeply about putting our broken lives back together.

Originally, the Ark was the footstool of God in the place at which heaven and earth overlapped, where God dwelt with his people in the tabernacle. It was also the place God dealt with the sins of his people, where the blood of bulls and goats paid for individual and national sins—but only temporarily. You see, the Ark was always meant as a temporary measure to make things right between the sinner and the Sinned-Against—between humans and God. The Jewish writer of the Book of Hebrews made this clear when he spoke of the former Temple and its treasures being "symbols" and "copies" of a greater reality: Jesus Christ.

Silas made this point in his speech to Lucas Pryce. What he makes plain, and why the Ark no longer matters, is that God has forged a new relationship, written a new covenant with humanity in the blood of Jesus. If the Ark has been replaced by the cross of Christ as the altar upon which the sins of humanity have been atoned, that means no more sacrifice is needed! If the former method for atonement under the old covenant disappeared through God's divine direction, if he himself created the circumstances of the hidden Ark, perhaps that was God's way of saying how to find atonement for sins and salvation—completely apart from the Ark and the old covenant.

As Farhad said, from the very first upright steps that Homo Sapiens took upon the earth, salvation from death and the bliss of an afterlife paradise has been the longing of the collective consciousness. The mystery has always been the *how*. That's the magic, the beauty of the Christian faith: God offered himself to do what we couldn't do ourselves. We can know that we are right with him. Right now, today. In this life.

The Passion relics symbolize this message—with the scourging post and nails, the crown of thorns and True Cross. Whether or not they are genuine is beside the point, although it is true that some of the earliest church fathers thought they were. What is the point is that they serve as tangible memory-markers of that Good Friday in AD 33 when the final sacrifice for the sins of the world was made on those blood-soaked Roman boards of execution that held the limp, lifeless body of Jesus of Nazareth, the Christ. And because he paid our price in our place, we can know, without a shadow of a doubt, that all of the bad things we've done in rebellion against God and in selfishness against other people has been dealt with. As Hebrews 10 makes clear:

> *"For by a single offering Jesus Christ has perfected for*
> *all time those who are sanctified. And the Holy*
> *Spirit also testifies to us, for after saying,*
> *"This is the covenant that I will make with them*
> *after those days, says the Lord:*
> *I will put my laws in their hearts,*

and I will write them on their minds,"
he also adds,
"I will remember their sins and their lawless deeds
no more."
Where there is forgiveness of these, there is no longer
any offering for sin.

In other words, the hidden covenant has been replaced by a new covenant, forged in the blood of Jesus, and available for all as the foundation for their relationship with God, and a life of freedom from the weight of sin and agony of death.

Research is an important part of my process for creating compelling stories that entertain, inform, and inspire. Here are a few of the resources I used to research the Ark of the Covenant:

- Hancock, Graham. *The Sign and the Seal.* New York: Crown Publishers, 1992. www.bouma.us/ark1
- Haron, M. "The Disappearance of the Ark." *Israel Exploration Journal* 13, January (1963), 46-58. www.bouma.us/ark2
- Price, Randall. *In Search of Temple Treasures.* Eugene, OR: Harvest House Publishers, 1994. www.bouma.us/ark3
- Price, Randall. *Searching for the Ark of the Covenant.* Eugene, OR: Harvest House Publishers, 2005. www.bouma.us/ark4

ABOUT THE AUTHOR

J. A. Bouma is an emerging author of vintage faith fiction. As a former congressional staffer and pastor, and bestselling author of over thirty religious fiction and nonfiction books, he blends a love for ideas and adventure, exploration and discovery, thrill and thought. With graduate degrees in Bible and theology, he writes within the tension of faith and doubt, spirituality and theology, Church and culture, belief and practice, modern and vintage forms of Church, and the gritty drama that is our collective pilgrim story.

He also offers nonfiction resources on the Christian faith under Jeremy Bouma. His books and courses help people rediscover and retrieve the vintage Christian faith by connecting that faith in relevant ways to our 21st century world.

Jeremy lives in Grand Rapids, Michigan, with his wife, son, and daughter, and their rambunctious boxer-pug-terrier Zoe.

www.jabouma.com
jeremy@jabouma.com

 facebook.com/jaboumabooks
twitter.com/bouma
amazon.com/author/jabouma

THANK YOU!

A big thanks for joining Silas Grey and the rest of SEPIO on their
adventure saving the world!

Enjoy the story? Here's what you can do next:

If you loved the book and have a moment to spare, **a short review
is much appreciated.** Nothing fancy, just your honest take.
Spreading the word is probably the #1 way you can help
independent authors like me and help others enjoy the story.

**If you're ready for another adventure you can get the previous
book in the series for free!** All you have to do is join the insider's
group to be notified of specials and new releases by going to this
link: www.jabouma.com/free

GET YOUR FREE THRILLER

Building a relationship with my readers is one of my all-time favorite joys of writing! Once in a while I like to send out a newsletter with giveaways, free stories, pre-release content, updates on new books, and other bits on my stories.

Join my insider's group for updates, giveaways, and your free novel—a full-length action-adventure story in my *Order of Thaddeus* thriller series. Just tell me where to send it.

Follow this link to subscribe:
www.jabouma.com/free

ALSO BY J. A. BOUMA

J. A. Bouma is an emerging author of vintage faith fiction. You may also like these books that explore the tension of faith and doubt, spirituality and theology, Church and culture, belief and practice, modern and vintage forms of Church, and the gritty drama that is our collective pilgrim story.

Order of Thaddeus **Action-Adventure Thriller Series**

Holy Shroud • Book 1

The Thirteenth Apostle • Book 2

Hidden Covenant • Book 3

American God • Book 4

Grail of Power • Book 5

Printed in Poland
by Amazon Fulfillment
Poland Sp. z o.o., Wrocław

50244440R00199